All the Light We Cannot See

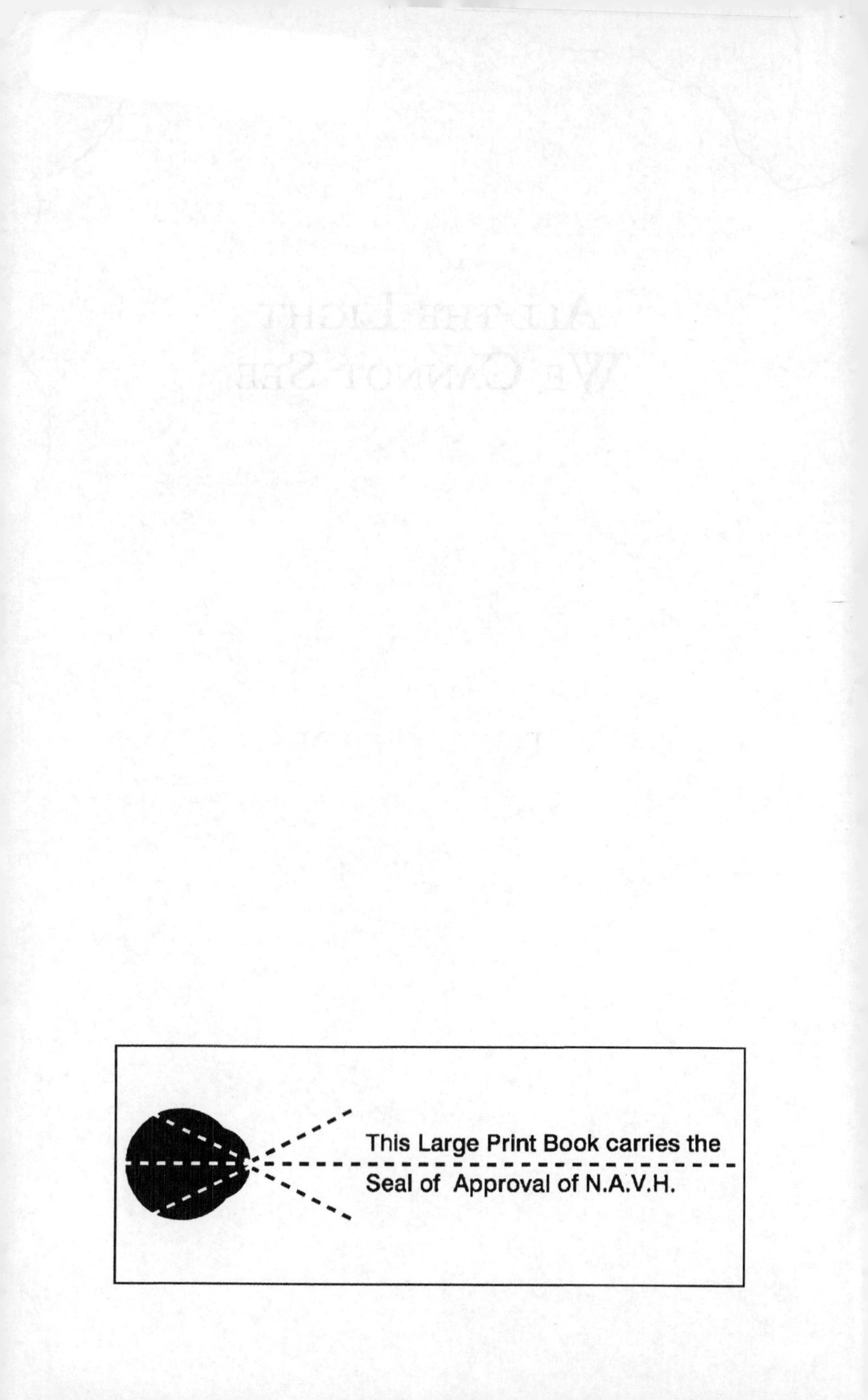
This Large Print Book carries the
Seal of Approval of N.A.V.H.

All the Light We Cannot See

Anthony Doerr

LARGE PRINT PRESS
A part of Gale, Cengage Learning

Farmington Hills, Mich • San Francisco • New York • Waterville, Maine
Meriden, Conn • Mason, Ohio • Chicago

Large Print Press, a part of Gale, Cengage Learning.

The text of this Large Print edition is unabridged.
Other aspects of the book may vary from the original edition.
Set in 16 pt. Plantin.

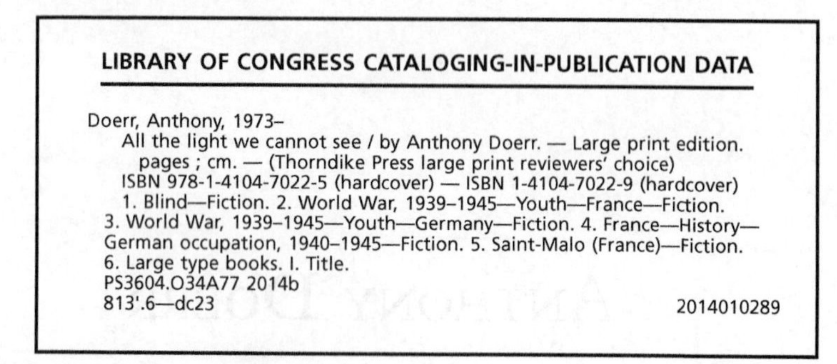
LIBRARY OF CONGRESS CATALOGING-IN-PUBLICATION DATA

Doerr, Anthony, 1973–
All the light we cannot see / by Anthony Doerr. — Large print edition.
pages ; cm. — (Thorndike Press large print reviewers' choice)
ISBN 978-1-4104-7022-5 (hardcover) — ISBN 1-4104-7022-9 (hardcover)
1. Blind—Fiction. 2. World War, 1939–1945—Youth—France—Fiction.
3. World War, 1939–1945—Youth—Germany—Fiction. 4. France—History—German occupation, 1940–1945—Fiction. 5. Saint-Malo (France)—Fiction.
6. Large type books. I. Title.
PS3604.O34A77 2014b
813'.6—dc23 2014010289

ISBN 13: 978-1-59413-815-7 (pbk.)
ISBN 10: 1-59413-815-X (pbk.)

Published in 2017 by arrangement with Scribner, a division of Simon & Schuster, Inc.

Print Number: 27 Print Year: 2023
Printed in Mexico

For Wendy Weil
1940–2012

In August 1944 the historic walled city of Saint-Malo, the brightest jewel of the Emerald Coast of Brittany, France, was almost totally destroyed by fire. . . . Of the 865 buildings within the walls, only 182 remained standing and all were damaged to some degree.

— Philip Beck

It would not have been possible for us to take power or to use it in the ways we have without the radio.

— Joseph Goebbels

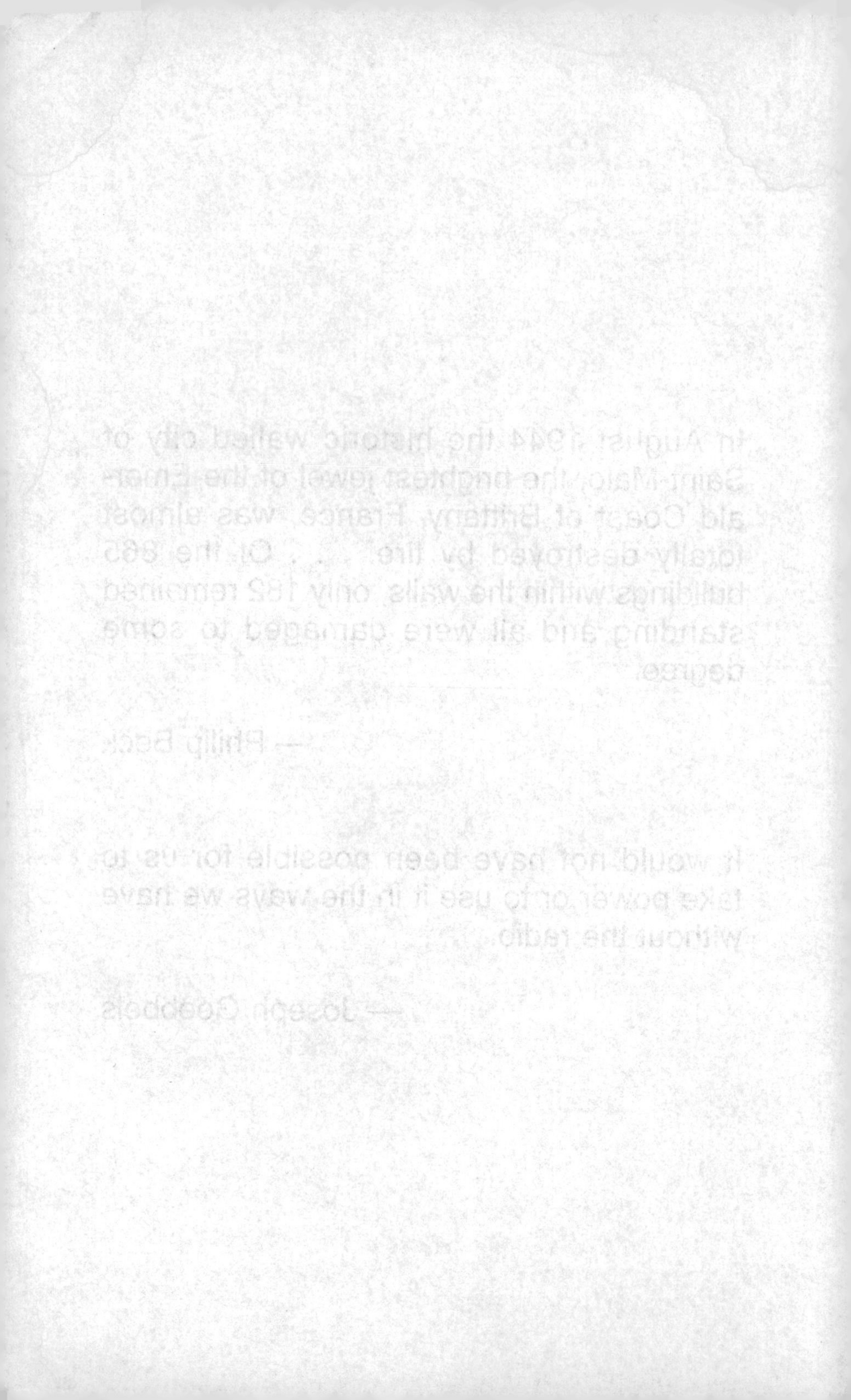

ZERO:
7 AUGUST 1944

LEAFLETS

At dusk they pour from the sky. They blow across the ramparts, turn cartwheels over rooftops, flutter into the ravines between houses. Entire streets swirl with them, flashing white against the cobbles. *Urgent message to the inhabitants of this town,* they say. *Depart immediately to open country.*

The tide climbs. The moon hangs small and yellow and gibbous. On the rooftops of beachfront hotels to the east, and in the gardens behind them, a half-dozen American artillery units drop incendiary rounds into the mouths of mortars.

Bombers

They cross the Channel at midnight. There are twelve and they are named for songs: *Stardust* and *Stormy Weather* and *In the Mood* and *Pistol-Packin' Mama.* The sea glides along far below, spattered with the countless chevrons of whitecaps. Soon enough, the navigators can discern the low moonlit lumps of islands ranged along the horizon.

France.

Intercoms crackle. Deliberately, almost lazily, the bombers shed altitude. Threads of red light ascend from anti-air emplacements up and down the coast. Dark, ruined ships appear, scuttled or destroyed, one with its bow shorn away, a second flickering as it burns. On an outermost island, panicked sheep run zigzagging between rocks.

Inside each airplane, a bombardier peers through an aiming window and counts to twenty. Four five six seven. To the bombardiers, the walled city on its granite headland, drawing ever closer, looks like an unholy tooth, something black and dangerous, a final abscess to be lanced away.

The Girl

In a corner of the city, inside a tall, narrow house at Number 4 rue Vauborel, on the sixth and highest floor, a sightless sixteen-year-old named Marie-Laure LeBlanc kneels over a low table covered entirely with a model. The model is a miniature of the city she kneels within, and contains scale replicas of the hundreds of houses and shops and hotels within its walls. There's the cathedral with its perforated spire, and the bulky old Château de Saint-Malo, and row after row of seaside mansions studded with chimneys. A slender wooden jetty arcs out from a beach called the Plage du Môle; a delicate, reticulated atrium vaults over the seafood market; minute benches, the smallest no larger than apple seeds, dot the tiny public squares.

Marie-Laure runs her fingertips along the centimeter-wide parapet crowning the ramparts, drawing an uneven star shape around the entire model. She finds the opening atop the walls where four ceremonial cannons point to sea. "Bastion de la Hollande," she whispers, and her fingers walk down a little staircase. "Rue des Cordiers. Rue Jacques Cartier."

In a corner of the room stand two galvanized buckets filled to the rim with water. Fill them up, her great-uncle has taught her, whenever you can. The bathtub on the third floor too. Who knows when the water will go out again.

Her fingers travel back to the cathedral spire. South to the Gate of Dinan. All evening she has been marching her fingers around the model, waiting for her great-uncle Etienne, who owns this house, who went out the previous night while she slept, and who has not returned. And now it is night again, another revolution of the clock, and the whole block is quiet, and she cannot sleep.

She can hear the bombers when they are three miles away. A mounting static. The hum inside a seashell.

When she opens the bedroom window, the noise of the airplanes becomes louder. Otherwise, the night is dreadfully silent: no engines, no voices, no clatter. No sirens. No footfalls on the cobbles. Not even gulls. Just a high tide, one block away and six stories below, lapping at the base of the city walls.

And something else.

Something rattling softly, very close. She eases open the left-hand shutter and runs her fingers up the slats of the right. A sheet of paper has lodged there.

She holds it to her nose. It smells of fresh ink. Gasoline, maybe. The paper is crisp; it has not been outside long.

Marie-Laure hesitates at the window in her stocking feet, her bedroom behind her, seashells arranged along the top of the armoire, pebbles along the baseboards. Her cane stands in the corner; her big Braille novel waits facedown on the bed. The drone of the airplanes grows.

The Boy

Five streets to the north, a white-haired eighteen-year-old German private named Werner Pfennig wakes to a faint staccato hum. Little more than a purr. Flies tapping at a far-off windowpane.

Where is he? The sweet, slightly chemical scent of gun oil; the raw wood of newly constructed shell crates; the mothballed odor of old bedspreads — he's in the hotel. Of course. L'hôtel des Abeilles, the Hotel of Bees.

Still night. Still early.

From the direction of the sea come whistles and booms; flak is going up.

An anti-air corporal hurries down the corridor, heading for the stairwell. "Get to the cellar," he calls over his shoulder, and Werner switches on his field light, rolls his blanket into his duffel, and starts down the hall.

Not so long ago, the Hotel of Bees was a cheerful address, with bright blue shutters on its facade and oysters on ice in its café and

Breton waiters in bow ties polishing glasses behind its bar. It offered twenty-one guest rooms, commanding sea views, and a lobby fireplace as big as a truck. Parisians on weekend holidays would drink aperitifs here, and before them the occasional emissary from the republic — ministers and vice ministers and abbots and admirals — and in the centuries before them, windburned corsairs: killers, plunderers, raiders, seamen.

Before that, before it was ever a hotel at all, five full centuries ago, it was the home of a wealthy privateer who gave up raiding ships to study bees in the pastures outside Saint-Malo, scribbling in notebooks and eating honey straight from combs. The crests above the door lintels still have bumblebees carved into the oak; the ivy-covered fountain in the courtyard is shaped like a hive. Werner's favorites are five faded frescoes on the ceilings of the grandest upper rooms, where bees as big as children float against blue backdrops, big lazy drones and workers with diaphanous wings — where, above a hexagonal bathtub, a single nine-foot-long queen, with multiple eyes and a golden-furred abdomen, curls across the ceiling.

Over the past four weeks, the hotel has become something else: a fortress. A detachment of Austrian anti-airmen has boarded up every window, overturned every bed. They've reinforced the entrance, packed the stairwells with crates of artillery shells. The hotel's fourth floor, where garden rooms with French balconies open directly onto the ramparts, has become home to an aging high-velocity anti-air gun called an 88 that can fire twenty-one-and-a-half-pound shells nine miles.

Her Majesty, the Austrians call their cannon, and for the past week these men have tended to it the way worker bees might tend to a queen. They've fed her oils, repainted her barrels, lubricated her wheels; they've arranged sandbags at her feet like offerings.

The royal *acht acht,* a deathly monarch meant to protect them all.

Werner is in the stairwell, halfway to the ground floor, when the 88 fires twice in quick succession. It's the first time he's heard the gun at such close range, and it sounds as if the top half of the hotel has torn off. He stumbles and throws his arms over his ears. The walls reverberate all the way down into the foundation, then back up.

Werner can hear the Austrians two floors up scrambling, reloading, and the receding screams of both shells as they hurtle above the ocean, already two or three miles away. One of the soldiers, he realizes, is singing. Or maybe it is more than one. Maybe they are all singing. Eight Luftwaffe men, none of whom will survive the hour, singing a love song to their queen.

Werner chases the beam of his field light

through the lobby. The big gun detonates a third time, and glass shatters somewhere close by, and torrents of soot rattle down the chimney, and the walls of the hotel toll like a struck bell. Werner worries that the sound will knock the teeth from his gums.

He drags open the cellar door and pauses a moment, vision swimming. "This is it?" he asks. "They're really coming?"

But who is there to answer?

Saint-Malo

Up and down the lanes, the last unevacuated townspeople wake, groan, sigh. Spinsters, prostitutes, men over sixty. Procrastinators, collaborators, disbelievers, drunks. Nuns of every order. The poor. The stubborn. The blind.

Some hurry to bomb shelters. Some tell themselves it is merely a drill. Some linger to grab a blanket or a prayer book or a deck of playing cards.

D-day was two months ago. Cherbourg has been liberated, Caen liberated, Rennes too. Half of western France is free. In the east, the Soviets have retaken Minsk; the Polish Home Army is revolting in Warsaw; a few newspapers have become bold enough to suggest that the tide has turned.

But not here. Not this last citadel at the edge of the continent, this final German strongpoint on the Breton coast.

Here, people whisper, the Germans have renovated two kilometers of subterranean corridors under the medieval walls; they have built new defenses, new conduits, new escape routes, underground complexes of bewildering intricacy. Beneath the peninsular fort of La Cité, across the river from the old city, there are rooms of bandages, rooms of ammunition, even an underground hospital, or so it is believed. There is air-conditioning, a two-hundred-thousand-liter water tank, a direct line to Berlin. There are flame-throwing booby traps, a net of pillboxes with periscopic sights; they have stockpiled enough ordnance to spray shells into the sea all day, every day, for a year.

Here, they whisper, are a thousand Germans ready to die. Or five thousand. Maybe more.

Saint-Malo: Water surrounds the city on four sides. Its link to the rest of France is tenuous: a causeway, a bridge, a spit of sand. We are Malouins first, say the people of Saint-Malo. Bretons next. French if there's anything left over.

In stormy light, its granite glows blue. At the highest tides, the sea creeps into basements at the very center of town. At the lowest tides, the barnacled ribs of a thousand shipwrecks stick out above the sea.

For three thousand years, this little promontory has known sieges.

But never like this.

A grandmother lifts a fussy toddler to her

chest. A drunk, urinating in an alley outside Saint-Servan, a mile away, plucks a sheet of paper from a hedge. *Urgent message to the inhabitants of this town,* it says. *Depart immediately to open country.*

Anti-air batteries flash on the outer islands, and the big German guns inside the old city send another round of shells howling over the sea, and three hundred and eighty Frenchmen imprisoned on an island fortress called National, a quarter mile off the beach, huddle in a moonlit courtyard peering up.

Four years of occupation, and the roar of oncoming bombers is the roar of what? Deliverance? Extirpation?

The clack-clack of small-arms fire. The gravelly snare drums of flak. A dozen pigeons roosting on the cathedral spire cataract down its length and wheel out over the sea.

Number 4 Rue Vauborel

Marie-Laure LeBlanc stands alone in her bedroom smelling a leaflet she cannot read. Sirens wail. She closes the shutters and relatches the window. Every second the airplanes draw closer; every second is a second lost. She should be rushing downstairs. She should be making for the corner of the kitchen where a little trapdoor opens into a cellar full of dust and mouse-chewed rugs and ancient trunks long unopened.

Instead she returns to the table at the foot of the bed and kneels beside the model of the city.

Again her fingers find the outer ramparts, the Bastion de la Hollande, the little staircase leading down. In this window, right here, in the real city, a woman beats her rugs every Sunday. From this window here, a boy once yelled, *Watch where you're going, are you blind?*

The windowpanes rattle in their housings. The anti-air guns unleash another volley. The earth rotates just a bit farther.

Beneath her fingertips, the miniature rue d'Estrées intersects the miniature rue Vauborel. Her fingers turn right; they skim doorways. One two three. Four. How many times has she done this?

Number 4: the tall, derelict bird's nest of a house owned by her great-uncle Etienne. Where she has lived for four years. Where she kneels on the sixth floor alone, as a dozen American bombers roar toward her.

She presses inward on the tiny front door, and a hidden catch releases, and the little house lifts up and out of the model. In her hands, it's about the size of one of her father's cigarette boxes.

Now the bombers are so close that the floor starts to throb under her knees. Out in the hall, the crystal pendants of the chandelier suspended above the stairwell chime. Marie-Laure twists the chimney of the miniature house ninety degrees. Then she slides off three wooden panels that make up its roof, and turns it over.

A stone drops into her palm.

It's cold. The size of a pigeon's egg. The shape of a teardrop.

Marie-Laure clutches the tiny house in one hand and the stone in the other. The room feels flimsy, tenuous. Giant fingertips seem about to punch through its walls.

"Papa?" she whispers.

Cellar

Beneath the lobby of the Hotel of Bees, a corsair's cellar has been hacked out of the bedrock. Behind crates and cabinets and pegboards of tools, the walls are bare granite. Three massive hand-hewn beams, hauled here from some ancient Breton forest and craned into place centuries ago by teams of horses, hold up the ceiling.

A single lightbulb casts everything in a wavering shadow.

Werner Pfennig sits on a folding chair in front of a workbench, checks his battery level, and puts on headphones. The radio is a steel-cased two-way transceiver with a 1.6-meter band antenna. It enables him to communicate with a matching transceiver upstairs, with two other anti-air batteries inside the walls of the city, and with the underground garrison command across the river mouth.

The transceiver hums as it warms. A spotter reads coordinates into the headpiece, and an artilleryman repeats them back. Werner rubs his eyes. Behind him, confiscated treasures are crammed to the ceiling: rolled tapestries, grandfather clocks, armoires, and giant landscape paintings crazed with cracks. On a shelf opposite Werner sit eight or nine plaster heads, the purpose of which he cannot guess.

The massive staff sergeant Frank Volkheimer comes down the narrow wooden stairs and ducks his head beneath the beams. He smiles gently at Werner and sits in a tall-backed armchair upholstered in golden silk with his rifle across his huge thighs, where it looks like little more than a baton.

Werner says, “It’s starting?”

Volkheimer nods. He switches off his field light and blinks his strangely delicate eyelashes in the dimness.

“How long will it last?”

“Not long. We’ll be safe down here.”

The engineer, Bernd, comes last. He is a little man with mousy hair and misaligned pupils. He closes the cellar door behind him and bars it and sits halfway down the wooden staircase with a damp look on his face, fear or grit, it’s hard to say.

With the door shut, the sound of the sirens softens. Above them, the ceiling bulb flickers.

Water, thinks Werner. I forgot water.

A second anti-air battery fires from a distant corner of the city, and then the 88 upstairs goes again, stentorian, deadly, and

Werner listens to the shell scream into the sky. Cascades of dust hiss out of the ceiling. Through his headphones, Werner can hear the Austrians upstairs still singing.

. . . auf d'Wulda, auf d'Wulda, da scheint d'Sunn a so gulda . . .

Volkheimer picks sleepily at a stain on his trousers. Bernd blows into his cupped hands. The transceiver crackles with wind speeds, air pressure, trajectories. Werner thinks of home: Frau Elena bent over his little shoes, double-knotting each lace. Stars wheeling past a dormer window. His little sister, Jutta, with a quilt around her shoulders and a radio earpiece trailing from her left ear.

Four stories up, the Austrians clap another shell into the smoking breech of the 88 and double-check the traverse and clamp their ears as the gun discharges, but down here Werner hears only the radio voices of his childhood. *The Goddess of History looked down to earth. Only through the hottest fires can purification be achieved.* He sees a forest of dying sunflowers. He sees a flock of blackbirds explode out of a tree.

Bombs Away

Seventeen eighteen nineteen twenty. Now the sea races beneath the aiming windows. Now rooftops. Two smaller aircraft line the corridor with smoke, and the lead bomber salvos its payload, and eleven others follow suit. The bombs fall diagonally; the bombers rise and scramble.

The underside of the sky goes black with flecks. Marie-Laure's great-uncle, locked with several hundred others inside the gates of Fort National, a quarter mile offshore, squints up and thinks, *Locusts,* and an Old Testament proverb comes back to him from some cobwebbed hour of parish school: *The locusts have no king, yet all of them go out in ranks.*

A demonic horde. Upended sacks of beans. A hundred broken rosaries. There are a thousand metaphors and all of them are inadequate: forty bombs per aircraft, four hundred and eighty altogether, seventy-two thousand pounds of explosives.

An avalanche descends onto the city. A hurricane. Teacups drift off shelves. Paintings slip off nails. In another quarter second, the sirens are inaudible. Everything is inaudible. The roar becomes loud enough to separate membranes in the middle ear.

The anti-air guns let fly their final shells. Twelve bombers fold back unharmed into the blue night.

On the sixth floor of Number 4 rue Vauborel, Marie-Laure crawls beneath her bed and clamps the stone and little model house to her chest.

In the cellar beneath the Hotel of Bees, the single bulb in the ceiling winks out.

One: 1934

Muséum National d'Histoire Naturelle

Marie-Laure LeBlanc is a tall and freckled six-year-old in Paris with rapidly deteriorating eyesight when her father sends her on a children's tour of the museum where he works. The guide is a hunchbacked old warder hardly taller than a child himself. He raps the tip of his cane against the floor for attention, then leads his dozen charges across the gardens to the galleries.

The children watch engineers use pulleys to lift a fossilized dinosaur femur. They see a stuffed giraffe in a closet, patches of hide wearing off its back. They peer into taxidermists' drawers full of feathers and talons and glass eyeballs; they flip through two-hundred-year-old herbarium sheets bedecked with orchids and daisies and herbs.

Eventually they climb sixteen steps into the Gallery of Mineralogy. The guide shows them agate from Brazil and violet amethysts and a meteorite on a pedestal that he claims is as ancient as the solar system itself. Then he leads them single file down two twisting staircases and along several corridors and stops outside an iron door with a single keyhole. "End of tour," he says.

A girl says, "But what's through there?"

"Behind this door is another locked door, slightly smaller."

"And what's behind that?"

"A third locked door, smaller yet."

"What's behind that?"

"A fourth door, and a fifth, on and on until you reach a thirteenth, a little locked door no bigger than a shoe."

The children lean forward. "And then?"

"Behind the thirteenth door" — the guide flourishes one of his impossibly wrinkled hands — "is the Sea of Flames."

Puzzlement. Fidgeting.

"Come now. You've never heard of the Sea of Flames?"

The children shake their heads. Marie-Laure squints up at the naked bulbs strung in three-yard intervals along the ceiling; each sets a rainbow-colored halo rotating in her vision.

The guide hangs his cane on his wrist and rubs his hands together. "It's a long story. Do you want to hear a long story?"

They nod.

He clears his throat. "Centuries ago, in the place we now call Borneo, a prince plucked a blue stone from a dry riverbed because he thought it was pretty. But on the way back to his palace, the prince was attacked by men on horseback and stabbed in the heart."

"Stabbed in the heart?"

"Is this true?"

A boy says, "Hush."

"The thieves stole his rings, his horse, everything. But because the little blue stone was clenched in his fist, they did not discover it. And the dying prince managed to crawl home. Then he fell unconscious for ten days. On the tenth day, to the amazement of his nurses, he sat up, opened his hand, and there was the stone.

"The sultan's doctors said it was a miracle, that the prince never should have survived such a violent wound. The nurses said the stone must have healing powers. The sultan's jewelers said something else: they said the stone was the largest raw diamond anyone had ever seen. Their most gifted stonecutter spent eighty days faceting it, and when he was done, it was a brilliant blue, the blue of tropical seas, but it had a touch of red at its center, like flames inside a drop of water. The sultan had the diamond fitted into a crown for the prince, and it was said that when the young prince sat on his throne and the sun hit him just so, he became so dazzling that visitors could not distinguish his figure from light itself."

"Are you sure this is true?" asks a girl.

"Hush," says the boy.

"The stone came to be known as the Sea of Flames. Some believed the prince was a deity, that as long as he kept the stone, he could not be killed. But something strange began to happen: the longer the prince wore his crown, the worse his luck became. In a month, he lost a brother to drowning and a second brother to snakebite. Within six months, his father died of disease. To make matters even worse, the sultan's scouts announced that a great army was gathering in the east.

"The prince called together his father's advisers. All said he should prepare for war, all but one, a priest, who said he'd had a dream. In the dream the Goddess of the Earth told him she'd made the Sea of Flames as a gift for her lover, the God of the Sea, and was sending the jewel to him through the river. But when the river dried up, and the prince plucked it out, the goddess became enraged. She cursed the stone and whoever kept it."

Every child leans forward, Marie-Laure along with them.

"The curse was this: the keeper of the stone would live forever, but so long as he kept it, misfortunes would fall on all those he loved one after another in unending rain."

"Live forever?"

"But if the keeper threw the diamond into

the sea, thereby delivering it to its rightful recipient, the goddess would lift the curse. So the prince, now sultan, thought for three days and three nights and finally decided to keep the stone. It had saved his life; he believed it made him indestructible. He had the tongue cut out of the priest's mouth."

"Ouch," says the youngest boy.

"Big mistake," says the tallest girl.

"The invaders came," says the warder, "and destroyed the palace, and killed everyone they found, and the prince was never seen again, and for two hundred years no one heard any more about the Sea of Flames. Some said the stone was recut into many smaller stones; others said the prince still carried the stone, that he was in Japan or Persia, that he was a humble farmer, that he never seemed to grow old.

"And so the stone fell out of history. Until one day, when a French diamond trader, during a trip to the Golconda Mines in India, was shown a massive pear-cut diamond. One hundred and thirty-three carats. Near-perfect clarity. As big as a pigeon's egg, he wrote, and as blue as the sea, but with a flare of red at its core. He made a casting of the stone and sent it to a gem-crazy duke in Lorraine, warning him of the rumors of a curse. But the duke wanted the diamond very badly. So the trader brought it to Europe, and the duke fitted it into the end of a walking stick and carried it everywhere."

"Uh-oh."

"Within a month, the duchess contracted a throat disease. Two of their favorite servants fell off the roof and broke their necks. Then the duke's only son died in a riding accident. Though everyone said the duke himself had never looked better, he became afraid to go out, afraid to accept visitors. Eventually he was so convinced that his stone was the accursed Sea of Flames that he asked the king to shut it up in his museum on the conditions that it be locked deep inside a specially built vault and the vault not be opened for two hundred years."

"And?"

"And one hundred and ninety-six years have passed."

All the children remain quiet a moment. Several do math on their fingers. Then they raise their hands as one. "Can we see it?"

"No."

"Not even open the first door?"

"No."

"Have *you* seen it?"

"I have not."

"So how do you know it's really there?"

"You have to believe the story."

"How much is it worth, Monsieur? Could it buy the Eiffel Tower?"

"A diamond that large and rare could in all likelihood buy five Eiffel Towers."

Gasps.

"Are all those doors to keep thieves from getting in?"

"Maybe," the guide says, and winks, "they're there to keep the curse from getting out."

The children fall quiet. Two or three take a step back.

Marie-Laure takes off her eyeglasses, and the world goes shapeless. "Why not," she asks, "just take the diamond and throw it into the sea?"

The warder looks at her. The other children look at her. "When is the last time," one of the older boys says, "you saw someone throw five Eiffel Towers into the sea?"

There is laughter. Marie-Laure frowns. It is just an iron door with a brass keyhole.

The tour ends and the children disperse and Marie-Laure is reinstalled in the Grand Gallery with her father. He straightens her glasses on her nose and plucks a leaf from her hair. "Did you have fun, *ma chérie*?"

A little brown house sparrow swoops out of the rafters and lands on the tiles in front of her. Marie-Laure holds out an open palm. The sparrow tilts his head, considering. Then it flaps away.

One month later she is blind.

Zollverein

Werner Pfennig grows up three hundred miles northeast of Paris in a place called Zollverein: a four-thousand-acre coal-mining complex outside Essen, Germany. It's steel country, anthracite country, a place full of holes. Smokestacks fume and locomotives trundle back and forth on elevated conduits and leafless trees stand atop slag heaps like skeleton hands shoved up from the underworld.

Werner and his younger sister, Jutta, are raised at Children's House, a clinker-brick two-story orphanage on Viktoriastrasse whose rooms are populated with the coughs of sick children and the crying of newborns and battered trunks inside which drowse the last possessions of deceased parents: patchwork dresses, tarnished wedding cutlery, faded ambrotypes of fathers swallowed by the mines.

Werner's earliest years are the leanest. Men brawl over jobs outside the Zollverein gates, and chicken eggs sell for two million reichsmarks apiece, and rheumatic fever stalks Children's House like a wolf. There is no butter or meat. Fruit is a memory. Some evenings, during the worst months, all the house directress has to feed her dozen wards are cakes made from mustard powder and water.

But seven-year-old Werner seems to float. He is undersized and his ears stick out and he speaks with a high, sweet voice; the whiteness of his hair stops people in their tracks. Snowy, milky, chalky. A color that is the absence of color. Every morning he ties his shoes, packs newspaper inside his coat as insulation against the cold, and begins interrogating the world. He captures snowflakes, tadpoles, hibernating frogs; he coaxes bread from bakers with none to sell; he regularly appears in the kitchen with fresh milk for the babies. He makes things too: paper boxes, crude biplanes, toy boats with working rudders.

Every couple of days he'll startle the directress with some unanswerable query: "Why do we get hiccups, Frau Elena?"

Or: "If the moon is so big, Frau Elena, how come it looks so little?"

Or: "Frau Elena, does a bee know it's going to die if it stings somebody?"

Frau Elena is a Protestant nun from Alsace who is more fond of children than of supervision. She sings French folk songs in a screechy falsetto, harbors a weakness for sherry, and regularly falls asleep standing up. Some nights she lets the children stay up late while she tells them stories in French about her girlhood cozied up against mountains, snow six feet deep on rooftops, town criers and creeks smoking in the cold and frost-dusted vineyards: a Christmas-carol world.

"Can deaf people hear their heartbeat, Frau Elena?"

"Why doesn't glue stick to the inside of the bottle, Frau Elena?"

She'll laugh. She'll tousle Werner's hair; she'll whisper, "They'll say you're too little, Werner, that you're from nowhere, that you shouldn't dream big. But I believe in you. I think you'll do something great." Then she'll send him up to the little cot he has claimed for himself in the attic, pressed up beneath the window of a dormer.

Sometimes he and Jutta draw. His sister sneaks up to Werner's cot, and together they lie on their stomachs and pass a single pencil back and forth. Jutta, though she is two years younger, is the gifted one. She loves most of all to draw Paris, a city she has seen in exactly one photograph, on the back cover of one of Frau Elena's romance novels: mansard roofs, hazy apartment blocks, the iron lattice of a distant tower. She draws twisting white skyscrapers, complicated bridges, flocks of figures beside a river.

Other days, in the hours after lessons,

Werner tows his little sister through the mine complex in a wagon he has assembled from cast-off parts. They rattle down the long gravel lanes, past pit cottages and trash barrel fires, past laid-off miners squatting all day on upturned crates, motionless as statues. One wheel regularly clunks off and Werner crouches patiently beside it, threading back the bolts. All around them, the figures of second-shift workers shuffle into warehouses while first-shift workers shuffle home, hunched, hungry, blue-nosed, their faces like black skulls beneath their helmets. "Hello," Werner will chirp, "good afternoon," but the miners usually hobble past without replying, perhaps without even seeing him, their eyes on the muck, the economic collapse of Germany looming over them like the severe geometry of the mills.

Werner and Jutta sift through glistening piles of black dust; they clamber up mountains of rusting machines. They tear berries out of brambles and dandelions out of fields. Sometimes they manage to find potato peels or carrot greens in trash bins; other afternoons they collect paper to draw on, or old toothpaste tubes from which the last dregs can be squeezed out and dried into chalk. Once in a while Werner tows Jutta as far as the entrance to Pit Nine, the largest of the mines, wrapped in noise, lit like the pilot at the center of a gas furnace, a five-story coal elevator crouched over it, cables swinging, hammers banging, men shouting, an entire mapful of pleated and corrugated industry stretching into the distance on all sides, and they watch the coal cars trundling up from the earth and the miners spilling out of warehouses with their lunch pails toward the mouth of the elevator like insects toward a lighted trap.

"Down there," Werner whispers to his sister. "That's where Father died."

And as night falls, Werner pulls little Jutta wordlessly back through the close-set neighborhoods of Zollverein, two snowy-haired children in a bottomland of soot, bearing their paltry treasures to Viktoriastrasse 3, where Frau Elena stares into the coal stove, singing a French lullaby in a tired voice, one toddler yanking her apron strings while another howls in her arms.

KEY POUND

Congenital cataracts. Bilateral. Irreparable. “Can you see this?” ask the doctors. “Can you see this?” Marie-Laure will not see anything for the rest of her life. Spaces she once knew as familiar — the four-room flat she shares with her father, the little tree-lined square at the end of their street — have become labyrinths bristling with hazards. Drawers are never where they should be. The toilet is an abyss. A glass of water is too near, too far; her fingers too big, always too big.

What is blindness? Where there should be a wall, her hands find nothing. Where there should be nothing, a table leg gouges her shin. Cars growl in the streets; leaves whisper in the sky; blood rustles through her inner ears. In the stairwell, in the kitchen, even beside her bed, grown-up voices speak of despair.

“Poor child.”

“Poor Monsieur LeBlanc.”

“Hasn’t had an easy road, you know. His

father dead in the war, his wife dead in childbirth. And now this?"

"Like they're cursed."

"Look at her. Look at him."

"Ought to send her away."

Those are months of bruises and wretchedness: rooms pitching like sailboats, half-open doors striking Marie-Laure's face. Her only sanctuary is in bed, the hem of her quilt at her chin, while her father smokes another cigarette in the chair beside her, whittling away at one of his tiny models, his little hammer going tap tap tap, his little square of sandpaper making a rhythmic, soothing rasp.

The despair doesn't last. Marie-Laure is too young and her father is too patient. There are, he assures her, no such things as curses. There is luck, maybe, bad or good. A slight inclination of each day toward success or failure. But no curses.

Six mornings a week he wakes her before dawn, and she holds her arms in the air while he dresses her. Stockings, dress, sweater. If there's time, he makes her try to knot her shoes herself. Then they drink a cup of coffee together in the kitchen: hot, strong, as much sugar as she wants.

At six forty she collects her white cane from the corner, loops a finger through the back of her father's belt, and follows him down three flights and up six blocks to the museum.

He unlocks Entrance #2 at seven sharp. Inside are the familiar smells: typewriter ribbons, waxed floors, rock dust. There are the familiar echoes of their footfalls crossing the Grand Gallery. He greets a night guard, then a warder, always the same two words repeated back: *Bonjour, bonjour.*

Two lefts, one right. Her father's key ring jingles. A lock gives way; a gate swings open.

Inside the key pound, inside six glass-fronted cabinets, thousands of iron keys hang from pegs. There are blanks and skeletons, barrel-stem keys and saturn-bow keys, elevator keys and cabinet keys. Keys as long as Marie-Laure's forearm and keys shorter than her thumb.

Marie-Laure's father is principal locksmith for the National Museum of Natural History. Between the laboratories, warehouses, four separate public museums, the menagerie, the greenhouses, the acres of medicinal and decorative gardens in the Jardin des Plantes, and a dozen gates and pavilions, her father estimates there are twelve thousand locks in the entire museum complex. No one else knows enough to disagree.

All morning he stands at the front of the key pound and distributes keys to employees: zookeepers coming first, office staff arriving in a rush around eight, technicians and librarians and scientific assistants trooping in next, scientists trickling in last. Everything is numbered and color-coded. Every employee from custodians to the director must carry his or her keys at all times. No one is allowed to leave his respective building with keys, and no one is allowed to leave keys on a desk. The museum possesses priceless jade from the thirteenth century, after all, and cavansite from India and rhodochrosite from Colorado; behind a lock her father has designed sits a Florentine dispensary bowl carved from lapis lazuli that specialists travel a thousand miles every year to examine.

Her father quizzes her. Vault key or padlock key, Marie? Cupboard key or dead bolt key? He tests her on the locations of displays, on the contents of cabinets. He is continually placing some unexpected thing into her hands: a lightbulb, a fossilized fish, a flamingo feather.

For an hour each morning — even Sundays — he makes her sit over a Braille workbook. *A* is one dot in the upper corner. *B* is two dots in a vertical line. *Jean. Goes. To. The. Baker. Jean. Goes. To. The. Cheese. Maker.*

In the afternoons he takes her on his rounds. He oils latches, repairs cabinets, polishes escutcheons. He leads her down hallway after hallway into gallery after gallery. Narrow corridors open into immense libraries; glass doors give way to hothouses overflowing with the smells of humus, wet newspaper, and lobelia. There are carpenters' shops, taxidermists' studios, acres of shelves and specimen drawers, whole museums within the museum.

Some afternoons he leaves Marie-Laure in the laboratory of Dr. Geffard, an aging mollusk expert whose beard smells permanently of damp wool. Dr. Geffard will stop whatever he is doing and open a bottle of Malbec and tell Marie-Laure in his whispery voice about reefs he visited as a young man: the Seychelles, Belize, Zanzibar. He calls her Laurette; he eats a roasted duck every day at 3 P.M.; his mind accommodates a seemingly inexhaustible catalog of Latin binomial names.

On the back wall of Dr. Geffard's lab are cabinets that contain more drawers than she can count, and he lets her open them one after another and hold seashells in her hands — whelks, olives, imperial volutes from Thailand, spider conchs from Polynesia — the museum possesses more than ten thousand specimens, over half the known species in the world, and Marie-Laure gets to handle most of them.

"Now that shell, Laurette, belonged to a violet sea snail, a blind snail that lives its whole life on the surface of the sea. As soon as it is released into the ocean, it agitates the water to make bubbles, and binds those bubbles with mucus, and builds a raft. Then it blows around, feeding on whatever floating aquatic invertebrates it encounters. But if it ever loses its raft, it will sink and die . . ."

A *Carinaria* shell is simultaneously light and heavy, hard and soft, smooth and rough. The murex Dr. Geffard keeps on his desk can entertain her for a half hour, the hollow spines, the ridged whorls, the deep entrance; it's a forest of spikes and caves and textures; it's a kingdom.

Her hands move ceaselessly, gathering, probing, testing. The breast feathers of a stuffed and mounted chickadee are impossibly soft, its beak as sharp as a needle. The pollen at the tips of tulip anthers is not so much powder as it is tiny balls of oil. To really touch something, she is learning — the bark of a sycamore tree in the gardens; a pinned stag beetle in the Department of Etymology; the exquisitely polished interior of a scallop shell in Dr. Geffard's workshop — is to love it.

At home, in the evenings, her father stows their shoes in the same cubby, hangs their coats on the same hooks. Marie-Laure crosses six evenly spaced friction strips on the kitchen tiles to reach the table; she follows a strand of twine he has threaded from the table to the toilet. He serves dinner on a round plate and describes the locations of different foods by the hands of a clock. Potatoes at six o'clock, *ma chérie.* Mushrooms at three. Then he lights a cigarette and goes to work on his miniatures at a workbench in the corner of the kitchen. He is building a scale model of their entire neighborhood, the tall-windowed houses, the rain gutters, the *laverie* and *boulangerie* and the little *place* at the end of the street with its four benches and ten trees. On warm nights Marie-Laure opens her bedroom window and listens to the evening as it settles over the balconies and gables and chimneys, languid and peaceful, until the real neighborhood and the miniature one get mixed up in her mind.

Tuesdays the museum is closed. Marie-Laure and her father sleep in; they drink coffee thick with sugar. They walk to the Panthéon, or to a flower market, or along the Seine. Every so often they visit the bookshop. He hands her a dictionary, a journal, a magazine full of photographs. "How many pages, Marie-Laure?"

She runs a nail along the edge.

"Fifty-two?" "Seven hundred and five?" "One hundred thirty-nine?"

He sweeps her hair back from her ears; he swings her above his head. He says she is his *émerveillement.* He says he will never leave her, not in a million years.

Radio

Werner is eight years old and ferreting about in the refuse behind a storage shed when he discovers what looks like a large spool of thread. It consists of a wire-wrapped cylinder sandwiched between two discs of pinewood. Three frayed electrical leads sprout from the top. One has a small earphone dangling from its end.

Jutta, six years old, with a round face and a mashed cumulus of white hair, crouches beside her brother. "What is that?"

"I think," Werner says, feeling as though some cupboard in the sky has just opened, "we just found a radio."

Until now he has seen radios only in glimpses: a big cabinet wireless through the lace curtains of an official's house; a portable unit in a miners' dormitory; another in the church refectory. He has never touched one.

He and Jutta smuggle the device back to Viktoriastrasse 3 and appraise it beneath an electric lamp. They wipe it clean, untangle the snarl of wires, wash mud out of the earphone.

It does not work. Other children come and stand over them and marvel, then gradually lose interest and conclude it is hopeless. But Werner carries the receiver up to his attic dormer and studies it for hours. He disconnects everything that will disconnect; he lays its parts out on the floor and holds them one by one to the light.

Three weeks after finding the device, on a sun-gilded afternoon when perhaps every other child in Zollverein is outdoors, he notices that its longest wire, a slender filament coiled hundreds of times around the central cylinder, has several small breaks in it. Slowly, meticulously, he unwraps the coil, carries the entire looped mess downstairs, and calls Jutta inside to hold the pieces for him while he splices the breaks. Then he rewraps it.

"Now let's try," he whispers, and presses the earphone against his ear and runs what he has decided must be the tuning pin back and forth along the coil.

He hears a fizz of static. Then, from somewhere deep inside the earpiece, a stream of consonants issues forth. Werner's heart pauses; the voice seems to echo in the architecture of his head.

The sound fades as quickly as it came. He shifts the pin a quarter inch. More static.

Another quarter inch. Nothing.

In the kitchen, Frau Elena kneads bread. Boys shout in the alley. Werner guides the tuning pin back and forth.

Static, static.

He is about to hand the earphone to Jutta when — clear and unblemished, about halfway down the coil — he hears the quick, drastic strikes of a bow dashing across the strings of a violin. He tries to hold the pin perfectly still. A second violin joins the first. Jutta drags herself closer; she watches her brother with outsize eyes.

A piano chases the violins. Then woodwinds. The strings sprint, woodwinds fluttering behind. More instruments join in. Flutes? Harps? The song races, seems to loop back over itself.

"Werner?" Jutta whispers.

He blinks; he has to swallow back tears. The parlor looks the same as it always has: two cribs beneath two Latin crosses, dust floating in the open mouth of the stove, a dozen layers of paint peeling off the baseboards. A needlepoint of Frau Elena's snowy Alsatian village above the sink. Yet now there is music. As if, inside Werner's head, an infinitesimal orchestra has stirred to life.

The room seems to fall into a slow spin. His sister says his name more urgently, and he presses the earphone to her ear.

"Music," she says.

He holds the pin as stock-still as he can. The signal is weak enough that, though the earphone is six inches away, he can't hear any trace of the song. But he watches his sister's face, motionless except for her eyelids, and in the kitchen Frau Elena holds her flour-whitened hands in the air and cocks her head, studying Werner, and two older boys rush in and stop, sensing some change in the air, and the little radio with its four terminals and trailing aerial sits motionless on the floor between them all like a miracle.

Take Us Home

Usually Marie-Laure can solve the wooden puzzle boxes her father creates for her birthdays. Often they are shaped like houses and contain some hidden trinket. Opening them involves a cunning series of steps: find a seam with your fingernails, slide the bottom to the right, detach a side rail, remove a hidden key from inside the rail, unlock the top, and discover a bracelet inside.

For her seventh birthday, a tiny wooden chalet stands in the center of the kitchen table where the sugar bowl ought to be. She slides a hidden drawer out of the base, finds a hidden compartment beneath the drawer, takes out a wooden key, and slots the key inside the chimney. Inside waits a square of Swiss chocolate.

"Four minutes," says her father, laughing. "I'll have to work harder next year."

For a long time, though, unlike his puzzle boxes, his model of their neighborhood makes little sense to her. It is not like the real world. The miniature intersection of rue de Mirbel and rue Monge, for example, just a block from their apartment, is nothing like the real intersection. The real one presents an amphitheater of noise and fragrance: in the fall it smells of traffic and castor oil, bread from the bakery, camphor from Avent's pharmacy, delphiniums and sweet peas and roses from the flower stand. On winter days it swims with the odor of roasting chestnuts; on summer evenings it becomes slow and drowsy, full of sleepy conversations and the scraping of heavy iron chairs.

But her father's model of the same intersection smells only of dried glue and sawdust. Its streets are empty, its pavements static; to her fingers, it serves as little more than a tiny and insufficient facsimile. He persists in asking Marie-Laure to run her fingers over it, to recognize different houses, the angles of streets. And one cold Tuesday in December, when Marie-Laure has been blind for over a year, her father walks her up rue Cuvier to the edge of the Jardin des Plantes.

"Here, *ma chérie,* is the path we take every morning. Through the cedars up ahead is the Grand Gallery."

"I know, Papa."

He picks her up and spins her around three times. "Now," he says, "you're going to take us home."

Her mouth drops open.

"I want you to think of the model, Marie."

"But I can't possibly!"

"I'm one step behind you. I won't let anything happen. You have your cane. You know where you are."

"I do not!"

"You do."

Exasperation. She cannot even say if the gardens are ahead or behind.

"Calm yourself, Marie. One centimeter at a time."

"It's far, Papa. Six blocks, at least."

"Six blocks is exactly right. Use logic. Which way should we go first?"

The world pivots and rumbles. Crows shout, brakes hiss, someone to her left bangs something metal with what might be a hammer. She shuffles forward until the tip of her cane floats in space. The edge of a curb? A pond, a staircase, a cliff? She turns ninety degrees. Three steps forward. Now her cane finds the base of a wall. "Papa?"

"I'm here."

Six paces seven paces eight. A roar of noise — an exterminator just leaving a house, pump bellowing — overtakes them. Twelve paces farther on, the bell tied around the handle of a shop door rings, and two women come out, jostling her as they pass.

Marie-Laure drops her cane; she begins to cry.

Her father lifts her, holds her to his narrow chest.

"It's so big," she whispers.

"You can do this, Marie."

She cannot.

Something Rising

While the other children play hopscotch in the alley or swim in the canal, Werner sits alone in his upstairs dormer, experimenting with the radio receiver. In a week he can dismantle and rebuild it with his eyes closed. Capacitor, inductor, tuning coil, earpiece. One wire goes to ground, the other to sky. Nothing he's encountered before has made so much sense.

He harvests parts from supply sheds: snips of copper wire, screws, a bent screwdriver. He charms the druggist's wife into giving him a broken earphone; he salvages a solenoid from a discarded doorbell, solders it to a resistor, and makes a loudspeaker. Within a month he manages to redesign the receiver entirely, adding new parts here and there and connecting it to a power source.

Every evening he carries his radio downstairs, and Frau Elena lets her wards listen for an hour. They tune in to newscasts, concerts, operas, national choirs, folk shows, a dozen children in a semicircle on the furniture, Frau Elena among them, hardly more substantial than a child herself.

We live in exciting times, says the radio. *We make no complaints. We will plant our feet firmly in our earth, and no attack will move us.*

The older girls like musical competitions, radio gymnastics, a regular spot called *Seasonal Tips for Those in Love* that makes the younger children squeal. The boys like plays, news bulletins, martial anthems. Jutta likes jazz. Werner likes everything. Violins, horns, drums, speeches — a mouth against a microphone in some faraway yet simultaneous evening — the sorcery of it holds him rapt.

Is it any wonder, asks the radio, *that courage, confidence, and optimism in growing measure fill the German people? Is not the flame of a new faith rising from this sacrificial readiness?*

Indeed it does seem to Werner, as the weeks go by, that something new is rising. Mine production increases; unemployment drops. Meat appears at Sunday supper. Lamb, pork, wieners — extravagances unheard of a year before. Frau Elena buys a new couch upholstered in orange corduroy, and a range with burners in black rings; three new Bibles arrive from the consistory in Berlin; a laundry boiler is delivered to the back door. Werner gets new trousers; Jutta gets her own pair of shoes. Working telephones ring in the houses of neighbors.

One afternoon, on the walk home from school, Werner stops outside the drugstore and presses his nose to a tall window: five dozen inch-tall storm troopers march there, each toy man with a brown shirt and tiny red armband, some with flutes, some with drums, a few officers astride glossy black stallions. Above them, suspended from a wire, a tin-plate clockwork aquaplane with wooden pontoons and a rotating propeller makes an electric, hypnotizing orbit. Werner studies it through the glass for a long time, trying to understand how it works.

Night falls, autumn in 1936, and Werner carries the radio downstairs and sets it on the sideboard, and the other children fidget in anticipation. The receiver hums as it warms. Werner steps back, hands in pockets. From the loudspeaker, a children's choir sings, *We hope only to work, to work and work and work, to go to glorious work for the country.* Then a state-sponsored play out of Berlin begins: a story of invaders sneaking into a village at night.

All twelve children sit riveted. In the play, the invaders pose as hook-nosed department-store owners, crooked jewelers, dishonorable bankers; they sell glittering trash; they drive established village businessmen out of work. Soon they plot to murder German children in their beds. Eventually a vigilant and humble neighbor catches on. Police are called: big handsome-sounding policemen with splendid voices. They break down the doors. They drag the invaders away. A patriotic march plays. Everyone is happy again.

Light

Tuesday after Tuesday she fails. She leads her father on six-block detours that leave her angry and frustrated and farther from home than when they started. But in the winter of her eighth year, to Marie-Laure's surprise, she begins to get it right. She runs her fingers over the model in their kitchen, counting miniature benches, trees, lampposts, doorways. Every day some new detail emerges — each storm drain, park bench, and hydrant in the model has its counterpart in the real world.

Marie-Laure brings her father closer to home before making a mistake. Four blocks three blocks two. And one snowy Tuesday in March, when he walks her to yet another new spot, very close to the banks of the Seine, spins her around three times, and says, "Take us home," she realizes that, for the first time since they began this exercise, dread has not come trundling up from her gut.

Instead she squats on her heels on the

sidewalk.

The faintly metallic smell of the falling snow surrounds her. *Calm yourself. Listen.*

Cars splash along streets, and snowmelt drums through runnels; she can hear snowflakes tick and patter through the trees. She can smell the cedars in the Jardin des Plantes a quarter mile away. Here the Metro hurtles beneath the sidewalk: that's the Quai Saint-Bernard. Here the sky opens up, and she hears the clacking of branches: that's the narrow stripe of gardens behind the Gallery of Paleontology. This, she realizes, must be the corner of the quay and rue Cuvier.

Six blocks, forty buildings, ten tiny trees in a square. This street intersects this street intersects this street. One centimeter at a time.

Her father stirs the keys in his pockets. Ahead loom the tall, grand houses that flank the gardens, reflecting sound.

She says, "We go left."

They start up the length of the rue Cuvier. A trio of airborne ducks threads toward them, flapping their wings in synchrony, making for the Seine, and as the birds rush overhead, she imagines she can feel the light settling over their wings, striking each individual feather.

Left on rue Linné. Right on rue Daubenton. Three storm drains four storm drains five. Approaching on the left will be the open ironwork fence of the Jardin des Plantes, its thin spars like the bars of a great birdcage.

Across from her now: the bakery, the butcher, the delicatessen.

"Safe to cross, Papa?"

"It is."

Right. Then straight. They walk up their street now, she is sure of it. One step behind her, her father tilts his head up and gives the sky a huge smile. Marie-Laure knows this even though her back is to him, even though he says nothing, even though she is blind — Papa's thick hair is wet from the snow and standing in a dozen angles off his head, and his scarf is draped asymmetrically over his shoulders, and he's beaming up at the falling snow.

They are halfway up the rue des Patriarches. They are outside their building. Marie-Laure finds the trunk of the chestnut tree that grows past her third-floor window, its bark beneath her fingers.

Old friend.

In another half second her father's hands are in her armpits, swinging her up, and Marie-Laure smiles, and he laughs a pure, contagious laugh, one she will try to remember all her life, father and daughter turning in circles on the sidewalk in front of their apartment house, laughing together while snow sifts through the branches above.

Our Flag Flutters Before Us

In Zollverein, in the spring of Werner's tenth year, the two oldest boys at Children's House — thirteen-year-old Hans Schilzer and fourteen-year-old Herribert Pomsel — shoulder secondhand knapsacks and goose-step into the woods. When they come back, they are members of the Hitler Youth.

They carry slingshots, fashion spears, rehearse ambushes from behind snowbanks. They join a bristling gang of miners' sons who sit in the market square, sleeves rolled up, shorts hiked to their hips. "Good evening," they cry at passersby. "Or *heil* Hitler, if you prefer!"

They give each other matching haircuts and wrestle in the parlor and brag about the rifle training they're preparing for, the gliders they'll fly, the tank turrets they'll operate. *Our flag represents the new era,* chant Hans and Herribert, *our flag leads us to eternity.* At meals they chide younger children for admiring anything foreign: a British car advertisement, a French picture book.

Their salutes are comical; their outfits verge on ridiculous. But Frau Elena watches the boys with wary eyes: not so long ago they were feral toddlers skulking in their cots and crying for their mothers. Now they've become adolescent thugs with split knuckles and postcards of the führer folded into their shirt pockets.

Frau Elena speaks French less and less frequently whenever Hans and Herribert are present. She finds herself conscious of her accent. The smallest glance from a neighbor can make her wonder.

Werner keeps his head down. Leaping over bonfires, rubbing ash beneath your eyes, picking on little kids? Crumpling Jutta's drawings? Far better, he decides, to keep one's presence small, inconspicuous. Werner has been reading the popular science magazines in the drugstore; he's interested in wave turbulence, tunnels to the center of the earth, the Nigerian method of relaying news over distances with drums. He buys a notebook and draws up plans for cloud chambers, ion detectors, X-ray goggles. What about a little motor attached to the cradles to rock the babies to sleep? How about springs stretched along the axles of his wagon to help him pull it up hills?

An official from the Labor Ministry visits Children's House to speak about work opportunities at the mines. The children sit at his feet in their cleanest clothes. All boys, without exception, explains the man, will go to work for the mines once they turn fifteen. He speaks of glories and triumphs and how fortunate they'll be to have fixed employment. When he picks up Werner's radio and sets it back down without commenting, Werner feels the ceiling slip lower, the walls constrict.

His father down there, a mile beneath the house. Body never recovered. Haunting the tunnels still.

"From your neighborhood," the official says, "from your soil, comes the might of our nation. Steel, coal, coke. Berlin, Frankfurt, Munich — they do not exist without this place. You supply the foundation of the new order, the bullets in its guns, the armor on its tanks."

Hans and Herribert examine the man's leather pistol belt with dazzled eyes. On the sideboard, Werner's little radio chatters.

It says, *Over these three years, our leader has had the courage to face a Europe that was in danger of collapse . . .*

It says, *He alone is to be thanked for the fact that, for German children, a German life has once again become worth living.*

Around the World in Eighty Days

Sixteen paces to the water fountain, sixteen back. Forty-two to the stairwell, forty-two back. Marie-Laure draws maps in her head, unreels a hundred yards of imaginary twine, and then turns and reels it back in. Botany smells like glue and blotter paper and pressed flowers. Paleontology smells like rock dust, bone dust. Biology smells like formalin and old fruit; it is loaded with heavy cool jars in which float things she has only had described for her: the pale coiled ropes of rattlesnakes, the severed hands of gorillas. Entomology smells like mothballs and oil: a preservative that, Dr. Geffard explains, is called naphthalene. Offices smell of carbon paper, or cigar smoke, or brandy, or perfume. Or all four.

She follows cables and pipes, railings and ropes, hedges and sidewalks. She startles people. She never knows if the lights are on.

The children she meets brim with questions: Does it hurt? Do you shut your eyes to sleep? How do you know what time it is?

It doesn't hurt, she explains. And there is no darkness, not the kind they imagine. Everything is composed of webs and lattices and upheavals of sound and texture. She walks a circle around the Grand Gallery, navigating between squeaking floorboards; she hears feet tramp up and down museum staircases, a toddler squeal, the groan of a weary grandmother lowering herself onto a bench.

Color — that's another thing people don't expect. In her imagination, in her dreams, everything has color. The museum buildings are beige, chestnut, hazel. Its scientists are lilac and lemon yellow and fox brown. Piano chords loll in the speaker of the wireless in the guard station, projecting rich blacks and complicated blues down the hall toward the key pound. Church bells send arcs of bronze careening off the windows. Bees are silver; pigeons are ginger and auburn and occasionally golden. The huge cypress trees she and her father pass on their morning walk are shimmering kaleidoscopes, each needle a polygon of light.

She has no memories of her mother but imagines her as white, a soundless brilliance. Her father radiates a thousand colors, opal, strawberry red, deep russet, wild green; a smell like oil and metal, the feel of a lock tumbler sliding home, the sound of his key rings chiming as he walks. He is an olive green when he talks to a department head, an escalating series of oranges when he speaks to Mademoiselle Fleury from the greenhouses, a bright red when he tries to cook. He glows sapphire when he sits over his workbench in the evenings, humming almost inaudibly as he works, the tip of his cigarette gleaming a prismatic blue.

She gets lost. Secretaries or botanists, and once the director's assistant, bring her back to the key pound. She is curious; she wants to know the difference between an alga and a lichen, a *Diplodon charruanus* and a *Diplodon delodontus.* Famous men take her by the elbow and escort her through the gardens or guide her up stairwells. "I have a daughter too," they'll say. Or "I found her among the hummingbirds."

"Toutes mes excuses," her father says. He lights a cigarette; he plucks key after key out of her pockets. "What," he whispers, "am I going to do with you?"

On her ninth birthday, when she wakes, she finds two gifts. The first is a wooden box with no opening she can detect. She turns it this way and that. It takes her a little while to realize one side is spring-loaded; she presses it and the box flips open. Inside waits a single cube of creamy Camembert that she pops directly into in her mouth.

"Too easy!" her father says, laughing.

The second gift is heavy, wrapped in paper

and twine. Inside is a massive spiral-bound book. In Braille.

"They said it's for boys. Or very adventurous girls." She can hear him smiling.

She slides her fingertips across the embossed title page. *Around. The. World. In. Eighty. Days.* "Papa, it's too expensive."

"That's for me to worry about."

That morning Marie-Laure crawls beneath the counter of the key pound and lies on her stomach and sets all ten fingertips in a line on a page. The French feels old-fashioned, the dots printed much closer together than she is used to. But after a week, it becomes easy. She finds the ribbon she uses as a bookmark, opens the book, and the museum falls away.

Mysterious Mr. Fogg lives his life like a machine. Jean Passepartout becomes his obedient valet. When, after two months, she reaches the novel's last line, she flips back to the first page and starts again. At night she runs her fingertips over her father's model: the bell tower, the display windows. She imagines Jules Verne's characters walking along the streets, chatting in shops; a half-inch-tall baker slides speck-sized loaves in and out of his ovens; three minuscule burglars hatch plans as they drive slowly past the jeweler's; little grumbling cars throng the rue de Mirbel, wipers sliding back and forth. Behind a fourth-floor window on the rue des

Patriarches, a miniature version of her father sits at a miniature workbench in their miniature apartment, just as he does in real life, sanding away at some infinitesimal piece of wood; across the room is a miniature girl, skinny, quick-witted, an open book in her lap; inside her chest pulses something huge, something full of longing, something unafraid.

The Professor

"You have to swear," Jutta says. "Do you swear?" Amid rusted drums and shredded inner tubes and wormy creek-bottom muck, she has discovered ten yards of copper wire. Her eyes are bright tunnels.

Werner glances at the trees, the creek, back to his sister. "I swear."

Together they smuggle the wire home and loop it back and forth through nail holes in the eave outside the attic window. Then they attach it to their radio. Almost immediately, on a shortwave band, they can hear someone talking in a strange language full of *z*'s and *s*'s. "Is it Russian?"

Werner thinks it's Hungarian.

Jutta is all eyes in the dimness and heat. "How far away is Hungary?"

"A thousand kilometers?"

She gapes.

Voices, it turns out, streak into Zollverein from all over the continent, through the clouds, the coal dust, the roof. The air swarms with them. Jutta makes a log to match a scale that Werner draws on the tuning coil, carefully spelling the name of each city they manage to receive. *Verona 65, Dresden 88, London 100.* Rome. Paris. Lyon. Late-night shortwave: province of ramblers and dreamers, madmen and ranters.

After prayers, after lights-out, Jutta sneaks up to her brother's dormer; instead of drawing together, they lie hip to hip listening till midnight, till one, till two. They hear British news reports they cannot understand; they hear a Berlin woman pontificating about the proper makeup for a cocktail party.

One night Werner and Jutta tune in to a scratchy broadcast in which a young man is talking in feathery, accented French about light.

The brain is locked in total darkness, of course, children, says the voice. *It floats in a clear liquid inside the skull, never in the light. And yet the world it constructs in the mind is full of light. It brims with color and movement. So how, children, does the brain, which lives without a spark of light, build for us a world full of light?*

The broadcast hisses and pops.

"What is this?" whispers Jutta.

Werner does not answer. The Frenchman's voice is velvet. His accent is very different from Frau Elena's, and yet his voice is so ardent, so hypnotizing, that Werner finds he can understand every word. The Frenchman talks about optical illusions, electromagnetism; there's a pause and a peal of static, as though a record is being flipped, and then he enthuses about coal.

Consider a single piece glowing in your family's stove. See it, children? That chunk of coal was once a green plant, a fern or reed that lived one million years ago, or maybe two million, or maybe one hundred million. Can you imagine one hundred million years? Every summer for the whole life of that plant, its leaves caught what light they could and transformed the sun's energy into itself. Into bark, twigs, stems. Because plants eat light, in much the way we eat food. But then the plant died and fell, probably into water, and decayed into peat, and the peat was folded inside the earth for years upon years — eons in which something like a month or a decade or even your whole life was just a puff of air, a snap of two fingers. And eventually the peat dried and became like stone, and someone dug it up, and the coal man brought it to your house, and maybe you yourself carried it to the stove, and now that sunlight — sunlight one hundred million years old — is heating your home tonight . . .

Time slows. The attic disappears. Jutta disappears. Has anyone ever spoken so intimately about the very things Werner is most curious about?

Open your eyes, concludes the man, *and see what you can with them before they close forever,* and then a piano comes on, playing a lonely song that sounds to Werner like a golden boat traveling a dark river, a progression of harmonies that transfigures Zollverein: the houses turned to mist, the mines filled in, the smokestacks fallen, an ancient sea spilling through the streets, and the air streaming with possibility.

Sea of Flames

Rumors circulate through the Paris museum, moving fast, as quick and brightly colored as scarves. The museum is considering displaying a certain gemstone, a jewel more valuable than anything else in all the collections.

"Word has it," Marie-Laure overhears one taxidermist telling another, "the stone is from Japan, it's very ancient, it belonged to a shogun in the eleventh century."

"I hear," the other says, "it came out of our own vaults. That it's been here all along, but for some legal reason we weren't allowed to show it." One day it's a cluster of rare magnesium hydroxy carbonate; the next it's a star sapphire that will set a man's hand on fire if he touches it. Then it becomes a diamond, definitely a diamond. Some people call it the Shepherd's Stone, others call it the Khon-Ma, but soon enough everyone is calling it the Sea of Flames.

Marie-Laure thinks: Four years have passed.

"Evil," says a warder in the guard station. "Brings sorrow on anyone who carries it. I heard all nine previous owners have committed suicide."

A second voice says, "I heard that anyone who holds it in his ungloved hand dies within a week."

"No, no, if you hold it, you *cannot* die, but the people around you die within a month. Or maybe it's a year."

"I better get my hands on that!" says a third, laughing.

Marie-Laure's heart races. Ten years old, and onto the black screen of her imagination she can project anything: a sailing yacht, a sword battle, a Colosseum seething with color. She has read *Around the World in Eighty Days* until the Braille is soft and fraying; for this year's birthday, her father has bought her an even fatter book: Dumas's *The Three Musketeers.*

Marie-Laure hears that the diamond is pale green and as big as a coat button. Then she hears it's as big as a matchbook. A day later it's blue and as big as a baby's fist. She envisions an angry goddess stalking the halls, sending curses through the galleries like poison clouds. Her father says to tamp down her imagination. Stones are just stones and rain is just rain and misfortune is just bad luck. Some things are simply more rare than others, and that's why there are locks.

"But, Papa, do you believe it's real?"

"The diamond or the curse?"

"Both. Either."

"They're just stories, Marie."

And yet whenever anything goes wrong, the staff whispers that the diamond has caused it. The electricity fails for an hour: it's the diamond. A leaky pipe destroys an entire rack of pressed botanical samples: it's the diamond. When the director's wife slips on ice in the Place des Vosges and breaks her wrist in two places, the museum's gossip machine explodes.

Around this time, Marie-Laure's father is summoned upstairs to the director's office. He's there for two hours. When else in her memory has her father been called to the director's office for a two-hour meeting? Not once.

Almost immediately afterward, her father begins working deep within the Gallery of Mineralogy. For weeks he wheels carts loaded with various pieces of equipment in and out of the key pound, working long after the museum has closed, and every night he returns to the key pound smelling of brazing alloy and sawdust. Each time she asks to accompany him, he demurs. It would be best, he says, if she stayed in the key pound with her Braille workbooks, or upstairs in the mollusk laboratory.

She pesters him at breakfast. "You're building a special case to display that diamond. Some kind of transparent safe."

Her father lights a cigarette. "Please get your book, Marie. Time to go."

Dr. Geffard's answers are hardly better. "You know how diamonds — how all crystals — grow, Laurette? By adding microscopic layers, a few thousand atoms every month, each atop the next. Millennia after millennia. That's how stories accumulate too. All the old stones accumulate stories. That little rock you're so curious about may have seen Alaric sack Rome; it may have glittered in the eyes of Pharaohs. Scythian queens might have danced all night wearing it. Wars might have been fought over it."

"Papa says curses are only stories cooked up to deter thieves. He says there are sixty-five million specimens in this place, and if you have the right teacher, each can be as interesting as the last."

"Still," he says, "certain things compel people. Pearls, for example, and sinistral shells, shells with a left-handed opening. Even the best scientists feel the urge now and then to put something in a pocket. That something so small could be so beautiful. Worth so much. Only the strongest people can turn away from feelings like that."

They are quiet a moment.

Marie-Laure says, "I heard that the diamond is like a piece of light from the original world. Before it fell. A piece of light rained to earth from God."

"You want to know what it looks like. That's why you're so curious."

She rolls a murex in her hands. Holds it to her ear. Ten thousand drawers, ten thousand whispers inside ten thousand shells.

"No," she says. "I want to believe that Papa hasn't been anywhere near it."

Open Your Eyes

Werner and Jutta find the Frenchman's broadcasts again and again. Always around bedtime, always midway through some increasingly familiar script.

Today let's consider the whirling machinery, children, that must engage inside your head for you to scratch your eyebrow . . . They hear a program about sea creatures, another about the North Pole. Jutta likes one on magnets. Werner's favorite is one about light: eclipses and sundials, auroras and wavelengths. *What do we call visible light? We call it color. But the electromagnetic spectrum runs to zero in one direction and infinity in the other, so really, children, mathematically, all of light is invisible.*

Werner likes to crouch in his dormer and imagine radio waves like mile-long harp strings, bending and vibrating over Zollverein, flying through forests, through cities, through walls. At midnight he and Jutta prowl the ionosphere, searching for that lavish, penetrating voice. When they find it, Werner feels as if he has been launched into a different existence, a secret place where great discoveries are possible, where an orphan from a coal town can solve some vital mystery hidden in the physical world.

He and his sister mimic the Frenchman's experiments; they make speedboats out of matchsticks and magnets out of sewing needles.

"Why doesn't he say where he is, Werner?"

"Maybe because he doesn't want us to know?"

"He sounds rich. And lonely. I bet he does these broadcasts from a huge mansion, big as this whole colony, a house with a thousand rooms and a thousand servants."

Werner smiles. "Could be."

The voice, the piano again. Perhaps it's Werner's imagination, but each time he hears one of the programs, the quality seems to degrade a bit more, the sound growing fainter: as though the Frenchman broadcasts from a ship that is slowly traveling farther away.

As the weeks pass, with Jutta asleep beside him, Werner looks out into the night sky, and restlessness surges through him. Life: it's happening beyond the mills, beyond the gates. Out there people chase questions of great importance. He imagines himself as a tall white-coated engineer striding into a laboratory: cauldrons steam, machinery rumbles, complex charts paper the walls. He carries a lantern up a winding staircase to a starlit observatory and looks through the eyepiece of a great telescope, its mouth pointed into the black.

Fade

Maybe the old tour guide was off his rocker. Maybe the Sea of Flames never existed at all, maybe curses *aren't* real, maybe her father is right: Earth is all magma and continental crust and ocean. Gravity and time. Stones are just stones and rain is just rain and misfortune is just bad luck.

Her father returns to the key pound earlier in the evenings. Soon he is taking Marie-Laure along on various errands again, teasing her about the mountains of sugar she spoons into her coffee or bantering with warders about the superiority of his brand of cigarettes. No dazzling new gemstone goes on exhibit. No plagues rain down upon museum employees; Marie-Laure does not succumb to snakebite or tumble into a sewer and break her back.

On the morning of her eleventh birthday, she wakes to find two new packages where the sugar bowl should be. The first is a lacquered wooden cube constructed entirely from sliding panels. It takes thirteen steps to open, and she discovers the sequence in under five minutes.

"Good Christ," says her father, "you're a safecracker!"

Inside the cube: two Barnier bonbons. She unwraps both and puts them in her mouth at the same time.

Inside the second package: a fat stack of pages with Braille on the cover. *Twenty. Thousand. Leagues. Under. The. Sea.*

"The bookseller said it's in two parts, and this is the first. I thought that next year, if we keep saving, we can get the second —"

She begins that instant. The narrator, a famed marine biologist named Pierre Aronnax, works at the same museum as her father! Around the world, he learns, ships are being rammed one after another. After a scientific expedition to America, Aronnax ruminates over the true nature of the incidents. Are they caused by a moving reef? A gigantic horned narwhal? A mythical kraken?

But I am letting myself be carried away by reveries which I must now put aside, writes Aronnax. *Enough of these phantasies.*

All day Marie-Laure lies on her stomach and reads. Logic, reason, pure science: these, Aronnax insists, are the proper ways to pursue a mystery. Not fables and fairy tales. Her fingers walk the tightropes of sentences; in her imagination, she walks the decks of the speedy two-funneled frigate called the *Abraham Lincoln.* She watches New York City recede; the forts of New Jersey salute her departure with cannons; channel markers bob in the swells. A lightship with twin beacons glides past as America recedes; ahead wait the great glittering prairies of the Atlantic.

The Principles of Mechanics

A vice minister and his wife visit Children's House. Frau Elena says they are touring orphanages.

Everyone washes; everyone behaves. Maybe, the children whisper, they are considering adopting. The oldest girls serve pumpernickel and goose liver on the house's last unchipped plates while the portly vice minister and his severe-looking wife inspect the parlor like lords come to tour some distasteful gnomish cottage. When supper is ready, Werner sits at the boys' end of the table with a book in his lap. Jutta sits with the girls at the opposite end, her hair frizzed and snarled and bright white, so she looks as if she has been electrified.

Bless us O Lord and these Thy gifts. Frau Elena adds a second prayer for the vice minister's benefit. Everyone falls to eating.

The children are nervous; even Hans Schilzer and Herribert Pomsel sit quietly in their brown shirts. The vice minister's wife sits so upright that it seems as if her spine is hewn from oak.

Her husband says, "And each of the children contributes?"

"Certainly. Claudia, for instance, made the bread basket. And the twins prepared the livers."

Big Claudia Förster blushes. The twins bat their eyelashes.

Werner's mind drifts; he is thinking about the book in his lap, *The Principles of Mechanics* by Heinrich Hertz. He discovered it in the church basement, water-stained and forgotten, decades old, and the rector let him bring it home, and Frau Elena let him keep it, and for several weeks Werner has been fighting through the thorny mathematics. Electricity, Werner is learning, can be static by itself. But couple it with magnetism, and suddenly you have movement — waves. Fields and circuits, conduction and induction. Space, time, mass. The air swarms with so much that is invisible! How he wishes he had eyes to see the ultraviolet, eyes to see the infrared, eyes to see radio waves crowding the darkening sky, flashing through the walls of the house.

When he looks up, everyone is staring at him. Frau Elena's eyes are alarmed.

"It's a book, sir," announces Hans Schilzer. He tugs it out of Werner's lap. The volume is heavy enough that he needs both hands to hold it up.

Several creases sharpen in the forehead of the vice minister's wife. Werner can feel his cheeks flush.

The vice minister extends a pudgy hand. "Give it here."

"Is it a Jew book?" says Herribert Pomsel. "It's a Jew book, isn't it?"

Frau Elena looks as if she's about to speak, then thinks better of it.

"Hertz was born in Hamburg," says Werner.

Jutta announces out of nowhere, "My brother is so quick at mathematics. He's quicker than every one of the schoolmasters. Someday he'll probably win a big prize. He says we'll go to Berlin and study under the great scientists."

The younger children gape; the oldest children snicker. Werner stares hard into his plate. The vice minister frowns as he turns pages. Hans Schilzer kicks Werner in the shin and coughs.

Frau Elena says, "Jutta, that's enough."

The vice minister's wife takes a forkful of liver and chews and swallows and touches her napkin to each corner of her mouth. The vice minister sets down *The Principles of Mechanics* and pushes it away, then glances at his palms as though it has made them dirty. He says, "The only place your brother is going, little girl, is into the mines. As soon as he turns fifteen. Same as every other boy in this house."

Jutta scowls, and Werner stares at the congealed liver on his plate with his eyes burning and something inside his chest compressing tighter and tighter, and for the rest of supper the only sound is of the children cutting and chewing and swallowing.

Rumors

New rumors arrive. They rustle along the paths of the Jardin des Plantes and wind through the museum galleries; they echo in high dusty redoubts where shriveled old botanists study exotic mosses. They say the Germans are coming.

The Germans, a gardener claims, have sixty thousand troop gliders; they can march for days without eating; they impregnate every schoolgirl they meet. A woman behind the ticket counter says the Germans carry fog pills and wear rocket belts; their uniforms, she whispers, are made of a special cloth stronger than steel.

Marie-Laure sits on a bench beside the mollusk display and trains her ears on passing groups. A boy blurts, "They have a bomb called the Secret Signal. It makes a sound, and everyone who hears it goes to the bathroom in their pants!"

Laughter.

"I hear they give out poisoned chocolate."

"I hear they lock up the cripples and morons everywhere they go."

Each time Marie-Laure relays another rumor to her father, he repeats "Germany" with a question mark after it, as if saying it for the very first time. He says the takeover of Austria is nothing to worry about. He says everyone remembers the last war, and no one is mad enough to go through that again. The director is not worrying, he says, and neither are the department heads, so neither should young girls who have lessons to learn.

It seems true: nothing changes but the day of the week. Every morning Marie-Laure wakes and dresses and follows her father through Entrance #2 and listens to him greet the night guard and the warder. *Bonjour bonjour. Bonjour bonjour.* The scientists and librarians still collect their keys in the mornings, still study their ancient elephants' teeth, their exotic jellyfish, their herbarium sheets. The secretaries still talk about fashion; the director still arrives in a two-tone Delage limousine; and every noon the African vendors still wheel their sandwich carts quietly down the halls with their whispers of rye and egg, rye and egg.

Marie-Laure reads Jules Verne in the key pound, on the toilet, in the corridors; she reads on the benches of the Grand Gallery and out along the hundred gravel paths of the gardens. She reads the first half of *Twenty*

Thousand Leagues Under the Sea so many times, she practically memorizes it.

The sea is everything. It covers seven tenths of the globe . . . The sea is only a receptacle for all the prodigious, supernatural things that exist inside it. It is only movement and love; it is the living infinite.

At night, in her bed, she rides in the belly of Captain Nemo's *Nautilus,* below the gales, while canopies of coral drift overhead.

Dr. Geffard teaches her the names of shells — *Lambis lambis, Cypraea moneta, Lophiotoma acuta* — and lets her feel the spines and apertures and whorls of each in turn. He explains the branches of marine evolution and the sequences of the geologic periods; on her best days, she glimpses the limitless span of millennia behind her: millions of years, tens of millions.

"Nearly every species that has ever lived has gone extinct, Laurette. No reason to think we humans will be any different!" Dr. Geffard pronounces this almost gleefully and pours wine into his glass, and she imagines his head as a cabinet filled with ten thousand little drawers.

All summer the smells of nettles and daisies and rainwater purl through the gardens. She and her father cook a pear tart and burn it by accident, and her father opens all the windows to let out the smoke, and she hears violin music rise from the street below. And yet by early autumn, once or twice a week, at certain moments of the day, sitting out in the Jardin des Plantes beneath the massive hedges or reading beside her father's workbench, Marie-Laure looks up from her book and believes she can smell gasoline under the wind. As if a great river of machinery is steaming slowly, irrevocably, toward her.

BIGGER FASTER BRIGHTER

Membership in the State Youth becomes mandatory. The boys in Werner's Kameradschaften are taught parade maneuvers and quizzed on fitness standards and required to run sixty meters in twelve seconds. Everything is glory and country and competition and sacrifice.

Live faithfully, the boys sing as they troop past the edges of the colony. *Fight bravely and die laughing.*

Schoolwork, chores, exercise. Werner stays up late listening to his radio or driving himself through the complicated math he copied out of *The Principles of Mechanics* before it was confiscated. He yawns at meals, is short-tempered with the younger children. "Are you feeling okay?" asks Frau Elena, peering into his face, and Werner looks away, saying, "Fine."

Hertz's theories are interesting but what he loves most is building things, working with his hands, connecting his fingers to the engine of his mind. Werner repairs a neighbor's sewing machine, the Children's House grandfather clock. He builds a pulley system to wind laundry from the sunshine back indoors, and a simple alarm made from a battery, a bell, and wire so that Frau Elena will know if a toddler has wandered outside. He invents a machine to slice carrots: lift a lever, nineteen blades drop, and the carrot falls apart into twenty neat cylinders.

One day a neighbor's wireless goes out, and Frau Elena suggests Werner have a look. He unscrews the back plate, waggles the tubes back and forth. One is not seated properly, and he fits it back into its groove. The radio comes back to life, and the neighbor shrieks with delight. Before long, people are stopping by Children's House every week to ask for the radio repairman. When they see thirteen-year-old Werner come down from the attic, rubbing his eyes, shocks of white hair sticking up off his head, homemade toolbox hanging from his fist, they stare at him with the same skeptical smirk.

The older sets are the easiest to fix: simpler circuitry, uniform tubes. Maybe it's wax dripping from the condenser or charcoal built up on a resistor. Even in the newest sets, Werner can usually puzzle out a solution. He dismantles the machine, stares into its circuits, lets his fingers trace the journeys of electrons. Power source, triode, resistor, coil. Loudspeaker. His mind shapes itself around the problem, disorder becomes order, the obstacle reveals itself, and before long the radio is fixed.

Sometimes they pay him a few marks. Sometimes a coal mother cooks him sausages or wraps biscuits in a napkin to take home to his sister. Before long Werner can draw a map in his head of the locations of nearly every radio in their district: a homemade crystal set in the kitchen of a druggist; a handsome ten-valve radiogram in the home of a department head that was giving his fingers a shock every time he tried to change the channel. Even the poorest pit houses usually possess a state-sponsored Volksemfänger VE301, a mass-produced radio stamped with an eagle and a swastika, incapable of shortwave, marked only for German frequencies.

Radio: it ties a million ears to a single mouth. Out of loudspeakers all around Zollverein, the staccato voice of the Reich grows like some imperturbable tree; its subjects lean toward its branches as if toward the lips of God. And when God stops whispering, they become desperate for someone who can put things right.

Seven days a week the miners drag coal into the light and the coal is pulverized and fed into coke ovens and the coke is cooled in huge quenching towers and carted to the blast furnaces to melt iron ore and the iron is refined into steel and cast into billets and loaded onto barges and floated off into the great hungry mouth of the country. *Only through the hottest fires,* whispers the radio, *can purification be achieved. Only through the harshest tests can God's chosen rise.*

Jutta whispers, "A girl got kicked out of the swimming hole today. Inge Hachmann. They said they wouldn't let us swim with a half-breed. Unsanitary. A half-breed, Werner. Aren't we half-breeds too? Aren't we half our mother, half our father?"

"They mean half-Jew. Keep your voice down. We're not half-Jews."

"We must be half something."

"We're whole German. We're not half anything."

Herribert Pomsel is fifteen years old now, off in a miners' dormitory, working the second shift as a firedamper, and Hans Schilzer has become the oldest boy in the house. Hans does push-ups by the hundreds; he plans to attend a rally in Essen. There are fistfights in the alleys, rumors that Hans has set a car on fire. One night Werner hears him downstairs, shouting at Frau Elena. The front door slams; the children toss in their beds; Frau Elena paces the parlor, her slippers whispering left, whispering right. Coal cars grind past in the wet dark. Machinery hums in the distance: pistons throbbing, belts turning. Smoothly. Madly.

Mark of the Beast

November 1939. A cold wind sends the big dry leaves of plane trees rolling down the gravel lanes of the Jardin des Plantes. Marie-Laure is rereading *Twenty Thousand Leagues* — *I could make out long ribbons of sea wrack, some globular and others tubular, laurenciae, cladostephae with their slender foliage* — not far from the rue Cuvier gate when a group of children comes tramping through the leaves.

A boy's voice says something; several other boys laugh. Marie-Laure lifts her fingers from her novel. The laughter spins, turns. The first voice is suddenly right beside her ear. "They're mad for blind girls, you know."

His breath is quick. She extends her arm into the space beside her but contacts nothing.

She cannot say how many others are with him. Three or four, perhaps. His is the voice of a twelve- or thirteen-year-old. She stands and hugs her huge book against her chest, and she can hear her cane roll along the edge of the bench and clatter to the ground.

Someone else says, "They'll probably take the blind girls before they take the gimps."

The first boy moans grotesquely. Marie-Laure raises her book as if to shield herself.

The second boy says, "Make them do things."

"Nasty things."

An adult's voice in the distance calls out, "Louis, Peter?"

"Who are you?" hisses Marie-Laure.

"Bye-bye, blind girl."

Then: quiet. Marie-Laure listens to the trees rustle; her blood swarms. For a long and panicked minute, she crawls among the leaves at the foot of the bench until her fingers find her cane.

Stores sell gas masks. Neighbors tape cardboard to their windows. Each week fewer visitors come to the museum.

"Papa?" Marie-Laure asks. "If there's a war, what will happen to us?"

"There won't be a war."

"But what if there is?"

His hand on her shoulder, the familiar clanking of keys on his belt. "Then we will be fine, *ma chérie.* The director has already filed a dispensation to keep me out of the reserves. I'm not going anywhere."

But she hears the way he turns newspaper pages, snapping them with urgency. He lights cigarette after cigarette; he hardly stops working. Weeks pass and the trees go bare and her father doesn't ask her to walk in the gardens once. If only they had an impregnable submarine like the *Nautilus.*

The smoky voices of office girls swirl past the open window of the key pound. "They creep into apartments at night. They booby-trap kitchen cupboards, toilet bowls, brassieres. Go to open your panty drawer, and you get your fingers blown off."

She has nightmares. Silent Germans row up the Seine in synchrony; their skiffs glide as if through oil. They fly noiselessly beneath the bridge trestles; they have beasts with them on chains; their beasts leap out of the boats and sprint past the massifs of flowers, down the rows of hedges. They sniff the air on the steps to the Grand Gallery. Slavering. Ravenous. They surge into the museum, scatter into the departments. The windows go black with blood.

Dear Professor I dont know if youre getting these letters or if the radio station will forward this or is there even a radio station? We havent heard you in two months at least. Did you stop broadcasting or maybe is the problem ours? Theres a new radio transmitter in Brandenburg called the Deutschlandsender 3 my brother says it is three hundred thirty-something meters tall the second-tallest man-made construction in the world. It pushes basically everything else off the dial. Old Frau Stresemann, shes one of our neighbors, she says she can hear Deutschlandsender broadcasts in her tooth fillings. My brother said its possible if you have an antenna and a rectifier and something to serve as a speaker. He said you can use a section of wire fence to pick up radio signals, so maybe the silver in a tooth can too. I like to think about that.

Dont you Professor? Songs in your teeth? Frau Elena says we have to come straight home from school now. She says were not Jews but were poor and thats almost as dangerous. Its a criminal offense now to tune into a foreign broadcast. You can get hard labor for it, things like breaking rocks fifteen hours a day. Or making nylon stockings or going down in the pits. No one will help me mail this letter not even my brother so I will do it myself.

Good Evening. Or *Heil* Hitler if You Prefer.

His fourteenth birthday arrives in May. It's 1940 and no one laughs at the Hitler Youth now. Frau Elena prepares a pudding and Jutta wraps a piece of quartz in newspaper and the twins, Hannah and Susanne Gerlitz, march around the room impersonating soldiers. A five-year-old — Rolf Hupfauer — sits in the corner of the sofa, eyelids slipping heavily over his eyes. A new arrival — a baby girl — sits in Jutta's lap and gums her fingers. Out the window, beyond the curtains, the flame atop the waste stack, high in the distance, flaps and shivers.

The children sing and devour the pudding, Frau Elena says, "Time's up," and Werner switches off his receiver. Everyone prays. His whole body feels heavy as he carries the radio up to the dormer. In the alleys, fifteen-year-old boys are making their way toward mine elevators, queuing up with their helmets and lamps outside the gates. He tries to imagine their descent, sporadic and muted lights passing and receding, cables rattling, everyone quiet, sinking down to that permanent darkness where men claw at the earth with a half mile of rock hunched on top of them.

One more year. Then they'll give him a helmet and lamp and stuff him into a cage with the others.

It has been months since he last heard the Frenchman on the shortwave. A year since he held that water-stained copy of *The Principles of Mechanics.* Not so long ago he let himself dream of Berlin and its great scientists: Fritz Haber, inventor of fertilizer; Hermann Staudinger, inventor of plastics. Hertz, who made the invisible visible. All the great men doing things out there. *I believe in you,* Frau Elena used to say. *I think you'll do something great.* Now, in his nightmares, he walks the tunnels of the mines. The ceiling is smooth and black; slabs of it descend over him as he treads. The walls splinter; he stoops, crawls. Soon he cannot raise his head, move his arms. The ceiling weighs ten trillion tons; it gives off a permeating cold; it drives his nose into the floor. Just before he wakes, he feels a splintering at the back of his skull.

Rainwater purls from cloud to roof to eave. Werner presses his forehead to the window of the dormer and peers through the drops, the roof below just one among a cluster of wet rooftops, hemmed in by the vast walls of the cokery and smelter and gasworks, the winding tower silhouetted against the sky, mine and mill running on and on, acre after acre, beyond his range of sight, to the villages, the cities, the ever-quickening, ever-expanding machine that is Germany. And a million men ready to set down their lives for it.

Good evening, he thinks. Or *heil* Hitler. Everyone is choosing the latter.

Bye-Bye, Blind Girl

The war drops its question mark. Memos are distributed. The collections must be protected. A small cadre of couriers has begun moving things to country estates. Locks and keys are in greater demand than ever. Marie-Laure's father works until midnight, until one. Every crate must be padlocked, every transport manifest kept in a secure place. Armored trucks rumble at the loading docks. There are fossils to be safeguarded, ancient manuscripts; there is jade from the thirteenth century and cavansite from India and rhodochrosite from Colorado; there are pearls, gold nuggets, a sapphire as big as a mouse. There might be, thinks Marie-Laure, the Sea of Flames.

From a certain angle, the spring seems so calm: warm, tender, each night redolent and composed. And yet everything radiates tension, as if the city has been built upon the skin of a balloon and someone is inflating it toward the breaking point.

Bees work the blooming aisles of the Jardin des Plantes. The plane trees drop their seeds and huge drifts of fluff gather on the walkways.

If they attack, why would they attack, they would be crazy to attack.

To retreat is to save lives.

Deliveries stop. Sandbags appear around the museum gates. A pair of soldiers on the roof of the Gallery of Paleontology peer over the gardens with binoculars. But the huge bowl of the sky remains untracked: no zeppelins, no bombers, no superhuman paratroopers, just the last songbirds returning from their winter homes, and the quicksilver winds of spring transmuting into the heavier, greener breezes of summer.

Rumor, light, air. That May seems more beautiful than any Marie-Laure can remember. On the morning of her twelfth birthday, there is no puzzle box in place of the sugar bowl when she wakes; her father is too busy. But there is a book: the second Braille volume of *Twenty Thousand Leagues Under the Sea,* as thick as a sofa cushion.

A thrill rides all the way into the nails of her fingers. "How — ?"

"You're welcome, Marie."

The walls of their flat tremble with the dragging of furniture, the packing of trunks, the nailing shut of windows. They walk to the museum, and her father remarks distractedly to the warder who meets them at the door, "They say we are holding the river."

Marie-Laure sits on the floor of the key pound and opens her book. When part one left off, Professor Aronnax had traveled only six thousand leagues. So many left to go. But something strange happens: the words do not connect. She reads, *During the entire day, a formidable school of sharks followed the ship,* but the logic that is supposed to link each word to the next fails her.

Someone says, "Has the director left?"

Someone else says, "Before the end of the week."

Her father's clothes smell of straw; his fingers reek of oil. Work, more work, then a few hours of exhausted sleep before returning to the museum at dawn. Trucks carry off skeletons and meteorites and octopi in jars and herbarium sheets and Egyptian gold and South African ivory and Permian fossils.

On the first of June, airplanes fly over the city, extremely high, crawling through the stratus clouds. When the wind is down and nobody is running an engine nearby, Marie-Laure can stand outside the Gallery of Zoology and hear them: a mile-high purr. The following day, the radio stations begin disappearing. The warders in the guards' station whack the side of their wireless and tilt it this way and that, but only static comes out of its speaker. As if each relay antenna were a candle flame and a pair of fingers came along and pinched it out.

Those last nights in Paris, walking home with her father at midnight, the huge book clasped against her chest, Marie-Laure thinks she can sense a shiver beneath the air, in the pauses between the chirring of the insects, like the spider cracks of ice when too much weight is set upon it. As if all this time the city has been no more than a scale model built by her father and the shadow of a great hand has fallen over it.

Didn't she presume she would live with her father in Paris for the rest of her life? That she would always sit with Dr. Geffard in the afternoons? That every year, on her birthday, her father would present her with another puzzle and another novel, and she would read all of Jules Verne and all of Dumas and maybe even Balzac and Proust? That her father would always hum as he fashioned little buildings in the evenings, and she would always know how many paces from the front door to the bakery (forty) and how many more to the brasserie (thirty-two), and there would always be sugar to spoon into her coffee when she woke?

Bonjour, bonjour.

Potatoes at six o'clock, Marie. Mushrooms at three.

Now? What will happen now?

Making Socks

Werner wakes past midnight to find eleven-year-old Jutta kneeling on the floor beside his cot. The shortwave is in her lap and a sheet of drawing paper is on the floor beside her, a many-windowed city of her imagination half-articulated on the page.

Jutta removes the earpiece and squints. In the twilight, her wild volutions of hair look more radiant than ever: a struck match.

"In Young Girls League," she whispers, "they have us making socks. Why so many socks?"

"The Reich must need socks."

"For what?"

"For feet, Jutta. For the soldiers. Let me sleep." As though on cue, a young boy — Siegfried Fischer — cries out downstairs once, then twice more, and Werner and Jutta wait to hear Frau Elena's feet on the stairs and her gentle ministrations and the house fall quiet once more.

"All you want to do are mathematics problems," Jutta whispers. "Play with radios. Don't you want to understand what's happening?"

"What are you listening to?"

She crosses her arms and puts the earphone back and does not answer.

"Are you listening to something you're not supposed to be listening to?"

"What do you care?"

"It's dangerous, is why I care."

She puts her finger in her other ear.

"The other girls don't seem to mind," he whispers. "Making socks. Collecting newspapers and all that."

"We're dropping bombs on Paris," she says. Her voice is loud, and he resists an urge to clap his hand over her mouth.

Jutta stares up, defiant. She looks as if she is being raked by some invisible arctic wind. "That's what I'm listening to, Werner. Our airplanes are bombing Paris."

Flight

All across Paris, people pack china into cellars, sew pearls into hems, conceal gold rings inside book bindings. The museum workspaces are stripped of typewriters. The halls become packing yards, their floors strewn with straw and sawdust and twine.

At noon the locksmith is summoned to the director's office. Marie-Laure sits cross-legged on the floor of the key pound and tries to read her novel. Captain Nemo is about to take Professor Aronnax and his companions on an underwater stroll through oyster beds to hunt for pearls, but Aronnax is afraid of the prospect of sharks, and though she longs to know what will happen, the sentences disintegrate across the page. Words devolve into letters, letters into unintelligible bumps. She feels as if big mitts have been drawn over each hand.

Down the hall, at the guards' station, a warder twists the knobs of the wireless back and forth but finds only hiss and crackle.

When he shuts it off, quiet closes over the museum.

Please let this be a puzzle, an elaborate game Papa has constructed, a riddle she must solve. The first door, a combination lock. The second, a dead bolt. The third will open if she whispers a magic word through its keyhole. Crawl through thirteen doors, and everything will return to normal.

Out in the city, church bells strike one. One thirty. Still her father does not return. At some point, several distinct thumps travel into the museum from the gardens or the streets beyond, as if someone is dropping sacks of cement mix out of the clouds. With each impact, the thousands of keys in their cabinets quiver on their pegs.

Nobody moves up or down the corridor. A second series of concussions arrives — closer, larger. The keys chime and the floor creaks and she thinks she can smell threads of dust cascading from the ceiling.

"Papa?"

Nothing. No warders, no janitors, no carpenters, no clop-clop-clop of a secretary's heels crossing the hall.

They can march for days without eating. They impregnate every schoolgirl they meet.

"Hello?" How quickly her voice is swallowed, how empty the halls sound. It terrifies her.

A moment later, there are clanking keys and

footfalls and her father's voice calls her name. Everything happens quickly. He drags open big, low drawers; he jangles dozens of key rings.

"Papa, I heard —"

"Hurry."

"My book —"

"Better to leave it. It's too heavy."

"Leave my book?"

He pulls her out the door and locks the key pound. Outside, waves of panic seem to be traveling the rows of trees like tremors from an earthquake.

Her father says, "Where is the watchman?"

Voices near the curb: soldiers.

Marie-Laure's senses feel scrambled. Is that the rumble of airplanes? Is that the smell of smoke? Is someone speaking German?

She can hear her father exchange a few words with a stranger and hand over some keys. Then they are moving past the gate onto the rue Cuvier, brushing through what might be sandbags or silent police officers or something else newly planted in the middle of the sidewalk.

Six blocks, thirty-eight storm drains. She counts them all. Because of the sheets of wood veneer her father has tacked over its windows, their apartment is stuffy and hot. "This will just take a moment, Marie-Laure. Then I'll explain." Her father shoves things into what might be his canvas rucksack. *Food,* she thinks, trying to identify everything by its sound. Coffee. Cigarettes. Bread?

Something thumps again and the window-panes tremble. Their dishes rattle in the cupboards. Automobile horns bleat. Marie-Laure goes to the model neighborhood and runs her fingers over the houses. Still there. Still there. Still there.

"Go to the toilet, Marie."

"I don't have to."

"It may be a while until you can go again."

He buttons her into her winter overcoat, though it is the middle of June, and they bustle downstairs. On the rue des Patriarches, she hears a distant stamping, as though thousands of people are on the move. She walks beside her father with her cane telescoped in one fist, her other hand on his rucksack, everything disconnected from logic, as in nightmares.

Right, left. Between turns run long stretches of paving stones. Soon they are walking streets, she is sure, that she has never been on, streets beyond the boundaries of her father's model. Marie-Laure has long since lost count of her strides when they reach a crowd dense enough that she can feel heat spilling off of it.

"It will be cooler on the train, Marie. The director has arranged tickets for us."

"Can we go in?"

"The gates are locked."

The crowd gives off a nauseating tension.

"I'm scared, Papa."

"Keep hold of me."

He leads her in a new direction. They cross a seething thoroughfare, then go up an alley that smells like a muddy ditch. Always there is the muted rattling of her father's tools inside his rucksack and the distant and incessant honking of automobile horns.

In a minute they find themselves amid another throng. Voices echo off a high wall; the smell of wet garments crowds her. Somewhere someone shouts names through a bullhorn.

"Where are we, Papa?"

"Gare Saint-Lazare."

A baby cries. She smells urine.

"Are there Germans, Papa?"

"No, *ma chérie.*"

"But soon?"

"So they say."

"What will we do when they get here?"

"We will be on a train by then."

In the space to her right, a child screeches. A man with panic in his voice demands the crowd make way. A woman nearby moans, "Sebastien? Sebastien?" over and over.

"Is it night yet?"

"It's only now getting dark. Let's rest a moment. Save our breath."

Someone says, "The Second Army mauled, the Ninth cut off. France's best fleets wasted."

Someone says, "We will be overrun."

Trunks slide across tiles and a little dog yaps and a conductor's whistle blows and some kind of big machinery coughs to a start and then dies. Marie-Laure tries to calm her stomach.

"But we have tickets, for God's sake!" shouts someone behind her.

There is a scuffle. Hysteria ripples through the crowd.

"What does it look like, Papa?"

"What, Marie?"

"The station. The night."

She hears the sparking of his lighter, the suck and flare of tobacco as his cigarette ignites.

"Let's see. The whole city is dark. No streetlights, no lights in windows. There are projector lights moving through the sky now and then. Looking for airplanes. There's a woman in a gown. And another carrying a stack of dishes."

"And the armies?"

"There are no armies, Marie."

His hand finds hers. Her fear settles slightly. Rain trickles through a downspout.

"What are we doing now, Papa?"

"Hoping for a train."

"What is everybody else doing?"

"They're hoping too."

Herr Siedler

A knock after curfew. Werner and Jutta are doing schoolwork with a half-dozen other children at the long wooden table. Frau Elena pins her party insignia through her lapel before opening the door.

A lance corporal with a pistol on his belt and a swastika band on his left arm steps in from the rain. Beneath the low ceiling of the room, the man looks absurdly tall. Werner thinks of the shortwave radio tucked into the old wooden first-aid cabinet beneath his cot. He thinks: *They know.*

The lance corporal looks around the room — the coal stove, the hanging laundry, the undersize children — with equal measures of condescension and hostility. His handgun is black; it seems to draw all the light in the room toward it.

Werner risks a single glance at his sister. Her attention stays fixed on the visitor. The corporal picks up a book from the parlor table — a children's book about a talking train — and turns every one of its pages before dropping it. Then he says something that Werner can't hear.

Frau Elena folds her hands over her apron, and Werner can see she has done so to keep them from shaking. "Werner," she calls in a slow, dreamlike voice, without taking her eyes from the corporal. "This man says he has a wireless in need of —"

"Bring your tools," the man says.

On the way out, Werner looks back only once: Jutta's forehead and palms are pressed against the glass of the living room window. She is backlit and too far away and he cannot read her expression. Then the rain obscures her.

Werner is half the corporal's height and has to take two strides for every one of the man's. He follows past company houses and the sentry at the bottom of the hill to where the mining officials reside. Rain falls slant through the lights. The few people they pass give the corporal a wide berth.

Werner risks no questions. With every heartbeat comes a sharp longing to run.

They approach the gate of the largest house in the colony, a house he has seen a thousand times but never so close. A large crimson flag, heavy with rainwater, hangs from the sill of an upstairs window.

The corporal raps on a rear door. A maid in a high-waisted dress takes their coats, expertly flips off the water, and hangs them on a brass-footed rack. The kitchen smells of cake.

The corporal steers Werner into a dining room where a narrow-faced woman with three fresh daisies stuck through her hair sits in a chair turning the pages of a magazine. “Two wet ducks,” she says, and looks back at her magazine. She does not ask them to sit.

A thick red carpet sucks at the soles of Werner’s brogues; electric bulbs burn in a chandelier above the table; roses twine across the wallpaper. A fire smolders in the fireplace. On all four walls hang framed tintypes of glowering ancestors. Is this where they arrest boys whose sisters listen to foreign radio stations? The woman turns pages of her magazine, one after another. Her fingernails are bright pink.

A man comes down the stairs wearing an extremely white shirt. “Christ, he is little, isn’t he?” he says to the lance corporal. “You’re the famous radio repairman?” The man’s thick black hair looks lacquered to his skull. “Rudolf Siedler,” he says. He dismisses the corporal with a slight wag of his chin.

Werner tries to exhale. Herr Siedler buttons his cuffs and examines himself in a smoky mirror. His eyes are profoundly blue. “Well. Not a long-winded boy, are you? There’s the offending device.” He points to a massive American Philco in the adjacent room. "Two fellows have looked at it already. Then we heard about you. Worth a try, right? She" — he nods at the woman — "is desperate to hear her program. News bulletins too, of course."

He says this in such a way that Werner understands the woman does not really wish to listen to news bulletins. She does not look up. Herr Siedler smiles as if to say: *You and I, son, we know history takes a longer course, don't we?* His teeth are very small. "Take your time with it."

Werner squats in front of the set and tries to calm his nerves. He switches it on, waits for the tubes to warm, then runs the dial carefully down the band, right to left. He runs the knob back toward the right. Nothing.

It is the finest radio he has ever laid hands on: an inclined control panel, magnetic tuning, big as an icebox. Ten-tube, all-wave, superheterodyne, with fancy gadrooned moldings and a two-tone walnut cabinet. It has shortwave, wide frequencies, a big attenuator — this radio costs more than everything at Children's House put together. Herr Siedler could probably hear Africa if he wanted to.

Green and red spines of books line the walls. The lance corporal is gone. In the next room, Herr Siedler stands in a pool of lamplight, talking into a black telephone.

They are not arresting him. They merely

want him to fix this radio.

Werner unscrews the backing and peers inside. The tubes are all intact, and nothing looks amiss. "All right," he mumbles to himself. "Think." He sits cross-legged; he examines the circuitry. The man and the woman and the books and the rain recede until there is only the radio and its tangle of wires. He tries to envision the bouncing pathways of electrons, the signal chain like a path through a crowded city, RF signal coming in here, passing through a grid of amplifiers, then to variable condensers, then to transformer coils . . .

He sees it. There are two breaks in one of the resistance wires. Werner peers over the top of the set: to his left, the woman reads her magazine; to his right, Herr Siedler speaks into the telephone. Every so often Herr Siedler runs his thumb and finger along the crease in his pin-striped trousers, sharpening it.

Could two men have missed something so simple? It feels like a gift. So easy! Werner rewinds the resistance track and splices the wires and plugs in the radio. When he turns it on, he half expects fire to leap out of the machine. Instead: the smoky murmur of a saxophone.

At the table the woman puts down her magazine and sets all ten fingers on her cheeks. Werner climbs out from behind the radio. For a moment his mind is clear of all feeling save triumph.

"He fixed it just by thinking!" the woman exclaims. Herr Siedler covers the mouthpiece of the telephone receiver and looks over. "He sat there like a little mouse and thought, and in half a minute it was fixed!" She flourishes her brilliant fingernails and breaks into child-like laughter.

Herr Siedler hangs up the phone. The woman crosses into the sitting room and kneels in front of the radio — she is barefoot, and her smooth white calves show beneath the hem of her skirt. She rotates the knob. There is a sputter, then a torrent of bright music. The radio produces a vivid, full sound: Werner has never heard another like it.

"Oh!" Again she laughs.

Werner gathers his tools. Herr Siedler stands in front of the radio and seems about to pat him on the head. "Outstanding," he says. He ushers Werner to the dining table and calls for the maid to bring cake. Immediately it appears: four wedges on a plain white plate. Each is dusted with confectioners' sugar and topped by a dollop of whipped cream. Werner gapes. Herr Siedler laughs. "Cream is forbidden. I know. But" — he puts a forefinger to his lips — "there are ways around such things. Go on."

Werner takes a piece. Powdered sugar cascades down his chin. In the other room the woman twists the dial, and voices sermonize from the speaker. She listens awhile, then applauds, kneeling there in her bare feet. The stern faces in the tintypes stare down.

Werner eats one piece of cake, then another, then takes a third. Herr Siedler watches with his head slightly cocked, amused, considering something. "You do have a look, don't you? And that hair. Like you've had a terrible shock. Who is your father?"

Werner shakes his head.

"Right. Children's House. Silly me. Have another. Get some more cream on it, now."

The woman claps again. Werner's stomach gives a creaking sound. He can feel the man's eyes on him.

"People say it must not be a great posting, here at the mines," says Herr Siedler. "They say: 'Wouldn't you rather be in Berlin? Or France? Wouldn't you rather be a captain at the front, watching the lines advance, away from all this' " — he waves his hand at the window — " 'soot?' But I tell them I live at the center of it all. I tell them this is where the fuel is coming from, the steel too. This is the furnace of the country."

Werner clears his throat. "We act in the interest of peace." It is, verbatim, a sentence he and Jutta heard on Deutschlandsender radio three days before. "In the interest of the world."

Herr Siedler laughs. Again Werner is impressed with how numerous and tiny his teeth are.

"You know the greatest lesson of history? It's that history is whatever the victors say it is. That's the lesson. Whoever wins, that's who decides the history. We act in our own self-interest. Of course we do. Name me a person or a nation who does not. The trick is figuring out where your interests are."

A single slice of cake remains. The radio purrs and the woman laughs and Herr Siedler looks almost nothing, Werner decides, like his neighbors, their guarded, anxious faces — faces of people accustomed to watching loved ones disappear every morning into pits. His face is clean and committed; he is a man supremely confident in his privileges. And five yards away kneels this woman with varnished fingernails and hairless calves — a woman so entirely removed from Werner's previous experience that it is as if she is from a different planet. As if she has stepped out of the big Philco itself.

"Good with tools," Herr Siedler is saying. "Smart beyond your years. There are places for a boy like you. General Heissmeyer's schools. Best of the best. Teach the mechanical sciences too. Code breaking, rocket propulsion, all the latest."

Werner does not know where to set his gaze. "We do not have money."

"That's the genius of these institutions.

They want the working classes, laborers. Boys who aren't stamped by" — Herr Siedler frowns —"middle-class garbage. The cinemas and so forth. They want industrious boys. Exceptional boys."

"Yes, sir."

"Exceptional," he repeats, nodding, talking as if only to himself. He gives a whistle and the lance corporal returns, helmet in hand. The soldier's eyes flit to the remaining piece of cake and then away. "There's a recruiting board in Essen," Herr Siedler is saying. "I'll write you a letter. And take this." He hands Werner seventy-five marks, and Werner tucks the bills into his pocket as quickly as he can.

The corporal laughs. "Looks like it burned his fingers!"

Herr Siedler's attention is somewhere else. "I will send Heissmeyer a letter," he repeats. "Good for us, good for you. We act in the interest of the world, eh?" He winks. Then the corporal gives Werner a curfew pass and shows him out.

Werner walks home oblivious to the rain, trying to absorb the immensity of what has happened. Nine herons stand like flowers in the canal beside the coking plant. A barge sounds its outcast horn and coal cars trundle to and fro and the regular thudding of the hauling machine reverberates through the gloom.

At Children's House, everyone has been

put to bed. Frau Elena sits just inside the entryway with a mountain of laundered stockings in her lap and the bottle of kitchen sherry between her feet. Behind her, at the table, Jutta watches Werner with electric intensity.

Frau Elena says, "What did he want?"

"He only wanted me to fix a radio."

"Nothing more?"

"No."

"Did they have questions? About you? Or the children?"

"No, Frau Elena."

Frau Elena lets out a huge breath, as if she has not exhaled these past two hours. *"Dieu merci."* She rubs her temples with both hands. "You can go to bed now, Jutta," she says.

Jutta hesitates.

"I fixed it," says Werner.

"That's a good boy, Werner." Frau Elena takes a long pull of sherry and her eyes close and her head rocks back. "We saved you some supper." Jutta walks to the stairs, uncertainty in her eyes.

In the kitchen, everything looks coal-stained and cramped. Frau Elena brings a plate; on it sits a single boiled potato cut in two.

"Thank you," says Werner. The taste of the cake is still in his mouth. The pendulum swings on and on in the old grandfather clock. The cake, the whipped cream, the thick carpet, the pink fingernails and long calves of Fräulein Siedler — these sensations whirl through Werner's head as if on a carousel. He remembers towing Jutta to Pit Nine, where their father disappeared, evening after evening, as if their father might come shuffling out of the elevators.

Light, electricity, ether. Space, time, mass. Heinrich Hertz's *Principles of Mechanics.* Heissmeyer's famous schools. *Code breaking, rocket propulsion, all the latest.*

Open your eyes, the Frenchman on the radio used to say, *and see what you can with them before they close forever.*

"Werner?"

"Yes, Frau?"

"Aren't you hungry?"

Frau Elena: as close to a mother as he will ever have. Werner eats, though he is not hungry. Then he gives her the seventy-five marks, and she blinks at the amount and gives fifty back.

Upstairs, after he has heard Frau Elena go to the toilet and climb into her own bed and the house has become utterly quiet, Werner counts to one hundred. Then he rises from his cot and takes the little shortwave radio out of the first-aid box — six years old and bristling with his modifications, replacement wires, a new solenoid, Jutta's notations orbiting the tuning coil — and carries it into the alley behind the house and crushes it with a brick.

Exodus

Parisians continue to press through the gates. By 1 A.M., the gendarmes have lost control, and no trains have arrived or departed in over four hours. Marie-Laure sleeps on her father's shoulder. The locksmith hears no whistles, no rattling couplings: no trains. At dawn he decides it will be better to go on foot.

They walk all morning. Paris thins steadily into low houses and stand-alone shops broken by long strands of trees. Noon finds them picking their way through deadlocked traffic on a new motorway near Vaucresson, a full ten miles west of their apartment, as far from home as Marie-Laure has ever been.

At the crest of a low hill, her father looks over his shoulder: vehicles are backed up as far as he can see, carryalls and vans, a sleek new cloth-top wraparound V-12 wedged between two mule carts, some cars with wooden axles, some run out of gasoline, some with households of furniture strapped to the roof, a few with entire bristling farmyards crammed onto trailers, chickens and pigs in cages, cows clomping alongside, dogs panting against windshields.

The entire procession slogs past at little more than walking speed. Both lanes are clogged — everyone staggers west, away. A woman bicycles wearing dozens of costume necklaces. A man tows a leather armchair on a handcart, a black kitten cleaning itself on the center cushion. Women push baby carriages crammed with china, birdcages, crystalware. A man in a tuxedo walks along calling, "For the love of God, let me through," though no one steps aside, and he moves no more quickly than anyone else.

Marie-Laure stays at her father's hip with her cane in her fist. With each step, another disembodied question spins around her: *How far to Saint-Germain? Is there food, Auntie? Who has fuel?* She hears husbands yelling at wives; she hears that a child has been run over by a truck on the road ahead. In the afternoon a trio of airplanes race past, loud and fast and low, and people crouch where they walk and some scream and others clamber into the ditch and put their faces in the weeds.

By dusk they are west of Versailles. Marie-Laure's heels are bleeding and her stockings are torn and every hundred steps she stumbles. When she declares that she can walk no farther, her father carries her off the road, traveling uphill through mustard flowers until they reach a field a few hundred yards from a small farmhouse. The field has been mowed only halfway, the cut hay left unraked and unbaled. As though the farmer has fled in the middle of his work.

From his rucksack the locksmith produces a loaf of bread and some links of white sausage and they eat these quietly and then he lifts her feet into his lap. In the gloaming to the east, he can make out a gray line of traffic herded between the edges of the road. The thin and stupefied bleating of automobile horns. Someone calls as if to a missing child and the wind carries the sound away.

"Is something on fire, Papa?"

"Nothing is on fire."

"I smell smoke."

He pulls off her stockings to inspect her heels. In his hands, her feet are as light as birds.

"What is that noise?"

"Grasshoppers."

"Is it dark?"

"Getting there now."

"Where will we sleep?"

"Here."

"Are there beds?"

"No, *ma chérie.*"

"Where are we going, Papa?"

"The director has given me the address of someone who will help us."

"Where?"

"A town called Evreux. We are going to see a man named Monsieur Giannot. He is a friend of the museum's."

"How far is Evreux?"

"It will take us two years of walking to get there."

She seizes his forearm.

"I am teasing, Marie. Evreux is not so far. If we find transportation, we will be there tomorrow. You will see."

She manages to stay quiet for a dozen heartbeats. Then she says, "But for now?"

"For now we will sleep."

"With no beds?"

"With the grass as our beds. You might like it."

"In Evreux we will have beds, Papa?"

"I expect so."

"What if he does not want us to stay there?"

"He will want us."

"What if he does not?"

"Then we will go visit my uncle. Your great-uncle. In Saint-Malo."

"Uncle Etienne? You said he was crazy."

"He is partially crazy, yes. He is maybe seventy-six percent crazy."

She does not laugh. "How far is Saint-Malo?"

"Enough questions, Marie. Monsieur Giannot will want us to stay in Evreux. In big soft beds."

"How much food do we have, Papa?"
"Some. Are you still hungry?"
"I'm not hungry. I want to save the food."
"Okay. Let's save the food. Let's be quiet now and rest."
She lies back. He lights another cigarette. Six to go. Bats dive and swoop through clouds of gnats, and the insects scatter and re-form once more. *We are mice,* he thinks, *and the sky swirls with hawks.*
"You are very brave, Marie-Laure."
The girl has already fallen asleep. The night darkens. When his cigarette is gone, he eases Marie-Laure's feet to the ground and covers her with her coat and opens the rucksack. By touch, he finds his case filled with woodworking tools. Tiny saws, tacks, gouges, carving chisels, fine-gritted sandpapers. Many of these tools were his grandfather's. From beneath the lining of the case, he withdraws a small bag made of heavy linen and cinched with a drawstring. All day he has restrained himself from checking on it. Now he opens the bag and upends its contents onto his palm.
In his hand, the stone is about the size of a chestnut. Even at this late hour, in the quarter-light, it glows a majestic blue. Strangely cold.
The director said there would be three decoys. Added to the real diamond, that makes four. One would stay behind at the

museum. Three others would be sent in three different directions. One south with a young geologist. Another north with the chief of security. And one is here, in a field west of Versailles, inside the tool case of Daniel Le-Blanc, principal locksmith for the Muséum National d'Histoire Naturelle.

Three fakes. One real. It is best, the director said, that no man knows whether he carries the real diamond or a reproduction. And everyone, he said, giving them each a grave look, should behave as if he carries the real thing.

The locksmith tells himself that the diamond he carries is not real. There is no way the director would knowingly give a tradesman a one-hundred-and-thirty-three-carat diamond and let him walk out of Paris with it. And yet as he stares at it, he cannot keep his thoughts from the question: *Could it be?*

He scans the field. Trees, sky, hay. Darkness falling like velvet. Already a few pale stars. Marie-Laure breathes the measured breath of sleep. *Everyone should behave as if he carries the real thing.* The locksmith reties the stone inside the bag and slips it back into his rucksack. He can feel its tiny weight there, as though he has slipped it inside his own mind: a knot.

Hours later, he wakes to see the silhouette of an airplane blot stars as it hurtles east. It makes a soft tearing sound as it passes overhead. Then it disappears. The ground concusses a moment later.

A corner of the night sky, beyond a wall of trees, blooms red. In the lurid, flickering light, he sees that the airplane was not alone, that the sky teems with them, a dozen swooping back and forth, racing in all directions, and in a moment of disorientation, he feels that he's looking not up but down, as though a spotlight has been shined into a wedge of bloodshot water, and the sky has become the sea, and the airplanes are hungry fish, harrying their prey in the dark.

▪ ▪ ▪ ▪

Two:
8 August 1944

▪ ▪ ▪ ▪

SAINT-MALO

Doors soar away from their frames. Bricks transmute into powder. Great distending clouds of chalk and earth and granite spout into the sky. All twelve bombers have already turned and climbed and realigned high above the Channel before roof slates blown into the air finish falling into the streets.

Flames scamper up walls. Parked automobiles catch fire, as do curtains and lampshades and sofas and mattresses and most of the twenty thousand volumes in the public library. The fires pool and strut; they flow up the sides of the ramparts like tides; they splash into alleys, over rooftops, through a carpark. Smoke chases dust; ash chases smoke. A newsstand floats, burning.

From cellars and crypts throughout the city, Malouins send up oaths: *Lord God safeguard this town its people don't overlook us in your name please amen.* Old men clutch hurricane lamps; children shriek; dogs yowl. In an instant, four-hundred-year-old beams in row houses are ablaze. One section of the old city, tucked against the western walls, becomes a firestorm in which the spires of flames, at their highest, reach three hundred feet. The appetite for oxygen is such that objects heavier than housecats are dragged into the flames. Shop signs swing toward the heat from their brackets; a potted hedge comes sliding across the rubble and capsizes. Swifts, flushed from chimneys, catch fire and swoop like blown sparks out over the ramparts and extinguish themselves in the sea.

On the rue de la Crosse, the Hotel of Bees becomes almost weightless for a moment, lifted in a spiral of flame, before it begins to rain in pieces back to the earth.

NUMBER 4 RUE VAUBOREL

Marie-Laure curls into a ball beneath her bed with the stone in her left fist and the little house in her right. Nails in the timbers shriek and sigh. Bits of plaster and brick and glass cascade onto the floor, onto the model city on the table, and onto the mattress above her head.

"Papa Papa Papa Papa," Marie-Laure is saying, but her body seems to have detached itself from her voice, and her words make a faraway, desolate cadence. The notion occurs to her that the ground beneath Saint-Malo has been knitted together all along by the root structure of an immense tree, located at the center of the city, in a square no one ever walked her to, and the massive tree has been uprooted by the hand of God and the granite is coming with it, heaps and clumps and clods of stones pulling away as the trunk comes up, followed by the fat tendrils of roots — the root structure like another tree turned upside down and shoved into the soil, isn't that how

Dr. Geffard might have described it? — the ramparts crumbling, streets leaking away, block-long mansions falling like toys.

Slowly, gratefully, the world settles. From outside comes a light tinkling, fragments of glass, perhaps, falling into the streets. It sounds both beautiful and strange, as though gemstones were raining from the sky.

Wherever her great-uncle is, could he have survived this?

Could anyone?

Has she?

The house creaks, drips, groans. Then comes a sound like wind in tall grass, only hungrier. It pulls at the curtains, at the delicate parts inside her ears.

She smells smoke and knows. Fire. The glass has shattered out of her bedroom window, and what she hears is the sound of something burning beyond the shutters. Something huge. The neighborhood. The entire town.

The wall, floor, and underside of her bed remain cool. The house is not yet in flames. But for how long?

Calm yourself, she thinks. Concentrate on filling your lungs, draining them. Filling them again. She stays under her bed. She says, *"Ce n'est pas la réalité."*

Hotel of Bees

What does he remember? He saw the engineer Bernd close the cellar door and sit on the stairs. He saw gigantic Frank Volkheimer, in the golden armchair, pick at something on his trousers. Then the ceiling bulb blinked out and Volkheimer switched on his field light and a roar leaped down upon them, a sound so loud it was like a weapon itself, consuming everything, quaking the very crust of the earth, and for an instant all Werner could see was Volkheimer's light go skittering away like a frightened beetle.

They were thrown. For an instant or an hour or a day — who could guess how long? — Werner was back in Zollverein, standing above a grave a miner had dug for two mules at the edge of a field, and it was winter and Werner was no older than five, and the skin of the mules had grown nearly translucent, so that their bones were hazily visible inside, and little clods of dirt were stuck to their open eyes, and he was hungry enough to wonder if there was anything left on them worth eating.

He heard the blade of a shovel strike pebbles.

He heard his sister inhale.

Then, as though some retaining cord had reached its limit, something yanked him back into the cellar beneath the Hotel of Bees.

The floor has stopped shaking, but the sound has not diminished. He clamps his palm to his right ear. The roar remains, the buzzing of a thousand bees, very close.

"Is there noise?" he asks, but cannot hear himself ask it. The left side of his face is wet. The headphones he was wearing are gone. Where is the workbench, where is the radio, what are these weights on top of him?

From his shoulders, chest, and hair, he plucks hot pieces of stone and wood. Find the field light, check on the others, check on the radio. Check on the exit. Figure out what has gone wrong with his hearing. These are the rational steps. He tries to sit up, but the ceiling has become lower, and he strikes his head.

Heat. Getting hotter. He thinks: We are locked inside a box, and the box has been pitched into the mouth of a volcano.

Seconds pass. Maybe they are minutes. Werner stays on his knees. Light. Then the others. Then the exit. Then his hearing. Probably the Luftwaffe men upstairs are already scrabbling through wreckage to help. But he cannot find his field light. He cannot even stand up.

In the absolute blackness, his vision is webbed with a thousand traveling wisps of red and blue. Flames? Phantoms? They lick along the floor, then rise to the ceiling, glowing strangely, serenely.

"Are we dead?" he shouts into the dark. "Have we died?"

Down Six Flights

The roar of the bombers has hardly faded when an artillery shell whistles over the house and makes a dull crash as it explodes not far away. Objects patter onto the roof — shell fragments? cinders? — and Marie-Laure says aloud, "You are too high in the house," and forces herself out from beneath the bed. Already she has lingered too long. She returns the stone inside the model house and restores the wooden panels that make up its roof and twists the chimney back into place and puts the house into the pocket of her dress.

Where are her shoes? She crawls around the floor, but her fingers feel only bits of wood and what might be shards of window glass. She finds her cane and goes in her stocking feet out the door and down the hall. The smell of smoke is stronger out here. The floor still cool, walls still cool. She relieves herself in the sixth-floor toilet and checks her instinct to flush, knowing the toilet will not refill, and double-checks the air to make sure it does not feel warm before continuing.

Six paces to the stairwell. A second shell screeches overhead, and Marie-Laure shrieks, and the chandelier above her head chimes as the shell detonates somewhere deeper in the city.

Rain of bricks, rain of pebbles, slower rain of soot. Eight curving stairs to the bottom; the second and fifth steps creak. Pivot around the newel, eight more stairs. Fourth floor. Third. Here she checks the trip wire her great-uncle built beneath the telephone table on the landing. The bell is suspended and the wire remains taut, running vertically through the hole he has drilled in the wall. No one has come or gone.

Eight paces down the hall into the third-floor bathroom. The bathtub is full. Things float in it, flakes of ceiling plaster, maybe, and there's grit on the floor beneath her knees, but she puts her lips to its surface and drinks her fill. As much as she can.

Back to the stairwell and down to the second floor. Then the first: grapevines carved into the banister. The coatrack has toppled over. Fragments of something sharp are in the hall — crockery, she decides, from the hutch in the dining room — and she steps as lightly as she can.

Down here, some of the windows must have blown out as well: she smells more smoke. Her great-uncle's wool coat hangs from the hook in the foyer; she puts it on. No sign of her shoes here either — what has she done with them? The kitchen is a welter of fallen shelves and pots. A cookbook lies facedown in her path like a shotgunned bird. In the cupboard, she finds a half-loaf of bread, what's left from the day before.

Here, in the center of the floor, the cellar door with its metal ring. She slides aside the small dining table and heaves open the hatch.

Home of mice and damp and the stink of stranded shellfish, as if a huge tide swept in decades ago and took its time draining away. Marie-Laure hesitates over the open door, smelling the fires from outside and the clammy, almost opposite smell washing up from the bottom. Smoke: her great-uncle says it is a suspension of particles, billions of drifting carbon molecules. Bits of living rooms, cafés, trees. People.

A third artillery shell screams toward the city from the east. Again Marie-Laure feels for the model house in the pocket of her dress. Then she takes the bread and her cane and starts down the ladder and pulls the trapdoor shut.

Trapped

A light emerges, a light not kindled, Werner prays, by his own imagination: an amber beam wandering the dust. It shuttles across debris, illuminates a fallen hunk of wall, lights up a twisted piece of shelving. It roves over a pair of metal cabinets that have been warped and mauled as if a giant hand has reached down and torn each in half. It shines on spilled toolboxes and broken pegboards and a dozen unbroken jars full of screws and nails.

Volkheimer. He has his field light and is swinging its beam repeatedly over a welter of compacted wreckage in the far corner — stones and cement and splintered wood. It takes Werner a moment to realize that this is the stairwell.

What is left of the stairwell.

That whole corner of the cellar is gone. The light hovers there another moment, as if allowing Werner to absorb their situation, then veers to the right and wobbles toward something nearby, and in the reflected light, through skeins of dust, Werner can see the huge silhouette of Volkheimer ducking and stumbling as he moves between hanging rebar and pipes. Finally the light settles. With the flashlight in his mouth, in those granular, high-slung shadows, Volkheimer lifts pieces of brick and mortar and plaster, chunk after chunk, shredded boards and slabs of stucco — there is something beneath all of this, Werner sees, buried under these heavy things, a form coming into shape.

The engineer. Bernd.

Bernd's face is white with dust, but his eyes are two voids and his mouth is a maroon hole. Though Bernd is screaming, through the serrated roar lodged in his ears, Werner cannot hear him. Volkheimer lifts the engineer — the older man like a child in the staff sergeant's arms, the field light gripped in Volkheimer's teeth — and crosses the ruined space with him, ducking again to avoid the hanging ceiling, and sets him in the golden armchair still upright in the corner, now powdered white.

Volkheimer puts his big hand on Bernd's jaw and gently closes the man's mouth. Werner, only a few feet away, hears no change in the air.

The structure around them gives off another tremor, and hot dust cascades everywhere.

Soon Volkheimer's light is making a circuit

of what is left of the roof. The three huge wooden beams have cracked, but none has given way entirely. Between them the stucco is spiderwebbed, and pipes poke through in two places. The light veers behind him and illuminates the capsized workbench, the crushed case of their radio. Finally it finds Werner. He raises a palm to block it.

Volkheimer approaches; his big solicitous face presses close. Broad, familiar, deep-sunk eyes beneath the helmet. High cheekbones and long nose, flared at the tip like the knobs at the bottom of a femur. Chin like a continent. With slow care, Volkheimer touches Werner's cheek. His fingertip comes away red.

Werner says, "We have to get out. We have to find another way out."

Out? say Volkheimer's lips. He shakes his head. *There is no other way out.*

■ ■ ■ ■

Three: June 1940

■ ■ ■ ■

CHÂTEAU

Two days after fleeing Paris, Marie-Laure and her father enter the town of Evreux. Restaurants are either boarded up or thronged. Two women in evening gowns hunch hip to hip on the cathedral steps. A man lies facedown between market stalls, unconscious or worse.

No mail service. Telegraph lines down. The most recent newspaper is thirty-six hours old. At the prefecture, a queue for gasoline coupons snakes out the door and around the block.

The first two hotels are full. The third will not unlock the door. Every so often the locksmith catches himself glancing over his shoulder.

"Papa," Marie-Laure is mumbling. Bewildered. "My feet."

He lights a cigarette: three left. "Not much farther now, Marie."

On the western edge of Evreux, the road empties and the countryside levels out. He checks and rechecks the address the director has given him. *Monsieur François Giannot. 9 rue St. Nicolas.* But Monsieur Giannot's house, when they reach it, is on fire. In the windless dusk, sullen heaps of smoke pump upward through the trees. A car has crashed into a corner of the gatehouse and torn the gate off its hinges. The house — or what remains of it — is grand: twenty French windows in the facade, big freshly painted shutters, manicured hedges out front. *Un château.*

"I smell smoke, Papa."

He leads Marie-Laure up the gravel. His rucksack — or perhaps it is the stone deep inside — seems to grow heavier with each step. No puddles gleam in the gravel, no fire brigade swarms out front. Twin urns are toppled on the front steps. A burst chandelier sprawls across the entry stairs.

"What is burning, Papa?"

A boy comes toward them out of the smoky twilight, no older than Marie-Laure, streaked with ash, pushing a wheeled dining cart through the gravel. Silver tongs and spoons hanging from the cart chime and clank, and the wheels clatter and wallow. A little polished cherub grins at each corner.

The locksmith says, "Is this the house of François Giannot?"

The boy acknowledges neither question nor questioner as he passes.

"Do you know what happened to — ?"

The clanging of the cart recedes.

Marie-Laure yanks the hem of his coat. "Papa, please."

In her coat against the black trees, her face looks paler and more frightened than he has ever seen it. Has he ever asked so much of her?

"A house has burned, Marie. People are stealing things."

"What house?"

"The house we have come so far to reach."

Over her head, he can see the smoldering remains of door frames glow and fade with the passage of the breeze. A hole in the roof frames the darkening sky.

Two more boys emerge from the soot carrying a portrait in a gilded frame, twice as tall as they are, the visage of some long-dead great-grandfather glowering at the night. The locksmith holds up his palms to delay them. "Was it airplanes?"

One says, "There's plenty more inside." The canvas of the painting ripples.

"Do you know the whereabouts of Monsieur Giannot?"

The other says, "Ran off yesterday. With the rest. London."

"Don't tell him anything," says the first.

The boys jog down the driveway with their prize and are swallowed by the gloom.

"London?" whispers Marie-Laure. "The

friend of the director is in London?"

Sheets of blackened paper scuttle past their feet. Shadows whisper in the trees. A ruptured melon lolls in the drive like an amputated head. The locksmith is seeing too much. All day, mile after mile, he let himself imagine they would be greeted with food. Little potatoes with hot cores into which he and Marie-Laure would plunge forkfuls of butter. Shallots and mushrooms and hard-boiled eggs and béchamel. Coffee and cigarettes. He would hand Monsieur Giannot the stone, and Giannot would pull brass lorgnettes out of his breast pocket and fit their lenses over his calm eyes and tell him: real or fake. Then Giannot would bury it in the garden or conceal it behind a hidden panel somewhere in his walls, and that would be that. Duty fulfilled. *Je ne m'en occupe plus.* They would be given a private room, take baths; maybe someone would wash their clothes. Maybe Monsieur Giannot would tell humorous stories about his friend the director, and in the morning the birds would sing and a fresh newspaper would announce the end of the invasion, reasonable concessions. He would go back to the key pound, spend his evenings installing little sash windows in little wooden houses. *Bonjour, bonjour.* Everything as before.

But nothing is as before. The trees seethe and the house smolders, and standing in the gravel of the driveway, the daylight nearly finished, the locksmith has an unsettling thought: Someone might be coming for us. Someone might know what I carry.

He leads Marie-Laure back to the road at a trot.

"Papa, my feet."

He swings the rucksack around to his front and wraps her arms around his neck and carries her on his back. They pass the smashed gatehouse and the crashed car and turn not east toward the center of Evreux but west. Figures bicycle past. Pinched faces streaked with suspicion or fear or both. Perhaps it is the locksmith's own eyes that have been streaked.

"Not so quickly," begs Marie-Laure.

They rest in weeds twenty paces off the road. There is only plunging night and owls calling from the trees and bats straining insects above a roadside ditch. A diamond, the locksmith reminds himself, is only a piece of carbon compressed in the bowels of the earth for eons and driven to the surface in a volcanic pipe. Someone facets it, someone polishes it. It can harbor a curse no more than a leaf can, or a mirror, or a life. There is only chance in this world, chance and physics.

Anyway, what he carries is nothing more than a piece of glass. A diversion.

Behind him, over Evreux, a wall of clouds ignites once, twice. Lightning? On the road ahead, he can make out several acres of uncut hay and the gentle profiles of unlit farm buildings — a house and barn. No movement.

"Marie, I see a hotel."

"You said the hotels were full."

"This one looks friendly. Come. It's not far."

Again he carries his daughter. One more half mile. The windows of the house stay unlit as they approach. Its barn sits a hundred yards beyond. He tries to listen above the rush of blood in his ears. No dogs, no torches. Probably the farmers too have fled. He sets Marie-Laure in front of the barn doors and knocks softly and waits and knocks again.

The padlock is a brand-new single-latch Burguet; with his tools he picks it easily. Inside are oats and water buckets and horseflies flying sleepy loops but no horses. He opens a stall and helps Marie-Laure into the corner and pulls off her shoes.

"Voilà," he says. "One of the guests has just brought his horses into the lobby, so it may smell for a moment. But now the porters are hurrying him out. See, there he goes. Goodbye, horse! Go sleep in the stables, please!"

Her expression is faraway. Lost.

A vegetable garden waits behind the house. In the dimness he can make out roses, leeks, lettuces. Strawberries, most still green. Tender white carrots with black earth clotted in their fibers. Nothing stirs: no farmer materializes in a window with a rifle. The locksmith brings back a shirtful of vegetables and fills a tin bucket at a spigot and eases shut the barn door and feeds his daughter in the dark. Then he folds his coat, lays her head on it, and wipes her face with his shirt.

Two cigarettes left. Inhale, exhale.

Walk the paths of logic. Every outcome has its cause, and every predicament has its solution. Every lock its key. You can go back to Paris or you can stay here or you can go on.

From outside comes the soft hooting of owls. Distant grumbling of thunder or ordnance or both. He says, "This hotel is very cheap, *ma chérie.* The innkeeper behind the desk said our room was forty francs a night but only twenty francs if we made our own bed." He listens to her breathe. "So I said, 'Oh, we can make our own bed.' And he said, 'Right, I'll get you some nails and wood.' "

Marie-Laure still does not smile. "Now we go find Uncle Etienne?"

"Yes, Marie."

"Who is seventy-six percent crazy?"

"He was with your grandfather — his brother — when he died. In the war. 'Got a bit of gas in the head' is how they used to say it. Afterward he saw things."

"What kind of things?"

Creaking rumble of thunder closer now. The barn quakes lightly.

"Things that were not there."

Spiders draw their webs between rafters. Moths flap against the windows. It starts to rain.

Entrance Exam

Entrance exams for the National Political Institutes of Education are held in Essen, eighteen miles south of Zollverein, inside a sweltering dance hall where a trio of truck-sized radiators is plugged in to the back wall. One of the radiators clangs and steams all day despite various attempts to shut it down. War ministry flags as big as tanks hang from the rafters.

There are one hundred recruits, all boys. A school representative in a black uniform arranges them in ranks four deep. Medals chime on his chest as he paces. "You are," he declares, "attempting to enter the most elite schools in the world. The exams will last eight days. We will take only the purest, only the strongest." A second representative distributes uniforms: white shirts, white shorts, white socks. The boys shuck their clothes where they stand.

Werner counts twenty-six others in his age group. All but two are taller than he is. All but three are blond. None of them wear eyeglasses.

The boys spend that entire first morning in their new white outfits, filling out questionnaires on clipboards. There is no noise save the scribbling of pencils and the pacing of examiners and the clunking of the huge radiator.

Where was your grandfather born? What color are your father's eyes? Has your mother ever worked in an office? Of one hundred and ten questions about his lineage, Werner can accurately answer only sixteen. The rest are guesses.

Where is your mother from?

There are no options for past tense. He writes: *Germany.*

Where is your father from?

Germany.

What languages does your mother speak?

German.

He remembers Frau Elena as she looked early this morning, standing in her nightdress beside the hall lamp, fussing over his bag, all the other children asleep. She seemed lost, dazed, as if she could not absorb how quickly things were changing around her. She said she was proud. She said Werner should do his best. "You're a smart boy," she said. "You'll do well." She kept adjusting and readjusting his collar. When he said, "It's only a week," her eyes filled slowly, as if some internal flood were gradually overwhelming her.

In the afternoon, the recruits run. They crawl under obstacles, do push-ups, scale ropes suspended from the ceiling — one hundred children passing sleek and interchangeable in their white uniforms like livestock before the eyes of the examiners. Werner comes in ninth in the shuttle runs. He comes in second to last on the rope climb. He will never be good enough.

In the evening, the boys spill out of the hall, some met by proud-looking parents with automobiles, others vanishing purposefully in twos and threes into the streets: all seem to know where they're going. Werner makes his way alone to a spartan hostel six blocks away, where he rents a bed for two marks a night and lies among muttering itinerants and listens to the pigeons and bells and shuddering traffic of Essen. It is the first night he has spent outside of Zollverein, and he cannot stop thinking of Jutta, who has not spoken to him since discovering he smashed their radio. Who stared at him with so much accusation in her face that he had to look away. Her eyes said, *You are betraying me,* but wasn't he protecting her?

On the second morning, there are raciological exams. They require little of Werner except to raise his arms or keep from blinking while an inspector shines a penlight into the tunnels of his pupils. He sweats and shifts. His heart pounds unreasonably. An onion-breathed technician in a lab coat measures the distance between Werner's temples, the circumference of his head, and the thickness and shape of his lips. Calipers are used to evaluate his feet, the length of his fingers, and the distance between his eyes and his navel. They measure his penis. The angle of his nose is quantified with a wooden protractor.

A second technician gauges Werner's eye color against a chromatic scale on which sixty or so shades of blue are displayed. Werner's color is *himmelblau,* sky blue. To assess his hair color, the man snips a lock of hair from Werner's head and compares it to thirty or so other locks clipped to a board, arrayed darkest to lightest.

"Schnee," the man mutters, and makes a notation. Snow. Werner's hair is lighter than the lightest color on the board.

They test his vision, draw his blood, take his fingerprints. By noon he wonders if there is anything left for them to measure.

Verbal exams come next. How many Nationalpolitische Erziehungsanstalten are there? Twenty. Who are our greatest Olympians? He does not know. What is the birthday of the führer? April 20. Who is our greatest writer, what is the Treaty of Versailles, which is the nation's fastest airplane?

Day three involves more running, more climbing, more jumping. Everything is timed. The technicians, school representatives, and examiners — each wearing uniforms in subtly different shades — scribble on pads of graph paper with a very narrow gauge, and sheet after sheet of this paper gets closed into leather binders with a gold lightning bolt stamped on the front.

The recruits speculate in eager whispers.

"I hear the schools have sailboats, falconries, rifle ranges."

"I hear they will take only seven from each age group."

"I hear it's only four."

They speak of the schools with yearning and bravado; they want desperately to be selected. Werner tells himself: *So do I. So do I.*

And yet at other times, despite his ambitions, he is visited by instants of vertigo; he sees Jutta holding the smashed pieces of their radio and feels uncertainty steal into his gut.

The recruits scale walls; they run wind sprint after wind sprint. On the fifth day, three quit. On the sixth, four more give up. Each hour the dance hall seems to grow progressively warmer, so by the eighth day, the air, walls, and floor are saturated with the hot, teeming odor of boys. For their final test, each of the fourteen-year-olds is forced to climb a ladder haphazardly nailed to a wall.

Once at the top, twenty-five feet above the floor, their heads in the rafters, they are supposed to step onto a tiny platform, close their eyes, and leap off, to be caught in a flag held by a dozen of the other recruits.

First to go is a stout farm kid from Herne. He scales the ladder quickly enough, but as soon as he's on the platform high above everyone else, his face goes white. His knees wobble dangerously.

Someone mutters, "Pussy."

The boy beside Werner whispers, "Afraid of heights."

An examiner watches dispassionately. The boy on the platform peeks over the edge as if into a swirling abyss and shuts his eyes. He sways back and forth. Interminable seconds pass. The examiner peers at his stopwatch. Werner clutches the hem of the flag.

Soon most everyone in the dance hall has stopped to watch, even recruits in other age groups. The boy sways twice more, until it's clear he's about to faint. Even then no one moves to help him.

When he goes over, he goes sideways. The recruits on the ground manage to swing the flag around in time, but his weight tears the edges out of their hands, and he hits the floor arms first with a sound like a bundle of kindling breaking over a knee.

The boy sits up. Both of his forearms are bent at nauseating angles. He blinks at them curiously for a moment, as if scanning his memory for a clue that might explain how he got there.

Then he starts to scream. Werner looks away. Four boys are ordered to carry the injured one out.

One by one, the remaining fourteen-year-olds climb the ladder and tremble and leap. One sobs the whole way. Another sprains an ankle when he hits. The next waits at least two full minutes before jumping. The fifteenth boy looks out across the dance hall as if staring into a bleak, cold sea, then climbs back down.

Werner watches from his place on the flag. When his turn comes, he tells himself, he must not waver. On the undersides of his eyelids he sees the interlaced ironwork of Zollverein, the fire-breathing mills, men teeming out of elevator shafts like ants, the mouth of Pit Nine, where his father was lost. Jutta in the parlor window, sealed behind the rain, watching him follow the corporal to Herr Siedler's house. The taste of whipped cream and powdered sugar and the smooth calves of Herr Siedler's wife.

Exceptional. Unexpected.

We will take only the purest, only the strongest.

The only place your brother is going, little girl, is into the mines.

Werner scampers up the ladder. The rungs

have been roughly sawed, and his palms take splinters the whole way. From the top, the crimson flag with its white circle and black cross looks unexpectedly small. A pale ring of faces stares up. It's even hotter up here, torrid, and the smell of perspiration makes him light-headed.

Without hesitating, Werner steps to the edge of the platform and shuts his eyes and jumps. He hits the flag in its exact center, and the boys holding its edges give a collective groan.

He rolls to his feet, uninjured. The examiner clicks his stopwatch, scribbles on his clipboard, looks up. Their eyes meet for a half second. Maybe less. Then the man goes back to his notations.

"*Heil* Hitler!" yells Werner.

The next boy starts up the ladder.

Brittany

In the morning an ancient furniture lorry stops for them. Her father lifts her into its bed, where a dozen people nestle beneath a waxed canvas tarp. The engine roars and pops; the truck rarely accelerates past walking speed.

A woman prays in a Norman accent; someone shares pâté; everything smells of rain. No Stukas swoop over them, machine guns blazing. No one in the truck has even seen a German. For half the morning, Marie-Laure tries to convince herself that the previous days have been some elaborate test concocted by her father, that the truck is moving not away from Paris but toward it, that tonight they'll return home. The model will be on its bench in the corner, and the sugar bowl will be in the center of the kitchen table, its little spoon resting on the rim. Out the open windows, the cheese seller on the rue des Patriarches will lock his door and shutter up those marvelous smells, as he has done nearly every evening she can remember, and the leaves of the chestnut tree will clatter and murmur, and her father will boil coffee and draw her a hot bath, and say, "You did well, Marie-Laure. I'm proud."

The truck bounces from highway to country road to dirt lane. Weeds brush its flanks. Well after midnight, west of Cancale, they run out of fuel.

"Not much farther," her father whispers.

Marie-Laure shuffles along half-asleep. The road seems hardly wider than a path. The air smells like wet grain and hedge trimmings; in the lulls between their footfalls, she can hear a deep, nearly subsonic roar. She tugs her father to a stop. "Armies."

"The ocean."

She cocks her head.

"It's the ocean, Marie. I promise."

He carries her on his back. Now the barking of gulls. Smell of wet stones, of bird shit, of salt, though she never knew salt to have a smell. The sea murmuring in a language that travels through stones, air, and sky. What did Captain Nemo say? *The sea does not belong to tyrants.*

"We're crossing into Saint-Malo now," says her father, "the part they call the city within the walls." He narrates what he sees: a portcullis, defensive walls called ramparts, granite mansions, a steeple above rooftops. The echoes of his footfalls ricochet off tall houses and rain back onto them, and he labors beneath her weight, and she is old enough to suspect that what he presents as quaint and welcoming might in truth be harrowing and strange.

Birds make strangled cries overhead. Her father turns left, right. It feels to Marie-Laure as if they have wound these past four days toward the center of a bewildering maze, and now they are tiptoeing past the pickets of some final interior cell. Inside which a terrible beast might slumber.

"Rue Vauborel," her father says between pants. "Here, it must be. Or here?" He pivots, retraces their steps, climbs an alley, then turns around.

"Is there no one to ask?"

"There's not a single light, Marie. Everyone is asleep or pretending to be."

Finally they reach a gate, and he sets her down on a curbstone and pushes an electric buzzer, and she can hear it ring deep within a house. Nothing. He presses again. Again nothing. He presses a third time.

"This is the house of your uncle?"

"It is."

"He doesn't know us," she says.

"He's sleeping. As we should be."

They sit with their backs to the gate. Wrought iron and cool. A heavy wooden door just behind it. She leans her head on his shoulder; he pulls off her shoes. The world seems to sway gently back and forth, as though the town is drifting lightly away. As though back onshore, all of France is left to bite its fingernails and flee and stumble and weep and wake to a numb, gray dawn, unable to believe what is happening. Who do the roads belong to now? And the fields? The trees?

Her father takes his final cigarette from his shirt pocket and lights it.

From deep inside the house behind them come footfalls.

Madame Manec

As soon as her father says his name, the breathing on the other side of the door becomes a gasp, a held breath. The gate screeches; a door behind it gives way. "Jesus's mother," says a woman's voice. "You were so small —"

"My daughter, Madame. Marie-Laure, this is Madame Manec."

Marie-Laure attempts a curtsy. The hand that cups her cheek is strong: the hand of a geologist or a gardener.

"My God, there are none so distant that fate cannot bring them together. But, dear child, your stockings. And your heels! You must be famished."

They step into a narrow entry. Marie-Laure hears the gate clang shut, then the woman latching the door behind them. Two dead bolts, one chain. They are led into a room that smells of herbs and rising dough: a kitchen. Her father unbuttons her coat, helps her sit. "We are very grateful, I understand how late it is," he is saying, and the old woman — Madame Manec — is brisk, efficient, evidently overcoming her initial amazement; she brushes off their thank-yous; she scoots Marie-Laure's chair toward a tabletop. A match is struck; water fills a pot; an icebox clicks open and shut. There is the hum of gas and the tick-tick of heating metal. In another moment, a warm towel is on Marie-Laure's face. A jar of cool, sweet water in front of her. Each sip a blessing.

"Oh, the town is absolutely stuffed," Madame Manec is saying in her fairy-tale drawl as she moves about. She seems short; she wears blocky, heavy shoes. Hers is a low voice, full of pebbles — a sailor's voice or a smoker's. "Some can afford hotels or rentals, but many are in the warehouses, on straw, not enough to eat. I'd take them in, but your uncle, you know, it might upset him. There's no diesel, no kerosene, British ships long gone. They burned everything they left behind, at first I couldn't believe any of it, but Etienne, he has the wireless going nonstop —"

Eggs crack. Butter pops in a hot pan. Her father is telling an abridged story of their flight, train stations, fearful crowds, omitting the stop in Evreux, but soon all of Marie-Laure's attention is absorbed by the smells blooming around her: egg, spinach, melting cheese.

An omelet arrives. She positions her face over its steam. "May I please have a fork?"

The old woman laughs: a laugh Marie-Laure warms to immediately. In an instant a fork is fitted into her hand.

The eggs taste like clouds. Like spun gold. Madame Manec says, "I think she likes it," and laughs again.

A second omelet soon appears. Now it is her father who eats quickly. "How about peaches, dear?" murmurs Madame Manec, and Marie-Laure can hear a can opening, juice slopping into a bowl. Seconds later, she's eating wedges of wet sunlight.

"Marie," murmurs her father, "your manners."

"But they're —"

"We have plenty, you go ahead, child. I make them every year." When Marie-Laure has eaten two full cans of peaches, Madame Manec cleans Marie-Laure's feet with a rag and shakes out her coat and clanks dishes into a sink and says, "Cigarette?" and her father groans with gratitude and a match flares and the grown-ups smoke.

A door opens, or a window, and Marie-Laure can hear the hypnotic voice of the sea.

"And Etienne?" says her father.

Madame says, "Shuts himself up like a corpse one day, eats like an albatross the next."

"He still does not — ?"

"Not for twenty years."

Probably the grown-ups are mouthing more to each other. Probably Marie-Laure should be more curious — about her great-uncle who sees things that are not there, about the fate of everyone and everything she has ever known — but her stomach is full, her blood has become a warm golden flow through her arteries, and out the open window, beyond the walls, the ocean crashes, only a bit of stacked stone left between her and it, the rim of Brittany, the farthest windowsill of France — and maybe the Germans are advancing as inexorably as lava, but Marie-Laure is slipping into something like a dream, or perhaps it's the memory of one: she's six or seven years old, newly blind, and her father is sitting in the chair beside her bed, whittling away at some tiny piece of wood, smoking a cigarette, and evening is settling over the hundred thousand rooftops and chimneys of Paris, and all the walls around her are dissolving, the ceilings too, the whole city is disintegrating into smoke, and at last sleep falls over her like a shadow.

You Have Been Called

Everyone wants to hear Werner's stories. What were the exams like, what did they make you do, tell us everything. The youngest children tug his sleeves; the older ones are deferential. This snowy-haired dreamer plucked out of the soot.

"They said they'd accept only two from my age group. Maybe three." From the far end of the table, he can feel the heat of Jutta's attention. With the rest of the money from Herr Siedler, he purchased a People's Receiver for thirty-four marks eighty: a two-valve low-powered radio even cheaper than the state-sponsored Volksemfängers he has repaired in the houses of neighbors. Unmodified, its receiver can haul in only the big long-wave nationwide programs from Deutchlandsender. Nothing else. Nothing foreign.

The children shout, delighted, as he presents it. Jutta shows no interest.

Martin Sachse asks, "Was there loads of math?"

"Was there cheeses? Was there cakes?"

"Did they let you shoot rifles?"

"Did you ride in tanks? I bet you rode in tanks."

Werner says, "I didn't know the answers to half their questions. I'll never get in."

But he does. Five days after he returns from Essen, the letter is hand-delivered to Children's House. An eagle and cross on a crisp envelope. No stamp. Like a dispatch from God.

Frau Elena is doing laundry. The little boys are clustered around the new radio: a half-hour program called *Kids' Club.* Jutta and Claudia Förster have taken three of the younger girls to a puppet show in the market; Jutta has spoken no more than six words to Werner since his return.

You have been called, says the letter. Werner is to report to the National Political Institute of Education #6 at Schulpforta. He stands in the parlor of Children's House, trying to absorb it. Cracked walls, sagging ceiling, twin benches that have borne child after child after child for as long as the mine has made orphans. He has found a way out.

Schulpforta. Tiny dot on the map, near Naumburg, in Saxony. Two hundred miles east. Only in his most intrepid dreams did he allow himself to hope that he might travel so far. He carries the sheet of paper in a daze to the alley where Frau Elena boils sheets amid billows of steam.

She rereads it several times. "We can't pay."

"We don't need to."

"How far?"

"Five hours by train. They've already paid the fare."

"When?"

"Two weeks."

Frau Elena: strands of hair stuck to her cheeks, maroon aprons under her eyes, pink rims around her nostrils. Thin crucifix against her damp throat. Is she proud? She rubs her eyes and nods absently. "They'll celebrate this." She hands the letter back and stares down the alley at the dense ranks of clotheslines and coalbins.

"Who, Frau?"

"Everyone. The neighbors." She laughs a sudden and startling laugh. "People like that vice minister. The man who took your book."

"Not Jutta."

"No. Not Jutta."

He rehearses in his head the argument he will present to his sister. *Pflicht.* It means duty. Obligation. Every German fulfilling his function. Put on your boots and go to work. *Ein Volk, ein Reich, ein Führer.* We all have parts to play, little sister. But before the girls arrive, news of his acceptance has reverberated through the block. Neighbors come over one after another and exclaim and wag their chins. Coal wives bring pig knuckles and cheese; they pass around Werner's acceptance letter; the ones who can read, read it aloud to the ones who cannot, and Jutta comes home to a crowded, exhilarated room. The twins — Hannah and Susanne Gerlitz — sprint laps around the sofa, looped up in the excitement, and six-year-old Rolf Hupfauer sings *Rise! Rise! All glory to the fatherland!* and several of the other children join in, and Werner doesn't see Frau Elena speak to Jutta in the corner of the parlor, doesn't see Jutta run upstairs.

At the dinner bell, she does not come down. Frau Elena asks Hannah Gerlitz to lead the prayer, and tells Werner she'll talk to Jutta, that he ought to stay downstairs, all these people are here for him. Every few breaths, the words flare in his mind like sparks: *You have been called.* Each minute that passes is one fewer in this house. In this life.

After the meal, little Siegfried Fischer, no older than five, walks around the table and tugs Werner's sleeve and hands him a photograph he has torn from a newspaper. In the picture, six fighter-bombers float above a mountain range of clouds. Spangles of sun are frozen midglide across the airplanes' fuselages. The scarves of the pilots stretch backward.

Siegfried Fischer says, "You'll show them, won't you?" His face is fierce with belief; it seems to draw a circle around all the hours

Werner has spent at Children's House, hoping for something more.

"I will," Werner says. The eyes of all the children are on him. "Absolutely I will."

OCCUPER

Marie-Laure wakes to church bells: two three four five. Faint smell of mildew. Ancient down pillows with all the loft worn out. Silk wallpaper behind the lumpy bed where she sits. When she stretches out both arms, she can almost touch walls on either side.

The reverberations of the bells cease. She has slept most of the day. What is the muffled roar she hears? Crowds? Or is it still the sea?

She sets her feet on the floor. The wounds on the backs of her heels pulse. Where is her cane? She shuffles so she does not bash her shins on something. Behind curtains, a window rises out of her reach. Opposite the window, she finds a dresser whose drawers open only partway before striking the bed.

The weather in this place: you can feel it between your fingers.

She gropes through a doorway into what? A hall? Out here the roar is fainter, barely a murmur.

"Hello?"

Quiet. Then a bustling far below, the heavy shoes of Madame Manec climbing flights of narrow, curving steps, her smoker's lungs coming closer, third floor, fourth — how tall is this house? — now Madame's voice is calling, "Mademoiselle," and she is taken by the hand, led back into the room in which she woke, and seated on the edge of the bed. "Do you need to use the toilet? You must, then a bath, you had an excellent sleep, your father is in town trying the telegraph office, though I assured him that'll be about as profitable as trying to pick feathers out of molasses. Are you hungry?"

Madame Manec plumps pillows, flaps the quilt. Marie-Laure tries to concentrate on something small, something concrete. The model back in Paris. A single seashell in Dr. Geffard's laboratory.

"Does this whole house belong to my great-uncle Etienne?"

"Every room."

"How does he pay for it?"

Madame Manec laughs. "You get right to it, don't you? Your great-uncle inherited the house from his father, who was your great-grandfather. He was a very successful man with plenty of money."

"You knew him?"

"I have worked here since Master Etienne was a little boy."

"My grandfather too? You knew him?"

"I did."

"Will I meet Uncle Etienne now?"

Madame Manec hesitates. "Probably not."

"But he is here?"

"Yes, child. He is always here."

"Always?"

Madame Manec's big, thick hands enfold hers. "Let's see about the bath. Your father will explain when he returns."

"But Papa doesn't explain anything. He says only that Uncle was in the war with my grandfather."

"That's right. But your great-uncle, when he came home" — Madame hunts for the proper phrasing — "he was not the same as when he left."

"You mean he was more scared of things?"

"I mean lost. A mouse in a trap. He saw dead people passing through the walls. Terrible things in the corners of the streets. Now your great-uncle does not go outdoors."

"Not ever?"

"Not for years. But Etienne is a wonder, you'll see. He knows everything."

Marie-Laure listens to the house timbers creak and the gulls cry and the gentle roar breaking against the window. "Are we high in the air, Madame?"

"We are on the sixth floor. It's a good bed, isn't it? I thought you and your papa would be able to rest well here."

"Does the window open?"

"It does, dear. But it is probably best to leave it shuttered while —"

Marie-Laure is already standing atop the bed, running her palms along the wall. "Can one see the sea from it?"

"We're supposed to keep shutters and windows closed. But maybe just for a minute." Madame Manec turns a handle, pulls in the two hinged panes of the window, and nudges open the shutter. Wind: immediate, bright, sweet, briny, luminous. The roar rises and falls.

"Are there snails out there, Madame?"

"Snails? In the ocean?" Again that laugh. "As many as raindrops. You're interested in snails?"

"Yes yes yes. I have found tree snails and garden snails. But I have never found marine snails."

"Well," says Madame Manec. "You've turned up in the right place."

Madame draws a warm bath in a third-floor tub. From the tub, Marie-Laure listens to her shut the door, and the cramped bathroom groan beneath the weight of the water, and the walls creak, as if she were in a cabin inside Captain Nemo's *Nautilus.* The pain in her heels fades. She lowers her head below the level of the water. To never go outdoors! To hide for decades inside this strange, narrow house!

For dinner she is buttoned into a starchy

dress from some bygone decade. They sit at the square kitchen table, her father and Madame Manec at opposite sides, knees pressed to knees, windows jammed shut, shutters drawn. A wireless set mumbles the names of ministers in a harried, staccato voice — de Gaulle in London, Pétain replacing Reynaud. They eat fish stewed with green tomatoes. Her father reports that no letters have been delivered or collected in three days. Telegraph lines are not functioning. The newest newspaper is six days old. On the radio, the announcer reads public service classifieds.

Monsieur Cheminoux refugeed in Orange seeks his three children, left with luggage at Ivry-sur-Seine.

Francis in Genève seeks any information about Marie-Jeanne, last seen at Gentilly.

Mother sends prayers to Luc and Albert, wherever they are.

L. Rabier seeks news of his wife, last seen at Gare d'Orsay.

A. Cotteret wants his mother to know he is safe in Laval.

Madame Meyzieu seeks whereabouts of six daughters, sent by train to Redon.

"Everybody has misplaced someone," murmurs Madame Manec, and Marie-Laure's father switches off the wireless, and the tubes click as they cool. Upstairs, faintly, the same voice keeps reading names. Or is it her imagination? She hears Madame Manec stand and collect the bowls and her father exhale cigarette smoke as though it is very heavy in his lungs and he is glad to be rid of it.

That night she and her father wind up the twisting staircase and go to bed side by side on the same lumpy bed in the same sixth-floor bedroom with the fraying silk wallpaper. Her father fusses with his rucksack, with the door latch, with his matches. Soon enough there is the familiar smell of his cigarettes: Gauloises *bleues.* She hears wood pop and groan as the two halves of the window pull open. The welcome hiss of wind washes in, or maybe it's the sea and the wind, her ears unable to unbraid the two. With it come the scents of salt and hay and fish markets and distant marshes and absolutely nothing that smells to her of war.

"Can we visit the ocean tomorrow, Papa?"

"Probably not tomorrow."

"Where is Uncle Etienne?"

"I expect he's in his room on the fifth floor."

"Seeing things that are not there?"

"We are lucky to have him, Marie."

"Lucky to have Madame Manec too. She's a genius with food, isn't she, Papa? She is maybe just a little bit better at cooking than you are?"

"Just a very little bit better."

Marie-Laure is glad to hear a smile enter

his voice. But beneath it she can sense his thoughts fluttering like trapped birds. "What does it mean, Papa, they'll *occupy* us?"

"It means they'll park their trucks in the squares."

"Will they make us speak their language?"

"They might make us advance our clocks by one hour."

The house creaks. Gulls cry. He lights another cigarette.

"Is it like *occupation,* Papa? Like the sort of job a person does?"

"It's like military control, Marie. That's enough questions for now."

Quiet. Twenty heartbeats. Thirty.

"How can one country make another change its clocks? What if everybody refuses?"

"Then a lot of people will be early. Or late."

"Remember our apartment, Papa? With my books and our model and all those pinecones on the windowsill?"

"Of course."

"I lined up the pinecones largest to smallest."

"They're still there."

"Do you think so?"

"I know so."

"You do not know so."

"I do not know so. I believe so."

"Are German soldiers climbing into our beds right now, Papa?"

"No."

Marie-Laure tries to lie very still. She can almost hear the machinery of her father's mind churning inside his skull. "It will be okay," she whispers. Her hand finds his forearm. "We will stay here awhile and then we will go back to our apartment and the pinecones will be right where we left them and *Twenty Thousand Leagues Under the Sea* will be on the floor of the key pound where we left it and no one will be in our beds."

The distant anthem of the sea. The clopping of someone's boot heels on cobbles far below. She wants very badly for her father to say, Yes, that's it absolutely, *ma chérie,* but he says nothing.

Don't Tell Lies

He cannot concentrate on schoolwork or simple conversations or Frau Elena's chores. Every time he shuts his eyes, some vision of the school at Schulpforta overmasters him: vermilion flags, muscular horses, gleaming laboratories. The best boys in Germany. At certain moments he sees himself as an emblem of possibility to which all eyes have turned. Though at other moments, flickering in front of him, he sees the big kid from the entrance exams: his face gone bloodless atop the platform high above the dance hall. How he fell. How no one moved to help him.

Why can't Jutta be happy for him? Why, even at the moment of his escape, must some inexplicable warning murmur in a distant region of his mind?

Martin Sachse says, "Tell us again about the hand grenades!"

Siegfried Fischer says, "And the falconries!"

Three times he readies his argument and three times Jutta turns on a heel and strides away. Hour after hour she helps Frau Elena with the smaller children or walks to the market or finds some other excuse to be helpful, to be busy, to be out.

"She won't listen," Werner tells Frau Elena.

"Keep trying."

Before he knows it, there's only one day before his departure. He wakes before dawn and finds Jutta asleep in her cot in the girls' dormitory. Her arms are wrapped around her head and her wool blanket is twisted around her midsection and her pillow is jammed into the crack between mattress and wall — even in sleep, a tableau of friction. Above her bed are papered her fantastical pencil drawings of Frau Elena's village, of Paris with a thousand white towers beneath whirling flocks of birds.

He says her name.

She twines herself tighter into her blanket.

"Will you walk with me?"

To his surprise, she sits up. They step outside before anyone else is awake. He leads her without speaking. They climb one fence, then another. Jutta's untied shoelaces trail behind her. Thistles bite their knees. The rising sun makes a pinhole on the horizon.

They stop at the edge of an irrigation canal. In winters past, Werner used to tow her in their wagon to this very spot, and they would watch skaters race along the frozen canal, farmers with blades fixed to their feet and frost caked in their beards, five or six rushing by all at once, tightly packed, in the midst of an eight- or nine-mile race between towns. The look in the skaters' eyes was of horses who have run a long way, and it was always exciting for Werner to see them, to feel the air disturbed by their speed, to hear their skates clapping along, then fading — a sensation as if his soul might tear free of his body and go sparking off with them. But as soon as they'd continued around the bend and left behind only the white etchings of their skates in the ice, the thrill would fade, and he'd tow Jutta back to Children's House feeling lonely and forsaken and more trapped in his life than before.

He says, "No skaters came last winter."

His sister gazes into the ditch. Her eyes are mauve. Her hair is snarled and untamable and perhaps even whiter than his. *Schnee.*

She says, "None'll come this year either."

The mine complex is a smoldering black mountain range behind her. Even now Werner can hear a mechanical drumbeat thudding in the distance, first shift going down in the elevators as the owl shift comes up — all those boys with tired eyes and soot-stained faces rising in the elevators to meet the sun — and for a moment he apprehends a huge and terrible presence looming just beyond the morning.

"I know you're angry —"

"You'll become just like Hans and Herribert."

"I won't."

"Spend enough time with boys like that and you will."

"So you want me to stay? Go down in the mines?"

They watch a bicyclist far down the path. Jutta clamps her hands in her armpits. "You know what I used to listen to? On our radio? Before you ruined it?"

"Hush, Jutta. Please."

"Broadcasts from Paris. They'd say the opposite of everything Deutschlandsender says. They'd say we were devils. That we were committing *atrocities*. Do you know what *atrocities* means?"

"Please, Jutta."

"Is it right," Jutta says, "to do something only because everyone else is doing it?"

Doubts: slipping in like eels. Werner shoves them back. Jutta is barely twelve years old, still a child.

"I'll write you letters every week. Twice a week if I can. You don't have to show them to Frau Elena if you don't want to."

Jutta shuts her eyes.

"It's not forever, Jutta. Two years, maybe. Half the boys who get admitted don't manage to graduate. But maybe I'll learn something; maybe they'll teach me to be a proper engineer. Maybe I can learn to fly an airplane, like little Siegfried says. Don't shake your head, we've always wanted to see the inside of an airplane, haven't we? I'll fly us west, you and me, Frau Elena too if she wants. Or we could take a train. We'll ride through forests and *villages de montagnes,* all those places Frau Elena talked about when we were small. Maybe we could ride all the way to Paris."

The burgeoning light. The tender hissing of the grass. Jutta opens her eyes but doesn't look at him. "Don't tell lies. Lie to yourself, Werner, but don't lie to me."

Ten hours later, he's on a train.

Etienne

For three days she does not meet her great-uncle. Then, feeling her way to the toilet on the fourth morning after their arrival, she steps on something small and hard. She crouches and locates it with her fingers.

Whorled and smooth. A sculpture of vertical folds incised by a tapering spiral. The aperture broad and oval. She whispers, "A whelk."

One stride in front of the first shell, she finds another. Then a third and a fourth. The trail of seashells arcs past the toilet and down a flight to the closed fifth-floor door she knows by now is his. Beyond which issues the concerted whispers of pianos playing. A voice says, "Come in."

She expects fustiness, an elderly funk, but the room smells mildly of soap and books and dried seaweed. Not unlike Dr. Geffard's laboratory.

"Great-Uncle?"

"Marie-Laure." His voice is low and soft, a

piece of silk you might keep in a drawer and pull out only on rare occasions, just to feel it between your fingers. She reaches into space, and a cool bird-boned hand takes hers. He is feeling better, he says. "I am sorry I have not been able to meet you sooner."

The pianos plink along softly; it sounds as if a dozen are playing all at once, as if the sound comes from every point of the compass.

"How many radios do you have, Uncle?"

"Let me show you." He brings her hands to a shelf. "This one is stereo. Heterodyne. I assembled it myself." She imagines a diminutive pianist, dressed in a tuxedo, playing inside the machine. Next he places her hands on a big cabinet radio, then on a third no bigger than a toaster. Eleven sets in all, he says, boyish pride slipping into his voice. "I can hear ships at sea. Madrid. Brazil. London. I heard Pakistan once. Here at the edge of the city, so high in the house, we get superb reception."

He lets her dig through a box of fuses, another of switches. He leads her to bookshelves next: the spines of hundreds of books; a birdcage; beetles in matchboxes; an electric mousetrap; a glass paperweight inside which, he says, a scorpion has been entombed; jars of miscellaneous fuses; a hundred more things she cannot identify.

He has the entire fifth floor — one big

room, except for the landing — to himself. Three windows open onto the rue Vauborel in the front, three more onto the alley in the back. There is a small and ancient bed, his coverlet smooth and tight. A tidy desk, a davenport.

"That's the tour," he says, almost whispering. Her great-uncle seems kind, curious, and entirely sane. Stillness: this is what he radiates more than anything else. The stillness of a tree. Of a mouse blinking in the dark.

Madame Manec brings sandwiches. Etienne doesn't have any Jules Verne, but he does have Darwin, he says, and reads to her from *The Voyage of the "Beagle,"* translating English to French as he goes — *the variety of species among the jumping spiders appears almost infinite . . .* Music spirals out of the radios, and it is splendid to drowse on the davenport, to be warm and fed, to feel the sentences hoist her up and carry her somewhere else.

Six blocks away at the telegraph office, Marie-Laure's father presses his face to the window to watch two German motorcycles with sidecars roar through the Porte Saint-Vincent. The shutters of the town are drawn, but between slats, over sills, a thousand eyes peer out. Behind the motorcycles roll two trucks. In the rear glides a single black Mercedes. Sunlight flashes from the hood ornaments and chrome fittings as the little procession grinds to a stop on the ringed gravel drive in front of the soaring lichen-streaked walls of the Château de Saint-Malo. An elderly, preternaturally tanned man — the mayor, somebody explains — waits with a white handkerchief in his big sailor's hands, a barely perceptible shake showing in his wrists.

The Germans climb out of their vehicles, more than a dozen of them. Their boots gleam and their uniforms are tidy. Two carry carnations; one urges along a beagle on a rope. Several gaze openmouthed up at the facade of the château.

A short man in a field captain's uniform emerges from the backseat of the Mercedes and brushes something invisible from the sleeve of his coat. He exchanges a few words with a thin aide-de-camp, who translates to the mayor. The mayor nods. Then the short man disappears through the huge doors. Minutes later, the aide-de-camp flings open the shutters of an upstairs window and gazes a moment across the rooftops before unfurling a crimson flag over the brick and securing its eyelets to the sill.

Jungmänner

It's a castle out of a storybook: eight or nine stone buildings sheltered below hills, rust-colored roofs, narrow windows, spires and turrets, weeds sprouting from between roof tiles. A pretty little river winds through athletics fields. Not in the clearest hour of Zollverein's clearest day has Werner breathed air so unadulterated by dust.

A one-armed bunk master sets forth rules in a belligerent torrent. "This is your parade uniform, this is your field uniform, this is your gym uniform. Suspenders crossed in the back, parallel in the front. Sleeves rolled to the elbow. Each boy is to carry a knife in a scabbard on the right side of the belt. Raise your right arm when you wish to be called upon. Always align in rows of ten. No books, no cigarettes, no food, no personal possessions, nothing in your locker but uniforms, boots, knife, polish. No talking after lights-out. Letters home will be posted on Wednesdays. You will strip away your weakness, your cowardice, your hesitation. You will become like a waterfall, a volley of bullets — you will all surge in the same direction at the same pace toward the same cause. You will forgo comforts; you will live by duty alone. You will eat country and breathe nation."

Do they understand?

The boys shout that they do. There are four hundred of them, plus thirty instructors and fifty more on the staff, NCOs and cooks, groomsmen and groundskeepers. Some cadets are as young as nine. The oldest are seventeen. Gothic faces, sharp noses, pointed chins. Blue eyes, all of them.

Werner sleeps in a tiny dormitory with seven other fourteen-year-olds. The bunk above belongs to Frederick: a reedy boy, thin as a blade of grass, skin as pale as cream. Frederick is new too. He's from Berlin. His father is assistant to an ambassador. When Frederick speaks, his attention floats up, as though he's scanning the sky for something.

He and Werner eat their first meal in their starchy new uniforms at a long wooden table in the refectory. Some boys talk in whispers, some sit alone, some gulp food as if they have not eaten in days. Through three arched windows, dawn sends a sheaf of hallowed golden rays.

Frederick flutters his fingers and asks, "Do you like birds?"

"Sure."

"Do you know about hooded crows?"
Werner shakes his head.

"Hooded crows are smarter than most mammals. Even monkeys. I've seen them put nuts they can't crack in the road and wait for cars to run over them to get at the kernel. Werner, you and I are going to be great friends, I'm sure of it."

A portrait of the führer glowers over every classroom. Learning happens on backless benches, at wooden tables grooved by the boredom of countless boys before them — squires, monks, conscripts, cadets. On Werner's first day, he walks past the half-open door of the technical sciences laboratory and glimpses a room as big as Zollverein's drugstore lined with brand-new sinks and glass-fronted cabinets inside which wait sparkling beakers and graduated cylinders and balances and burners. Frederick has to urge him along.

On their second day, a withered phrenologist gives a presentation to the entire student body. The lights in the refectory dim, a projector whirs, and a chart full of circles appears on the far wall. The old man stands beneath the projection screen and whisks the tip of a billiards cue through the grids. "White circles represent pure German blood. Circles with black indicate the proportion of foreign blood. Notice group two, number five." He raps the screen with his cue and it ripples. "Marriage between a pure German and one-quarter Jew is still permissible, you see?"

A half hour later, Werner and Frederick are reading Goethe in poetics. Then they're magnetizing needles in field exercises. The bunk master announces schedules of byzantine complication: Mondays are for mechanics, state history, racial sciences. Tuesdays are for horsemanship, orienteering, military history. Everyone, even the nine-year-olds, will be taught to clean, break down, and fire a Mauser rifle.

Afternoons, they lash themselves into a snarl of cartridge belts and run. Run to the troughs; run to the flag; run up the hill. Run carrying each other on your backs, run carrying your rifle above your head. Run, crawl, swim. Then more running.

The star-flooded nights, the dew-soaked dawns, the hushed ambulatories, the enforced asceticism — never has Werner felt part of something so single-minded. Never has he felt such a hunger to belong. In the rows of dormitories are cadets who talk of alpine skiing, of duels, of jazz clubs and governesses and boar hunting; boys who employ curse words with virtuosic skill and boys who talk about cigarettes named for cinema stars; boys who speak of "telephoning the colonel" and boys who have baronesses for mothers. There are boys who have been admitted not because they are good at anything in particular but because their fathers work for ministries. And the way they talk: "One mustn't expect figs from thistles!" "I'd pollinate her in a blink, you shit!" "Bear up and funk it, boys!" There are cadets who do everything right — perfect posture, expert marksmanship, boots polished so perfectly that they reflect clouds. There are cadets who have skin like butter and irises like sapphires and ultra-fine networks of blue veins laced across the backs of their hands. For now, though, beneath the whip of the administration, they are all the same, all *Jungmänner.* They hustle through the gates together, gulp fried eggs in the refectory together, march across the quadrangle, perform roll call, salute the colors, shoot rifles, run, bathe, and suffer together. They are each a mound of clay, and the potter that is the portly, shiny-faced commandant is throwing four hundred identical pots.

We are young, they sing, *we are steadfast, we have never compromised, we have so many castles yet to storm.*

Werner sways between exhaustion, confusion, and exhilaration. That his life has been so wholly redirected astounds him. He keeps any doubts at bay by memorizing lyrics or the routes to classrooms, by holding before his eyes a vision of the technical sciences laboratory: nine tables, thirty stools; coils, variable capacitors, amplifiers, batteries, soldering irons locked away in those gleaming cabinets.

Above him, kneeling on his bunk, Frederick peers out the open window through a pair of antique field glasses and makes a record on the bed rail of birds he has sighted. One notch under *red-necked grebe.* Six notches under *thrush nightingale.* Out on the grounds, a group of ten-year-olds is carrying torches and swastika flags toward the river. The procession pauses, and a gust of wind tears at the torch flames. Then they march on, their song swirling up through the window like a bright, pulsing cloud.

O take me, take me up into the ranks
so that I do not die a common death!
I do not want to die in vain, what
I want is to fall on the sacrificial mound.

VIENNA

Sergeant Major Reinhold von Rumpel is forty-one years old, not so old that he cannot be promoted. He has moist red lips; pale, almost translucent cheeks like fillets of raw sole; and an instinct for correctness that rarely fails him. He has a wife who suffers his absences without complaint, and who arranges porcelain kittens by color, lightest to darkest, on two different shelves in their drawing room in Stuttgart. He also has two daughters whom he has not seen in nine months. The eldest, Veronika, is deeply earnest. Her letters to him include phrases like *sacred resolve, proud accomplishments,* and *unparalleled in history.*

Von Rumpel's particular gift is for diamonds: he can facet and polish stones as well as any Aryan jeweler in Europe, and he often spots fakes at a glance. He studied crystallography in Munich, apprenticed as a polisher in Antwerp, has even been — one glorious afternoon — to Charterhouse Street in

London, to an unmarked diamond house, where he was asked to turn out his pockets and ushered up three staircases and through three locked doors and seated at a table where a man with a mustache waxed to knife-points let him examine a ninety-two-carat raw diamond from South Africa.

Before the war, the life of Reinhold von Rumpel was pleasant enough: he was a gemologist who ran an appraisal business out of a second-story shop behind Stuttgart's old chancellery. Clients would bring in stones and he'd tell them what they were worth. Sometimes he'd recut diamonds or consult on high-level faceting projects. If occasionally he cheated a customer, he told himself that was part of the game.

Because of the war, his job has expanded. Now Sergeant Major von Rumpel has the chance to do what no one has done in centuries — not since the Mogul Dynasty, not since the Khans. Perhaps not in history. The capitulation of France is only weeks past, and already he has seen things he did not dream he would see in six lifetimes. A seventeenth-century globe as big around as a small car, with rubies to mark volcanoes, sapphires clustered at the poles, and diamonds for world capitals. He has held — held! — a dagger handle at least four hundred years old, made of white jade and inlaid with emeralds. Just yesterday, on the road to Vienna, he took possession of a five-hundred-and-seventy-piece china set with a single marquise-cut diamond set into the rim of every single dish. Where the police confiscated these treasures and from whom, he does not ask. Already he has personally packed them into a crate and belted it shut and numbered it with white paint and seen it loaded inside a train car where it sits under twenty-four-hour guard.

Waiting to be sent to high command. Waiting for more.

This particular summer afternoon, in a dusty geological library in Vienna, Sergeant Major von Rumpel follows an underweight secretary wearing brown shoes, brown stockings, a brown skirt, and a brown blouse through stacks of periodicals. The secretary sets down a step stool, climbs, reaches.

Tavernier's 1676 *Travels in India.*

P. S. Pallas's 1793 *Travels Through the Southern Provinces of the Russian Empire.*

Streeter's 1898 *Precious Stones and Gems.*

Rumor is that the führer is compiling a wish list of precious objects from all around Europe and Russia. They say he intends to remake the Austrian town of Linz into an empyrean city, the cultural capital of the world. A vast promenade, mausoleum, acropolis, planetarium, library, opera house — everything marble and granite, everything profoundly clean. At its core, he plans a kilometer-long museum: a trove of the greatest achievements in human culture.

The document is real, von Rumpel has heard. Four hundred pages.

He sits at a table in the stacks. He tries to cross his legs but a slight swelling troubles his groin today: odd, though not painful. The mousy librarian brings books. He pages slowly through the Tavernier, the Streeter, Murray's *Sketches of Persia.* He reads entries on the three-hundred-carat Orloff diamond from Moscow, the Nur-al-Ain, the forty-eight-and-a-half-carat Dresden Green. Toward evening, he finds it. The story of a prince who could not be killed, a priest who warned of a goddess's wrath, a French prelate who believed he'd bought the same stone centuries later.

Sea of Flames. Grayish blue with a red hue at its center. Recorded at one hundred and thirty-three carats. Either lost or willed to the king of France in 1738 on the condition that it be locked away for two hundred years.

He looks up. Suspended lamps, rows of spines fading off into dusty gold. All of Europe, and he aims to find one pebble tucked inside its folds.

THE *BOCHES*

Her father says their weapons gleam as if they have never been fired. He says their boots are clean and their uniforms spotless. He says they look as if they have just stepped out of air-conditioned train cars.

The townswomen who stop by Madame Manec's kitchen door in ones and twos say the Germans (they refer to them as the *Boches*) buy every postcard on every pharmacy rack; they say the *Boches* buy straw dolls and candied apricots and stale cakes from the window of the confectionery. The *Boches* buy shirts from Monsieur Verdier and lingerie from Monsieur Morvan; the *Boches* require absurd quantities of butter and cheese; the *Boches* have guzzled down every bottle of champagne the *caviste* would sell them.

Hitler, the women whisper, is touring Parisian monuments.

Curfews are installed. Music that can be heard outdoors is banned. Public dances are banned. The country is in mourning and we must behave respectfully, announces the mayor. Though what authority he retains is not clear.

Every time she comes within earshot, Marie-Laure hears the *fsst* of her father lighting another match. His hands flutter between his pockets. Mornings he alternates between Madame Manec's kitchen, the tobacco shop, and the post office, where he waits in interminable queues to use the telephone. Afternoons he repairs things around Etienne's house — a loose cabinet door, a squeaking stair board. He asks Madame Manec about the reliability of the neighbors. He flips the locking clasp on his tool case over and over until Marie-Laure begs him to stop.

One day Etienne sits with Marie-Laure and reads to her in his feathery voice; the next he suffers from what he calls a headache and sequesters himself inside his study behind a locked door. Madame Manec sneaks Marie-Laure chocolate bars, slices of cake; this morning they squeeze lemons into glasses full of water and sugar, and she lets Marie-Laure drink as much as she likes.

"How long will he stay in there, Madame?"

"Sometimes just a day or two," Madame Manec says. "Sometimes longer."

One week in Saint-Malo becomes two. Marie begins to feel that her life, like *Twenty Thousand Leagues Under the Sea,* has been interrupted halfway through. There was volume 1, when Marie-Laure and her father lived in Paris and went to work, and now there is volume 2, when Germans ride motorcycles through these strange, narrow streets and her uncle vanishes inside his own house.

"Papa, when will we leave?"

"As soon as I hear from Paris."

"Why do we have to sleep in this little bedroom?"

"I'm sure we could clean out a downstairs room if you'd like."

"What about the room across the hall from us?"

"Etienne and I agreed we would not use it."

"Why not?"

"It belonged to your grandfather."

"When can I go to the sea?"

"Not today, Marie."

"Can't we go for a walk around the block?"

"It's too dangerous."

She wants to shriek. What dangers await? When she opens her bedroom window, she hears no screams, no explosions, only the calls of birds that her great-uncle calls gannets, and the sea, and the occasional throb of an airplane as it passes far overhead.

She spends her hours learning the house. The first floor belongs to Madame Manec: clean, navigable, full of visitors who come through the kitchen door to trade in small-town scandal. There's the dining room, the foyer, a hutch full of antique dishes in the hall that tremble whenever anyone walks past, and a door off the kitchen that leads to Madame's room: a bed, a sink, a chamber pot.

Eleven winding steps lead to the second floor, which is full of the smells of faded grandeur: an old sewing room, a former maid's room. Right here on the landing, Madame Manec tells her, pallbearers dropped the coffin carrying Etienne's great-aunt. "The coffin flipped over, and she slid down the whole flight. They were all horrified, but she looked entirely unaffected!"

More clutter on the third floor: boxes of jars, metal disks, and rusty jigsaws; buckets of what might be electrical components; engineering manuals in piles around a toilet. By the fourth floor, things are piled everywhere, in the rooms and corridors and along the staircase: baskets of what must be machine parts, shoe boxes loaded with screws, antique dollhouses built by her great-grandfather. Etienne's huge study colonizes the entire fifth floor, alternately deeply quiet or else full of voices or music or static.

Then there's the sixth floor: her grandfather's tidy bedroom on the left, toilet straight ahead, the little room where she sleeps with her father on the right. When the wind is blowing, which it almost always is, with the walls groaning and the shutters banging, the rooms overloaded and the staircase wound tightly up through its center, the house seems the material equivalent of her uncle's inner being: apprehensive, isolated, but full of cobwebby wonders.

In the kitchen, Madame Manec's friends fuss over Marie-Laure's hair and freckles. In Paris, the women say, people are waiting in line five hours for a loaf of bread. People are eating pets, crushing pigeons with bricks for soup. There is no pork, no rabbit, no cauliflower. The headlights of cars are all painted blue, they say, and at night the city is as quiet as a graveyard: no buses, no trains, hardly any gasoline. Marie-Laure sits at the square table, a plate of cookies in front of her, and imagines the old women with veiny hands and milky eyes and oversize ears. From the kitchen window comes the *wit wit wit* of a barn swallow, footfalls on ramparts, halyards clinking against masts, hinges and chains creaking in the harbor. Ghosts. Germans. Snails.

HAUPTMANN

A rosy-cheeked and diminutive instructor of technical sciences named Dr. Hauptmann peels off his brass-buttoned coat and hangs it over the back of a chair. He orders the cadets in Werner's class to collect hinged metal boxes from a locked cabinet at the back of the laboratory.

Inside each are gears, lenses, fuses, springs, shackles, and resistors. There's a fat coil of copper wire, a tiny instrument hammer, and a two-terminal battery as big as a shoe — finer equipment than Werner has had access to in his life. The little professor stands at the chalkboard drawing a wiring schematic for a simple Morse-code practice circuit. He sets down his chalk, presses his slender fingertips together, five to five, and asks the boys to assemble the circuit with the parts in their kits. "You have one hour."

Most of the boys blanch. They dump everything out on the tables and poke gingerly at the parts as if at trinkets imported from some future age. Frederick plucks random pieces out of his box and holds them to the light.

For a moment Werner is back inside his attic room at Children's House, his head a swarm of questions. *What is lightning? How high could you jump if you lived on Mars? What is the difference between twice twenty-five and twice five and twenty?* Then he takes the battery, two rectangles of sheet metal, some penny nails, and the instrument hammer from his box. In under a minute, he has built an oscillator to match the schematic.

The little professor frowns. He tests Werner's circuit, which works.

"Right," he says, and stands in front of Werner's table and laces his hands behind his back. "Next take from your kit the disk-shaped magnet, a wire, a screw, and your battery." Though his instructions seem meant for the class, he looks at Werner alone. "That is all you may use. Who can build a simple motor?"

Some boys stir the parts in their kits half-heartedly. Most simply watch.

Werner feels Dr. Hauptmann's attention on him like a floodlight. He sticks the magnet to the screw's head and holds the screw's point to the positive terminal on the battery. When he runs the wire from the negative side of the battery to the head of the screw, both the screw and the magnet start to spin. The operation takes him no more than fifteen seconds.

Dr. Hauptmann's mouth is partially open. His face is flushed, adrenalized. "What is your name, cadet?"

"Pfennig, sir."

"What else can you make?"

Werner studies the parts on his table. "A doorbell, sir? Or a Morse beacon? An ohmmeter?"

The other boys crane their necks. Dr. Hauptmann's lips are pink and his eyelids are improbably thin. As though he is watching Werner even when he blinks. He says, "Make them all."

Flying Couch

Posters go up in the market, on tree trunks in the Place Chateaubriand. Voluntary surrender of firearms. Anyone who does not cooperate will be shot. At noon the following day, various Bretons troop in to drop off weapons, farmers on mule carts from miles away, plodding old sailors with antique pistols, a few hunters with outrage in their eyes gazing at the floor as they turn in their rifles.

In the end it's a pathetic pile, maybe three hundred weapons in all, half of them rusted. Two young gendarmes pile them into the back of a truck and drive up the narrow street and across the causeway and are gone. No speeches, no explanations.

"Please, Papa, can't I go out?"

"Soon, little dove." But he is distracted; he smokes so much it is as if he is turning himself into ash. Lately he stays up working frenetically on a model of Saint-Malo that he claims is for her, adding new houses every day, framing ramparts, mapping streets, so that she can learn the town the way she learned their neighborhood in Paris. Wood, glue, nails, sandpaper: rather than comforting her, the noises and smells of his manic diligence make her more anxious. Why will she have to learn the streets of Saint-Malo? How long will they be here?

In the fifth-floor study, Marie-Laure listens to her great-uncle read another page of *The Voyage of the "Beagle."* Darwin has hunted rheas in Patagonia, studied owls outside Buenos Aires, and scaled a waterfall in Tahiti. He pays attention to slaves, rocks, lightning, finches, and the ceremony of pressing noses in New Zealand. She loves especially to hear about the dark coasts of South America with their impenetrable walls of trees and offshore breezes full of the stink of rotting kelp and the cries of whelping seals. She loves to imagine Darwin at night, leaning over the ship's rail to stare into bioluminescent waves, watching the tracks of penguins marked by fiery green wakes.

"Bonsoir," she says to Etienne, standing on the davenport in his study. "I may be only a girl of twelve, but I am a brave French explorer who has come to help you with your adventures."

Etienne adopts a British accent. "Good evening, mademoiselle, why don't you come to the jungle with me and eat these butterflies, they are as big as dinner plates and may not be poisonous, who knows?"

"I would love to eat your butterflies, Monsieur Darwin, but first I will eat these cookies."

Other evenings they play Flying Couch. They climb onto the davenport and sit side by side, and Etienne says, "Where to tonight, mademoiselle?"

"The jungle!" Or: "Tahiti!" Or: "Mozambique!"

"Oh, it's a long journey this time," Etienne will say in an entirely new voice, smooth, velvety, a conductor's drawl. "That's the Atlantic Ocean far below, it's shining under the moonlight, can you smell it? Feel how cold it is up here? Feel the wind in your hair?"

"Where are we now, Uncle?"

"We're in Borneo, can't you tell? We're skimming the treetops now, big leaves are glimmering below us, and there are coffee bushes over there, smell them?" and Marie-Laure will indeed smell something, whether because her uncle is passing coffee grounds beneath her nose, or because they really are flying over the coffee trees of Borneo, she does not want to decide.

They visit Scotland, New York City, Santiago. More than once they put on winter coats and visit the moon. "Can't you feel how lightweight we are, Marie? You can move by hardly twitching a muscle!" He sets her in his wheeled desk chair and pants as he whirls her in circles until she cannot laugh anymore for the pain of it.

"Here, try some nice fresh moon flesh," he says, and into her mouth goes something that tastes a lot like cheese. Always at the end they sit side by side again and pound the cushions, and slowly the room rematerializes around them. "Ah," he says, more quietly, his accent fading, the faintest touch of dread returning to his voice, "here we are. Home."

The Sum of Angles

Werner is summoned to the office of the technical sciences professor. A trio of sleek long-legged hounds swirl around him as he enters. The room is lit by a pair of green-shaded banker's lamps, and in the shadows Werner can see shelves crowded with encyclopedias, models of windmills, miniature telescopes, prisms. Dr. Hauptmann stands behind his big desk wearing his brass-buttoned coat, as though he too has just arrived. Tight curls frame his ivory forehead; he tugs off his leather gloves one finger at a time. "Drop a log on the fire, please."

Werner tacks across the room and stirs the coals to life. In the corner, he realizes, sits a third person, a massive figure camped sleepily in an armchair intended for a much smaller man. He is Frank Volkheimer, an upperclassman, seventeen years old, a colossal boy from some boreal village, a legend among the younger cadets. Supposedly Volkheimer has carried three first-years across the river by holding them above his head; supposedly he has lifted the tail end of the commandant's automobile high enough to slip a jack under the axle. There is a rumor that he crushed a communist's windpipe with his hands. Another that he grabbed the muzzle of a stray dog and cut out its eyes just to inure himself to the suffering of other beings.

They call him the Giant. Even in the low, flickering light, Werner sees that veins climb Volkheimer's forearms like vines.

"A student has never built the motor," says Hauptmann, his back partially to Volkheimer. "Not without help."

Werner does not know how to reply, so he does not. He pokes the fire one last time, and sparks rise up the chimney.

"Can you do trigonometry, cadet?"

"Only what I have been able to teach myself, sir."

Hauptmann takes a sheet of paper from a drawer and writes on it. "Do you know what this is?"

Werner squints.

$$\ell = \frac{d}{\tan \alpha} + \frac{d}{\tan \beta}$$

"A formula, sir."

"Do you comprehend its uses?"

"I believe it is a way to use two known points to find the location of a third and unknown point."

Hauptmann's blue eyes glitter; he looks like someone who has discovered something very valuable lying right in front of him on the ground. "If I give you the known points and a distance between them, cadet, can you solve it? Can you draw the triangle?"

"I believe so."

"Sit at my desk, Pfennig. Take my chair. Here is a pencil."

When he sits in the desk chair, the toes of Werner's boots do not reach the ground. The fire pumps heat into the room. Block out giant Frank Volkheimer with his mammoth boots and cinder-block jaw. Block out the little aristocratic professor pacing in front of the hearth and the late hour and the dogs and the shelves brimming with interesting things. There is only this.

$$\tan\alpha = \sin\alpha / \cos\alpha$$

$$\text{and } \sin(\alpha+\beta) = \sin\alpha\cos\beta + \cos\alpha\sin\beta$$

Now *d* can be moved to the front of the equation.

$$d = \frac{\ell\sin\alpha\ \sin\beta}{\sin(\alpha+\beta)}$$

Werner plugs Hauptmann's numbers into the equation. He imagines two observers in a field pacing out the distance between them, then leveling their eyes on a far-off landmark: a sailing ship or a smokestack. When Werner asks for a slide rule, the professor slips one onto the desk immediately, having expected the request. Werner takes it without looking and begins to calculate the sines.

Volkheimer watches. The little doctor paces, hands behind his back. The fire pops. The only sounds are the breathing of the dogs and clicking of the slide rule's cursor.

Eventually Werner says, "Sixteen point four three, Herr Doktor." He draws the triangle and labels the distances of each segment and passes the paper back. Hauptmann checks something in a leather book. Volkheimer shifts slightly in his chair; his gaze is both interested and indolent. The professor presses one of his palms flat to the desk while reading, frowning absently, as though waiting for a thought to pass. Werner is seized with a sudden and foreboding dread, but then Hauptmann looks back at him, and the feeling subsides.

"It says in your application papers that when you leave here, you wish to study electrical mechanics in Berlin. And you are an orphan, is that correct?"

Another glance at Volkheimer. Werner nods. "My sister —"

"A scientist's work, cadet, is determined by two things. His interests and the interests of his time. Do you understand?"

"I think so."

"We live in exceptional times, cadet."

A thrill enters Werner's chest. Firelit rooms lined with books — these are the places in which important things happen.

"You will work in the laboratory after dinner. Every night. Even Sundays."

"Yes, sir."

"Start tomorrow."

"Yes, sir."

"Volkheimer here will keep an eye out for you. Take these biscuits." The professor produces a tin with a bow on it. "And breathe, Pfennig. You cannot hold your breath every time you're in my laboratory."

"Yes, sir."

Cold air whistles through the halls, so pure it makes Werner dizzy. A trio of moths swim against the ceiling of his bunkroom. He unlaces his boots and folds his trousers in the dark and sets the tin of biscuits on top. Frederick peers over the edge of his bunk. "Where did you go?"

"I got cookies," whispers Werner.

"I heard an eagle owl tonight."

"Hush," hisses a boy two bunks down.

Werner passes up a biscuit. Frederick whispers: "Do you know about them? They're really rare. Big as gliders. This one was probably a young male looking for new territory. He was in one of the poplar trees beside the parade ground."

"Oh," says Werner. Greek letters move across the undersides of his eyelids: isosceles triangles, betas, sine curves. He sees himself in a white coat, striding past machines.

Someday he'll probably win a big prize.

Code breaking, rocket propulsion, all the latest.

We live in exceptional times.

From the hall come the clicking boot heels of the bunk master. Frederick tips back onto his bunk. "I couldn't see him," he whispers, "but I heard him perfectly."

"Shut your face!" says a second boy. "You'll get us thrashed."

Frederick says nothing more. Werner stops chewing. The bunk master's boots go quiet: either he is gone or he has paused outside the door. Out on the grounds, someone is splitting wood, and Werner listens to the ringing of the sledgehammer against the wedge and the quick, frightened breaths of the boys all around him.

THE PROFESSOR

Etienne is reading Darwin to Marie-Laure when he stops midsyllable.

"Uncle?"

He breathes nervously, out of pursed lips, as if blowing on a spoonful of hot soup. He whispers, "Someone's here."

Marie-Laure can hear nothing. No footfalls, no knocks. Madame Manec whisks a broom across the landing one floor up. Etienne hands her the book. She can hear him unplug a radio, then tangle himself in its cords. "Uncle?" she says again, but he is leaving his study, floundering downstairs — are they in danger? — and she follows him to the kitchen, where she can hear him laboring to slide the kitchen table out of the way.

He pulls up a ring in the center of the floor. Beneath a hatch waits a square hole out of which washes a damp, frightening smell. "One step down, hurry now."

Is this a cellar? What has her uncle seen? She has set one foot on the top rung of a ladder when the blocky shoes of Madame Manec come clomping into the kitchen. "Really, Master Etienne, please!"

Etienne's voice from below: "I heard something. Someone."

"You are frightening her. It is nothing, Marie-Laure. Come now."

Marie-Laure backs out. Below her, her great-uncle whispers nursery rhymes to himself.

"I can sit with him for a bit, Madame. Maybe we could read some more of our book, Uncle?"

The cellar, she gathers, is merely a dank hole in the ground. They sit awhile on a rolled carpet with the trapdoor open and listen to Madame Manec hum as she makes tea in the kitchen above them. Etienne trembles lightly beside her.

"Did you know," says Marie-Laure, "that the chance of being hit by lightning is one in one million? Dr. Geffard taught me that."

"In one year or in one lifetime?"

"I'm not sure."

"You should have asked."

Again those quick, pursed exhalations. As though his whole body urges him to flee.

"What happens if you go outside, Uncle?"

"I get uneasy." His voice is almost inaudible.

"But what makes you uneasy?"

"Being outside."

"What part?"

"Big spaces."

"Not all spaces are big. Your street is not that big, is it?"

"Not as big as the streets you are used to."

"You like eggs and figs. And tomatoes. They were in our lunch. They grow outside."

He laughs softly. "Of course they do."

"Don't you miss the world?"

He is quiet; so is she. Both ride spirals of memory.

"I have the whole world here," he says, and taps the cover of Darwin. "And in my radios. Right at my fingertips."

Her uncle seems almost a child, monastic in the modesty of his needs and wholly independent of any sort of temporal obligations. And yet she can tell he is visited by fears so immense, so multiple, that she can almost feel the terror pulsing inside him. As though some beast breathes all the time at the windowpanes of his mind.

"Could you read some more, please?" she asks, and Etienne opens the book and whispers, *"Delight itself is a weak term to express the feelings of a naturalist who, for the first time, has wandered by himself into a Brazilian forest . . ."*

After a few paragraphs, Marie-Laure says without preamble, "Tell me about that bedroom upstairs. Across from the one I sleep in."

He stops. Again his quick, nervous breaths.

"There's a little door at the back of it," she says, "but it's locked. What's through there?"

He is silent for long enough that she worries she has upset him. But then he stands, and his knees crack like twigs.

"Are you getting one of your headaches, Uncle?"

"Come with me."

They wind all the way up the stairs. On the sixth-floor landing, they turn left, and he pushes open the door to what was once her grandfather's room. She has already run her hands over its contents many times: a wooden oar nailed to a wall, a window dressed with long curtains. Single bed. Model ship on a shelf. At the back stands a wardrobe so large, she cannot reach its top nor stretch her arms wide enough to touch both sides at once.

"These are his things?"

Etienne unlatches the little door beside the wardrobe. "Go on."

She gropes through. Dry, confined heat. Mice scuttle. Her fingers find a ladder.

"It leads to the garret. It's not high."

Seven rungs. At the top, she stands; she has the sense of a long slope-walled space pressed beneath the gable of the roof. The peak of the ceiling is just taller than she is.

Etienne climbs up behind her and takes her

hand. Her feet find cables on the floor. They snake between dusty boxes, overwhelm a sawhorse; he leads her through a thicket of them to what feels like an upholstered piano bench at the far end, and helps her sit.

"This is the attic. That's the chimney in front of us. Put your hands on the table; there you are." Metal boxes cover the tabletop: tubes, coils, switches, meters, at least one gramophone. This whole part of the attic, she realizes, is some sort of machine. The sun bakes the slates above their heads. Etienne secures a headset over Marie-Laure's ears. Through the headphones, she can hear him turn a crank, switch on something, and then, as if positioned directly in the center of her head, a piano plays a sweet, simple song.

The song fades, and a staticky voice says, *Consider a single piece glowing in your family's stove. See it, children? That chunk of coal was once a green plant, a fern or reed that lived one million years ago, or maybe two million, or maybe one hundred million . . .*

After a little while, the voice gives way to the piano again. Her uncle pulls off the headset. "As a boy," he says, "my brother was good at everything, but his voice was what people commented on most. The nuns at St. Vincent's wanted to build choirs around it. We had a dream together, Henri and I, to make recordings and sell them. He had the voice and I had the brains and back then everyone wanted gramophones. And hardly anyone was making programs for children. So we contacted a recording company in Paris, and they expressed interest, and I wrote ten different scripts about science, and Henri rehearsed them, and finally we started recording. Your father was just a boy, but he would come around to listen. It was one of the happiest times of my life."

"Then there was the war."

"We became signalmen. Our job, mine and your grandfather's, was to knit telegraph wires from command positions at the rear to field officers at the front. Most nights the enemy would shoot pistol flares called 'very lights' over the trenches, short-lived stars suspended in the air from parachutes, meant to illuminate possible targets for snipers. Every soldier within reach of the glare would freeze while it lasted. Some hours, eighty or ninety of these flares would go off, one after another, and the night would turn stark and strange in that magnesium glow. It would be so quiet, the only sound the fizzling of the flares, and then you'd hear the whistle of a sniper's bullet streak out of the darkness and bury itself in the mud. We would stay as close together as we could. But I'd become paralyzed sometimes; I could not move any part of my body, not even my fingers. Not even my eyelids. Henri would stay right beside me and whisper those scripts, the ones we recorded. Sometimes all night. Over and over. As though weaving some kind of protective screen around us. Until morning came."

"But he died."

"And I did not."

This, she realizes, is the basis of his fear, all fear. That a light you are powerless to stop will turn on you and usher a bullet to its mark.

"Who built all of this, Uncle? This machine?"

"I did. After the war. Took me years."

"How does it work?"

"It's a radio transmitter. This switch here" — he guides her hand to it — "powers up the microphone, and this one runs the phonograph. Here's the premodulation amplifier, and these are the vacuum tubes, and these are the coils. The antenna telescopes up along the chimney. Twelve meters. Can you feel the lever? Think of energy as a wave and the transmitter as sending out smooth cycles of those waves. Your voice creates a disruption in those cycles . . ."

She stops listening. It's dusty and confusing and mesmerizing all at once. How old must all this be? Ten years? Twenty? "What did you transmit?"

"The recordings of my brother. The gramophone company in Paris wasn't interested anymore, but every night I played the ten recordings we'd made, until most of them were worn out. And his song."

"The piano?"

"Debussy's 'Clair de Lune.' " He touches a metal cylinder with a sphere stuck on top. "I'd just tuck the microphone into the bell of the gramophone, and *voilà.*"

She leans over the microphone, says, "Hello out there." He laughs his feathery laugh. "Did it ever reach any children?" she asks.

"I don't know."

"How far can it transmit, Uncle?"

"Far."

"To England?"

"Easily."

"To Paris?"

"Yes. But I wasn't trying to reach England. Or Paris. I thought that if I made the broadcast powerful enough, my brother would hear me. That I could bring him some peace, protect him as he had always protected me."

"You'd play your brother's own voice to him? After he died?"

"And Debussy."

"Did he ever talk back?"

The attic ticks. What ghosts sidle along the walls right now, trying to overhear? She can almost taste her great-uncle's fright in the air.

"No," he says. "He never did."

To My Dear Sister Jutta —

Some of the boys whisper that Dr. Hauptmann is connected to very powerful ministers. He won't answer But he wants me to assist him all the time! I go to his workshop in the evenings and he sets me to work on circuits for a radio he is testing. Trigonometry too. He says to be as creative as I can; he says creativity fuels the Reich. He has this big upperclassman, they call him the Giant, stand over me with a stopwatch to test how fast I can calculate. Triangles triangles triangles. I probably do fifty calculations a night. They don't tell me why. You would not believe the copper wire here; they have Everyone gets out of the way when the Giant comes through.

Dr. Hauptmann says we can do anything,

build anything. He says the führer has collected scientists to help him control the weather. He says the führer will develop a rocket that can reach Japan. He says the führer will build a city on the moon.

To My Dear Sister Jutta —

Today in field exercises the commandant told us about Reiner Schicker. He was a young corporal and his captain needed someone to go behind enemy lines to map their defenses. The captain asked for volunteers and Reiner Schicker was the only one who stood up. But the next day Reiner Schicker got caught. The very next day! The Poles captured him and tortured him with electricity. They gave him so much electricity that his brain liquefied, said the commandant, but before they did, Reiner Schicker said something amazing. He said, "I only regret that I have but one life to lose for my country."

Everyone says there is a great test coming. A test harder than all the other tests.

Frederick says that story about Reiner Schicker is

Just being around the Giant — his name is Frank Volkheimer — means the other boys treat me with respect. I come up only to his waist practically. He seems a man, not a boy. He possesses the loyalty of Reiner Schicker. In his hands and heart and bones. Please tell Frau Elena I am eating lots here but that no one makes flour cakes like hers or at all really. Tell little Siegfried to look lively. I think of you every day. *Sieg heil.*

To My Dear Sister Jutta —

Yesterday was Sunday and for field exercises we went into the forest. Most hunters are at the front so the woods are full of marten and deer. The other boys sat in the blinds and talked about magnificent victories and how soon we will cross the Channel and destroy the ████████ ████████████████ and Dr. Hauptmann's dogs came back with three rabbits one for each but Frederick, he came back with about a thousand berries in his shirt and his sleeves were ripped from the brambles and his binocular bag was torn open and I said, You're going to catch hell and he looked down at his clothes like he'd never seen them before! Frederick knows all the birds just by hearing them. Above the lake we heard skylarks and lapwings and plovers and a harrier hen and probably ten others I've forgotten. You would like Frederick I think. He sees what other people don't. Hope your cough is better and Frau Elena's too. *Sieg heil.*

Perfumer

His name is Claude Levitte but everyone calls him Big Claude. For a decade he has run a parfumerie on the rue Vauborel: a straggling business that prospers only when the cod are being salted and the stones of the town itself begin to stink.

But new opportunities have arrived, and Big Claude is not one to miss an opportunity. He is paying farmers near Cancale to butcher lambs and rabbits; Claude buckles the meat into his wife's matching vinyl suitcases and carries them himself by train to Paris. It is easy: some weeks he can make as much as five hundred francs. Supply and demand. There is always paperwork, of course; some official up the chain catches a whiff and wants a percentage. It takes a mind like Claude's to navigate the complexities of the business.

Today he is overheating; sweat trickles down his back and sides. Saint-Malo roasts. October is here, and bright cold winds ought to pour off the ocean; leaves ought to tumble down the alleys. But the wind has come and gone. As if deciding it did not like the changes here.

All afternoon Claude hunkers inside his shop above the hundreds of little bottles of florals and orientals and *fougères* in his vitrine, pinks and carmines and baby blues, and no one enters, and an oscillating electric fan blows across his face to the left, then to the right, and he does not read or move at all except to periodically reach a hand beneath his stool and grab a handful of biscuits from a round tin and stuff them into his mouth.

Around four P.M., a small company of German soldiers strolls up the rue Vauborel. They are lean, salmon-faced, and earnest; they have serious eyes; they carry their weapons barrel-down, slinging them over their shoulders like clarinets. They laugh to one another and seem touched underneath their helmets with a beneficent gold.

Claude understands that he ought to resent them, but he admires their competence and manners, the clean efficiency with which they move. They always seem to be going somewhere and never doubt that it is the right place to be going. Something his own country has lacked.

The soldiers turn down the rue St. Philippe and are gone. Claude's fingers trace ovals across the top of his vitrine. Upstairs his wife runs a vacuum cleaner; he can hear it coursing round and round. He is nearly asleep when he sees the Parisian who has been living three doors down exit the house of Etienne LeBlanc. A thin beak-nosed man who skulks outside the telegraph office, whittling little wooden boxes.

The Parisian walks in the same direction as the German soldiers, placing the heel of one foot against the toe of the other. He reaches the end of the street, scribbles something on a pad, turns one hundred and eighty degrees, and walks back. When he reaches the end of the block, he stares up at the Sajers' house and makes several more notes. Glancing up, glancing down. Measuring. Biting the eraser of his pencil as though uneasy.

Big Claude goes to the window. This too could be an opportunity. Occupation authorities will want to know that a stranger is pacing off distances and making drawings of houses. They will want to know what he looks like, who is sponsoring this activity. Who has sanctioned it.

This is good. This is excellent.

Time of the Ostriches

Still they do not return to Paris. Still she does not go outside. Marie-Laure counts every day she has been shut up in Etienne's house. One hundred and twenty. One hundred and twenty-one. She thinks of the transmitter in the attic, how it sent her grandfather's voice flying over the sea — *Consider a single piece glowing in your family's stove* — sailing like Darwin from Plymouth Sound to Cape Verde to Patagonia to the Falkland Islands, over waves, across borders.

"Once you're done with the model," she asks her father, "does that mean I can go out?"

His sandpaper does not stop.

The stories Madame Manec's visitors bring into the kitchen are terrifying and difficult to believe. Parisian cousins nobody has heard from in decades now write letters begging for capons, hams, hens. The dentist is selling wine through the mail. The perfumer is slaughtering lambs and carrying them in suitcases on the train to Paris, where he sells the meat for an enormous profit.

In Saint-Malo, people are fined for locking their doors, for keeping doves, for hoarding meat. Truffles disappear. Sparkling wine disappears. No eye contact. No chatter in doorways. No sunbathing, no singing, no lovers strolling the ramparts in the evenings — such rules are not written down, but they may as well be. Icy winds whirl in from the Atlantic and Etienne barricades himself inside his brother's old room and Marie-Laure endures the slow rain of hours by running her fingers over his seashells down in his study, ordering them by size, by species, by morphology, checking and rechecking their order, trying to make sure she has not mis-sorted a single one.

Surely she could go out for a half hour? On the arm of her father? And yet each time her father refuses, a voice echoes up from a chamber of her memory: *They'll probably take the blind girls before they take the gimps.*

Make them do things.

Outside the city walls, a few military boats cruise to and fro, and the flax is bundled and shipped and woven into rope or cables or parachute cord, and airborne gulls drop oysters or mussels or clams, and the sudden clatter on the roof makes Marie-Laure bolt upright in bed. The mayor announces a new tax, and some of Madame Manec's friends mutter that he has sold them out, that they need *un homme à poigne,* but others ask what the mayor is supposed to do. It becomes known as the time of the ostriches.

"Do we have our heads in the sand, Madame? Or do they?"

"Maybe everybody does," she murmurs.

Madame Manec has taken to falling asleep at the table beside Marie-Laure. It takes her a long time to carry meals the five flights to Etienne's room, wheezing the whole way. Most mornings, Madame is baking before anyone is awake; at midmorning she goes out into the city, cigarette in her mouth, to bring cakes or pots of stew to the sick or the stranded, and upstairs Marie-Laure's father works on the model, sanding, nailing, cutting, measuring, each day working more frenetically than the last, as if against some deadline known only to him.

Weakest

The warrant officer in charge of field exercises is the commandant, an overzealous schoolmaster named Bastian with an expansive walk and a round belly and a coat quivering with war medals. His face is scarred from smallpox, and his shoulders look as though they've been hewn from soft clay. He wears hobnailed jackboots every second of every day, and the cadets joke that he kicked his way out of the womb with them.

Bastian demands that they memorize maps, study the angle of the sun, cut their own belts from cowhide. Every afternoon, whatever the weather, he stands in a field bawling statesown dicta: "Prosperity depends on ferocity. The only things that keep your precious grandmothers in their tea and cookies are the fists at the end of your arms."

An antique pistol dangles from his belt; the most eager cadets look up at him with shining eyes. To Werner, he looks capable of severe and chronic violence.

"The corps is a body," he explains, twirling a length of rubber hose so that its tip whirs inches from a boy's nose. "No different from a man's body. Just as we ask you to each drive the weakness from your own bodies, so you must also learn to drive the weaknesses from the corps."

One October afternoon, Bastian plucks a pigeon-toed boy from the line. "You'll be first. Who are you?"

"Bäcker, sir."

"Bäcker. Tell us, Bäcker. Who is the weakest member of this group?"

Werner quails. He is smaller than every cadet in his year. He tries to expand his chest, stand as tall as he can. Bäcker's gaze rakes across the rows. "Him, sir?"

Werner exhales; Bäcker has chosen a boy far to Werner's right, one of the few boys with black hair. Ernst Somebody. A safe enough choice: Ernst is in fact a slow runner. A boy who has yet to grow into his horsey legs.

Bastian calls Ernst forward. The boy's bottom lip trembles as he turns to face the group.

"Getting all weepy won't help," says Bastian, and gestures vaguely to the far end of the field, where a line of trees cuts across the weeds. "You'll have a ten-second head start. Make it to me before they make it to you. Got it?"

Ernst neither nods nor shakes his head. Bastian feigns frustration. "When I raise my left hand, you run. When I raise my right hand, the rest of you fools run." Off Bastian waddles, rubber hose around his neck, pistol swinging at his side.

Sixty boys wait, breathing. Werner thinks of Jutta with her opalescent hair and quick eyes and blunt manners: she would never be mistaken for the weakest. Ernst Somebody is shaking everywhere now, all the way down to his wrists and ankles. When Bastian is maybe two hundred yards away, he turns and raises his left hand.

Ernst runs with his arms nearly straight and his legs wide and unhinged. Bastian counts down from ten. "Three," yells his faraway voice. "Two. One." At zero, his right arm goes up and the group unleashes. The dark-haired boy is at least fifty yards in front of them, but immediately the pack begins to gain.

Hurrying, scampering, running hard, fifty-nine fourteen-year-olds chase one. Werner keeps to the center of the group as it strings out, his heart beating in dark confusion, wondering where Frederick is, why they're chasing this boy, and what they're supposed to do if they catch him.

Except in some atavistic part of his brain, he knows exactly what they'll do.

A few outrunners are exceptionally fast; they gain on the lone figure. Ernst's limbs pump furiously, but he clearly is not accustomed to sprinting, and he loses steam.

The grass waves, the trees are transected by sunlight, the pack draws closer, and Werner feels annoyed: Why couldn't Ernst be faster? Why hasn't he practiced? How did he make it through the entrance exams?

The fastest cadet is lunging for the back of the boy's shirt. He almost has him. Black-haired Ernst is going to be caught, and Werner wonders if some part of him wants it to happen. But the boy makes it to the commandant a split second before the others come pounding past.

Mandatory Surrender

Marie-Laure has to badger her father three times before he'll read the notice aloud: *Members of the population must relinquish all radio receivers now in their possession. Radio sets are to be delivered to 27 rue de Chartres before tomorrow noon. Anyone failing to carry out this order will be arrested as a saboteur.*

No one says anything for a moment, and inside Marie-Laure, an old anxiety lumbers to its feet. "Is he — ?"

"In your grandfather's old room," says Madame Manec.

Tomorrow noon. Half the house, thinks Marie-Laure, is taken up by wireless receivers and the parts that go into them.

Madame Manec raps on the door to Henri's room and receives no reply. In the afternoon they box up the equipment in Etienne's study, Madame and Papa unplugging radios and lowering them into crates, Marie-Laure sitting on the davenport listening to the sets go off one by one: the old Radiola Five; a

G.M.R. Titan; a G.M.R. Orphée. A Delco thirty-two-volt farm radio that Etienne had shipped all the way from the United States in 1922.

Her father wraps the largest in cardboard and uses an ancient wheeled dolly to thump it down the stairs. Marie-Laure sits with her fingers going numb in her lap and thinks of the machine in the attic, its cables and switches. A transmitter built to talk to ghosts. Does it qualify as a radio receiver? Should she mention it? Do Papa and Madame Manec know? They seem not to. In the evening, fog moves into the city, trailing a cold, fishy smell, and they eat potatoes and carrots in the kitchen and Madame Manec leaves a dish outside Henri's door and taps but the door does not open and the food remains untouched.

"What," asks Marie-Laure, "will they do with the radios?"

"Send them to Germany," says Papa.

"Or pitch them in the sea," says Madame Manec. "Come, child, drink your tea. It's not the end of the world. I'll put an extra blanket on your bed tonight."

In the morning Etienne remains shut inside his brother's room. If he knows what is happening in his house, Marie-Laure cannot tell. At ten A.M. her father starts wheeling loads to the rue de Chartres, one trip, two trips, three, and when he comes back and loads the dolly with the last radio, Etienne still has not appeared. Marie-Laure holds Madame Manec's hand as she listens to the gate clang shut, to the cart's axle bounce as her father pushes it down the rue Vauborel, and to the silence that reinstalls itself after he's gone.

Museum

Sergeant Major Reinhold von Rumpel wakes early. He upholsters himself in his uniform, pockets his loupe and tweezers, rolls up his white gloves. By six A.M. he's in the hotel lobby in full dress, polish on his shoes, pistol case snapped shut. The hotelkeeper brings him bread and cheese in a basket made from dark wicker, covered nicely with a cotton napkin: everything shipshape.

There is great pleasure in being out in the city before the sun is up, streetlights glowing, the hum of a Parisian day commencing. As he walks up the rue Cuvier and turns into the Jardin des Plantes, the trees look misty and significant: parasols held up just for him.

He likes being early.

At the entrance to the Grand Gallery, two night warders stiffen. They glance at the stripes on his collar patch and sleeves; the cords in their throats tighten. A small man in black flannel comes down the staircase apologizing in German; he says he is the assistant director. He did not expect the sergeant major for another hour.

"We can speak French," says von Rumpel.

Behind him scurries a second man with eggshell skin and an evident terror of eye contact.

"We would be honored to show you the collections, Sergeant Major," breathes the assistant director. "This is the mineralogist, Professor Hublin." Hublin blinks twice, gives the impression of a penned animal. The pair of warders watch from the end of the corridor.

"May I take your basket?"

"It's no trouble."

The Gallery of Mineralogy is so long, von Rumpel can hardly see the end of it. In sections, display case after display case sits vacant, little shapes on their felted shelves marking the silhouettes of whatever has been removed. Von Rumpel strolls with his basket on his arm, forgetting to do anything but look. What treasures they left behind! A gorgeous set of yellow topaz crystals on a gray matrix. A great pink hunk of beryl like a crystallized brain. A violet column of tourmaline from Madagascar that looks so rich he cannot resist the urge to stroke it. Bournonite; apatite on muscovite; natural zircon in a spray of colors; dozens more minerals he cannot name. These men, he thinks, probably handle more gemstones in a week than he has seen in his lifetime.

Each piece is registered in huge organizational folios that have taken centuries to amass. The pallid Hublin shows him pages. "Louis XIII began the collection as a Cabinet of Medicines, jade for kidneys, clay for the stomach, and so on. There were already two hundred thousand entries in the catalog by 1850, a priceless mineral heritage . . ."

Every now and then von Rumpel pulls his notebook from his pocket and makes a notation. He takes his time. When they reach the end, the assistant director laces his fingers across his belt. "We hope you are impressed, Sergeant Major? You enjoyed your tour?"

"Very much." The electric lights in the ceiling are far apart, and the silence in the huge space is oppressive. "But," he says, enunciating very slowly, "what about the collections that are not on public display?"

The assistant director and the mineralogist exchange a glance. "You have seen everything we can show you, Sergeant Major."

Von Rumpel keeps his voice polite. Civilized. Paris is not Poland, after all. Waves must be made carefully. Things cannot simply be seized. What did his father used to say? *See obstacles as opportunities, Reinhold. See obstacles as inspirations.* "Is there somewhere," he says, "we can talk?"

The assistant director's office occupies a dusty third-floor corner that overlooks the gardens: walnut-paneled, underheated, decorated with pinned butterflies and beetles in alternating frames. On the wall behind his half-ton desk hangs the only image: a charcoal portrait of the French biologist Jean-Baptiste Lamarck.

The assistant director sits behind the desk, and von Rumpel sits in front with his basket between his feet. The mineralogist stands. A long-necked secretary brings tea.

Hublin says, "We are always acquiring, yes? All across the world, industrialization endangers mineral deposits. We collect as many types of minerals as exist. To a curator, none is superior to any other."

Von Rumpel laughs. He appreciates that they are trying to play the game. But don't they understand that the winner has already been determined? He sets down his cup of tea and says, "I would like to see your most protected specimens. I am most specifically interested in a specimen I believe you have only recently brought out from your vaults."

The assistant director sweeps his left hand through his hair and releases a blizzard of dandruff. "Sergeant Major, the minerals you've seen have aided discoveries in electrochemistry, in the fundamental laws of mathematical crystallography. The role of a national museum is to operate above the whims and fashions of collectors, to safeguard for future generations the —"

Von Rumpel smiles. "I will wait."

"You misunderstand us, monsieur. You have seen everything we can show you."

"I will wait to see what you cannot show me."

The assistant director peers into his tea. The mineralogist shifts from foot to foot; he appears to be wrestling with an interior fury.

"I am quite gifted at waiting," von Rumpel says in French. "It is my one great skill. I was never much good at athletics or mathematics, but even as a boy, I possessed unnatural patience. I would wait with my mother while she got her hair styled. I would sit in the chair and wait for hours, no magazine, no toys, not even swinging my legs back and forth. All the mothers were very impressed."

Both Frenchmen fidget. Beyond the door of the office, what ears listen? "Please sit if you'd like," von Rumpel says to Hublin, and pats the chair next to him. But Hublin does not sit. Time passes. Von Rumpel swallows the last of his tea and sets the cup very carefully on the edge of the assistant director's desk. Somewhere an electric fan whirs to life, runs awhile, and shuts down.

Hublin says, "It's not clear what we're waiting for, Sergeant Major."

"I'm waiting for you to be truthful."

"If I might —"

"Stay," says von Rumpel. "Sit. I'm sure if one of you were to call out instructions, the mademoiselle who looks like a giraffe will hear, will she not?"

The assistant director crosses and recrosses his legs. By now it is past noon. "Perhaps you would like to see the skeletons?" tries the assistant director. "The Hall of Man is quite spectacular. And our zoological collection is beyond —"

"I would like to see the minerals you do not reveal to the public. One in particular."

Hublin's throat splotches pink and white. He does not take a seat. The assistant director seems resigned to an impasse and pulls a thick perfect-bound stack of paper from a drawer and begins to read. Hublin shifts as if to leave, but von Rumpel merely says, "Please, stay until we have resolved this."

Waiting, thinks von Rumpel, is a kind of war. You simply tell yourself that you must not lose. The assistant director's telephone rings, and he reaches to pick it up, but von Rumpel holds up a hand, and the phone rings ten or eleven times and then falls quiet. What might be a full half hour passes, Hublin staring at his shoelaces, the assistant director making occasional notes in his manuscript with a silver pen, von Rumpel remaining completely motionless, and then there is a distant tapping on the door.

"Gentlemen?" comes the voice.

Von Rumpel calls, "We are fine, thank you."

The assistant director says, "I have other

matters to attend to, Sergeant Major."

Von Rumpel does not raise his voice. "You will wait here. Both of you. You will wait here with me until I see what I have come to see. And then we will all go back to our important jobs."

The mineralogist's chin trembles. The fan starts again, then dies. A five-minute timer, guesses von Rumpel. He waits for it to start and die one more time. Then he lifts his basket into his lap. He points to the chair. His voice is gentle. "Sit, Professor. You will be more comfortable."

Hublin does not sit. Two o'clock out in the city, and bells toll in a hundred churches. Walkers down on the paths. The last of autumn's leaves spiraling to earth.

Von Rumpel unrolls the napkin across his lap, lifts out the cheese. He breaks the bread slowly, sending a rich cascade of crust onto his napkin. As he chews, he can almost hear their guts rumbling. He offers them nothing. When he finishes, he wipes the corners of his mouth. "You read me wrong, messieurs. I am not an animal. I am not here to raze your collections. They belong to all of Europe, to all of humanity, do they not? I am here only for something small. Something smaller than the bone of your kneecaps." He looks at the mineralogist as he says it. Who looks away, crimson.

The assistant director says, "This is absurd,

Sergeant Major."

Von Rumpel folds his napkin and places it back in the basket and sets the basket on the ground. He licks the tip of his finger and picks the crumbs off his tunic one by one. Then he looks directly at the assistant director. "The Lycée Charlemagne, is that right? On the rue Charlemagne?"

The skin around the assistant director's eyes stretches.

"Where your daughter goes to school?" Von Rumpel turns in his chair. "And the College Stanislas, isn't it, Dr. Hublin? Where your twin sons attend? On the rue Notre-Dame des Champs? Wouldn't those handsome boys be preparing to walk home right now?"

Hublin sets his hands on the back of the empty chair beside him, and his knuckles become very white.

"One with a violin and the other a viola, am I correct? Crossing all those busy streets. That is a long walk for ten-year-old boys."

The assistant director is sitting very upright. Von Rumpel says, "I know it is not here, messieurs. Not even the lowest janitor would be so stupid as to leave the diamond here. But I would like to see where you have kept it. I would like to know what sort of place you believe is safe enough."

Neither of the Frenchmen says anything. The assistant director resumes looking at his manuscript, though it is clear to von Rumpel that he is no longer reading. At four o'clock the secretary raps on the door and again von Rumpel sends her away. He practices concentrating only on blinking. Pulse in his neck. Tock tock tock tock. Others, he thinks, would do this with less finesse. Others would use scanners, explosives, pistol barrels, muscle. Von Rumpel uses the cheapest of materials, only minutes, only hours.

Five bells. The light leaches out of the gardens.

"Sergeant Major, please," says the assistant director. His hands flat on his desk. Looking up now. "It is very late. I must relieve myself."

"Feel free." Von Rumpel gestures with one hand at a metal trash can beside the desk.

The mineralogist wrinkles his face. Again the phone rings. Hublin chews his cuticles. Pain shows in the assistant director's face. The fan whirs. Out in the gardens, the daylight unwinds from the trees and still von Rumpel waits.

"Your colleague," he says to the mineralogist, "he's a logical man, isn't he? He doubts the legends. But you, you seem more fiery. You don't want to believe, you tell yourself not to believe. But you do believe." He shakes his head. "You've held the diamond. You've felt its power."

"This is ridiculous," says Hublin. His eyes roll like a frightened colt's. "This is not civilized behavior. Are our children safe,

Sergeant Major? I demand that you let us determine if our children are safe."

"A man of science, and yet you believe the myths. You believe in the might of reason, but you also believe in fairy tales. Goddesses and curses."

The assistant director inhales sharply. "Enough," he says. "Enough."

Von Rumpel's pulse soars: has it already happened? So easily? He could wait two more days, three, while ranks of men broke against him like waves.

"Are our children safe, Sergeant Major?"

"If you wish them to be."

"May I use the telephone?"

Von Rumpel nods. The assistant director reaches for the handset, says "Sylvie" into it, listens awhile, then sets it down. The woman enters with a ring of keys. From a drawer inside the assistant director's desk, she produces another key on a chain. Simple, elegant, long-shafted.

A small locked door at the back of the main-floor gallery. It takes two keys to open it, and the assistant director seems inexperienced with the lock. They lead von Rumpel down a corkscrewing stone staircase; at the bottom, the assistant director unlocks a second gate. They wind through warrens of hallways, past a warder who drops his newspaper and sits ramrod straight as they pass. In an unassuming storeroom filled with dropcloths and pallets and crates, behind a sheet of plywood, the mineralogist reveals a simple combination safe that the assistant director opens rather easily.

No alarms. Only the one guard.

Inside the safe is a second, far more interesting box. It is heavy enough that it requires both the assistant director and the mineralogist to lift it out.

Elegant, its joinery invisible. No brand name, no combination dial. It is presumably hollow but with no discernible hinges, no nails, no attachment points; it looks like a solid block of highly polished wood. Custom work.

The mineralogist fits a key into a tiny, almost invisible hole on the bottom; when it turns, two more tiny keyholes open on the opposite side. The assistant director inserts matching keys into those holes; they unlock what looks like five different shafts.

Three overlapping cylinder locks, each dependent on the next.

"Ingenious," whispers von Rumpel.

The entire box falls gently open.

Inside sits a small felt bag.

He says, "Open it."

The mineralogist looks at the assistant director. The assistant director picks up the bag and unties its throat and upends a wrapped bundle into his palm. With a single finger, he nudges apart the folds. Inside lies a blue stone as big as a pigeon's egg.

The Wardrobe

Townspeople who violate blackout are fined or rounded up for questioning, though Madame Manec reports that at the Hôtel-Dieu, lamps burn all night long, and German officers go stumbling in and out at every hour, tucking in shirts and adjusting trousers. Marie-Laure keeps herself awake, waiting to hear her uncle stir. Finally she hears the door across the hall tick open and feet brush the boards. She imagines a storybook mouse creeping out from its hole.

She climbs out of bed, trying not to wake her father, and crosses into the hall. "Uncle," she whispers. "Don't be afraid."

"Marie-Laure?" His very smell like that of coming winter, a tomb, the heavy inertia of time.

"Are you well?"

"Better."

They stand on the landing. "There was a notice," says Marie-Laure. "Madame has left it on your desk."

"A notice?"

"Your radios."

He descends to the fifth floor. She can hear him sputtering. Fingers traveling across his newly empty shelves. Old friends gone. She prepares for shouts of anger but catches half-hyperventilated nursery rhymes instead: . . . *à la salade je suis malade au céleri je suis guéri . . .*

She takes his elbow, helps him to the davenport. He is still murmuring, trying to talk himself off some innermost ledge, and she can feel fear pumping off him, virulent, toxic; it reminds her of fumes billowing off the vats of formalin in the Department of Zoology.

Rain taps at the windowpanes. Etienne's voice comes from a long way off. "All of them?"

"Not the radio in the attic. I did not mention it. Does Madame Manec know about it?"

"We have never spoken of it."

"Is it hidden, Uncle? Could someone see it if the house were searched?"

"Who would search the house?"

A silence follows.

He says, "We could still turn it in. Say we overlooked it?"

"The deadline was yesterday at noon."

"They might understand."

"Uncle, do you really believe they will

understand that you have overlooked a transmitter that can reach England?"

More agitated breaths. The wheeling of the night on its silent trunnions. "Help me," he says. He finds an automobile jack in a third-floor room, and together they go up to the sixth floor and shut the door of her grandfather's room and kneel beside the massive wardrobe without risking the light of a single candle. He slides the jack under the wardrobe and cranks up the left side. Under its feet he slips folded rags; then he jacks up the other side and does the same. "Now, Marie-Laure, put your hands here. And push." With a thrill, she understands: they are going to park the wardrobe in front of the little door leading to the attic.

"All your might, ready? One two three."

The huge wardrobe slides an inch. The heavy mirrored doors knock lightly as it glides. She feels as if they are pushing a house across ice.

"My father," says Etienne, panting, "used to say Christ Himself could not have carried this wardrobe up here. That they must have built the house around it. Another now, ready?"

They push, rest, push, rest. Eventually the wardrobe settles in front of the little door, and the entrance to the attic is walled off. Etienne jacks up each foot again, pulls out the rags, and sinks to the floor, breathing hard, and Marie-Laure sits beside him. Before dawn rolls across the city, they are asleep.

Blackbirds

Roll call. Breakfast. Phrenology, rifle training, drills. Black-haired Ernst leaves the school five days after he is chosen as the weakest in Bastian's exercise. Two others leave the following week. Sixty becomes fifty-seven. Every evening Werner works in Dr. Hauptmann's lab, alternately plugging numbers into triangulation formulas or engineering: Hauptmann wants him to improve the efficiency and power of a directional radio transceiver he is designing. It needs to be quickly retuned to transmit on multiple frequencies, the little doctor says, and it needs to be able to measure the angle of the transmissions it receives. Can Werner manage this?

He reconfigures nearly everything in the design. Some nights Hauptmann grows talkative, explaining the role of a solenoid or resistor in great detail, even classifying a spider hanging from a rafter, or enthusing about gatherings of scientists in Berlin, where practically every conversation, he says, seems to unveil some new possibility. Relativity, quantum mechanics — on such nights he seems happy enough talking about whatever Werner asks.

Yet the very next night, Hauptmann's manner will be frighteningly closed; he invites no questions and supervises Werner's work in silence. That Dr. Hauptmann might have ties so far up — that the telephone on his desk connects him with men a hundred miles away who could probably wag a finger and send a dozen Messerschmitts streaming up from an airfield to strafe some city — intoxicates Werner.

We live in exceptional times.

He wonders if Jutta has forgiven him. Her letters consist mostly of banalities — *we are busy; Frau Elena says hello* — or else arrive in his bunkroom so full of censor marks that their meaning has disintegrated. Does she grieve over his absence? Or has she calcified her feelings, protected herself, as he is learning to do?

Volkheimer, like Hauptmann, seems full of contradictions. To the other boys, the Giant is a brute, an instrument of pure strength, and yet sometimes, when Hauptmann is away in Berlin, Volkheimer will disappear into the doctor's office and return with a Grundig tube radio and hook up the shortwave antenna and fill the lab with classical music.

Mozart, Bach, even the Italian Vivaldi. The more sentimental, the better. The huge boy will lean back in a chair, so that it makes squeaking protestations beneath his bulk, and let his eyelids slip to half-mast.

Why always triangles? What is the purpose of the transceiver they are building? What two points does Hauptmann know, and why does he need to know the third?

"It's only numbers, cadet," Hauptmann says, a favorite maxim. "Pure math. You have to accustom yourself to thinking that way."

Werner tries out various theories on Frederick, but Frederick, he's learning, moves about as if in the grip of a dream, his trousers too big around the waist, the hems already falling out. His eyes are both intense and vague; he hardly seems to realize when he misses targets in marksmanship. Most nights Frederick murmurs to himself before falling asleep: bits of poems, the habits of geese, bats he's heard swooping past the windows.

Birds, always birds.

". . . now, arctic terns, Werner, they fly from the south pole to the north pole, true navigators of the globe, probably the most migratory creatures ever to live, seventy thousand kilometers a year . . ."

A metallic wintery light settles over the stables and vineyard and rifle range, and songbirds streak over the hills, great scattershot nets of passerines on their way south, a migratory throughway running right over the spires of the school. Once in a while a flock descends into one of the huge lindens on the grounds and seethes beneath its leaves.

Some of the senior boys, sixteen- and seventeen-year-olds, cadets who are allowed freer access to ammunition, develop a fondness for firing volleys into the trees to see how many birds they can hit. The tree looks uninhabited and calm; then someone fires, and its crown shatters in all directions, a hundred birds exploding into flight in a half second, shrieking as though the whole tree has flown apart.

In the dormitory window one night, Frederick rests his forehead against the glass. "I hate them. I hate them for that."

The dinner bell rings, and everyone trots off, Frederick coming in last with his taffy-colored hair and wounded eyes, bootlaces trailing. Werner washes Frederick's mess tin for him; he shares homework answers, shoe polish, sweets from Dr. Hauptmann; they run next to each other during field exercises. A brass pin weighs lightly on each of their lapels; one hundred and fourteen hobnailed boots spark against pebbles on the trail. The castle with its towers and battlements looms below them like some misty vision of foregone glory. Werner's blood gallops through his ventricles, his thoughts on Hauptmann's transceiver, on solder, fuses, batteries, antennas; his boot and Frederick's touch the ground at the exact same moment.

SSG35 A NA513 NL WUX
DUPLICATE OF TELEPHONED TELEGRAM

10 DECEMBER 1940

M. DANIEL LEBLANC
SAINT-MALO FRANCE

= RETURN TO PARIS END OF MONTH = TRAVEL SECURELY =

Bath

One final burst of frenetic gluing and sanding, and Marie-Laure's father has completed the model of Saint-Malo. It is unpainted, imperfect, striped with a half-dozen different types of wood, and missing details. But it's complete enough for his daughter to use if she must: the irregular polygon of the island framed by ramparts, each of its eight hundred and sixty-five buildings in place.

He feels ragged. For weeks logic has been failing him. The stone the museum has asked him to protect is not real. If it were, the museum would have sent men already to collect it. Why then, when he puts a magnifying glass to it, do its depths reveal tiny daggers of flames? Why does he hear footfalls behind him when there are none? And why does he find himself entertaining the brainless notion that the stone he carries in the linen sachet in his pocket has brought him misfortune, has put Marie-Laure in danger, may indeed have precipitated the whole invasion of France?

Idiotic. Ludicrous.

He has tried every test he can think of without involving another soul.

Tried folding it between pieces of felt and striking it with a hammer — it did not shatter.

Tried scratching it with a halved pebble of quartz — it did not scratch.

Tried holding it to candle flame, drowning it, boiling it. He has hidden the jewel under the mattress, in his tool case, in his shoe. For several hours one night, he tucked it into Madame Manec's geraniums in a window flower box, then convinced himself the geraniums were wilting and dug the stone out.

This afternoon a familiar face looms in the train station, maybe four or five back in the queue. He has seen this man before, pudgy, sweating, multi-chinned. They lock eyes; the man's gaze slides away.

Etienne's neighbor. The perfumer.

Weeks ago, while taking measurements for the model, the locksmith saw this same man atop the ramparts pointing a camera out to sea. Not a man to trust, Madame Manec said. But he is just a man waiting in line to buy a ticket.

Logic. The principles of validity. Every lock has its key.

For more than two weeks, the director's telegram has echoed in his head. Such a maddeningly ambiguous choice for that final directive — *Travel securely.* Does it mean to bring the stone or leave it behind? Bring Marie-Laure or leave her behind? Travel by train? Or by some other, theoretically more secure means?

And what if, the locksmith considers, the telegram was not sent from the director at all?

Round and round the questions run. When it is his turn at the window, he buys a ticket for a single passenger on the morning train to Rennes and then on to Paris and walks the narrow, sunless streets back to the rue Vauborel. He will go do this and then it will be over. Back to work, staff the key pound, lock things away. In a week, he will ride unburdened back to Brittany and collect Marie-Laure.

For supper Madame Manec serves stew and baguettes. Afterward he leads Marie-Laure up the rickety flights of stairs to the third-floor bath. He fills the big iron tub and turns his back as she undresses. "Use as much soap as you'd like," he says. "I bought extra." The train ticket remains folded in his pocket like a betrayal.

She lets him wash her hair. Over and over Marie-Laure trawls her fingers through the suds, as though trying to gauge their weight. There has always been a sliver of panic in him, deeply buried, when it comes to his daughter: a fear that he is no good as a father, that he is doing everything wrong. That he never quite understood the rules. All those Parisian mothers pushing buggies through the Jardin des Plantes or holding up cardigans in department stores — it seemed to him that those women nodded to each other as they passed, as though each possessed some secret knowledge that he did not. How do you ever know for certain that you are doing the right thing?

There is pride, too, though — pride that he has done it alone. That his daughter is so curious, so resilient. There is the humility of being a father to someone so powerful, as if he were only a narrow conduit for another, greater thing. That's how it feels right now, he thinks, kneeling beside her, rinsing her hair: as though his love for his daughter will outstrip the limits of his body. The walls could fall away, even the whole city, and the brightness of that feeling would not wane.

The drain moans; the cluttered house crowds in close. Marie turns up her wet face. "You're leaving. Aren't you?"

He is glad, just now, that she cannot see him.

"Madame told me about the telegram."

"I won't be long, Marie. A week. Ten days at most."

"When?"

"Tomorrow. Before you wake."

She leans over her knees. Her back is long and white and split by the knobs of her vertebrae. She used to fall asleep holding his index finger in her fist. She used to sprawl with her books beneath the key pound bench and move her hands like spiders across the pages.

"Am I to stay here?"

"With Madame. And Etienne."

He hands her a towel and helps her climb onto the tile and waits outside while she puts on her nightgown. Then he walks her up to the sixth floor and into their little room, though he knows she does not need to be guided, and he sits on the edge of the bed and she kneels beside the model and sets three fingers on the steeple of the cathedral.

He finds the hairbrush, does not bother turning on the lamp.

"Ten days, Papa?"

"At most." The walls creak; the window between the curtains is black; the town prepares to sleep. Somewhere out there, German U-boats glide above underwater canyons, and thirty-foot squid ferry their huge eyes through the cold dark.

"Have we ever spent a night apart?"

"No." His gaze flits through the unlit room. The stone in his pocket seems almost to pulse. If he manages to sleep tonight, what will he dream?

"Can I go out while you are gone, Papa?"

"Once I get back. I promise."

As tenderly as he can, he draws the brush through the damp strands of his daughter's hair. Between strokes, they can hear the sea wind rattle the window.

Marie-Laure's hands whisper across the houses as she recites the names of the streets. "Rue des Cordiers, rue Jacques Cartier, rue Vauborel."

He says, "You'll know them all in a week."

Marie-Laure's fingers rove to the outer ramparts. The sea beyond. "Ten days," she says.

"At most."

Weakest (#2)

December sucks the light from the castle. The sun hardly clears the horizon before sinking away. Snow falls once, twice, then stays locked over the lawns. Has Werner ever seen snow this white, snow that was not fouled immediately with ash and coal dust? The only emissaries from the outside world are the occasional songbird who lands in the lindens beyond the quadrangle, blown astray by distant storm or battle or both, and two callow-faced corporals who come into the refectory every week or so — always after the prayer, always just as the boys have placed the first morsel of dinner in their mouths — to pass beneath the blazonry and stop behind a cadet and whisper in his ear that his father has been killed in action.

Other nights a prefect yells *Achtung!* and the boys stand at their benches and Bastian the commandant waddles in. The boys look down at their food in silence while Bastian walks the rows, trailing a single index finger across their backs. "Homesick? We mustn't trouble ourselves over our homes. In the end we all come home to the führer. What other home matters?"

"No other!" shout the boys.

Every afternoon, no matter the weather, the commandant blows his whistle and the fourteen-year-olds trot outside and he looms over them with his coat stretched across his belly and his medals chiming and the rubber hose twirling. "There are two kinds of death," he says, the clouds of his breath plunging out into the cold. "You can fight like a lion. Or you can go as easy as lifting a hair from a cup of milk. The nothings, the nobodies — they die easy." He sweeps his eyes along the ranks and swings his hose and widens his eyes dramatically. "How will you boys die?"

One windy afternoon he pulls Helmut Rödel out of line. Helmut is a small, unpromising child from the south who keeps his hands balled in fists nearly all his waking hours.

"And who is it, Rödel? In. Your. Opinion. Who is the weakest member of the corps?" The commandant twirls the hose. Helmut Rödel takes no time. "Him, sir."

Werner feels something heavy fall through him. Rödel is pointing directly at Frederick.

Bastian calls Frederick forward. If fear darkens his friend's face, Werner cannot see it. Frederick looks distracted. Almost philosophical. Bastian drapes his hose around his neck and trudges across the field, snow to his shins, taking his time, until he is little more than a dark lump at the far edge. Werner tries to make eye contact with Frederick, but his eyes are a mile away.

The commandant raises his right arm and yells, "Ten!" and the wind frays the word across the long expanse. Frederick blinks several times, as he often does when addressed in class, waiting for his internal life to catch up with his external one.

"Nine!"

"Run," hisses Werner.

Frederick is a decent runner, faster than Werner, but the commandant seems to count quickly this afternoon, and Frederick's head start has been abbreviated, and the snow hampers him, and he cannot be over twenty yards away when Bastian raises his left arm.

The boys explode into movement. Werner runs with the others, trying to stay in the back of the pack, their rifles beating in syncopation against their backs. Already the fastest of the boys seem to be running faster than usual, as though tired of being outrun.

Frederick runs hard. But the fastest boys are greyhounds, harvested from all over the nation for their speed and eagerness to obey, and they seem to Werner to be running more fervently, more conclusively, than they have before. They are impatient to find out what will happen if someone is caught.

Frederick is fifteen strides from Bastian when they haul him down.

The group coalesces around the frontrunners as Frederick and his pursuers get to their feet, all of them pasted with snow. Bastian strides up. The cadets encircle their instructor, chests heaving, many with their hands on their knees. The breath of the boys pulses out before them in a collective fleeting cloud that is stripped away quickly by the wind. Frederick stands in the middle, panting and blinking his long eyelashes.

"It usually does not take so long," says Bastian mildly, almost as if to himself. "For the first to be caught."

Frederick squints at the sky.

Bastian says, "Cadet, are you the weakest?"

"I don't know, sir."

"You don't know?" A pause. Into Bastian's face flows an undercurrent of antagonism. "Look at me when you speak."

"Some people are weak in some ways, sir. Others in other ways."

The commadant's lips thin and his eyes narrow and an expression of slow and intense malice rises in his face. As though a cloud has drifted away and for a moment Bastian's true, deformed character has come glaring through. He pulls the hose from around his neck and hands it to Rödel.

Rödel blinks up at his bulk. "Go on, then,"

prods Bastian. In some other context, he might be encouraging a reluctant boy to step into cold water. "Do him some good."

Rödel looks down at the hose: black, three feet long, stiff in the cold. What might be several seconds pass, though they feel to Werner like hours, and the wind tears through the frosted grass, sending zephyrs and wisps of snow sirening off across the white, and a sudden nostalgia for Zollverein rolls through him in a wave: boyhood afternoons wandering the soot-stained warrens, towing his little sister in the wagon. Muck in the alleys, the hoarse shouts of work crews, the boys in their dormitory sleeping head to toe while their coats and trousers hang from hooks along the walls. Frau Elena's midnight passage among the beds like an angel, murmuring, *I know it's cold. But I'm right beside you, see?*

Jutta, close your eyes.

Rödel steps forward and swings the hose and smacks Frederick with it across the shoulder. Frederick takes a step backward. The wind slashes across the field. Bastian says, "Again."

Everything becomes soaked in a hideous and wondrous slowness. Rödel rears back and strikes. This time he catches Frederick on the jaw. Werner forces his mind to keep sending up images of home: the laundry; Frau Elena's overworked pink fingers; dogs in the alleys; steam blowing from stacks — every part of him wants to scream: is this not wrong?

But here it is right.

It takes such a long time. Frederick withstands a third blow. "Again," commands Bastian. On the fourth, Frederick throws up his arms and the hose smacks against his forearms and he stumbles. Rödel swings again, and Bastian says, "In your shining example, Christ, lead the way, ever and always," and the whole afternoon turns sideways, torn open; Werner watches the scene recede as though observing it from the far end of a tunnel: a small white field, a group of boys, bare trees, a toy castle, none of it any more real than Frau Elena's stories about her Alsatian childhood or Jutta's drawings of Paris. Six more times he hears Rödel swing and the hose whistle and the strangely dead smack of the rubber striking Frederick's hands, shoulders, and face.

Frederick can walk for hours in the woods, can identify warblers fifty yards away simply by hearing their song. Frederick hardly ever thinks of himself. Frederick is stronger than he is in every imaginable way. Werner opens his mouth but closes it again; he drowns; he shuts his eyes, his mind.

At some point the beating stops. Frederick is facedown in the snow.

"Sir?" says Rödel, panting. Bastian takes back the length of hose from Rödel and drapes it around his neck and reaches underneath his belly to hitch up his belt. Werner kneels beside Frederick and turns him onto his side. Blood is running from his nose or eye or ear, maybe all three. One of his eyes is already swollen shut; the other remains open. His attention, Werner realizes, is on the sky. Tracing something up there.

Werner risks a glance upward: a single hawk, riding the wind.

Bastian says, "Up."

Werner stands. Frederick does not move.

Bastian says, "Up," more quietly this time, and Frederick gets to a knee. He stands, wobbling. His cheek is gashed and leaks tendrils of blood. Splotches of moisture show on his back from where the snow has melted into his shirt. Werner gives Frederick his arm.

"Cadet, are you the weakest?"

Frederick does not look at the commandant. "No, sir."

Hawk still gyring up there. The portly commandant chews on a thought for a moment. Then his clear voice rings out, flying above the company, urging them into a run. Fifty-seven cadets cross the grounds and jog up the snowy path into the forest. Frederick runs in his place beside Werner, his left eye swelling, twin networks of blood peeling back across his cheeks, his collar wet and brown.

The branches seethe and clatter. All fifty-seven boys sing in unison.

We shall march onwards,
Even if everything crashes down in pieces;
For today the nation hears us,
And tomorrow the whole world!

Winter in the forests of old Saxony. Werner does not risk another glance toward his friend. He quick-steps through the cold, an unloaded five-round rifle over his shoulder. He is almost fifteen years old.

The Arrest of the Locksmith

They seize him outside of Vitré, hours from Paris. Two policemen in plain clothes bundle him off a train while a dozen passengers stare. He is questioned in a van and again in an ice-cold mezzanine office decorated with poorly executed watercolors of oceangoing steamers. The first interrogators are French; an hour later they become German. They brandish his notebook and tool case. They hold up his key ring and count seven different skeleton keys. What do these unlock, they want to know, and how do you employ these tiny files and saws? What about this notebook full of architectural measurements?

A model for my daughter.

Keys for the museum where I work.

Please.

They frog-march him to a cell. The door's lock and hinges are so big and antiquarian, they must be Louis XIV. Maybe Napoleon. Any hour now the director or his people will show up and explain everything. Certainly this will happen.

In the morning the Germans run him through a second, more laconic spell of questioning while a typist clatters away in the corner. They seem to be accusing him of plotting to destroy the Château de Saint-Malo, though why they might believe this is not clear. Their French is barely adequate and they seem more interested in their questions than his answers. They deny access to paper, to linens, to a telephone. They have photographs of him.

He yearns for cigarettes. He lies faceup on the floor and imagines himself kissing Marie-Laure once on each eye while she sleeps. Two days after his arrest, he is driven to a holding pen a few miles outside Strasbourg. Through fence slats, he watches a column of uniformed schoolgirls walk double-file in the winter sunshine.

Guards bring prepackaged sandwiches, hard cheese, sufficient water. In the pen, maybe thirty others sleep on straw laid atop frozen mud. Mostly French but some Belgians, four Flemings, two Walloons. All have been accused of crimes they speak of only with reticence, anxious about what traps might lurk within any question he puts to them. At night they trade rumors in whispers. "We will only be in Germany for a few months," someone says, and the word goes twisting down the line.

"Merely to help with spring planting while their men are at war."

"Then they'll send us home."

Each man thinks this is impossible and then: It might be true. Just a few months. Then home.

No officially appointed lawyer. No military tribunal. Marie-Laure's father spends three days shivering in the holding pen. No rescue arrives from the museum, no limousine from the director grinds up the lane. They will not let him write letters. When he demands to use a telephone, the guards don't bother to laugh. "Do you know the last time *we* used a telephone?" Every hour is a prayer for Marie-Laure. Every breath.

On the fourth day, all the prisoners are piled onto a cattle truck and driven east. "We are close to Germany," the men whisper. They can glimpse it on the far side of the river. Low clumps of naked trees bracketed by snow-dusted fields. Black rows of vineyards. Four disconnected strands of gray smoke melt into a white sky.

The locksmith squints. Germany? It looks no different from this side of the river.

It may as well be the edge of a cliff.

Four: 8 August 1944

The Fort of La Cité

Sergeant Major von Rumpel climbs a ladder in the dark. He can feel the lymph nodes on either side of his neck compressing his esophagus and trachea. His weight like a rag on the rungs.

The two gunners inside the periscope turret watch from beneath the rims of their helmets. Not offering help, not saluting. The turret is crowned with a steel dome and is used primarily to range larger guns positioned farther below. It offers views of the sea to the west; the cliffs below, all strung with entangling wire; and directly across the water, a half mile away, the burning city of Saint-Malo.

Artillery has stopped for the moment, and the predawn fires inside the walls take on a steady middle life, an adulthood. The western edge of the city has become a holocaust of crimson and carmine from which rise multiple towers of smoke. The largest has curdled into a pillar like the cloud of tephra and ash and steam that billows atop an erupting volcano. From afar, the smoke appears strangely solid, as though carved from luminous wood. All along its perimeter, sparks rise and ash falls and administrative documents flutter: utility plans, purchase orders, tax records.

With binoculars, von Rumpel watches what might be bats go flaming and careening out over the ramparts. A geyser of sparks erupts deep within a house — an electrical transformer or hoarded fuel or maybe a delayed-action bomb — and it looks to him as if lightning lashes the town from within.

One of the gunners makes unimaginative comments about the smoke, a dead horse he can see at the base of the walls, the intensity of certain quadrants of fire. As though they are noblemen in grandstands viewing fortress warfare in the years of the Crusaders. Von Rumpel tugs his collar against the bulges in his throat, tries to swallow.

The moon sets and the eastern sky lightens, the hem of night pulling away, taking stars with it one by one until only two are left. Vega, maybe. Or Venus. He never learned.

"Church spire is gone," says the second gunner.

A day ago, above the zigzag rooftops, the cathedral spire pointed straight up, higher than everything else. Not this morning. Soon the sun is above the horizon and the orange of flames gives way to the black of smoke, rising along the western walls and blowing like a caul across the citadel.

Finally, for a few seconds, the smoke parts long enough for von Rumpel to peer into the serrated maze of the city and pick out what he's looking for: the upper section of a tall house with a broad chimney. Two windows visible, the glass out. One shutter hanging, three in place.

Number 4 rue Vauborel. Still intact. Seconds pass; smoke veils it again.

A single airplane tracks across the deepening blue, incredibly high. Von Rumpel retreats down the long ladder into the tunnels of the fort below. Trying not to limp, not to think of the bulges in his groin. In the underground commissary, men sit against the walls spooning oatmeal from their upturned helmets. The electric lights cast them in alternating pools of glare and shadow.

Von Rumpel sits on an ammunition box and eats cheese from a tube. The colonel in charge of defending Saint-Malo has made speeches to these men, speeches about valor, about how any hour the Hermann Göring Division will break the American line at Avranches, how reinforcements will pour in from Italy and possibly Belgium, tanks and Stukas, truckloads of fifty-millimeter mortars, how the people of Berlin believe in them like a nun believes in God, how no one will abandon his post and if he does he'll be executed as a deserter, but von Rumpel is thinking now of the vine inside of him. A black vine that has grown branches through his legs and arms. Gnawing his abdomen from the inside. Here in this peninsular fortress just outside Saint-Malo, cut off from the retreating lines, it seems only a matter of time until Canadians and Brits and the bright American eyes of the Eighty-third Division will be swarming the city, scouring the homes for marauding Huns, doing whatever it is they do when they take prisoners.

Only a matter of time until the black vine chokes off his heart.

"What?" says a soldier beside him.

Von Rumpel sniffs. "I do not think I said anything."

The soldier squints back into the oatmeal in his helmet.

Von Rumpel squeezes out the last of the vile, salty cheese and drops the empty tube between his feet. The house is still there. His army still holds the city. For a few hours the fires will burn, and then the Germans will swarm like ants back to their positions and fight for another day.

He will wait. Wait and wait and wait, and when the smoke clears, he will go in.

Atelier de Réparation

Bernd the engineer squirms in pain, grinding his face into the back of the golden armchair. Something wrong with his leg and something worse with his chest.

The radio is hopeless. The power cable has been severed and the lead to the aboveground antenna is lost and Werner would not be surprised if the selector panel is broken. In the weakening amber of Volkheimer's field light, he stares at one crushed plug after another.

The bombing seems to have destroyed the hearing in his left ear. His right, as far as he can tell, is gradually coming back. Beyond the ringing, he begins to hear.

Ticking of fires as they cool.

Groaning of the hotel above.

Strange miscellaneous dripping.

And Volkheimer as he hacks intermittently, insanely, at the rubble blocking the stairwell. Volkheimer's technique, apparently, is this: he crouches beneath the buckled ceiling, panting, holding a piece of twisted rebar in one hand. He switches on his flashlight and scans the packed stairwell for anything he might drag out of it. Memorizing positions. Then he switches off the light, to preserve its battery, and goes at his task in the darkness. When the light comes back on, the mess of the stairwell looks the same. An impacted welter of metal and brickwork and timber so thick that it's hard to believe twenty men could get through.

Please, Volkheimer says. Whether he knows he is saying it aloud or not, Werner cannot say. But Werner hears it in his right ear like a distant prayer. *Please. Please.* As though everything in the war to this point was tolerable to twenty-one-year-old Frank Volkheimer but not this final injustice.

The fires above ought to have sucked the last oxygen out of this hole by now. They all should have asphyxiated. Debts paid, accounts settled. And yet they breathe. The three splintered beams in the ceiling hold up God knows what load: ten tons of carbonized hotel and the corpses of eight anti-aircraft men and untold unexploded ordnance. Maybe Werner for his ten thousand small betrayals and Bernd for his innumerable crimes and Volkheimer for being the instrument, the executor of the orders, the blade of the Reich — maybe the three of them have some greater price to pay, some final sentence to be handed down.

First a corsair's cellar, built to safeguard gold, weapons, an eccentric's beekeeping equipment. Then a wine cellar. Then a handyman's nook. *Atelier de réparation,* thinks Werner, a chamber in which to make reparations. As appropriate a place as any. Certainly there would be people in the world who believe these three have reparations to make.

Two Cans

When Marie-Laure wakes, the little model house is pinned beneath her chest, and she is sweating through her great-uncle's coat.

Is it dawn? She climbs the ladder and presses her ear to the trapdoor. No more sirens. Maybe the house burned to the ground while she slept. Or else she slept through the last hours of the war and the city has been liberated. There could be people in the streets: volunteers, gendarmes, fire brigades. Even Americans. She should go up through the trapdoor and walk out the front door onto the rue Vauborel.

But what if Germany has held the city? What if Germans are right now marching from house to house, shooting whomever they please?

She will wait. At any moment Etienne could be making his way toward her, fighting with his last breath to reach her.

Or he is crouched somewhere, cradling his head. Seeing demons.

Or he is dead.

She tells herself to save the bread, but she is famished and the loaf is getting stale, and before she knows it, she has finished it.

If only she had brought her novel down with her.

Marie-Laure roves the cellar in her stocking feet. Here's a rolled rug, its hollow filled with what smell like wood shavings: mice. Here's a crate that contains old papers. Antique lamp. Madame Manec's canning supplies. And here, at the back of a shelf near the ceiling, two small miracles. Full cans! Hardly any food remains in the entire kitchen — only cornmeal and a sheaf of lavender and two or three bottles of skunked Beaujolais — but down here in the cellar, two heavy cans.

Peas? Beans? Corn kernels, maybe. Not oil, she prays; aren't oil cans smaller? When she shakes them, they offer no clues. Marie-Laure tries to calculate the chances that one might contain Madame Manec's peaches, the white peaches from Languedoc that she'd buy by the crate and peel and quarter and boil with sugar. The whole kitchen would fill with their smell and color, Marie-Laure's fingers sticky with them, a kind of rapture.

Two cans Etienne missed.

But to raise one's hopes is to risk their falling further. Peas. Or beans. These would be more than welcome. She deposits one can in each pocket of her uncle's coat, and checks again for the little house in the pocket of her dress, and sits on a trunk and clasps her cane in both hands and tries not to think about her bladder.

Once, when she was eight or nine, her father took her to the Panthéon in Paris to describe Foucault's pendulum. Its bob, he said, was a golden sphere shaped like a child's top. It swung from a wire that was sixty-seven meters long; because its trajectory changed over time, he explained, it proved beyond all doubt that the earth rotated. But what Marie-Laure remembered, standing at the rail as it whistled past, was her father saying that Foucault's pendulum would never stop. It would keep swinging, she understood, after she and her father left the Panthéon, after she had fallen asleep that night. After she had forgotten about it, and lived her entire life, and died.

Now it is as if she can hear the pendulum in the air in front of her: that huge golden bob, as wide across as a barrel, swinging on and on, never stopping. Grooving and regrooving its inhuman truth into the floor.

NUMBER 4 RUE VAUBOREL

Ashes, ashes: snow in August. The shelling resumed sporadically after breakfast, and now, around six P.M., has ceased. A machine gun fires somewhere, a sound like a chain of beads passing through fingers. Sergeant Major von Rumpel carries a canteen, a half dozen ampules of morphine, and his field pistol. Over the seawall. Over the causeway toward the huge smoldering bulwark of Saint-Malo. Out in the harbor, the jetty has been shattered in multiple places. A half-submerged fishing boat drifts stern up.

Inside the old city, mountains of stone blocks, sacks, shutters, branches, iron grille-work, and chimney pots fill the rue de Dinan. Smashed flower boxes and charred window frames and shattered glass. Some buildings still smoke, and though von Rumpel keeps a damp handkerchief pressed over his mouth and nose, he has to stop several times to gather his breath.

Here a dead horse, starting to bloat. Here a

chair upholstered in striped green velvet. Here the torn shreds of a canopy proclaim a brasserie. Curtains swing idly from broken windows in the strange, flickering light; they unnerve him. Swallows fly to and fro, looking for lost nests, and someone very far away might be screaming, or it might be the wind. The blasts have stripped many shop signs off their brackets, and the gibbets hang forsaken.

A schnauzer trots after him, whining. No one shouts down from a window to warn him away from mines. Indeed, in four blocks he sees only one soul, a woman outside what was, the day before, the movie-house. Dustpan in one hand, broom nowhere to be seen. She looks up at him, dazed. Through an open door behind her, rows of seats have crumpled beneath great slabs of ceiling. Beyond them, the screen stands unblemished, not even stained by smoke.

"Show's not till eight," she says in her Breton French, and he nods as he limps past. On the rue Vauborel, vast quantities of slate tiles have slid off roofs and detonated in the streets. Scraps of burned paper float overhead. No gulls. Even if the house has caught fire, he thinks, the diamond will be there. He will pluck it from the ashes like a warm egg.

But the tall, slender house remains nearly unscathed. Eleven windows on the facade, most of the glass out. Blue window frames, old granite of grays and tans. Four of its six flower boxes hang on. The mandated list of occupants clings to its front door.

M. Etienne LeBlanc, age 63.

Mlle Marie-Laure LeBlanc, age 16.

All the dangers he is willing to endure. For the Reich. For himself.

No one stops him. No shells come whistling in. Sometimes the eye of a hurricane is the safest place to be.

What They Have

When is it day and when night? Time seems better measured by flashes: Volkheimer's field light flicks off, flicks on.

Werner watches Volkheimer's ash-dusted face in the reflected glow, his ministrations as he leans over Bernd. *Drink,* says Volkheimer's mouth as he holds his canteen to Bernd's lips, and shadows lunge across the broken ceiling like a circle of wraiths preparing to feast.

Bernd twists his face away, panic in his eyes, and tries to examine his leg.

The flashlight switches off and the darkness rushes back.

In Werner's duffel, he has his childhood notebook, his blanket, and dry socks. Three rations. This is all the food they have. Volkheimer has none. Bernd has none. They have only two canteens of water, each half-empty. Volkheimer has also discovered a bucket of paintbrushes in a corner with some watery sludge in the bottom, but how desperate will they have to become to drink that?

Two stick grenades: Model 24s, one in each of the side pockets of Volkheimer's coat. Hollow wood handles on the bottom, high-explosive charges in a steel can on top — handheld bombs the boys at Schulpforta called potato mashers. Twice already Bernd has begged Volkheimer to try one on the impacted mess of the stairwell, to see if they can blast their way out. But to use a grenade down here, in such close quarters, beneath rubble presumably littered with live 88-millimeter shells, would be suicide.

Then there's the rifle: Volkheimer's bolt-action Karabiner 98K, loaded with five rounds. Enough, thinks Werner. Plenty. They would need only three, one for each.

Sometimes, in the darkness, Werner thinks the cellar may have its own faint light, perhaps emanating from the rubble, the space going a bit redder as the August day above them progresses toward dusk. After a while, he is learning, even total darkness is not quite darkness; more than once he thinks he can see his spread fingers when he passes them in front of his eyes.

Werner thinks of his childhood, the skeins of coal dust suspended in the air on winter mornings, settling on windowsills, in the children's ears, in their lungs, except down here in this hole, the white dust is the inverse, as if he is trapped in some deep mine that is the same but also the opposite of the one that killed his father.

Dark again. Light again. Volkheimer's antic ash-dusted face materializes in front of Werner, his rank insignia partially torn off one shoulder. With the beam of his field light, he shows Werner that he is holding two bent screwdrivers and a box of electrical fuses. "The radio," he says into Werner's good ear. "Have you slept at all?"

Volkheimer turns the light onto his own face. *Before we run out of battery,* says his mouth.

Werner shakes his head. The radio is hopeless. He wants to close his eyes, forget, give up. Wait for the rifle barrel to touch his temple. But Volkheimer wants to make an argument that life is worth living.

The filaments of the bulb inside his field light glow yellow: weaker already. Volkheimer's illuminated mouth is red against the blackness. *We are running out of time,* his lips say. The building groans. Werner sees green grass, crackling flies, sunlight. The gates of a summer estate opening wide. When death comes for Bernd, it might as well come for him also. Save a second trip.

Your sister, says Volkheimer. *Think of your sister.*

Trip Wire

Her bladder will not hold much longer. She scales the cellar steps and holds her breath and hears nothing for thirty heartbeats. Forty. Then she pushes open the trapdoor and climbs into the kitchen.

No one shoots her. She hears no explosions.

Marie-Laure crunches over the fallen kitchen shelves and crosses into Madame Manec's tiny apartment, the two cans swinging heavily in her great-uncle's coat. Throat stinging, nostrils stinging. The smoke slightly thinner in here.

She relieves herself in the bedpan at the foot of Madame Manec's bed. Pulls up her stockings and rebuttons her great-uncle's coat. Is it afternoon? She wishes for the thousandth time that she could talk to her father. Would it be better to go out into the city, especially if it is still daylight, and try to find someone?

A soldier would help her. Anyone would. Though even as the thought rises, she doubts it.

The unsteady feeling in her legs, she knows, stems from hunger. In the tumult of the kitchen, she cannot find a can opener, but she does find a paring knife in Madame Manec's knife drawer and the large coarse brick Madame used to prop open the fireplace grate.

She will eat whatever is inside one of the two cans. Then she will wait a bit longer in case her uncle comes home, in case she hears anyone pass by, the town crier, a fireman, an American serviceman with gallantry on his mind. If she hears no one by the time she is hungry again, she will go out into what is left of the street.

First she climbs to the third floor to drink from the bathtub. With her lips against its surface, she takes long inward pulls. Pooling, burbling in her gut. A trick she and Etienne have learned over a hundred insufficient meals: before you eat, drink as much water as you can, and you will feel full more quickly. "At least, Papa," she says out loud, "I was smart about the water."

Then she sits on the third-floor landing with her back against the telephone table. She braces one of the cans between her thighs, holds the point of the knife against its lid, and raises the brick to tap down on the knife handle. But before she can bring the brick down, the trip wire behind her jerks, and the bell rings, and someone enters the house.

▪ ▪ ▪ ▪

FIVE: JANUARY 1941

▪ ▪ ▪ ▪

January Recess

The commandant makes a speech about virtue and family and the emblematic fire that Schulpforta boys carry everywhere they go, a bowl of pure flame to stoke the nation's hearths, führer this and führer that, his words crashing into Werner's ears in a familiar battery, one of the most daring boys muttering afterward, "Oh, I've got a hot bowl of something in my core."

In the bunk room, Frederick leans over the rim of his bed. His face presents a map of purples and yellows. "Why don't you come to Berlin? Father will be working, but you could meet Mother."

For two weeks Frederick has limped around bruised and slow-footed and puffy, and not once has he spoken to Werner with anything more than his own gentle brand of distracted kindness. Not once has he accused Werner of betrayal, even though Werner did nothing while Frederick was beaten and has done nothing since: did not hunt down Rödel or point a rifle at Bastian or bang indignantly on Dr. Hauptmann's door, demanding justice. As if Frederick understands already that both have been assigned to their specific courses, that there is no deviating now.

Werner says, "I don't have —"

"Mother will pay your fare." Frederick tilts back up and stares at the ceiling. "It's nothing."

The train ride is a sleepy six-hour epic, every hour their rickety car shunted onto a siding to let trains full of soldiers, headed for the front, hurry past. Finally Werner and Frederick disembark at a dim charcoal-colored station and climb a long flight of stairs, each step painted with the same exclamation — *Berlin smokes Junos!* — and rise into the streets of the largest city Werner has ever seen.

Berlin! The very name like two sharp bells of glory. Capital of science, seat of the führer, nursery to Bohr, Einstein, Staudinger, Bayer. Somewhere in these streets, plastic was invented, X-rays were discovered, continental drift was identified. What marvels does science cultivate here now? Superman soldiers, Dr. Hauptmann says, and weather-making machines and missiles that can be steered by men a thousand miles away.

The sky drops silver threads of sleet. Gray houses run in converging lines to the horizon, bunched as if to fend off cold. They pass shops stuffed with hanging meats and a drunk with a broken mandolin on his lap and a trio of streetwalkers huddled beneath an awning who catcall the boys in their uniforms.

Frederick leads them into a five-story town house one block off a pretty avenue called the Knesebeckstrasse. He rings #2 and a returning buzz echoes from inside and the door unlatches. They come into a dim foyer and stand before a pair of matched doors. Frederick presses a button and something high in the building rattles and Werner whispers, "You have an elevator?"

Frederick smiles. The machinery clangs downward and the lift clanks into place and Frederick pushes the wooden doors inward. Werner watches the interior of the building slide past in amazement. When they reach the second floor, he says, "Can we ride it again?"

Frederick laughs. They go down. Back up. Down, up, to the lobby a fourth time, and Werner is peering into the cables and weights above the car, trying to understand its mechanism, when a tiny woman enters the building and shakes out her umbrella. With her other hand, she carries a paper sack, and her eyes rapidly apprehend the boys' uniforms and the intense whiteness of Werner's hair and the livid bruises beneath Frederick's eyes. On the breast of her coat, a mustard-yellow star has been carefully stitched. Perfectly straight, one vertex down, another up. Drops fall like seeds from the tip of her umbrella.

"Good afternoon, Frau Schwartzenberger," says Frederick. He backs up against the wall of the elevator car and gestures for her to enter.

She squeezes into the lift and Werner steps in behind her. From the top of her sack juts a sheaf of withered greens. Her collar, he can see, is separating from the rest of the coat; threads are giving way. If she were to turn, their eyes would be a hand's width apart.

Frederick presses 2, then 5. No one speaks. The old woman rubs the trembling tip of an index finger across one eyebrow. The lift clangs up one floor. Frederick snaps open the cage and Werner follows him out. He watches the old woman's gray shoes rise past his nose. Already the door to #2 is opening, and an aproned woman with baggy arms and a downy face rushes out and embraces Frederick. She kisses him on both cheeks, then touches his bruises with her thumbs.

"It's all right, Franny, horseplay."

The apartment is sleek and shiny, full of deep carpets that swallow noise. Big rear windows look out into the hearts of four leafless lindens. Sleet still falling outside.

"Mother isn't home yet," Franny says, smoothing down her apron with both palms. Her eyes stay on Frederick. "You're sure you're all right?"

Frederick says, "Of course," and together he and Werner pad into a warm, clean-smelling bedroom and Frederick slides open a drawer, and when he turns around, he's wearing eyeglasses with black frames. He looks at Werner shyly. "Oh, come on, you didn't already know?"

With his glasses on, Frederick's expression seems to ease; his face makes more sense — this, Werner thinks, is who he is. A soft-skinned boy in glasses with taffy-colored hair and the finest trace of a mustache needled across his lip. Bird lover. Rich kid.

"I barely hit anything in marksmanship. You really didn't know?"

"Maybe," says Werner. "Maybe I knew. How did you pass the eye exams?"

"Memorized the charts."

"Don't they have different ones?"

"I memorized all four. Father got them ahead of time. Mother helped me study."

"What about your binoculars?"

"They're prescription. Cost a fortune."

They sit in a big kitchen at a butcher's block with a marble cap. The maid named Franny emerges with a dark loaf and a round of cheese, and she smiles at Frederick as she sets it down. They talk about Christmas and how Frederick was sorry to miss it, and the maid passes out through a swinging door and returns with two white plates so delicate that they ring when she sets them down.

Werner's mind reels: A lift! A Jewess! A maid! Berlin! They retreat into Frederick's bedroom, which is populated with tin soldiers and model airplanes and wooden crates full of comic books. They lie on their stomachs and page through comics, feeling the pleasure of being outside of school, glancing at each other now and then as if curious to learn whether their friendship will continue to exist in another place.

Franny calls, "I'm going," and as soon as the door closes, Frederick takes Werner by the arm into the living room and climbs a ladder built along tall hardwood shelves and slides aside a large wicker basket and, from behind it, brings down a huge book: two volumes enfolded in golden slipcovers, each as big as a crib mattress. "Here." His voice glows; his eyes glow. "This is what I wanted to show you."

Inside are lush full-color paintings of birds. Two white falcons swoop over each other, beaks open. A bloodred flamingo holds its black-tipped beak over stagnant water. Resplendent geese stand on a headland and peer into a heavy sky. Frederick turns the pages with both hands. *Pipiry flycatcher. Buff-breasted merganser. Red-cockaded woodpecker.* Many of them larger in the book than in real life.

"Audubon," Frederick says, "was an American. Walked the swamps and woods for years, back when that whole country was just swamps and woods. He'd spend all day watching one individual bird. Then he'd shoot it and prop it up with wires and sticks and paint it. Probably knew more than any birder before or since. He'd eat most of the birds after he painted them. Can you imagine?" Frederick's voice trembles with ardency. Gazing up. "Those bright mists and your gun on your shoulder and your eyes set firmly in your head?"

Werner tries to see what Frederick sees: a time before photography, before binoculars. And here was someone willing to tramp out into a wilderness brimming with the unknown and bring back paintings. A book not so much full of birds as full of evanescence, of blue-winged, trumpeting mysteries.

He thinks of the Frenchman's radio program, of Heinrich Hertz's *Principles of Mechanics* — doesn't he recognize the thrill in Frederick's voice? He says, "My sister would love this."

"Father says we're not supposed to have it. Says we have to keep it hidden up there behind the basket because it's American and was printed in Scotland. It's just birds!"

The front door opens and footsteps clack across the foyer. Frederick hurries the volumes back inside their slipcovers; he calls, "Mother?" and a woman wearing a green ski suit with white stripes down the legs enters crying, "Fredde! Fredde!" She embraces her son and holds him back with straight arms while she runs a fingertip over a mostly healed cut along his forehead. Frederick looks off over her shoulder with a trace of panic on his face. Is he afraid that she'll see he was looking at the forbidden book? Or that she'll be angry about his bruises? She does not say anything but merely stares at her son, tangled in thoughts Werner cannot guess, then remembers herself.

"And you must be Werner!" The smile sweeps back onto her face. "Frederick has written lots about you! Look at that hair! Oh, we adore guests." She climbs the ladder and restores the heavy Audubon volumes to their shelf one at a time, as though putting away something irritating. The three of them sit at the vast oak table and Werner thanks her for the train ticket and she tells a story about a man she "ran into just now, unbelievable really," who apparently is a famous tennis player and every now and then she reaches across and squeezes Frederick's forearm. "You would have been absolutely amazed," she says more than once, and Werner studies his friend's face to gauge whether or not he would have been amazed, and Franny returns to set out wine and more Rauchkäse and for an hour Werner forgets about Schulpforta, about Bastian and the black rubber hose, about the Jewess upstairs — the *things* these people have! A violin on a stand in the corner and sleek furniture made from chromium steel and a brass telescope and a sterling silver chess set behind glass and this magnificent cheese that tastes like smoke has been stirred into butter.

Wine glows sleepily in Werner's stomach and sleet ticks down through the lindens when Frederick's mother announces that they are going out. "Tighten up your ties, won't you?" She applies powder beneath Frederick's eyes and they walk to a bistro, the kind of restaurant Werner has never dreamed of entering, and a boy in a white jacket, barely older than they are, brings more wine.

A constant stream of diners come to their table to shake Werner's and Frederick's hands and ask Frederick's mother in low sycophantic voices about her husband's latest advancement. Werner notices a girl in the corner, radiant, dancing by herself, throwing her face to the ceiling. Eyes closed. The food is rich, and every now and then Frederick's mother laughs, and Frederick absently touches the makeup on his face while his mother says, "Well, Fredde has all the best there at that school, all the best," and seemingly every minute some new face comes along and kisses Frederick's mother on both cheeks and whispers in her ear. When Werner overhears Frederick's mother say to a woman, "Oh, the Schwartzenberger crone will be gone by year's end, then we'll have the top floor, *du wirst schon sehen,*" he glances at Frederick, whose smudged eyeglasses have gone opaque in the candlelight, whose makeup looks strange and lewd now, as though it has intensified the bruises rather than concealed them, and a feeling of great uneasiness overtakes him. He hears Rödel swing the hose, the smack of it across Frederick's up-flung palms. He hears the voices of the boys in his Kameradschaften back in Zollverein sing, *Live faithfully, fight bravely, and die laughing.* The bistro is overcrowded; everyone's mouths move too quickly; the woman talking to Frederick's mother is wearing a nauseating quantity of perfume; and in the watery light it seems suddenly as if the scarf trailing from the dancing girl's neck is a noose.

Frederick says, "Are you all right?"

"Fine, it's delicious," but Werner feels something inside him screw tighter, tighter.

On the way home, Frederick and his mother walk ahead. She loops her slender arm through his and talks to him in a low voice. Fredde this, Fredde that. The street is empty, the windows dead, the electric signs switched off. Innumerable shops, millions sleeping in beds around them, and yet where are they all? As they reach Frederick's block, a woman in a dress, leaning against a building, bends over and vomits on the sidewalk.

In the town house, Frederick pulls on pajamas made of jelly-green silk and folds his glasses on the nightstand and climbs barefoot into his brass childhood bed. Werner gets into a trundle bed that Frederick's mother has apologized for three separate times, although its mattress is more comfortable than any he has slept on in his life.

The building falls quiet. Model automobiles glimmer on Frederick's shelves.

"Do you ever wish," whispers Werner, "that you didn't have to go back?"

"Father needs me to be at Schulpforta. Mother too. It doesn't matter what I want."

"Of course it matters. I want to be an engineer. And you want to study birds. Be like that American painter in the swamps. Why else do any of this if not to become who we want to be?"

A stillness in the room. Out there in the trees beyond Frederick's window hangs an alien light.

"Your problem, Werner," says Frederick, "is that you still believe you own your life."

When Werner wakes, it's well past dawn. His head aches and his eyeballs feel heavy. Frederick is already dressed, wearing trousers, an ironed shirt, and a necktie, kneeling against the window with his nose against the glass. "Gray wagtail." He points. Werner looks past him into the naked lindens.

"Doesn't look like much, does he?" murmurs Frederick. "Hardly a couple of ounces of feathers and bones. But that bird can fly to Africa and back. Powered by bugs and worms and desire."

The wagtail hops from twig to twig. Werner rubs his aching eyes. It's just a bird.

"Ten thousand years ago," whispers Frederick, "they came through here in the millions. When this place was a garden, one endless garden from end to end."

He Is Not Coming Back

Marie-Laure wakes and thinks she hears the shuffle of Papa's shoes, the clink of his key ring. Fourth floor fifth floor sixth. His fingers brush the doorknob. His body radiates a faint but palpable heat in the chair beside her. His little tools rasp across wood. He smells of glue and sandpaper and Gauloises *bleues.*

But it is only the house groaning. The sea throwing foam against rocks. Deceits of the mind.

On the twentieth morning without any word from her father, Marie-Laure does not get out of bed. She no longer cares that her great-uncle put on an ancient necktie and stood by the front door on two separate occasions and whispered weird rhymes to himself — *à la pomme de terre, je suis par terre; au haricot, je suis dans l'eau* — trying and failing to summon the courage to go out. She no longer begs Madame Manec to take her to the train station, to write another letter, to spend another futile afternoon at the prefecture trying to petition occupation authorities to locate her father. She becomes unreachable, sullen. She does not bathe, does not warm herself by the kitchen fire, ceases to ask if she can go outdoors. She hardly eats. "The museum says they're searching, child," whispers Madame Manec, but when she tries to press her lips to Marie-Laure's forehead, the girl jerks backward as if burned.

The museum replies to Etienne's appeals; they report that Marie-Laure's father never arrived.

"Never arrived?" says Etienne aloud.

This becomes the question that drags its teeth through Marie-Laure's mind. Why didn't he make it to Paris? If he couldn't, why didn't he return to Saint-Malo?

I will never leave you, not in a million years.

She wants only to go home, to stand in their four-room flat and hear the chestnut tree rustle outside her window; hear the cheese seller raise his awning; feel her father's fingers close around hers.

If only she had begged him to stay.

Now everything in the house scares her: the creaking stairs, shuttered windows, empty rooms. The clutter and silence. Etienne tries performing silly experiments to cheer her: a vinegar volcano, a tornado in a bottle. "Can you hear it, Marie? Spinning in there?" She does not feign interest. Madame Manec brings her omelets, cassoulet, brochettes of fish, fabricating miracles out of ration tickets and the dregs of her cupboards, but Marie-Laure refuses to eat.

"Like a snail," she overhears Etienne say outside her door. "Curled up so tight in there."

But she is angry. At Etienne for doing so little, at Madame Manec for doing so much, at her father for not being here to help her understand his absence. At her eyes for failing her. At everything and everyone. Who knew love could kill you? She spends hours kneeling by herself on the sixth floor with the window open and the sea hurling arctic air into the room, her fingers on the model of Saint-Malo slowly going numb. South to the Gate of Dinan. West to the Plage du Môle. Back to the rue Vauborel. Every second Etienne's house grows colder; every second it feels as if her father slips farther away.

Prisoner

One February morning, the cadets are roused from their beds at two A.M. and driven out into the glitter. In the center of the quadrangle, torches burn. Keg-chested Bastian waddles out with his bare legs showing beneath his coat.

Frank Volkheimer emerges from the shadows, dragging a tattered and skeletal man in mismatched shoes. Volkheimer sets him down beside the commandant, where a stake has been driven into the snow. Methodically Volkheimer ties the man's torso to the stake.

A vault of stars hangs overhead; the collective breath of the cadets mingles slowly, nightmarishly above the courtyard.

Volkheimer retreats; the commandant paces.

"You boys would not believe what a creature this is. What a foul beast, a centaur, an *Untermensch.*"

Everyone cranes to see. The prisoner's ankles are cuffed and his arms bound from wrists to forearms. His thin shirt has split at the seams and he gazes into some middle distance with hypothermic slackness. He looks Polish. Russian, maybe. Despite his fetters, he manages to sway lightly back and forth.

Bastian says, "This man escaped from a work camp. Tried to violate a farmhouse and steal a liter of fresh milk. He was stopped before he could do something more nefarious." He gestures vaguely beyond the walls. "This barbarian would tear out your throats in a second if we let him."

Since the visit to Berlin, a great dread has been blooming inside Werner's chest. It came gradually, as slow-moving as the sun's passage across the sky, but now he finds himself writing letters to Jutta in which he must skirt the truth, must contend that everything is fine when things do not feel fine. He descends into dreams in which Frederick's mother mutates into a leering, small-mouthed demon and lowers Dr. Hauptmann's triangles over his head.

A thousand frozen stars preside over the quad. The cold is invasive, mindless.

"This look?" Bastian says, and flourishes his fat hand. "The way he's got nothing left? A German soldier never reaches this point. There's a name for this look. It's called 'circling the drain.' "

The boys try not to shiver. The prisoner

blinks down at the scene as if from a very high perch. Volkheimer returns carrying a clattering raft of buckets; two other seniors uncoil a water hose across the quadrangle. Bastian explains: First the instructors. Then upperclassmen. Everyone will file past and soak the prisoner with a bucket of water. Every man in the school.

They start. One by one, each instructor takes a full bucket from Volkheimer and flings its contents at the prisoner a few feet away. Cheers rise into the frozen night.

At the first two or three dousings, the prisoner comes awake, rocking back on his heels. Vertical creases appear between his eyes; he looks like someone trying to remember something vital.

Among the instructors in their dark capes, Dr. Hauptmann goes past, his gloved fingers pinching his collar around his throat. Hauptmann accepts his bucket and throws a sheet of water and doesn't linger to watch it land.

The water keeps coming. The prisoner's face empties. He slumps over the ropes propping him up, and his torso slides down the stake, and every now and then Volkheimer comes out of the shadows, looming fantastically huge, and the prisoner straightens again.

The upperclassmen vanish inside the castle. The buckets make a muted, frozen clanking as they are refilled. The sixteen-year-olds finish. The fifteen-year-olds finish. The cheers lose their gusto and a pure longing to flee floods Werner. Run. Run.

Three boys until his turn. Two boys. Werner tries to float images in front of his eyes, but the only ones that come are wretched: the hauling machine above Pit Nine; the hunched miners walking as if they dragged the weight of enormous chains. The boy from the entrance exams trembling before he fell. Everyone trapped in their roles: orphans, cadets, Frederick, Volkheimer, the old Jewess who lives upstairs. Even Jutta.

When his turn arrives, Werner throws the water like all the others and the splash hits the prisoner in the chest and a perfunctory cheer rises. He joins the cadets waiting to be released. Wet boots, wet cuffs; his hands have become so numb, they do not seem his own.

Five boys later, it is Frederick's turn. Frederick, who clearly cannot see well without his glasses. Who has not been cheering when each bucketful of water finds its mark. Who is frowning at the prisoner as though he recognizes something there.

And Werner knows what Frederick is going to do.

Frederick has to be nudged forward by the boy behind him. The upperclassman hands him a bucket and Frederick pours it out on the ground.

Bastian steps forward. His face flares scarlet in the cold. "Give him another."

Again Frederick sloshes it onto the ice at his feet. He says in a small voice, "He is already finished, sir."

The upperclassman hands over a third pail. "Throw it," commands Bastian. The night steams, the stars burn, the prisoner sways, the boys watch, the commandant tilts his head. Frederick pours the water onto the ground. "I will not."

Plage du Môle

Marie-Laure's father has been missing without word for twenty-nine days. She wakes to Madame Manec's blocky pumps climbing to the third floor the fourth the fifth.

Etienne's voice on the landing outside his study: "Don't."

"He won't know."

"She is my responsibility."

Some unexpected steel emerges in Madame Manec's voice. "I cannot stand by one moment longer."

She climbs the last flight. Marie-Laure's door creaks open; the old woman crosses the floor and places her heavy-boned hand on Marie-Laure's forehead. "You're awake?"

Marie-Laure rolls herself into the corner and speaks through linens. "Yes, Madame."

"I'm taking you out. Bring your cane."

Marie-Laure dresses herself; Madame Manec meets her at the bottom of the stairs with a heel of bread. She ties a scarf over Marie-Laure's head, buttons her coat all the way to the collar, and opens the front door. Morning in late February, and the air smells rainy and calm.

Marie-Laure hesitates, listening. Her heart beats two four six eight.

"Hardly anyone is out yet, dear," whispers Madame Manec. "And we are doing nothing wrong."

The gate creaks.

"One step down, now straight on, that's it." The cobbled street presses up irregularly against Marie-Laure's shoes; the tip of her cane catches, vibrates, catches again. A light rain falls on rooftops, trickles through runnels, beads up on her scarf. Sound ricochets between the high houses; she feels, as she did in her first hour here, as if she has stepped into a maze.

Far above them, someone shakes a duster out a window. A cat mewls. What terrors gnash their teeth out here? What was Papa so anxious to protect her from? They make one turn, then a second, and then Madame Manec steers her left where Marie-Laure does not expect her to, where the city walls, furred with moss, have been scrolling along unbroken, and they're stepping through a gateway.

"Madame?"

They pass out of the city.

"Stairs here, mind yourself, one down, two, there you are, easy as cake . . ."

The ocean. The ocean! Right in front of her! So close all this time. It sucks and booms and splashes and rumbles; it shifts and dilates and falls over itself; the labyrinth of Saint-Malo has opened onto a portal of sound larger than anything she has ever experienced. Larger than the Jardin des Plantes, than the Seine, larger than the grandest galleries of the museum. She did not imagine it properly; she did not comprehend the scale.

When she raises her face to the sky, she can feel the thousand tiny spines of raindrops melt onto her cheeks, her forehead. She hears Madame Manec's raspy breathing, and the deep sounding of the sea among the rocks, and the calls of someone down the beach echoing off the high walls. In her mind she can hear her father polishing locks. Dr. Geffard walking along the rows of his drawers. Why didn't they tell her it would be like this?

"That's Monsieur Radom calling to his dog," says Madame Manec. "Nothing to worry about. Here's my arm. Sit down and take off your shoes. Roll up your coat sleeves."

Marie-Laure does as she is told. "Are they watching?"

"The *Boches*? So what if they are? An old woman and a girl? I'll tell them we're digging clams. What can they do?"

"Uncle says they've buried bombs in the beaches."

"Don't you worry about that. He is frightened of an ant."

"He says the moon pulls the ocean back."

"The moon?"

"Sometimes the sun pulls too. He says that around the islands, the tides make funnels that can swallow boats whole."

"We aren't going anywhere near there, dear. We're just on the beach."

Marie-Laure unwinds her scarf and Madame Manec takes it. Briny, weedy, pewter-colored air slips down her collar.

"Madame?"

"Yes?"

"What do I do?"

"Just walk."

She walks. Now there are cold round pebbles beneath her feet. Now crackling weeds. Now something smoother: wet, unwrinkled sand. She bends and spreads her fingers. It's like cold silk. Cold, sumptuous silk onto which the sea has laid offerings: pebbles, shells, barnacles. Tiny slips of wrack. Her fingers dig and reach; the drops of rain touch the back of her neck, the backs of her hands. The sand pulls the heat from her fingertips, from the soles of her feet.

A months-old knot inside Marie-Laure begins to loosen. She moves along the tide line, almost crawling at first, and imagines the beach stretching off in either direction, ringing the promontory, embracing the outer islands, the whole filigreed tracery of the

Breton coastline with its wild capes and crumbling batteries and vine-choked ruins. She imagines the walled city behind her, its soaring ramparts, its puzzle of streets. All of it suddenly as small as Papa's model. But what surrounds the model is not something her father conveyed to her; what's beyond the model is the most compelling thing.

A flock of gulls squalls overhead. Each of the hundred thousand tiny grains of sand in her fists grinds against its neighbor. She feels her father pick her up and spin her around three times.

No occupation soldier comes to arrest them; no one even speaks to them. In three hours Marie-Laure's numb fingers discover a stranded jellyfish, an encrusted buoy, and a thousand polished stones. She wades to her knees and soaks the hem of her dress. When Madame Manec finally leads her — damp and dazzled — back to the rue Vauborel, Marie-Laure climbs all five flights and raps on the door of Etienne's study and stands before him, wet sand stuck all over her face.

"You were gone a long time," he murmurs. "I worried."

"Here, Uncle." From her pockets, she brings up shells. Barnacles, cowries, thirteen lumps of quartz gritty with sand. "I brought you this. And this and this and this."

Lapidary

In three months, Sergeant Major von Rumpel has traveled to Berlin and Stuttgart; he has assessed the value of a hundred confiscated rings, a dozen diamond bracelets, a Latvian cigarette case in which a lozenge of blue topaz twinkled; now, back in Paris, he has slept at the Grand Hôtel for a week and sent forth his queries like birds. Every night the moment returns to him: when he clasped that pear-shaped diamond between his thumb and forefinger, made huge by the lens of his loupe, and believed he held the one-hundred-and-thirty-three-carat Sea of Flames.

He stared into the stone's ice-blue interior, where miniature mountain ranges seemed to send back fire, crimsons and corals and violets, polygons of color twinkling and coruscating as he rotated it, and he almost convinced himself that the stories were true, that centuries ago a sultan's son wore a crown that blinded visitors, that the keeper of the diamond could never die, that the fabled stone had caromed down through the pegs of history and dropped into his palm.

There was joy in that moment — triumph. But an unexpected fear mixed with it; the stone looked like something enchanted, not meant for human eyes. An object that, once looked at, could never be forgotten.

But. Eventually reason won out. The joints of the diamond's facets were not quite as sharp as they should have been. The girdle just slightly waxy. More telling, the stone betrayed no delicate cracks, no pinpoints, not a single inclusion. *A real diamond,* his father used to say, *is never entirely free of inclusions. A real diamond is never perfect.*

Had he expected it to be real? To be kept precisely where he wished it would be? To win such a victory in a single day?

Of course not.

One might think von Rumpel would be frustrated, but he is not. On the contrary, he feels quite hopeful. The museum would never have commissioned such a high-quality fake if they did not possess the real thing somewhere. Over the past weeks in Paris, in the hours between other tasks, he has narrowed a list of seven lapidaries to three, then to one: a half-Algerian named Dupont who came of age cutting opal. It appears Dupont was making money before the war by faceting spinels into false diamonds for dowagers and baronesses. Also for museums.

One February midnight, von Rumpel lets himself into Dupont's fastidious shop not far from Sacré-Coeur. He examines a copy of Streeter's *Precious Stones and Gems;* drawings of cleavage panes; trigonometric charts used for faceting. When he finds several painstaking iterations of a mold that match exactly the size and pear-cut shape of the stone in the vault at the museum, he knows he has his man.

At von Rumpel's request, Dupont is furnished with forged food-ration tickets. Now von Rumpel waits. He prepares his questions: Did you make other replicas? How many? Do you know who has them now?

On the last day of February 1941, a dapper little Gestapo man comes to him with the news that the unwitting Dupont has tried to use the forged tickets. He has been arrested. *Kinderleicht:* child's play.

It's an attractive and drizzly winter's night, scraps of melting snow shored up against the edges of the Place de la Concorde, the city looking ghostly, its windows jeweled with raindrops. A close-cropped corporal checks von Rumpel's identification and points him not to a cell but to a high-ceilinged third-story office where a typist sits behind a desk. On the wall behind her, a painted wisteria vine frays into a tangled modernist spray of color that makes von Rumpel uneasy.

Dupont is cuffed to a cheap dining chair in

the center of the room. His face has the color and polish of tropical wood. Von Rumpel expected a mélange of fear and indignation and hunger, but Dupont sits upright. One of the lenses of his eyeglasses is already fractured, but otherwise he looks well enough.

The typist twists her cigarette into an ashtray, a bright red smear of lipstick on its butt. The ashtray is full: fifty stubs squashed in there, limbless, somehow gory.

"You can go," says von Rumpel, nodding at her, and levels his attention on the lapidary.

"He cannot speak German, sir."

"We will be fine," he says in French. "Shut the door, please."

Dupont looks up, some gland within him leaching courage into his blood. Von Rumpel does not have to force the smile; it comes easily enough. He hopes for names, but all he needs is a number.

Dearest Marie-Laure —
We are in Germany now and it is fine. I've managed to find an angel who will try to get this to you. The winter firs and alders are very beautiful here. And — you are not going to believe this, but you will have to trust me — they serve us wonderful food. First-class: quail and duck and stewed rabbit. Chicken legs and potatoes fried with bacon and apricot tarts. Boiled beef with carrots. Coq au vin on rice. Plum tarts. Fruits and crème glacée. As much as we can eat. I so look forward to the meals!

Be polite to your uncle and Madame too. Thank them for reading this to you. And know that I am always with you, that I am right beside you.

Your Papa

Entropy

For a week the dead prisoner remains strapped to the stake in the courtyard, his flesh frozen gray. Boys stop and ask the corpse directions; someone dresses him in a cartridge belt and helmet. After several days, a pair of crows take to standing on his shoulders, chiseling away with their beaks, and eventually the custodian comes out with two third-year boys and they hack the corpse's feet out of the ice with a maul and tip him into a cart and roll him away.

Three times in nine days, Frederick is chosen as the weakest in field exercises. Bastian walks out farther than ever, and counts more quickly than ever, so that Frederick has to run four or five hundred yards, often through deep snow, and the boys race after him as if their lives depend on it. Each time he is caught; each time he is drubbed while Bastian looks on; each time Werner does nothing to stop it.

Frederick lasts seven blows before falling.

Then six. Then three. He never cries out and never asks to leave, and this in particular seems to make the commandant quake with homicidal frustration. Frederick's dreaminess, his otherness — it's on him like a scent, and everyone can smell it.

Werner tries to lose himself in his work in Hauptmann's lab. He has constructed a prototype of their transceiver and tests fuses and valves and handsets and plugs — but even in those late hours, it is as if the sky has dimmed and the school has become a darker, ever more diabolical place. His stomach bothers him. He gets diarrhea. He wakes in distant quarters of the night and sees Frederick in his bedroom in Berlin, wearing his eyeglasses and necktie, freeing trapped birds from the pages of a massive book.

You're a smart boy. You'll do well.

One evening when Hauptmann is down the hall in his office, Werner glances over at imperious, sleepy Volkheimer in the corner and says, "That prisoner."

Volkheimer blinks, stone turning to flesh. "They do that every year." He takes off his cap and runs one hand over the dense stubble of his hair. "They say he's a Pole, a Red, a Cossack. He stole liquor or kerosene or money. Every year it's the same."

Under the seams of the hour, boys struggle in a dozen different arenas. Four hundred children crawling along the edge of a razor.

"Always the same phrase too," Volkheimer adds. " 'Circling the drain.' "

"But was it decent to leave him out there like that? Even after he was dead?"

"Decency does not matter to them." Then Hauptmann's crisp boot heels come clicking into the room, and Volkheimer leans back into the corner, and his eye sockets refill with shadow, and Werner does not have the chance to ask him which *them* he means.

Boys leave dead mice in Frederick's boots. They call him a poof, Blowjob, countless other juvenile sobriquets. Twice, a fifth-year takes Frederick's field glasses and smears the lenses with excrement.

Werner tells himself that he tries. Every night he polishes Frederick's boots for him until they shine a foot deep — one less reason for a bunk master, or Bastian, or an upperclassman to jump on him. Sunday mornings in the refectory, they sit quietly in a sunbeam and Werner helps him with his schoolwork. Frederick whispers that in the spring, he hopes to find skylark nests in the grasses outside the school walls. Once he lifts his pencil and stares into space and says, "Lesser spotted woodpecker," and Werner hears a bird's distant thrumming travel across the grounds and through the wall.

In technical sciences, Dr. Hauptmann introduces the laws of thermodynamics. "Entropy, who can say what that is?"

The boys hunch over their desks. No one raises a hand. Hauptmann stalks the rows. Werner tries not to twitch a single muscle.

"Pfennig."

"Entropy is the degree of randomness or disorder in a system, Doctor."

His eyes fix on Werner's for a heartbeat, a glance both warm and chilling. "Disorder. You hear the commandant say it. You hear your bunk masters say it. There must be order. Life is chaos, gentlemen. And what we represent is an ordering to that chaos. Even down to the genes. We are ordering the evolution of the species. Winnowing out the inferior, the unruly, the chaff. This is the great project of the Reich, the greatest project human beings have ever embarked upon."

Hauptmann writes on the blackboard. The cadets inscribe the words into their composition books. *The entropy of a closed system never decreases. Every process must by law decay.*

The Rounds

Although Etienne continues to offer objections, Madame Manec walks Marie-Laure to the beach every morning. The girl knots her shoes herself, feels her way down the stairwell, and waits in the foyer with her cane in her fist while Madame Manec finishes up in the kitchen.

"I can find my own way," Marie-Laure says the fifth time they step out. "You don't have to lead."

Twenty-two paces to the intersection with the rue d'Estrées. Forty more to the little gate. Nine steps down and she's on the sand and the twenty thousand sounds of the ocean engulf her.

She collects pinecones dropped by trees who knows how far away. Thick hanks of rope. Slick globules of stranded polyps. Once a drowned sparrow. Her greatest pleasure is to walk to the north end of the beach at low tide and squat below an island that Madame Manec calls Le Grand Bé and let her fingers whisk around in the tidepools. Only then, with her toes and fingers in the cold sea, does her mind seem to fully leave her father; only then does she stop wondering how much of his letter was true, when he'll write again, why he has been imprisoned. She simply listens, hears, breathes.

Her bedroom fills with pebbles, seaglass, shells: forty scallops along the windowsill, sixty-one whelks along the top of the armoire. She arranges them by species whenever she can, then by size. Smallest on the left, largest on the right. She fills jars, pails, trays; the room assumes the smell of the sea.

Most mornings, after the beach, she makes the rounds with Madame Manec, going to the vegetable market, occasionally to the butcher's, then delivering food to whichever neighbors Madame Manec decides are most in need. They climb an echoing stairwell, rap on a door; an old woman invites them in, asks for news, insists all three of them drink a thimbleful of sherry. Madame Manec's energy, Marie-Laure is learning, is extraordinary; she burgeons, shoots off stalks, wakes early, works late, concocts bisques without a drop of cream, loaves with less than a cup of flour. They clomp together through the narrow streets, Marie-Laure's hand on the back of Madame's apron, following the odors of her stews and cakes; in such moments Madame seems like a great moving wall of rosebushes, thorny and fragrant and crackling with bees.

Still-warm bread to an ancient widow named Madame Blanchard. Soup to Monsieur Saget. Slowly Marie-Laure's brain becomes a three-dimensional map in which exist glowing landmarks: a thick plane tree in the Place aux Herbes; nine potted topiaries outside the Hôtel Continental; six stairs up a passageway called the rue du Connétable.

Several days a week, Madame brings food to Crazy Harold Bazin, a veteran of the Great War who sleeps in an alcove behind the library in sun or snow. Who lost his nose, left ear, and eye to shellfire. Who wears an enameled copper mask over half his face.

Harold Bazin loves to talk about the walls and warlocks and pirates of Saint-Malo. Over the centuries, he tells Marie-Laure, the city ramparts have kept out bloodthirsty marauders, Romans, Celts, Norsemen. Some say sea monsters. For thirteen hundred years, he says, the walls kept out bloodthirsty English sailors who would park their ships offshore and launch flaming projectiles at the houses, who would try to burn everything and starve everybody, who would stop at nothing to kill them all.

"The mothers of Saint-Malo," he says, "used to tell their children: Sit up straight. Mind your manners. Or an Englishman will come in the night to cut your throat."

"Harold, please," says Madame Manec. "You'll frighten her."

In March, Etienne turns sixty and Madame Manec stews little clams — *palourdes* — with shallots and serves them alongside mushrooms and quarters of two hard-boiled eggs: the only two eggs, she reports, she could find in the city. Etienne talks in his soft voice about the eruption of Krakatoa, how, in all of his earliest memories, ash from the East Indies turned the sunsets over Saint-Malo blood-red, big veins of crimson glowing above the sea every evening; and to Marie-Laure, her pockets lined with sand, her face aglow from wind, the occupation seems, for a moment, a thousand miles away. She misses Papa, Paris, Dr. Geffard, the gardens, her books, her pinecones — all are holes in her life. But over these past few weeks, her existence has become tolerable. At least, out on the beaches, her privation and fear are rinsed away by wind and color and light.

Most afternoons, after making the morning rounds with Madame, Marie-Laure sits on her bed with the window open and travels her hands over her father's model of the city. Her fingers pass the shipbuilder's sheds on the rue de Chartres, pass Madame Ruelle's bakery on the rue Robert Surcouf. In her imagination she hears the bakers sliding about on the flour-slick floor, moving in the way she imagines ice skaters must move, baking loaves in the same four-hundred-year-old oven that Monsieur Ruelle's great-great-grandfather used. Her fingers pass the cathedral steps — here an old man clips roses in a garden; here, beside the library, Crazy Harold Bazin murmurs to himself as he peers with his one eye into an empty wine bottle; here is the convent; here's the restaurant Chez Chuche beside the fish market; here's Number 4 rue Vauborel, its door slightly recessed, where downstairs Madame Manec kneels beside her bed, shoes off, rosary beads slipping through fingers, a prayer for practically every soul in the city. Here, in a fifth-floor room, Etienne walks beside his empty shelves, trailing his fingers over the places where his radios once stood. And somewhere beyond the borders of the model, beyond the borders of France, in a place her fingers cannot reach, her father sits in a cell, a dozen of his whittled models on a windowsill, a guard coming toward him with what she wants very badly to believe is a feast — *quail and duck and stewed rabbit. Chicken legs and potatoes fried with bacon and apricot tarts* — a dozen trays, a dozen platters, as much as he can eat.

Nadel Im Heuhaufen

Midnight. Dr. Hauptmann's hounds bound through frozen fields beside the school, drops of quicksilver skittering through the white. Behind them comes Hauptmann in his fur cap, walking with short strides as though counting paces over some great distance. In the rear comes Werner, carrying the pair of transceivers he and Hauptmann have been testing for months.

Hauptmann turns, his face bright. "Nice spot here, good sight lines, set it down, Pfennig. I've sent our friend Volkheimer ahead. He's somewhere on the hill." Werner sees no tracks, only a humped swale of glitter in the moonlight, and the white forest beyond.

"He has the KX transmitter in an ammunition box," Hauptmann says. "He is to conceal himself and broadcast steadily until we find him or his battery dies. Even I do not know where he is." He smacks his gloved hands together, and the dogs swirl around him, their breath smoking. "Ten square kilometers.

Locate the transmitter, locate our friend."

Werner looks out at the ten thousand snow-mantled trees. "Out there, sir?"

"Out there." Hauptmann draws a flask from his pocket and unscrews it without looking at it. "This is the fun part, Pfennig."

Hauptmann stamps a clearing in the snow, and Werner sets up the first transceiver, uses measuring tape to pace off two hundred meters, and sets up the second. He uncoils the grounding wires, raises the aerials, and switches them on. Already his fingers are numb.

"Try eighty meters, Pfennig. Typically teams won't know what band to search. But for tonight, our first field test, we'll cheat a bit."

Werner puts on the headset and fills his ears with static. He dials up the RF gain, adjusts the filter. Before long, he has tuned in both receivers to Volkheimer's transmitter pinging along. "I have him, sir."

Hauptmann starts smiling in earnest. The dogs caper and sneeze with excitement. From his coat he produces a grease pencil. "Just do it on the radio. Teams won't always have paper, not in the field."

Werner sketches out the equation on the metal casing of the transceiver and starts plugging in numbers. Hauptmann hands him a slide rule. In two minutes Werner has a vector and a distance: two and a half kilometers.

"And the map?" Hauptmann's little aristocratic face gleams with pleasure.

Werner uses a protractor and compass to draw the lines.

"Lead on, Pfennig."

Werner folds the map into his coat pocket, packs up the transceivers, and carries one in each hand like matching suitcases. Tiny snow crystals sift down through the moonlight. Soon the school and its outbuildings look like toys on the white plain below. The moon slips lower, a half-lidded eye, and the dogs stick close to their master, mouths steaming, and Werner sweats.

They drop into a ravine and climb out. One kilometer. Two.

"Sublimity," Hauptmann says, panting, "you know what that is, Pfennig?" He is tipsy, animated, almost prattling. Never has Werner seen him like this. "It's the instant when one thing is about to become something else. Day to night, caterpillar to butterfly. Fawn to doe. Experiment to result. Boy to man."

Far up a third climb, Werner unfolds the map and double-checks his bearings with a compass. Everywhere the silent trees gleam. No tracks save their own. The school lost behind them. "Shall I set out the transceivers again, sir?"

Hauptmann puts his fingers to his lips.

Werner triangulates again and sees how close they are to his original reading — under half a kilometer. He repacks the transceivers and picks up his pace, hunting now, on the scent, all three dogs sensing it too, and Werner thinks: I have found a way in, I am solving it, the numbers are becoming real. And the trees unload siftings of snow and the dogs freeze and twitch their noses, locked on a scent, pointing as if at a pheasant, and Hauptmann holds up a palm, and finally Werner, coming up through a gap between trees, laboring as he carries the big cases, sees the form of a man lying faceup in the snow, transmitter at his feet, antenna rising into the low branches.

The Giant.

The dogs tremble in their stances. Hauptmann keeps his palm up. With his other hand, he unholsters his pistol. "This close, Pfennig, you cannot hesitate."

Volkheimer's left side faces them. Werner can see the vapor of his breath rise and disperse. Hauptmann aims his Walther right at Volkheimer, and for a long and startling moment, Werner is certain that his teacher is about to shoot the boy, that they are in grave danger, every single cadet, and he cannot help but hear Jutta as she stood beside the canal: *Is it right to do something only because everyone else is doing it?* Something in Werner's soul shuts its scaly eyes, and the little professor raises his pistol and fires it into the sky.

Volkheimer leaps immediately into a squat, his head coming around as the hounds release toward him, and Werner's heart feels as if it has been blown to pieces in his chest.

Volkheimer's arms come up as the dogs charge him, but they know him; they are leaping on him in play, barking and scampering, and Werner watches the huge boy throw off the dogs as if they were housecats. Dr. Hauptmann laughs. His pistol smokes, and he takes a long drink from his flask and passes it to Werner, and Werner puts it to his lips. He has pleased his professor after all; the transceivers work; he is out in the luminous, starlit night feeling the stinging glow of brandy flow into his gut —

"This," says Hauptmann, "is what we're doing with the triangles."

The dogs circle and duck and romp. Hauptmann relieves himself beneath the trees. Volkheimer trudges toward Werner lugging the big KX transmitter; he grows ever larger; he rests a huge mittened hand on Werner's cap.

"It's only numbers," he says, quietly enough that Hauptmann cannot hear.

"Pure math, cadet," adds Werner, mimicking Hauptmann's clipped accent. He presses his gloved fingertips together, all five to five. "You have to accustom yourself to thinking that way."

It is the first time Werner has heard Volkheimer laugh, and his countenance changes; he becomes less menacing and more like a benevolent, humongous child. More like the person he becomes when he listens to music.

All the next day the pleasure of his success lingers in Werner's blood, the memory of how it seemed almost holy to him to walk beside big Volkheimer back to the castle, down through the frozen trees, past the rooms of sleeping boys ranked like gold bars in strong-rooms — Werner felt an almost fatherly protectiveness for the others as he undressed beside his bunk, as lumbering Volkheimer continued on toward the dormitories of the upperclassmen, an ogre among angels, a keeper crossing a field of gravestones at night.

Proposal

Marie-Laure sits in her customary spot in the corner of the kitchen, closest to the fireplace, and listens to the friends of Madame Manec complain.

"The price of mackerel!" says Madame Fontineau. "You'd think they had to sail to Japan for it!"

"I cannot remember," says Madame Hébrard, the postmistress, "what a proper plum tastes like."

"And these ridiculous shoe ration coupons," says Madame Ruelle, the baker's wife. "Theo has number 3,501 and they haven't even called 400!"

"It's not just the brothels on the rue Thévenard anymore. They're giving all the summer apartments to the freelancers."

"Big Claude and his wife are getting extra fat."

"Damned *Boches* have their lights on all day!"

"I cannot bear one more night stuck indoors with my husband."

Nine of them sit around the square table, knees pressed to knees. Ration card restrictions, abysmal puddings, the deteriorating quality of fingernail varnish — these are crimes they feel in their souls. To hear so many of them in a room together confuses and excites Marie-Laure: they are giddy when they should be serious, somber after jokes; Madame Hébrard cries over the nonavailability of Demerara sugar; another woman's complaint about tobacco disintegrates midsentence into hysterics about the phenomenal size of the perfumer's backside. They smell of stale bread, of stuffy living rooms crammed with dark titanic Breton furnishings.

Madame Ruelle says, "So the Gautier girl wants to get married. The family has to melt all its jewelry to get the gold for the wedding ring. The gold gets taxed thirty percent by occupation authorities. Then the jeweler's work is taxed another thirty percent. By the time they've paid him, there's no ring left!"

The exchange rate is a farce, the price of carrots indefensible, duplicity lives everywhere. Eventually Madame Manec deadbolts the kitchen door and clears her throat. The women fall quiet.

"We're the ones who make their world run," Madame Manec says. "You, Madame Guiboux, your son repairs their shoes. Madame Hébrard, you and your daughter sort their mail. And you, Madame Ruelle, your bakery makes much of their bread."

The air stretches tight; Marie-Laure has the sense that they are watching someone slide onto thin ice or hold a palm over a flame.

"What are you saying?"

"That we do something."

"Put bombs in their shoes?"

"Poop in the bread dough?"

Brittle laughter.

"Nothing so bold as all that. But we could do smaller things. Simpler things."

"Like what?"

"First I need to know if you're willing."

A charged silence ensues. Marie-Laure can feel them all poised there. Nine minds swinging slowly around. She thinks of her father — imprisoned for what? — and aches.

Two women leave, claiming obligations involving grandchildren. Others tug at their blouses and rattle their chairs as though the temperature of the kitchen has gone up. Six remain. Marie-Laure sits among them, wondering who will cave, who will tattle, who will be the bravest. Who will lie on her back and let her last breath curl up to the ceiling as a curse upon the invaders.

You Have Other Friends

"Look out, Pusswood," Martin Burkhard yells as Frederick crosses the quad. "I'm coming for you tonight!" He convulses his pelvis maniacally.

Someone defecates on Frederick's bunk. Werner hears Volkheimer's voice: *Decency does not matter to them.*

"Bed-shitter," spits a boy, "bring me my boots."

Frederick pretends not to hear.

Night after night Werner retreats into Hauptmann's laboratory. Three times now they have gone out into the snow to track down Volkheimer's transmitter, and each time they have found him more directly. During the most recent field test, Werner managed to set up the transceivers, find the transmission, and plot Volkheimer's location on the map in under five minutes. Hauptmann promises trips to Berlin; he unrolls schematics from an electronics factory in Austria and says, "Several ministries have demonstrated enthusiasm for our project."

Werner is succeeding. He is being loyal. He is being what everybody agrees is good. And yet every time he wakes and buttons his tunic, he feels he is betraying something.

One night he and Volkheimer trudge back through the slush, Volkheimer carrying the transmitter, both receivers, and the folded antenna under one arm. Werner walks behind, content to be in his shadow. The trees drip; their branches seem moments away from erupting into bloom. Spring. In two more months Volkheimer will be given his commission and go to war.

They stop a moment so Volkheimer can rest, and Werner bends to examine one of the transceivers, draws a little screwdriver from his pocket, and tightens a loose hinge plate. Volkheimer looks down at him with great tenderness. "What you could be," he says.

That night Werner climbs into bed and stares up at the underside of Frederick's mattress. A warm wind blows against the castle, and somewhere a shutter bangs and snowmelt trickles down the long downspouts. As quietly as he can manage, he whispers, "Are you awake?"

Frederick leans over the side of his bunk, and for a moment in the nearly complete darkness Werner believes they will finally say to each other what they have not been able to say.

"You could go home, you know, to Berlin. Leave this place."

Frederick only blinks.

"Your mother wouldn't mind. She'd probably like to have you around. Franny too. Just for a month. Even a week. As soon as you leave, the cadets will let up, and by the time you return, they'll have moved on to someone else. Your father wouldn't even have to know."

But Frederick tips back into his bed and Werner can no longer see him. His voice comes reflecting down from the ceiling.

"Maybe it'd be better if we aren't friends anymore, Werner." Too loud, dangerously loud. "I know it's a liability, walking with me, eating with me, always folding my clothes and shining my boots and tutoring me. You have your studies to think of."

Werner clenches his eyes. A memory of his attic bedroom swamps him: clicking of mouse feet in the walls, sleet tapping the window. The ceiling so sloped he could stand only in the spot closest to the door. And the feeling that somewhere just behind his vision, ranged like spectators in a gallery, his mother and father and the Frenchman from the radio were all watching him through the rattling window to see what he would do.

He sees Jutta's crestfallen face, bent over the pieces of their broken radio. He has the sensation that something huge and empty is about to devour them all.

"That's not what I meant," Werner says into his blanket. But Frederick says nothing more, and both boys lie motionless a long time, watching the blue spokes of moonlight rotate through the room.

Old Ladies' Resistance Club

Madame Ruelle, the baker's wife — a pretty-voiced woman who smells mostly of yeast but also sometimes of face powder or the sweet perfume of sliced apples — straps a stepladder to the roof of her husband's car and drives the Route de Carentan at dusk with Madame Guiboux and rearranges road signs with a ratchet set. They return drunk and laughing to the kitchen of Number 4 rue Vauborel.

"Dinan is now twenty kilometers to the north," says Madame Ruelle.

"Right in the middle of the sea!"

Three days later, Madame Fontineau overhears that the German garrison commander is allergic to goldenrod. Madame Carré, the florist, tucks great fistfuls of it into an arrangement headed for the château.

The women funnel a shipment of rayon to the wrong destination. They intentionally misprint a train timetable. Madame Hébrard, the postmistress, slides an important-looking letter from Berlin into her underpants, takes it home, and starts her evening fire with it.

They come spilling into Etienne's kitchen with gleeful reports that someone has heard the garrison commander sneezing, or that the dog shit placed on a brothel doorstep reached the target of a German's shoe bottom perfectly. Madame Manec pours sherry or cider or Muscadet; someone sits stationed by the door to serve as sentry. Small and stooped Madame Fontineau boasts that she tied up the switchboard at the château for an hour; dowdy and strapping Madame Guiboux says she helped her grandsons paint a stray dog the colors of the French flag and sent it running through the Place Chateaubriand.

The women cackle, thrilled. "What can I do?" asks the ancient widow Madame Blanchard. "I want to do something."

Madame Manec asks everyone to give Madame Blanchard their money. "You'll get it back," she says, "don't worry. Now, Madame Blanchard, you've had beautiful handwriting all your life. Take this fountain pen of Master Etienne's. On every five-franc note, I want you to write, *Free France Now.* No one can afford to destroy money, right? Once everyone has spent their bills, our little message will go out all over Brittany."

The women clap. Madame Blanchard squeezes Madame Manec's hand and wheezes and blinks her glossy eyes in pleasure.

Sometimes Etienne comes down grumbling, one shoe on, and the whole kitchen goes quiet while Madame Manec fixes his tea and sets it on a tray and Etienne carries it back upstairs. Then the women start up again, scheming, gabbling. Madame Manec brushes Marie-Laure's hair in long absent-minded strokes. "Seventy-six years old," she whispers, "and I can still feel like this? Like a little girl with stars in my eyes?"

Diagnosis

The military doctor takes Sergeant Major von Rumpel's temperature. Inflates the blood pressure cuff. Examines his throat with a penlight. This very morning von Rumpel inspected a fifteenth-century davenport and supervised its installment onto a railcar meant for Marshal Göring's hunting lodge. The private who brought it to him described plundering the villa they took it from; he called it "shopping."

The davenport makes von Rumpel think of an eighteenth-century Dutch tobacco box made out of brass and copper and encrusted with tiny diamonds that he examined earlier this week, and the tobacco box sends his thoughts, as inexorably as gravity, back to the Sea of Flames. In his weaker moments, he imagines walking in some future hour between arcades of pillars in the great Führermuseum at Linz, his heels clacking smartly on the marble, twilight cascading through high windows. He sees a thousand crystalline display cases, so clear they seem to float above the floor; inside them wait the world's mineral treasures, harvested from every hole on the globe: dioptase and topaz and amethyst and California rubellite.

What was the phrase? *Like stars flung off the brows of archangels.*

And in the very center of the gallery, a spotlight falls through the ceiling onto a pedestal; there, inside a glass cube, glows a small blue stone . . .

The doctor asks von Rumpel to lower his trousers. Though the business of war has not let up for even a day, von Rumpel has been happy for months. His responsibilities are doubling; there are not, it turns out, a lot of Aryan diamond experts in the Reich. Just three weeks ago, outside a tiny sun-streaked station west of Bratislava, he examined an envelope full of perfectly clear, well-faceted stones; behind him rumbled a truck full of paintings wrapped in paper and packed in straw. The guards whispered that a Rembrandt was in there, and pieces of a famous altarpiece from Cracow. All being sent to a salt mine somewhere deep beneath the Austrian village of Altaussee, where a mile-long tunnel drops into a glittering arcade filled with shelving three stories high, upon which the high command is stacking Europe's finest art. They will assemble everything under one unassailable roof, a temple to the human endeavor. Visitors will marvel at it for a thousand years.

The doctor probes his groin. "No pain?"

"None."

"Nor here?"

"None."

It would have been too much to hope for names from the lapidary in Paris. Dupont, after all, would not have known who had been given the replicas of the diamond; he had no insight into the last-second safeguards of the museum. But Dupont was of service nonetheless; von Rumpel needed a number, and he got it.

Three.

The doctor says, "You may dress," and washes his hands at a sink.

In the two months leading up to the invasion of France, Dupont fashioned three replicas for the museum. Did he use the real diamond to make them? He used a casting. He never saw the real diamond. Von Rumpel believed him.

Three replicas. Plus the real stone. Somewhere on this planet among its sextillion grains of sand.

Four stones, one of them in the basement of the museum, locked in a safe. Three more to find. There are moments when von Rumpel feels impatience rising in him like bile, but he forces himself to swallow it back. It will come.

He buckles his belt. The doctor says, "We

need to take a biopsy. You will want to telephone your wife."

WEAKEST (#3)

The scales of cruelty tip. Maybe Bastian exacts some final vendetta; maybe Frederick goes looking for his only way out. All Werner knows for certain is that one April morning he wakes to find three inches of slush on the ground and Frederick not in his bunk.

He does not show at breakfast or poetics or morning field exercises. Each story Werner hears contains its own flaws and contradictions, as though the truth is a machine whose gears are not meshing. First he hears that a group of boys took Frederick out and set up torches in the snow and told him to shoot the torches with his rifle — to prove he had adequate eyesight. Then Werner hears that they brought him charts for eye exams, and when he could not read them, they force-fed the charts to him.

But what does the truth matter in this place? Werner imagines twenty boys closing over Frederick's body like rats; he sees the fat, gleaming face of the commandant, throat spilling out of his collar, reclined like a king on some high-backed oak throne, while blood slowly fills the floor, rises past his ankles, past his knees . . .

Werner skips lunch and walks in a daze to the school's infirmary. He's risking detention or worse; it's a sunny, bright noon, but his heart is being crushed slowly in a vise, and everything is slow and hypnotic, and he watches his arm work as it pulls open the door as if he's peering through several feet of blue water.

A single bed with blood in it. Blood on the pillow and on the sheets and even on the enameled metal of the bed frame. Pink rags in a basin. Half-unrolled bandage on the floor. The nurse bustles over and grimaces at Werner. Outside of the kitchens, she is the only woman at the school.

"Why so much blood?" he asks.

She sets four fingers across her lips. Debating perhaps whether to tell him or pretend she does not know. Accusation or resignation or complicity.

"Where is he?"

"Leipzig. For surgery." She touches a round white button on her uniform with what might be an inconveniently trembling finger. Otherwise her manner is entirely stern.

"What happened?"

"Shouldn't you be at noontime meal?"

Each time he blinks, he sees the men of his

childhood, laid-off miners drifting through back alleys, men with hooks for fingers and vacuums for eyes; he sees Bastian standing over a smoking river, snow falling all around him. *Führer, folk, fatherland. Steel your body, steel your soul.*

"When will he be back?"

"Oh," she says, a soft enough word. She shakes her head.

A blue soapbox on the table. Above it a portrait of some foregone officer in a crumbling frame. Some previous boy sent through this place to die.

"Cadet?"

Werner has to sit on the bed. The nurse's face seems to occupy multiple distances, a mask atop a mask atop a mask. What is Jutta doing at this exact moment? Wiping the nose of some wailing newborn or collecting newspapers or listening to presentations from army nurses or darning another sock? Praying for him? Believing in him?

He thinks: I will never be able to tell her about this.

Dearest Marie-Laure —
The others in my cell are mostly kind. Some tell jokes. Here's one: Have you heard about the Wehrmacht exercise program? Yes, each morning you raise your hands above your head and leave them there!

Ha ha. My angel has promised to deliver this letter for me at great risk. It is very safe and nice to be out of the "Gasthaus" for a bit. We are building a road now and the work is good. My body is getting stronger. Today I saw an oak tree disguised as a chestnut tree. I think it is called a chestnut oak. I would like very much to ask some of the botanists in the gardens about it when we get home.

I hope you and Madame and Etienne will keep sending things. They say we will be allowed to receive one parcel each, so something has to get through eventually. I doubt they would let me keep any tools but it would be wonderful if they would. You absolutely would not believe how pretty it is here, *ma chérie,* and how far we are from danger. I am incredibly safe, as safe as safe can be.

Your Papa

Grotto

It's summer and Marie-Laure is sitting in the alcove behind the library with Madame Manec and Crazy Harold Bazin. Through his copper mask, through a mouthful of soup, Harold says, "I want to show you something."

He leads Marie-Laure and Madame Manec down what Marie-Laure thinks is the rue du Boyer, though it could be the rue Vincent de Gournay or the rue des Hautes Salles. They reach the base of the ramparts and turn right, following a lane Marie-Laure has not been on before. They descend two steps, pass through a curtain of hanging ivy, and Madame Manec says, "Harold, please, what is this?" The alley grows narrower and narrower until they must walk single file, the walls close on either side, and then they stop. Marie-Laure can feel stone blocks mounting vertically on both sides to brush their shoulders: they seem to rise forever. If her father has built this alley into his model, her fingers have not discovered it yet.

Harold rummages in his filthy trousers, breathing hard behind his mask. Where the wall of the ramparts should be, on their left, Marie-Laure hears a lock give way. A gate creaks open. "Watch your head," he says, and helps her through. They clamber down into a cramped, moist space that positively reeks of the sea. "We're beneath the wall. Twenty meters of granite on top of us."

Madame says, "Really, Harold, it's gloomy as a graveyard in here," but Marie-Laure ventures a bit farther, the soles of her shoes slipping, the floor angling down, and then her shoes touch water.

"Feel this," says Harold Bazin, and crouches and brings her hand to a curved wall which is completely studded with snails. Hundreds of them. Thousands.

"So many," she whispers.

"I don't know why. Maybe because they're safe from gulls? Here, feel this, I'll turn it over." Hundreds of tiny, squirming hydraulic feet beneath a horny, ridged top: a sea star. "Blue mussels here. And here's a dead stone crab, can you feel his claw? Watch your head now."

The surf breaks nearby; water purls past her shoes. Marie-Laure wades forward; the floor of the room is sandy, the water barely ankle-deep. From what she can tell, it's a low grotto, maybe four yards long and half as wide, shaped like a loaf of bread. At the far end is a thick grate through which lustrous, clear sea wind washes. Her fingertips discover barnacles, weeds, a thousand more snails. "What is this place?"

"Remember I told you about the dogs of the watch? A long time ago, city kennel keepers would keep the mastiffs in here, dogs as big as horses. At night a curfew bell would ring, and the dogs would be let loose onto the beaches to eat any sailor who dared come ashore. Somewhere beneath those mussels is a stone with the date 1165 scratched into it."

"But the water?"

"Even at the highest tides, it doesn't get more than waist-deep. Back then the tides might have been lower. We used to play in here as boys. Me and your grandfather. Sometimes your great-uncle too."

The tide flows past their feet. Everywhere mussels click and sigh. She thinks of the wild old seamen who lived in this town, smugglers and pirates, sailing over the dark seas, winding their ships between ten thousand reefs.

"Harold, we should go now," calls Madame Manec, her voice echoing. "This is no place for a young girl."

Marie-Laure calls, "It's fine, Madame." Hermit crabs. Anemones sending out a tiny jet of seawater when she pokes them. Galaxies of snails. A story of life immanent in each.

Finally Madame Manec coaxes them out of the kennel, and Crazy Harold leads Marie-

Laure back through the gate and locks it behind them. Before they reach the Place Broussais, Madame Manec walking out front, he taps Marie-Laure's shoulder. His whisper comes in her left ear; his breath smells like crushed insects. "Could you find that place again, do you think?"

"I think so."

He puts something iron in her hand. "Do you know what it is?"

Marie-Laure closes her fist. "It's a key."

Intoxicated

Every day there is word of another victory, another advance. Russia collapses like an accordion. In October the student body gathers around a big wireless to listen to the führer declare Operation Typhoon. German companies plant flags miles from Moscow; Russia will be theirs.

Werner is fifteen. A new boy sleeps in Frederick's bed. Sometimes at night, Werner sees Frederick when he is not there. His face appears over the edge of the upper bunk, or his silhouette presses binoculars to the windowpane. Frederick: who did not die but did not recover. Broken jaw, cracked skull, brain trauma. No one was punished, no one questioned. A blue automobile came to the school and Frederick's mother got out and walked into the commandant's residence and emerged soon afterward, tilted against the weight of Frederick's duffel bag, looking very small. She climbed back into the car and it drove away.

Volkheimer is gone; there are stories that he has become a fearsome sergeant in the Wehrmacht. That he led a platoon into the last town on the road to Moscow. Hacked off the fingers of dead Russians and smoked them in a pipe.

The newest crop of cadets grow wild in their urgency to prove themselves. They sprint, shout, hurl themselves over obstacles; in field exercises they play a game where ten boys get red armbands and ten get black. The game ends when one team has all twenty.

It seems to Werner as if all the boys around him are intoxicated. As if, at every meal, the cadets fill their tin cups not with the cold mineralized water of Schulpforta but with a spirit that leaves them glazed and dazzled, as if they ward off a vast and inevitable tidal wave of anguish only by staying forever drunk on rigor and exercise and gleaming boot leather. The eyes of the most bullheaded boys radiate a shining determination: every ounce of their attention has been trained to ferret out weakness. They study Werner with suspicion when he returns from Hauptmann's lab. They do not trust that he's an orphan, that he's often alone, that his accent carries a whisper of the French he learned as a child.

We are a volley of bullets, sing the newest cadets, *we are cannonballs. We are the tip of the sword.*

Werner thinks of home all the time. He

misses the sound of rain on the zinc roof above his dormer; the feral energy of the orphans; the scratchy singing of Frau Elena as she rocks a baby in the parlor. The smell of the coking plant coming in under the dawn, the first reliable smell of every day. Mostly he misses Jutta: her loyalty, her obstinacy, the way she always seems to recognize what is right.

Though in Werner's weaker moments, he resents those same qualities in his sister. Perhaps she's the impurity in him, the static in his signal that the bullies can sense. Perhaps she's the only thing keeping him from surrendering totally. If you have a sister back home, you're supposed to think of her as a pretty girl in a propaganda poster: rosy-cheeked, brave, steadfast. She's whom you fight for. Whom you die for. But Jutta? Jutta sends letters that the school censor blacks out almost completely. She asks questions that should not be asked. Only Werner's affiliation with Dr. Hauptmann — his privileged status as the favorite of the technical sciences professor — keeps him safe. A company in Berlin is producing their transceiver, and already some of their units are coming back from what Hauptmann calls "the field," blown apart or burned or drowned in mud or defective, and Werner's job is to rebuild them while Hauptmann talks into his telephone or writes requisitions for replacement parts or spends whole fortnights away from the school.

Weeks pass without a letter to Jutta. Werner writes four lines, a smattering of platitudes — *I am fine; I am so busy* — and hands it to the bunk master. Dread swamps him.

"You have minds," Bastian murmurs one evening in the refectory, each boy hunching almost imperceptibly farther over his food as the commandant's finger grazes the back of his uniform. "But minds are not to be trusted. Minds are always drifting toward ambiguity, toward questions, when what you really need is certainty. Purpose. Clarity. Do not trust your minds."

Werner sits in the lab late at night, alone again, and trolls the frequencies on the Grundig tube radio that Volkheimer used to borrow from Hauptmann's office, searching for music, for echoes, for what, he is not sure. He sees circuits break apart and re-form. He sees Frederick staring into his book of birds; he sees the furor of the mines at Zollverein, the shunting cars, the banging locks, the trundling conveyors, smokestacks silting the sky day and night; he sees Jutta slashing back and forth with a lit torch as darkness encroaches from all sides. Wind presses against the walls of the lab — wind, the commandant loves to remind them, that comes all the way from Russia, a Cossack wind, the wind of candle-eating barbarians with hogs' heads who will stop at nothing to drink the blood of German girls. Gorillas who must be wiped off the earth.

Static static.

Are you there?

Finally he shuts off the radio. Into the stillness come the voices of his masters, echoing from one side of his head while memory speaks from the other.

Open your eyes and see what you can with them before they close forever.

The Blade and the Whelk

The Hôtel-Dieu dining room is big and somber and full of people talking about U-boats off Gibraltar and the inequities of currency exchange and four-stroke marine diesel engines. Madame Manec orders two bowls of chowder that she and Marie-Laure promptly finish. She says she does not know what to do next — should they keep waiting? — so she orders two more.

At last a man in rustling clothing sits down with them. "You are sure your name is Madame Walter?"

Madame Manec says, "You are sure your name is René?"

A pause.

"And her?"

"My accomplice. She can tell if someone is lying just by hearing him speak."

He laughs. They talk about the weather. Sea air exudes from the man's clothes, as if he has been blown here by a gale. While he talks, he makes ungainly movements and bumps the table so that the spoons clatter in their bowls. Finally he says, "We admire your efforts, Madame."

The man who calls himself René starts talking extremely softly. Marie-Laure catches only phrases: "Look for special insignia on their license plates. *WH* for army, *WL* for air force, *WM* for navy. And you could note — or find someone who could — every vessel that comes in and out of the harbor. This information is very much in demand."

Madame Manec is quiet. If more is said that Marie-Laure cannot overhear — if there is a pantomime going on between them, notes passed, stratagems agreed upon — she cannot say. Some level of accord is reached, and soon enough she and Madame Manec are back in the kitchen at Number 4 rue Vauborel. Madame Manec clatters around in the cellar and hauls up canning supplies. This very morning, she announces, she has managed to procure what might be the last two crates of peaches in France. She hums as she helps Marie-Laure with the peeler.

"Madame?"

"Yes, Marie."

"What is a pseudonym?"

"It is a fake name, an alternate name."

"If I were to have one, what sort of name could I choose?"

"Well," says Madame Manec. She pits and quarters another peach. "You can be anything. You can be the Mermaid if you like. Or Daisy? Violet?"

"How about the Whelk? I think I would like to be the Whelk."

"The Whelk. That is an excellent pseudonym."

"And you, Madame? What would you like to be?"

"Me?" Madame Manec's knife pauses. Crickets sing in the cellar. "I think I would like to be the Blade."

"The Blade?"

"Yes." The perfume of the peaches makes a bright ruddy cloud.

"The Blade?" repeats Marie-Laure. Then they both start laughing.

Dear Werner,

Why don't you write? ████████ ████████████████ The foundries run day and night and the stacks never stop smoking and it's been cold here so everyone burns everything to stay warm. Sawdust, hard coal, soft coal, lime, garbage. War widows ████████ ████████████████ and every day there are more. I'm working at the laundry with the twins, Hannah and Susanne, and Claudia Förster, you remember her, we're mending tunics and trousers mostly. I'm getting better with a needle so at least I'm not pricking myself all the time. Right now I just finished my homework. Do you have homework? There are fabric shortages and people bring in slipcovers, curtains, old coats. Anything that can be used they say must be used. Just like all of us here. Ha. I found this under your old cot. Seems like you could use it.

Love,
Jutta

Inside the homemade envelope waits Werner's childhood notebook, his handwriting across the cover: *Questions.* Across its pages swarm boyhood drawings, inventions: an electric bed heater he wanted to build for Frau Elena; a bicycle with chains to drive both wheels. *Can magnets affect liquids? Why do boats float? Why do we feel dizzy when we spin?*

A dozen empty pages at the back. Juvenile enough, presumably, to make it past the censor.

Around him sounds the din of boots, clatter of rifles. Stocks on the ground, barrels against the wall. Grab cups off hooks, plates off racks. Queue up for boiled beef. Over him breaks a wave of homesickness so acute that he has to clamp his eyes.

Alive Before You Die

Madame Manec goes into Etienne's study on the fifth floor. Marie-Laure listens on the stairs.

"You could help," Madame says. Someone — likely Madame — opens a window, and the bright air of the sea washes onto the landing, stirring everything: Etienne's curtains, his papers, his dust, Marie-Laure's longing for her father.

Etienne says, "Please, Madame. Close the window. They are rounding up blackout offenders."

The window stays open. Marie-Laure creeps down another stair.

"How do you know whom they round up, Etienne? A woman in Rennes was given nine months in prison for naming one of her hogs Goebbels, did you know that? A palm reader in Cancale was shot for predicting de Gaulle would return in the spring. Shot!"

"Those are only rumors, Madame."

"Madame Hébrard says that a Dinard man

— a grandfather, Etienne — was given two years in prison for wearing the Cross of Lorraine under his collar. I heard they're going to turn the whole city into a big ammunition dump."

Her great-uncle laughs softly. "It all sounds like something a sixth-former would make up."

"Every rumor carries a seed of truth, Etienne."

All of Etienne's adult life, Marie-Laure realizes, Madame Manec has tended his fears. Skirted them, mitigated them. She creeps down one more stair.

Madame Manec is saying, "You know things, Etienne. About maps, tides, radios."

"It's already too dangerous, all those women in my house. People have eyes, Madame."

"Who?"

"The perfumer, for one."

"Claude?" She snorts. "Little Claude is too busy smelling himself."

"Claude is not so little anymore. Even I can see his family gets more than the others: more meat, more electricity, more butter. I know how such prizes are won."

"Then help us."

"I don't want to make trouble, Madame."

"Isn't doing nothing a kind of troublemaking?"

"Doing nothing is doing nothing."

"Doing nothing is as good as collaborating."

The wind gusts. In Marie-Laure's mind, it shifts and gleams, draws needles and thorns in the air. Silver then green then silver again.

"I know ways," says Madame Manec.

"What ways? Whom have you put your trust in?"

"You have to trust someone sometime."

"If your same blood doesn't run in the arms and legs of the person you're next to, you can't trust anything. And even then. It's not a person you wish to fight, Madame, it's a system. How do you fight a system?"

"You try."

"What would you have me do?"

"Dig out that old thing in the attic. You used to know more about radios than anyone in town. Anyone in Brittany, perhaps."

"They've taken all the receivers."

"Not all. People have hidden things everywhere. You'd only have to read numbers, is how I understand it, numbers on strips of paper. Someone — I don't know who, maybe Harold Bazin — will bring them to Madame Ruelle, and she'll collect them and bake the messages right into the bread. Right into it!" She laughs; to Marie-Laure, her voice sounds twenty years younger.

"Harold Bazin. You are trusting Harold Bazin? You are cooking secret codes into bread?"

"What fat Kraut is going to eat those awful

loaves? They take all the good flour for themselves. We bring home the bread, you transmit the numbers, then we burn the piece of paper."

"This is ridiculous. You act like children."

"It's better than not acting at all. Think of your nephew. Think of Marie-Laure."

Curtains flap and papers rustle and the two adults have a standoff in the study. Marie-Laure has crept so close to her great-uncle's doorway that she can touch the door frame.

Madame Manec says, "Don't you want to be alive before you die?"

"Marie is almost fourteen years old, Madame. Not so young, not during war. Fourteen-year-olds die the same as anybody else. But I want fourteen to be young. I want —"

Marie-Laure scoots back up a step. Have they seen her? She thinks of the stone kennel Crazy Harold Bazin led her to: the snails gathered in their multitudes. She thinks of the many times her father put her on his bicycle: she'd balance on the seat, and he would stand on the pedals, and they'd glide out into the roar of some Parisian boulevard. She'd hold his hips and bend her knees, and they'd fly between cars, down hills, through gauntlets of odor and noise and color.

Etienne says, "I am going back to my book, Madame. Shouldn't you be preparing dinner?"

No Out

In January 1942, Werner goes to Dr. Hauptmann in his glowing, firelit office, twice as warm as the rest of the castle, and asks to be sent home. The little doctor is sitting behind his big desk with an anemic-looking roasted bird on a dish in front of him. Quail or dove or grouse. Rolls of schematics on his right. His hounds splay on the rug before the fire.

Werner stands with his cap in his hands. Hauptmann shuts his eyes and runs a fingertip across one eyebrow. Werner says, "I will work to pay the train fare, sir."

The blue fretwork of veins in Hauptmann's forehead pulsates. He opens his eyes. "You?" The dogs look up as one, a three-headed hydra. "You who gets everything? Who comes here and listens to concerts and nibbles chocolates and warms yourself by the fire?"

A shred of roasted bird dances on Hauptmann's cheek. Perhaps for the first time, Werner sees in his teacher's thinning blond hair, in his black nostrils, in his small, almost elfin ears, something pitiless and inhuman, something determined only to survive.

"Perhaps you believe you are somebody now? Somebody of importance?"

Werner clenches his cap behind his back to keep his shoulders from quaking. "No, sir."

Hauptmann folds his napkin. "You are an orphan, Pfennig, with no allies. I can make you whatever I want to make you. A troublemaker, a criminal, an adult. I can send you to the front and make sure you are crouched in a trench in the ice until the Russians cut off your hands and feed them to you."

"Yes, sir."

"You will be given your orders when the school is ready to give you your orders. No sooner. We serve the Reich, Pfennig. It does not serve us."

"Yes, sir."

"You will come to the lab tonight. As usual."

"Yes, sir."

"No more chocolates. No more special treatment."

In the hall with the door shut behind him, Werner presses his forehead against the wall, and a vision of his father's last moments comes to him, the crushing press of the tunnels, the ceiling lowering. Jaw pinned against the floor. Skull splintering. I cannot go home, he thinks. And I cannot stay.

The Disappearance of Harold Bazin

Marie-Laure follows the odor of Madame Manec's soup through the Place aux Herbes and holds the warm pot outside the alcove behind the library while Madame raps on the door.

Madame says, "Where is Monsieur Bazin?"

"Must have moved on," says the librarian, though the doubt in his voice is only partially disguised.

"Where could Harold Bazin move to?"

"I'm not sure, Madame Manec. Please. It is cold."

The door closes. Madame Manec swears. Marie-Laure thinks of Harold Bazin's stories: lugubrious monsters made of sea foam, mermaids with fishy private parts, the romance of English sieges. "He'll be back," says Madame Manec, as much to herself as to Marie-Laure. But the next morning Harold Bazin is not back. Or the next.

Only half the group attends the following meeting.

"Do they think he was helping us?" whispers Madame Hébrard.

"Was he helping us?"

"I thought he was carrying messages."

"What sort of messages?"

"It is getting too dangerous."

Madame Manec paces; Marie-Laure can almost feel the heat of her frustration from across the room. "Leave, then." Her voice smolders. "All of you."

"Don't be rash," says Madame Ruelle. "We'll take a break, a week or two. Wait for things to settle."

Harold Bazin with his copper mask and boyish avidity and his breath like crushed insects. Where, Marie-Laure wonders, do they take people? The *"Gasthaus"* her father was taken to? Where they write letters home about wonderful food and mythical trees? The baker's wife claims they're sent to camps in the mountains. The grocer's wife says they're sent to nylon factories in Russia. It seems as likely to Marie-Laure that the people just disappear. The soldiers throw a bag over whomever they want to remove, run electricity through him, and then that person is gone, vanished. Expelled to some other world.

The city, thinks Marie-Laure, is slowly being remade into the model upstairs. Streets sucked empty one by one. Each time she steps outside, she becomes aware of all the windows above her. The quiet is fretful, unnatural. It's what a mouse must feel, she thinks, as it steps from its hole into the open blades of a meadow, never knowing what shadow might come cruising above.

EVERYTHING POISONED

New silk banners hang above the refectory tables, ablaze with slogans.

They say, *Disgrace is not to fall but to lie.*

They say, *Be slim and slender, as fast as a greyhound, as tough as leather, as hard as Krupp steel.*

Every few weeks another instructor vanishes, sucked up into the engine of the war. New instructors, elderly townsmen of unreliable sobriety and disposition, are brought in. All of them, Werner notices, are in some way broken: they limp, or are blind in one eye, or their faces are lopsided from strokes or the previous war. The cadets show less respect to the new instructors, who in turn have shorter tempers, and soon the school feels to Werner like a grenade with its pin pulled.

Strange things start happening with the electricity. It goes out for fifteen minutes, then surges. Clocks run fast, lightbulbs brighten, flare, and pop, and send a soft rain of glass falling into the corridors. Days of darkness ensue, the switches dead, the grid empty. The bunk rooms and showers become icy; for lighting, the caretaker resorts to torches and candles. All the gasoline is going to the war, and few cars come trundling through the school gates; food is delivered by the same withered mule, its ribs showing as it drags its cart.

More than once Werner slices the sausage on his plate to find pink worms squirming inside. The uniforms of the new cadets are stiffer and cheaper than his own; no longer do they have access to live ammunition for marksmanship. Werner would not be surprised if Bastian started handing out rocks and sticks.

And yet all the news is good. *We are at the gates to the Caucasus,* proclaims Hauptmann's radio, *we have taken oil fields, we will take Svalbard. We move with astounding speed. Five thousand seven hundred Russians killed, forty-five Germans lost.*

Every six or seven days, the same two pallid casualty assistance officers enter the refectory, and four hundred faces go ashen from the effort of not turning to watch. The boys move only their eyes, only their thoughts, tracking in their minds the passage of the two officers as they move between tables, seeking out the next boy whose father has been killed.

The cadet they stop behind often tries to

pretend that he doesn't notice their presence. He puts his fork in his mouth and chews, and usually it is then that the taller officer, a sergeant, sets a hand on the boy's shoulder. The boy looks up at them with a full mouth and an unsteady face, and follows the officers out, and the big oak double doors creak shut, and the lunchroom slowly exhales and edges back to life.

Reinhard Wöhlmann's father falls. Karl Westerholzer's father falls. Martin Burkhard's father falls, and Martin tells everybody — on the very same night his shoulder is tapped — that he is happy. "Doesn't everything," he says, "die at last and too soon? Who would not be honored to fall? To be a paving stone on the road to final victory?" Werner looks for uneasiness in Martin's eyes but cannot find it.

For Werner, doubts turn up regularly. Racial purity, political purity — Bastian speaks to a horror of any sort of corruption, and yet, Werner wonders in the dead of night, isn't life a kind of corruption? A child is born, and the world sets in upon it. Taking things from it, stuffing things into it. Each bite of food, each particle of light entering the eye — the body can never be pure. But this is what the commandant insists upon, why the Reich measures their noses, clocks their hair color.

The entropy of a closed system never decreases.

At night Werner stares up at Frederick's bunk, the thin slats, the miserable stained mattress. Another new boy sleeps up there, Dieter Ferdinand, a small muscular kid from Frankfurt who does everything he is told with a terrifying ferocity.

Someone coughs; someone else moans. A train sounds its lonesome whistle somewhere out beyond the lakes. To the east, always the trains move to the east, beyond the rims of the hills; they go to the huge trodden borderlands of the front. Even as he sleeps, the trains are moving. The catapults of history rattling past.

Werner laces his boots and sings the songs and marches the marches, acting less out of duty than out of a timeworn desire to be dutiful. Bastian walks the rows of boys at their dinners. "What's worse than death, boys?"

Some poor cadet is called to attention. "Cowardice!"

"Cowardice," agrees Bastian, and the boy sits while the commandant slogs forward, nodding to himself, pleased. Lately the commandant speaks more and more intimately of the führer and the latest thing — prayers, petroleum, loyalty — that he requires. The führer requires trustworthiness, electricity, boot leather. Werner is beginning to see, approaching his sixteenth birthday, that what the führer really requires is boys. Great rows of them walking to the conveyor belt to climb on. Give up cream for the führer, sleep for the führer, aluminum for the führer. Give up Reinhard Wöhlmann's father and Karl Westerholzer's father and Martin Burkhard's father.

In March 1942, Dr. Hauptmann calls Werner into his office. Half-packed crates litter the floor. The hounds are nowhere to be seen. The little man paces, and it is not until Werner announces himself that Hauptmann stops. He looks as if he is slowly being engulfed by something beyond his control. "I have been called to Berlin. They want me to continue my work there." Hauptmann lifts an hourglass from a shelf and sets it in a crate, and his pale silver-tipped fingers hang in the air.

"It will be as you dreamed, sir. The best equipment, the best minds."

"That is all," says Dr. Hauptmann.

Werner steps into the hall. Out on the snow-dusted quad, thirty first-formers jog in place, their breath showing in short-lived plumes. Chubby, slick-chinned, abominable Bastian yells something. He raises one short arm and the boys turn on their heels, raise their rifles above their heads, and run faster in place, their knees flashing in the moonlight.

VISITORS

The electric bell rings at Number 4 rue Vauborel. Etienne LeBlanc, Madame Manec, and Marie-Laure stop chewing at the same time, each thinking: They have found me out. The transmitter in the attic, the women in the kitchen, the hundred trips to the beach.

Etienne says, "You are expecting someone?"

Madame Manec says, "No one." The women would come to the kitchen door.

The bell rings again.

All three go to the foyer; Madame Manec opens the door.

French policemen, two of them. They are there, they explain, at the request of the Natural History Museum in Paris. The jarring of their boot heels on the boards of the foyer seems loud enough to shatter the windows. The first one is eating something — an apple, Marie-Laure decides. The second smells of shaving balm. And roasted meat. As if they have been feasting.

All five — Etienne, Marie-Laure, Madame

Manec, and the two men — sit in the kitchen around the square table. The men refuse a bowl of stew. The first clears his throat. "Right or wrong," he says, "he has been convicted of theft and conspiracy."

"All prisoners, political or otherwise," says the second, "are forced to do labor, even if they have not been sentenced to it."

"The museum has written to wardens and prison directors all over Germany."

"We do not yet know exactly which prison."

"We believe it could be Breitenau."

"We're certain they did not hold a proper tribunal."

Etienne's voice comes spiraling up from beside Marie-Laure. "Is that a good prison? I mean, one of the better ones?"

"I'm afraid there are no good German prisons."

A truck passes in the street. The sea folds onto the Plage du Môle fifty yards away. She thinks: They just say words, and what are words but sounds these men shape out of breath, weightless vapors they send into the air of the kitchen to dissipate and die. She says: "You have come all this way to tell us things we already know."

Madame Manec takes her hand.

Etienne murmurs, "We did not know about this place called Breitenau."

The first policeman says, "You told the

museum he has managed to smuggle out two letters?"

The second: "May we see them?"

Off goes Etienne, content to believe that someone is on the job. Marie-Laure ought to be happy too, but something makes her suspicious. She remembers something her father said back in Paris, on the first night of the invasion, as they waited for a train. *Everyone is looking out for himself.*

The first policeman snaps flesh off his apple with his teeth. Are they looking at her? To be so close to them makes her feel faint. Etienne returns with both letters, and she can hear the men passing the pages back and forth.

"Did he speak of anything before he left?"

"Of any particular activities or errands we should be aware of?"

Their French is good, very Parisian, but who knows where their loyalties lie? *If your same blood doesn't run in the arms and legs of the person you're next to, you can't trust anything.* Everything feels compressed and submarine to Marie-Laure just then, as if the five of them have been submerged into a murky aquarium overfull of fish, and their fins keep bumping as they shift about.

She says, "My father is not a thief."

Madame Manec's hand squeezes hers.

Etienne says, "He seemed concerned for his job, for his daughter. For France, of course. Who wouldn't be?"

"Mademoiselle," says the first man. He is talking directly to Marie-Laure. "Was there no specific thing he mentioned?"

"Nothing."

"He had many keys at the museum."

"He turned in his keys before he left."

"May we look at whatever he brought here with him?"

The second man adds, "His bags, perhaps?"

"He took his rucksack with him," says Marie-Laure, "when the director asked him to return."

"May we look anyway?"

Marie-Laure can feel the gravity in the room increase. What do they hope to find? She imagines the radio equipment high above her: microphone, transceiver, all those dials and switches and cables.

Etienne says, "You may."

They go into every room. Third floor fourth fifth. On the sixth, they stand in her grandfather's old bedroom and open the huge wardrobe with its heavy doors and cross the hall and stand over the model of Saint-Malo in Marie-Laure's room and whisper to each other and then tromp back downstairs.

They ask a total of one question: about three Free French flags rolled up in a second-floor closet. Why does Etienne have them?

"You put yourself in jeopardy keeping those," says the second policeman.

"You would not want the authorities to think you are terrorists," says the first. "People have been arrested for less." Whether this is offered as favor or threat remains unclear. Marie-Laure thinks: Do they mean Papa?

The policemen finish their search and say good night with perfect politeness and leave.

Madame Manec lights a cigarette.

Marie-Laure's stew is cold.

Etienne fumbles with the fireplace grate. He shoves the flags one after another into the fire. "No more. No more." He says the second louder than the first. "Not here."

Madame Manec's voice: "They found nothing. There is nothing to find."

The acrid smell of burning cotton fills the kitchen. Her great-uncle says, "You do what you like with your life, Madame. You have always been there for me, and I will try to be there for you. But you may no longer do these things in this house. And you may not do them with my great-niece."

To My Dear Sister Jutta —

It is very difficult now. Even paper is hard to

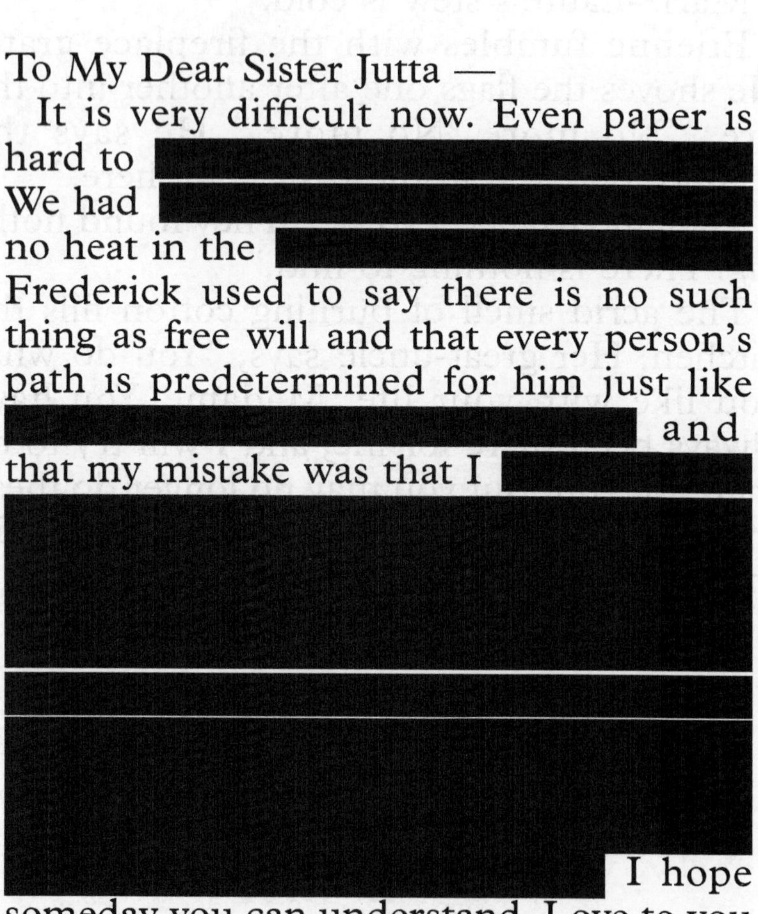

We had

no heat in the

Frederick used to say there is no such thing as free will and that every person's path is predetermined for him just like

and

that my mistake was that I

I hope someday you can understand. Love to you and Frau Elena too. *Sieg heil.*

The Frog Cooks

In the weeks to come, Madame Manec is perfectly cordial; she walks with Marie-Laure to the beach most mornings, takes her to the market. But she seems absent, asking how Marie-Laure and Etienne are doing with perfect courtesy, saying good morning as if they are strangers. Often she disappears for half a day.

Marie-Laure's afternoons become longer, lonelier. One evening she sits at the kitchen table while her great-uncle reads aloud.

The vitality which the snail's eggs possess surpasses belief. We have seen certain species frozen in solid blocks of ice, and yet regain their activity when subjected to the influences of warmth.

Etienne pauses. "We should make supper. It doesn't appear that Madame will be back tonight." Neither of them moves. He reads another page. *They have been kept for years in pill boxes, and yet on subjecting them to moisture, have crawled about appearing as well as ever . . . The shell may be broken, and even portions of it removed, and yet after a certain lapse of time the injured parts will be repaired by a deposition of shelly matter at the fractured parts.*

"There's hope for me yet!" says Etienne, and laughs, and Marie-Laure is reminded that her great-uncle was not always so fearful, that he had a life before this war and before the last one too; that he was once a young man who dwelled in the world and loved it as she does.

Eventually Madame Manec comes through the kitchen door and locks it behind her and Etienne says good evening rather coldly and after a moment Madame Manec says it back. Somewhere in the city, Germans are loading weapons or drinking brandy and history has become some nightmare from which Marie-Laure desperately wishes she could wake.

Madame Manec takes a pot from the hanging rack and fills it with water. Her knife falls through what sounds like potatoes, the blade striking the wooden cutting board beneath.

"Please, Madame," says Etienne. "Allow me. You are exhausted."

But he does not get up, and Madame Manec keeps chopping potatoes, and when she is done, Marie-Laure hears her push a load of them into the water with the back of her knife. The tension in the room makes

Marie-Laure feel dizzy, as if she can sense the planet rotating.

"Sink any U-boats today?" murmurs Etienne. "Blow up any German tanks?"

Madame Manec snaps open the door of the icebox. Marie-Laure can hear her rummage through a drawer. A match flares; a cigarette lights. Soon enough a bowl of undercooked potatoes appears before Marie-Laure. She feels around the tabletop for a fork but finds none.

"Do you know what happens, Etienne," says Madame Manec from the other side of the kitchen, "when you drop a frog in a pot of boiling water?"

"You will tell us, I am sure."

"It jumps out. But do you know what happens when you put the frog in a pot of cool water and then slowly bring it to a boil? You know what happens then?"

Marie-Laure waits. The potatoes steam.

Madame Manec says, "The frog cooks."

Orders

Werner is summoned by an eleven-year-old in full regalia to the commandant's office. He waits on a wooden bench in a slowly building panic. They must suspect something. Maybe they have discovered some fact about his parentage that even he doesn't know, something ruinous. He remembers when the lance corporal came through the door of Children's House to escort him to Herr Siedler's: the certainty that the instruments of the Reich could see through walls, through skin, into the very soul of each subject.

After several hours the commandant's assistant calls him in and sets down his ballpoint and looks across his desk as though Werner is one among a vast series of trivial problems he must put right. "It has come to our attention, cadet, that your age has been recorded incorrectly."

"Sir?"

"You are eighteen years old. Not sixteen, as you have claimed."

Werner puzzles. The absurdity is plain: he remains smaller than most of the fourteen-year-olds.

"Our former technical sciences professor, Dr. Hauptmann, has called our attention to the discrepancy. He has arranged that you will be sent to a special technology division of the Wehrmacht."

"A division, sir?"

"You have been here under false pretenses." His voice is oily and pleased; his chin is non-existent. Out a window the school band practices a triumphal march. Werner watches a Nordic-looking boy stagger beneath the weight of a tuba.

"The commandant urged disciplinary action, but Dr. Hauptmann suggested that you would be eager to offer your skills to the Reich." From behind his desk, the assistant produces a folded uniform — slate-gray, eagle on the breast, Litzen on the collar. Then a greenblack coal-scuttle helmet, obviously too large.

The band blares, then stops. The band instructor screams names.

The commandant's assistant says, "You are very lucky, cadet. To serve is an honor."

"When, sir?"

"You'll receive instructions within a fortnight. That is all."

Pneumonia

Breton spring, and a great onslaught of damp invades the coast. Fog on the sea, fog in the streets, fog in the mind. Madame Manec gets sick. When Marie-Laure holds her hand over Madame's chest, heat seems to steam up out of her sternum as though she cooks from the inside. Her breathing devolves into trains of oceanic coughs.

"I watch the sardines," murmurs Madame, "and the termites, and the crows . . ."

Etienne summons a doctor who prescribes rest, aspirin, and aromatic violet comfits. Marie-Laure sits with Madame through the worst of it, strange hours when the old woman's hands go very cold and she talks about being in charge of the world. She is in charge of everything, but no one knows. It is a tremendous burden, she says, to be responsible for every little thing, every infant born, every leaf falling from every tree, every wave that breaks onto the beach, every ant on its journey.

Deep in Madame's voice, Marie-Laure hears water: atolls and archipelagoes and lagoons and fjords.

Etienne proves to be a tender nurse. Washcloths, broth, now and then a page from Pasteur or Rousseau. His manner forgiving her all transgressions past and present. He wraps Madame in quilts, but eventually she shivers so deeply, so profoundly, that he takes the big heavy rag rug off the floor and lays it on top of her.

Dearest Marie-Laure —

Your parcels arrived, two of them, dated months apart. Joy is not a strong enough word. They let me keep the toothbrush and comb though not the paper they were wrapped in. Nor the soap. How I wish they would let us have soap! They said our next reposting would be to a chocolate factory but it was cardboard. All day we manufacture cardboard. What do they do with so much?

All my life, Marie-Laure, I have been the one carrying the keys. Now I hear them jangling in the mornings when they come for us, and every time I reach in my own pocket, only to find it empty.

When I dream, I dream I am in the museum.

Remember your birthdays? How there were always two things on the table when you woke? I'm sorry it turned out like this. If you ever wish to understand, look inside Etienne's house, inside the house. I know you will do the right thing. Though I wish the gift were better.

My angel is leaving, so if I can get this to you, I will. I do not worry about you because I know you are very smart and keeping yourself safe. I am safe too so you should not worry. Thank Etienne for reading this to you. Thank in your heart the brave soul who carries this letter away from me and on its way to you.

Your Papa

Treatments

Von Rumpel's doctor says that fascinating research is being done on mustard gases. That the anti-tumor properties of any number of chemicals are being explored. The prognosis is looking up: in test subjects, lymphoid tumors have been seen to reduce in size. But the injections make von Rumpel dizzy and weak. In the days following, he can hardly manage to comb his hair or convince his fingers to button his coat. His mind plays tricks, too: he walks into a room and forgets why he's there. He stares at a superior and forgets what the man just said. The sounds of passing cars are like the tines of forks dragged along his nerves.

Tonight he wraps himself in hotel blankets and orders soup and unwraps a bundle from Vienna. The mousy brown librarian has sent copies of the Tavernier and the Streeter and even — most remarkably — stencil duplicates of de Boodt's 1604 *Gemmarum et Lapidum Historia,* written entirely in Latin. Everything she could find concerning the Sea of Flames. Nine paragraphs total.

It takes all his concentration to bring the texts into focus. A goddess of the earth who fell in love with a god of the sea. A prince who recovered from catastrophic injuries, who ruled from within a blur of light. Von Rumpel closes his eyes and sees a flame-haired goddess charge through the tunnels of the earth, drops of flame glowing in her wake. He hears a priest with no tongue say, *The keeper of the stone will live forever.* He hears his father say, *See obstacles as opportunities, Reinhold. See obstacles as inspirations.*

Heaven

For a few weeks, Madame Manec gets better. She promises Etienne she will remember her age, not try to be everything to everyone, not fight the war by herself. One day in early June, almost exactly two years after the invasion of France, she and Marie-Laure walk through a field of Queen Anne's lace east of Saint-Malo. Madame Manec told Etienne that they were going to see if strawberries were available at the Saint-Servan market, but Marie-Laure is certain that when they stopped to greet a woman on the way here, Madame dropped off one envelope and picked up another.

At Madame's suggestion, they lie down in the weeds, and Marie-Laure listens to honeybees mine the flowers and tries to imagine their journeys as Etienne described them: each worker following a rivulet of odor, looking for ultraviolet patterns in the flowers, filling baskets on her hind legs with pollen grains, then navigating, drunk and heavy, all the way home.

How do they know what parts to play, those little bees?

Madame Manec takes off her shoes and lights a cigarette and lets out a contented groan. Insects drone: wasps, hoverflies, a passing dragonfly — Etienne has taught Marie-Laure to distinguish each by its sound.

"What's a roneo machine, Madame?"

"Something to help make pamphlets."

"What does it have to do with that woman we met?"

"Nothing to trouble yourself over, dear."

Horses nicker, and the wind comes off the sea gentle and cool and full of smells.

"Madame? What do I look like?"

"You have many thousands of freckles."

"Papa used to say they were like stars in heaven. Like apples in a tree."

"They are little brown dots, child. Thousands of little brown dots."

"That sounds ugly."

"On you, they are beautiful."

"Do you think, Madame, that in heaven we will really get to see God face-to-face?"

"We might."

"What if you're blind?"

"I'd expect that if God wants us to see something, we'll see it."

"Uncle Etienne says heaven is like a blanket babies cling to. He says people have flown airplanes ten kilometers above the earth and found no kingdoms there. No gates, no angels."

Madame Manec cracks off a ragged chain of coughs that sends tremors of fear through Marie-Laure. "You are thinking of your father," she finally says. "You have to believe your father will return."

"Don't you ever get tired of believing, Madame? Don't you ever want proof?"

Madame Manec rests a hand on Marie-Laure's forehead. The thick hand that first reminded her of a gardener's or a geologist's. "You must never stop believing. That's the most important thing."

The Queen Anne's lace sways on its taproots, and the bees do their steady work. If only life were like a Jules Verne novel, thinks Marie-Laure, and you could page ahead when you most needed to, and learn what would happen. "Madame?"

"Yes, Marie."

"What do you think they eat in heaven?"

"I'm not so sure they need to eat in heaven."

"Not eat! You would not like that, would you?"

But Madame Manec does not laugh the way Marie-Laure expects her to. She doesn't say anything at all. Her breath clatters in and out.

"Did I offend you, Madame?"

"No, child."

"Are we in danger?"

"No more than any other day."

The grasses toss and shimmy. The horses nicker. Madame Manec says, almost whispering, "Now that I think about it, child, I expect heaven is a lot like this."

Frederick

Werner spends the last of his money on train fare. The afternoon is bright enough, but Berlin seems not to want to accept the sunlight, as though its buildings have become gloomier and dirtier and more splotchy in the months since he last visited. Though perhaps what has changed are the eyes that see it.

Rather than ring the bell right away, Werner laps the block three times. The apartment windows are uniformly dark; whether unlit or blacked out, he cannot tell. At a certain point on each circuit, he passes a storefront filled with undressed mannequins, and though he knows each time that it is merely a trick of the light, he cannot stop his eyes from seeing them as corpses strung up by wires.

Finally he rings the bell for #2. No one buzzes down, and he notices from the nameplates that they are no longer in #2. Their name is on #5.

He rings. A returning buzz issues from inside.

The lift is out of order, so he walks up.

The door opens. Franny. With the downy face and swinging flaps of skin under her arms. She gives him a look that one trapped person gives another; then Frederick's mother swishes out of a side room wearing tennis clothes. "Why, Werner —"

She loses herself momentarily in troubled reverie, surrounded by sleek furniture, some of it wrapped in thick wool blankets. Does she blame him? Does she think he is partially responsible? Perhaps he is? But then she comes awake and kisses him on both cheeks, and her bottom lip quivers lightly. As if his materialization is preventing her from keeping certain shadows at bay.

"He won't know you. Don't try to make him remember. It will only upset him. But you are here. I suppose that's something. I was about to go, very sorry I cannot stay. Show him in, Franny."

The maid leads him into a grand drawing room, its ceilings aswirl with plaster flourishes, its walls painted a delicate eggshell blue. No paintings have been hung yet and the shelves wait empty and cardboard boxes stand open on the floor. Frederick sits at a glass-topped table at the back of the room, both table and boy looking small amid the clutter. His hair has been combed hard to one side, and his loose cotton shirt has bunched up behind his shoulders so that his collar is skewed. His eyes do not rise to meet his visitor's.

He wears his same old black-framed glasses. Someone has been feeding him, and the spoon rests on the glass table and blobs of porridge cling to Frederick's whiskers and his place mat, which is a woolen thing featuring happy pink-cheeked children in clogs. Werner cannot look at it.

Franny bends and pushes three more spoonfuls into Frederick's mouth and wipes his chin, folds up his place mat, and walks through a swinging door into what must be a kitchen. Werner stands with his hands crossed in front of his belt.

One year. More than that. Frederick has to shave now, Werner realizes. Or someone has to shave him.

"Hello, Frederick."

Frederick rolls his head back and looks toward Werner through his smudged lenses down the line of his nose.

"I'm Werner. Your mother said you might not remember? I'm your friend from school."

Frederick seems not so much to be looking at Werner as through him. On the table is a stack of paper, on top of which a thick and clumsy spiral has been drawn by a heavy hand.

"Did you make this?" Werner lifts the topmost drawing. Beneath that page is another, then another, thirty or forty spirals, each taking up a whole sheet, all in the same severe lead. Frederick drops his chin to his chest, possibly a nod. Werner glances around: a trunk, a box of linens, the pale blue of the walls and the rich white of the wainscot. Late sunlight glides through tall French windows, and the air tastes of silver polish. This fifth-floor apartment is indeed nicer than the second-floor one — the ceilings high and decorated with punched tin and stucco flourishes: fruits, flowers, banana leaves.

Frederick's lip is curled and his upper teeth show and a string of drool swings from his chin and touches the paper. Werner, unable to bear it a second longer, calls for the maid. Franny peeks out of the swinging door. "Where," he asks, "is that book? The one with the birds? In the gold slipcover?"

"I don't think we ever had a book like that."

"No, you did —"

Franny only shakes her head and laces her fingers across her apron.

Werner lifts the flaps of boxes, peering in. "Surely it's around here."

Frederick has begun to draw a new spiral on a blank sheet.

"Maybe in this?"

Franny stands beside Werner and plucks his wrist off the crate he is about to open. "I do not think," she repeats, "we ever had a book like that."

Werner's whole body has started to itch.

Out the huge windows, the lindens toss back and forth. The light fades. An unlit sign atop a building two blocks away reads, *Berlin smokes Junos.*

Franny has already retreated back into the kitchen.

Werner watches Frederick create another crude spiral, the pencil locked in his fist.

"I'm leaving Schulpforta, Frederick. They're changing my age and sending me to the front."

Frederick lifts the pencil, studying, then reapplies it.

"Less than a week."

Frederick works his mouth as if to chew air. "You look pretty," he says. He does not look directly at Werner, and his words are close to moans. "You look pretty, very pretty, Mama."

"I'm not your mama," hisses Werner. "Come on, now." Frederick's expression is entirely without artifice. Somewhere in the kitchen, the maid is listening. There is no other sound, not of traffic or airplanes or trains or radios or the specter of Frau Schwartzenberger rattling the cage of the elevator. No chanting no singing no silk banners no bands no trumpets no mother no father no slick-fingered commandant dragging a finger across his back. The city seems utterly still, as though everyone is listening, waiting for someone to slip.

Werner looks at the blue of the walls and thinks of *Birds of America,* yellow-crowned heron, Kentucky warbler, scarlet tanager, bird after glorious bird, and Frederick's gaze remains stuck in some terrible middle ground, each eye a stagnant pool into which Werner cannot bear to look.

RELAPSE

In late June 1942, for the first time since her fever, Madame Manec is not in the kitchen when Marie-Laure wakes. Could she already be at the market? Marie-Laure taps on her door, waits a hundred heartbeats. She opens the rear door and calls into the alley. Glorious warm June dawn. Pigeons and cats. Screech of laughter from a neighboring window.

"Madame?"

Her heart accelerates. She taps again on Madame Manec's door.

"Madame?"

When she lets herself in, she hears the rattle first. As though a weary tide stirs stones in the old woman's lungs. Sour odors of sweat and urine rise from the bed. Her hands find Madame's face, and the old woman's cheek is so hot that Marie-Laure's fingers recoil as though scalded. She scrambles upstairs, stumbling, shouting, "Uncle! Uncle!" the whole house turning scarlet in her mind, roof turning to smoke, flames chewing through walls.

Etienne crouches on his popping knees beside Madame, then scurries to the telephone and speaks a few words. He returns to Madame Manec's bedside at a trot. Over the next hour the kitchen fills with women, Madame Ruelle, Madame Fontineau, Madame Hébrard. The first floor becomes too crowded; Marie-Laure paces the staircase, up and down, up and down, as though working her way up and down the spire of an enormous seashell. The doctor comes and goes, the occasional woman closes her bony hand around Marie-Laure's shoulder, and at exactly two o'clock by the bonging of the cathedral bells, the doctor returns with a man who says nothing beyond good afternoon, who smells of dirt and clover, who lifts Madame Manec and carries her out into the street and sets her on a horse cart as though she is a bag of milled oats and the horse's shoes clop away and the doctor strips the bedsheets and Marie-Laure finds Etienne in the corner of the kitchen whispering: Madame is dead, Madame is dead.

■ ■ ■ ■

Six:
8 August 1944

■ ■ ■ ■

Someone in the House

A presence, an inhalation. Marie-Laure trains all of her senses on the entryway three flights below. The outer gate sighs shut, then the front door closes.

In her head, her father reasons: *The gate closed before the door, not after. Which means, whoever it is, he closed the gate first, then shut the door. He's inside.*

All the hairs on the back of her neck stand up.

Etienne knows he would have triggered the bell, Marie. Etienne would be calling for you already.

Boots in the foyer. Fragments of dishes crunching underfoot.

It is not Etienne.

The distress is so acute, it is almost unbearable. She tries to settle her mind, tries to focus on an image of a candle flame burning at the center of her rib cage, a snail drawn up into the coils of its shell, but her heart bangs in her chest and pulses of fear cycle up her spine, and she is suddenly uncertain whether a sighted person in the foyer can look up the curves of the stairwell and see all the way to the third floor. She remembers her great-uncle said that they would need to watch out for looters, and the air stirs with phantom blurs and rustles, and Marie-Laure imagines charging past the bathroom into the cob-webbed sewing room here on the third floor and hurling herself out the window.

Boots in the hall. The slide of a dish across the floor as it is kicked. A fireman, a neighbor, some German soldier hunting food?

A rescuer would be calling for survivors, ma chérie. *You have to move. You have to hide.*

The footfalls travel toward Madame Manec's room. They go slowly; maybe it's dark. Could it already be night?

Four or five or six or a million heartbeats roll by. She has her cane, Etienne's coat, the two cans, the knife, the brick. Model house in her dress pocket. The stone inside that. Water in the tub at the end of the hall.

Move. Go.

A pot or pan, presumably knocked off its hook in the bombing, wobbles on the kitchen tiles. He exits the kitchen. Returns to the foyer.

Stand, ma chérie. *Stand up now.*

She stands. With her right hand, she finds the railing. He is at the base of the stairs. She almost cries out. But then she recognizes —

just as he sets his foot on the first stair — that his stride is out of rhythm. One-pause-two one-pause-two. It is a walk she has heard before. The limp of a German sergeant major with a dead voice.

Go.

Marie-Laure takes each step as deliberately as she can. Grateful now that she does not have her shoes. Her heart knocks so furiously against the cage of her chest that she feels certain the man below will hear it.

Up to the fourth floor. Each step a whisper. The fifth. On the sixth-floor landing, she pauses beneath the chandelier and tries to listen. She hears the German climb three or four more stairs and take a brief asthmatic pause. Then on again. A wooden step complains beneath his weight; it sounds to her like a small animal being crushed.

He stops on what she believes is the third-floor landing. Where she was just sitting. Her warmth still there on the wood floor beside the telephone table. Her dissipated breath.

Where does she have left to run?

Hide.

To her left waits her grandfather's old room. To her right waits her little bedroom, the window glass blown out. Straight ahead is the toilet. Still the faint reek of smoke everywhere.

His footfalls cross the landing. One-pause-two one-pause-two. Wheezing. Climbing again.

If he touches me, she thinks, I will tear out his eyes.

She opens the door to her grandfather's bedroom and stops. Below her, the man pauses again. Has he heard her? Is he climbing more quietly? Out in the world waits a multitude of sanctuaries — gardens full of bright green wind; kingdoms of hedges; deep pools of forest shade through which butterflies float thinking only of nectar. She can get to none of them.

She finds the huge wardrobe at the far end of Henri's room and opens the two mirrored doors and parts the old shirts hanging inside and slides open the false door Etienne has built into its back. She squeezes into the tiny space where the ladder rises to the garret. Then she reaches back through the wardrobe, finds its doors, and closes them.

Protect me now, stone, if you are a protector.

Silently, says the voice of her father. *Make no noise.* With one hand, she finds the handle Etienne has rigged onto the false panel on the back of the wardrobe. She glides it shut, one centimeter at a time, until she hears it click into place, then takes a breath and holds it for as long as she can.

The Death of Walter Bernd

For an hour Bernd murmured gibberish. Then he went silent and Volkheimer said, "God, have mercy on your servant." But now Bernd sits up and calls for light. They feed him the last of the water in the first canteen. A single thread of it runs down through his whiskers and Werner watches it go.

Bernd sits in the glimmer of the field light and looks from Volkheimer to Werner. "On leave last year," he says, "I visited my father. He was old; he was old all my life. But now he seemed especially old. It took him forever just to cross his kitchen. He had a package of cookies, little almond cookies. He put them out on a plate, just the package lying crosswise. Neither of us ate any. He said, 'You don't have to stay. I'd like you to stay, but you don't have to. You probably have things to do. You can go off with your friends if you want to.' He kept saying that."

Volkheimer switches off the light, and Werner apprehends something excruciating held at bay there in the darkness.

"I left," says Bernd. "I went down the stairs and into the street. I had nowhere to go. Nobody to see. I didn't have any friends in that town. I had ridden trains all goddamn day to see him. But I left, just like that."

Then he's quiet. Volkheimer repositions him on the floor with Werner's blanket over him, and not long afterward, Bernd dies.

Werner works on the radio. Maybe he does it for Jutta, as Volkheimer suggested, or maybe he does it so he does not have to think about Volkheimer carrying Bernd into a corner and piling bricks onto his hands, his chest, his face. Werner holds the field light in his mouth and gathers what he can: a small hammer, three jars of screws, eighteen-gauge line cord from a shattered desk lamp. Inside a warped cabinet drawer, miraculously, he discovers a zinc-carbon eleven-volt battery with a black cat printed on the side. An American battery, its slogan offering nine lives. Werner spotlights it in the flickering orange glow, amazed. He checks its terminals. Still plenty of charge. When the field light battery dies, he thinks, we'll have this.

He rights the capsized table. Sets the crushed transceiver on top. Werner does not yet believe there is much promise in it, but maybe it's enough to give the mind something to do, a problem to solve. He adjusts Volkheimer's light in his teeth. Tries not to think about hunger or thirst, the stoppered void in his left ear, Bernd in the corner, the Austrians upstairs, Frederick, Frau Elena, Jutta, any of it.

Antenna. Tuner. Capacitor. His mind, while he works, is almost quiet, almost calm. This is an act of memory.

Sixth-Floor Bedroom

Von Rumpel limps through the rooms with their faded white moldings and ancient kerosene lamps and embroidered curtains and belle époque mirrors and ships in glass bottles and push-button electrical switches, all dead. Faint twilight angles through smoke and shutter slats in hazy red stripes.

Temple to the Second Empire, this house. A bathtub three-quarters full of cold water on the third floor. Deeply cluttered rooms on the fourth. No dollhouses yet. He climbs to the fifth floor, sweating. Worrying he got everything wrong. The weight in his gut swings pendulously. Here's a large ornate room crammed with trinkets and crates and books and mechanical parts. A desk, a bed, a divan, three windows on each side. No model.

To the sixth floor. On the left, a tidy bedroom with a single window and long curtains. A boy's cap hangs on the wall; at the back looms a massive wardrobe, mothballed shirts hung inside.

Back to the landing. Here's a little water closet, the toilet full of urine. Beyond it, a final bedroom. Seashells are lined along every available surface, shells on the sills and on the dresser and jars full of pebbles lined up on the floor, all arranged by some indiscernible system, and here, here! Here on the floor at the foot of the bed sits what he has been searching for, a wooden model of the city, nestled like a gift. As big as a dining table. Brimming with tiny houses. Except for flakes of plaster in its streets, the little city is entirely undamaged. The simulacrum now more whole than the original. A work of clear magnificence.

In the daughter's room. For her. Of course.

Von Rumpel feels as if he has come triumphantly to the end of a long journey, and as he sits on the edge of the bed, twin flares of pain riding up from his groin, he has the curious sensation of having been here before, of having lived in a room like this, slept in a lumpy bed like this, collected polished stones and arrayed them like this. As though somehow this whole set has been waiting for his return.

He thinks of his own daughters, how much they would love to see a city on a table. His youngest would want him to kneel beside her. *Let's imagine all the people having their supper,* she'd say. *Let's imagine us, Papa.*

Outside the broken window, outside the

latched shutters, Saint-Malo is so quiet that von Rumpel can hear the rustle of his own heartbeat shifting hairs in his inner ear. Smoke blowing over the roof. Ash falling lightly. Any moment the guns will start again. Gently now. It will be in here somewhere. It is just like the locksmith to repeat himself. The model — it will be inside the model.

Making the Radio

One end of wire Werner crimps around a shorn pipe standing diagonally up from the floor. With spit, he wipes clean the length of the wire and coils it a hundred times around the base of the pipe, making a new tuning coil. The other end he slings through a bent strut wedged into the congestion of timber, stone, and plaster that has become their ceiling.

Volkheimer watches from the shadows. A mortar shell explodes somewhere in the city, and a flurry of dust sifts down.

The diode goes between free ends of the two wires and meets the leads of the battery to complete the circuit. Werner runs the beam of Volkheimer's light over the entire operation. Ground, antenna, battery. Finally he braces the flashlight between his teeth and raises the twin leads of the earphone in front of his eyes and strips them against the threads of a screw and touches the naked ends to the diode. Invisibly, electrons bumble down the wires.

The hotel above them — what is left of it — makes a series of unearthly groans. Timber splinters, as though the rubble teeters on some final fulcrum. As though a single dragonfly could alight on it and trigger an avalanche that will bury them for good.

Werner presses the bud of the earphone into his right ear.

It does not work.

He turns over the dented radio case, peers into it. Raps Volkheimer's fading light back to life. Settle the mind. Envision the distribution of current. He rechecks the fuses, valves, plug pins; he toggles the receive/send switch, blows dust off the meter selector. Replaces the leads to the battery. Tries the earphone again.

And there it is, as if he is eight years old again, crouched beside his sister on the floor of Children's House: static. Rich and steady. In his memory, Jutta says his name, and on its tail comes a second, less expected image: twin ropes strung from the front of Herr Siedler's house, the great smooth crimson banner hanging from them, unsoiled, deeply red.

Werner scans frequencies by feel. No squelch, no snap of Morse code, no voices. Static static static static static. In his functioning ear, in the radio, in the air. Volkheimer's eyes stay on him. Dust floats through the feeble beam of the flashlight: ten thousand particles, turning softly, twinkling.

In the Attic

The German shuts the wardrobe doors and hobbles away, and Marie-Laure stays on the bottom rung of the ladder for a count of forty. Sixty. One hundred. The heart scrambling to deliver oxygenated blood, the mind scrambling to unravel the situation. A sentence Etienne once read aloud returns: *Even the heart, which in higher animals, when agitated, pulsates with increased energy, in the snail under similar excitement, throbs with a slower motion.*

Slow the heart. Flex your feet. Make no sound. She presses her ear to the false panel on the back of the wardrobe. What does she hear? Moths gnawing away at her grandfather's ancient smocks? Nothing.

Slowly, impossibly, Marie-Laure finds herself growing sleepy.

She feels for the cans in her pockets. How to open one now? Without making noise?

Only thing to do is climb. Seven rungs up into the long triangular tunnel of the garret.

The raw-timbered ceiling rises on both sides toward the peak, just higher than the top of her head.

Heat has lodged itself up here. No window, no exit. Nowhere else to run. No way out except the way she has come.

Her outstretched fingers find an old shaving bowl, an umbrella stand, and a crate full of who knows what. The attic floorboards beneath her feet are as wide across as her hands. She knows from experience how much noise a person walking on them makes.

Don't knock anything over.

If the German opens the wardrobe again and yanks aside the hanging clothes and squeezes through the door and climbs up into the attic, what will she do? Knock him on the head with the umbrella stand? Jab him with the paring knife?

Scream.

Die.

Papa.

She crawls along the center beam, from which the narrow planks of flooring emanate, toward the stone bulk of the chimney at the far end. The center beam is thickest and will be quieter. She hopes she has not become disoriented. She hopes he is not behind her, leveling a pistol at her back.

Bats cry almost inaudibly out the attic vent and somewhere far away, on a naval ship perhaps, or way out past Paramé, a heavy gun fires.

Crack. Pause. *Crack.* Pause. Then the long scream as the shell comes flying in, the *fhump* as it explodes on an outer island.

A ghastly creeping terror rises from a place beyond thoughts. Some innermost trapdoor she must leap upon immediately and lean against with all her weight and padlock shut. She takes off the coat and spreads it across the floor. She dares not pull herself up for fear of the noise her knees will make on the boards. Time passes. Nothing from downstairs. Could he have gone? So quickly?

Of course he is not gone. She knows, after all, why he is here.

To her left, several electrical cords wind along the floor. Just ahead is Etienne's box of old records. His wind-up Victrola. His old recording machine. The lever he uses to hoist the aerial alongside the chimney.

She hugs her knees to her chest and tries to breathe through her skin. Soundlessly, like a snail. She has the two cans. The brick. The knife.

Seven: August 1942

Prisoners

A dangerously underweight corporal in threadbare fatigues comes for Werner on foot. Long fingers, a thatch of thinning hair beneath his cap. One of his boots has lost its lace, and its tongue lolls cannibalistically. He says, "You're little."

Werner, in his new field tunic and oversize helmet and regulation *Gott mit uns* belt buckle, draws his shoulders back. The man squints at the huge school in the dawn, then bends and unzips Werner's duffel and rifles through the three carefully folded NPEA uniforms. He raises a pair of trousers against the light and seems disappointed that they are not remotely his size. After he closes the bag, he throws it over his shoulder; whether to keep or merely carry it, Werner cannot guess.

"I'm Neumann. They call me Two. There's another Neumann, the driver. He's One. Then there's the engineer and the sergeant and you, so for whatever it's worth, that's five again."

No trumpets, no ceremony. This is Werner's induction into the Wehrmacht. They walk the three miles from the school to the village. In a delicatessen, black flies swim over a half dozen tables. Neumann Two orders two plates of calves' liver and eats both, using dark little bread rolls to sop the blood. His lips shine. Werner waits for explanations — where they're going, what sort of unit he'll be joining — but none are forthcoming. The color of the arms displayed under the corporal's shoulder straps and collar tabs is wine-red, but Werner can't remember what that is supposed to signify. Armored infantry? Chemical warfare? The old frau collects the plates. Neumann Two removes a small tin from his coat, dumps three round pills on the table, and gulps them down. Then he puts the tin back inside his coat and looks at Werner. "Backache pills. You have money?"

Werner shakes his head. From a pocket Neumann Two pulls some crumpled and filthy reichsmarks. Before they leave, he asks the frau to bring a dozen hard-boiled eggs and hands Werner four.

From Schulpforta they ride a train through Leipzig and disembark at a switching station west of Lodz. Soldiers from an infantry battalion lie along the platform, all of them asleep, as though some enchantress has cast a spell over them. Their faded uniforms look spectral in the dimness, and their breathing seems synchronized, and the effect is ghostly and unnerving. Now and then a loudspeaker mutters destinations Werner has never heard of — *Grimma, Wurzen, Grossenhain* — though no trains come or go, and the men do not stir.

Neumann Two sits with his legs spread and eats eggs one after another, piling the shells into a tower inside his upturned cap. Dusk falls. A soft, tidal snoring issues from the sleeping company. Werner feels as though he and Neumann Two are the only souls awake in the world.

Well after dark, a whistle sounds in the east and the drowsing soldiers stir. Werner comes out of a half dream and sits up. Neumann Two is already upright beside him, palms cupped against each other, as though attempting to hold a sphere of darkness in the bowl of his hands.

Couplings rattle, brake blocks grind against wheels, and a train emerges from the gloom, moving fast. First comes a blacked-out locomotive, bolted over with armor, exhaling a thick geyser of smoke and steam. Behind the locomotive rumble a few closed cars and then a machine gun in a blister, two gunners crouching beside it.

All of the cars following the gunners' car are flatcars loaded with people. Some stand; more kneel. Two cars pass, three, four. Each car appears to have a wall of sacks along the front to serve as windbreak.

The rails below the platform shine dully as they bounce beneath the weight. Nine flatcars, ten, eleven. All full. The sacks, as they pass, seem strange: they look as though they have been sculpted out of gray clay. Neumann Two raises his chin. "Prisoners."

Werner tries to pick out individuals as the cars blur past: a sunken cheek, a shoulder, a glittering eye. Are they wearing uniforms? Many sit with their backs against the sacks at the front of the car: they look like scarecrows shipping west to be staked in some terrible garden. Some of the prisoners, Werner sees, are sleeping.

A face flashes past, pale and waxy, one ear pressed to the floor of the car.

Werner blinks. Those are not sacks. That is not sleep. Each car has a wall of corpses stacked in the front.

Once it becomes clear that the train will not stop, all the soldiers around them settle and close their eyes once more. Neumann Two yawns. Car after car the prisoners come, a river of human beings pouring out of the night. Sixteen seventeen eighteen: why count? Hundreds and hundreds of men. Thousands. Eventually from the darkness rushes a final flatcar where again the living recline on the dead, followed by the shadow of another gun in a blister and four or five gunners and then the train is gone.

The sound of the axles fades; silence seals itself back over the forest. Somewhere in that direction is Schulpforta with its dark spires, its bed wetters and sleepwalkers and bullies. Somewhere beyond that the groaning leviathan that is Zollverein. The rattling windows of Children's House. Jutta.

Werner says, "They were sitting on their dead?"

Neumann Two closes an eye and cocks his head like a rifleman aiming into the darkness where the train has receded. "Bang," he says. "Bang, bang."

The Wardrobe

In the days following the death of Madame Manec, Etienne does not come out of his study. Marie-Laure imagines him hunched on the davenport, mumbling children's rhymes and watching ghosts shuttle through the walls. Behind the door, his silence is so complete that she worries he has managed to depart the world altogether.

"Uncle? Etienne?"

Madame Blanchard walks Marie-Laure to St. Vincent's for Madame Manec's memorial. Madame Fontineau cooks enough potato soup to last a week. Madame Guiboux brings jam. Madame Ruelle, somehow, has baked a crumb cake.

Hours wear out and fall away. Marie-Laure sets a full plate outside Etienne's door at night and collects an empty plate in the morning. She stands alone in Madame Manec's room and smells peppermint, candle wax, six decades of loyalty. Housemaid, nurse, mother, confederate, counselor, chef

— what ten thousand things was Madame Manec to Etienne? To them all? German sailors sing a drunken song in the street, and a house spider over the stove spins a new web every night, and to Marie-Laure this is a double cruelty: that everything else keeps living, that the spinning earth does not pause for even an instant in its trip around the sun.

Poor child.

Poor Monsieur LeBlanc.

Like they're cursed.

If only her father would come through the kitchen door. Smile at the ladies, set his palms on Marie-Laure's cheeks. Five minutes with him. One minute.

After four days, Etienne comes out of his room. The stairs creak as he descends, and the women in the kitchen fall silent. In a grave voice, he asks everyone to please leave. "I needed time to say goodbye, and now I must look after myself and my niece. Thank you."

As soon as the kitchen door has closed, he turns the dead bolts and takes Marie-Laure's hands. "All the lights are off now. Very good. Please, stand over here."

Chairs slide away. The kitchen table slides away. She can hear him fumbling at the ring in the center of the floor: the trapdoor comes up. He goes down into the cellar.

"Uncle? What do you need?"

"This," he calls.

"What is it?"

"An electric saw."

She can feel something bright kindle in her abdomen. Etienne starts up the stairs, Marie-Laure trailing behind. Second floor, third, fourth fifth sixth, left turn into her grandfather's room. He opens the doors of the gigantic wardrobe, lifts out his brother's old clothes, and places them on the bed. He runs an extension cord out onto the landing and plugs it in. He says, "It will be loud."

She says, "Good."

Etienne climbs into the back of the wardrobe, and the saw yowls to life. The sound permeates the walls, the floor, Marie-Laure's chest. She wonders how many neighbors hear it, if somewhere a German at his breakfast has cocked his head to listen.

Etienne removes a rectangle from the back of the wardrobe, then cuts through the attic door behind it. He shuts down the saw and wriggles through the raw hole, up the ladder behind it, and into the garret. She follows. All morning Etienne crawls along the attic floor with cables and pliers and tools her fingers do not understand, weaving himself into the center of what she imagines as an intricate electronic net. He murmurs to himself; he fetches thick booklets or electrical components from various rooms on the lower stories. The attic creaks; houseflies draw electric-blue loops in the air. Late in the evening, Marie-Laure descends the ladder and falls asleep in her grandfather's bed to the sound of her great-uncle working above her.

When she wakes, barn swallows are chirring beneath the eaves and music is raining down through the ceiling.

"Clair de Lune," a song that makes her think of leaves fluttering, and of the hard ribbons of sand beneath her feet at low tide. The music slinks and rises and settles back to earth, and then the young voice of her long-dead grandfather speaks: *There are ninety-six thousand kilometers of blood vessels in the human body, children! Almost enough to wind around the earth two and a half times . . .*

Etienne comes down the seven ladder rungs and squeezes through the back of the wardrobe and takes her hands in his. Before he speaks, she knows what he will say. "Your father asked me to keep you safe."

"I know."

"This will be dangerous. It is not a game."

"I want to do it. Madame would want —"

"Tell it to me. Tell me the whole routine."

"Twenty-two paces down the rue Vauborel to the rue d'Estrées. Then right for sixteen storm drains. Left on the rue Robert Surcouf. Nine more storm drains to the bakery. I go to the counter and say, 'One ordinary loaf, please.' "

"How will she reply?"

"She will be surprised. But I am supposed to say, 'One ordinary loaf,' and she is supposed to say, 'And how is your uncle?' "

"She will ask about me?"

"She is supposed to. That's how she will know that you are willing to help. It's what Madame suggested. Part of the protocol."

"And you will say?"

"I will say, 'My uncle is well, thank you.' And I will take the loaf and put it in my knapsack and come home."

"This will happen even now? Without Madame?"

"Why wouldn't it?"

"How will you pay?"

"A ration ticket."

"Do we have any of those?"

"In the drawer downstairs. And you have money, don't you?"

"Yes. We have some money. How will you come back home?"

"Straight back."

"By which route?"

"Nine storm drains down the rue Robert Surcouf. Right on the rue d'Estrées. Sixteen drains back to the rue Vauborel. I know it all, Uncle, I have it memorized. I've been to the bakery three hundred times."

"You mustn't go anywhere else. You mustn't go to the beaches."

"I'll come directly back."

"You promise?"
"I promise."
"Then go, Marie-Laure. Go like the wind."

East

They ride in boxcars through Lodz, Warsaw, Brest. For miles, out the open door, Werner sees no sign of humans save the occasional railcar capsized beside the tracks, twisted and scarred by some kind of explosion. Soldiers clamber on and off, lean, pale, each carrying a pack, rifle, and steel helmet. They sleep despite noise, despite cold, despite hunger, as though desperate to stay removed from the waking world for as long as possible.

Rows of pines divide endless metal-colored plains. The day is sunless. Neumann Two wakes and urinates out the door and takes the pillbox from his coat and swallows two or three more tablets. "Russia," he says, though how he has marked the transition, Werner cannot guess.

The air smells of steel.

At dusk the train stops and Neumann Two leads Werner on foot through rows of ruined houses, beams and bricks lying in charred heaps. What walls stand are lined with the black crosshatchings of machine-gun fire. It's nearly dark when Werner is delivered to a musclebound captain dining alone on a sofa that consists of a wooden frame and springs. In a tin bowl, in the captain's lap, steams a cylinder of boiled gray meat. He studies Werner awhile without saying anything, wearing a look not of disappointment but tired amusement.

"Not making them any bigger, are they?"

"No, sir."

"How old are you?"

"Eighteen, sir."

The captain laughs. "Twelve, more like." He slices off a circle of meat and chews a long time and finally reaches into his mouth with two fingers and flings away a string of gristle. "You'll want to acquaint yourself with the equipment. See if you can do better than the last one they sent."

Neumann Two leads Werner to the open back of an unwashed Opel Blitz, a cross-country three-ton truck with a wooden shell built onto the back. Dented gasoline cans are strapped to one flank. Bullet trails have left wandering perforations down the other. The leaden dusk drains away. Neumann Two brings Werner a kerosene lantern. "Gadgets are inside."

Then he vanishes. No explanations. Welcome to war. Tiny moths swirl in the lantern light. Fatigue settles into every part of Werner.

Is this Dr. Hauptmann's idea of a reward or a punishment? He longs to sit on the benches in Children's House again, to hear Frau Elena's songs, to feel the heat pumping off the potbelly stove and the high voice of Siegfried Fischer rhapsodizing about U-boats and fighter planes, to see Jutta drawing at the far end of the table, sketching out the thousand windows of her imaginary city.

Inside the truck box lives a smell: clay, spilled diesel mixed with something putrid. Three square windows reflect the lantern light. It's a radio truck. On a bench along the left wall sit a pair of grimy listening decks the size of bed pillows. A folding RF antenna that can be raised and lowered from inside. Three headsets, a weapon rack, storage lockers. Wax pencils, compasses, maps. And here, in battered cases, wait two of the transceivers he designed with Dr. Hauptmann.

To see them all the way out here soothes him, as though he has turned and found an old friend floating beside him in the middle of the sea. He tugs the first transceiver from its case and unscrews the back plate. Its meter is cracked, several fuses are blown, and the transmitter plug is missing. He fishes for tools, a socket key, copper wire. He looks out the open door across the silent camp to where stars are spun in thousands across the sky.

Do Russian tanks wait out there? Training their guns on the lantern light?

He remembers Herr Siedler's big walnut Philco. Stare into the wires, concentrate, assess. Eventually a pattern will assert itself.

When he next looks up, a soft glow shows behind a line of distant trees, as if something is burning out there. Dawn. A half mile away, two boys with sticks slouch behind a drove of bony cattle. Werner is opening the second transceiver case when a giant appears in the back of the truck shell.

"Pfennig."

The man hangs his long arms from the top bar of the truck canopy; he eclipses the ruined village, the fields, the rising sun.

"Volkheimer?"

One Ordinary Loaf

They stand in the kitchen with the curtains drawn. She still feels the exhilaration of leaving the bakery with the warm weight of the loaf in her knapsack.

Etienne tears apart the bread. "There." He sets a tiny paper scroll, no bigger than a cowrie shell, in her palm.

"What does it say?"

"Numbers. Lots of them. The first three might be frequencies, I can't be sure. The fourth — twenty-three hundred — might be an hour."

"Will we do it now?"

"We'll wait until it is dark."

Etienne works wires up through the house, threading them behind walls, connecting one to a bell on the third floor, beneath the telephone table, another to a second bell in the attic, and a third to the front gate. Three times he has Marie-Laure test it: she stands in the street and swings open the outer gate, and from deep inside the house come two faint rings.

Next he builds a false back into the wardrobe, installing it on a sliding track so it can be opened from either side. At dusk they drink tea and chew the mealy, dense bread from the Ruelles' bakery. When it is fully dark, Marie-Laure follows her great-uncle up the stairs, through the sixth-floor room, and up the ladder into the attic. Etienne raises the heavy telescoping antenna alongside the line of the chimney. He flips switches, and the attic fills with a delicate crackle.

"Ready?" He sounds like her father when he was about to say something silly. In her memory, Marie-Laure hears the two policemen: *People have been arrested for less.* And Madame Manec: *Don't you want to be alive before you die?*

"Yes."

He clears his throat. He switches on the microphone and says, "567, 32, 3011, 50506, 110, 90, 146, 7751."

Off go the numbers, winging out across rooftops, across the sea, flying to who knows what destinations. To England, to Paris, to the dead.

He switches to a second frequency and repeats the transmission. A third. Then he shuts the whole thing off. The machine ticks as it cools.

"What do they mean, Uncle?"

"I don't know."

"Do they translate into words?"

"I suppose they must."

They go down the ladder and clamber out through the wardrobe. No soldiers wait in the hall with guns drawn. Nothing seems different at all. A line comes back to Marie-Laure from Jules Verne: *Science, my lad, is made up of mistakes, but they are mistakes which it is useful to make, because they lead little by little to the truth.*

Etienne laughs as though to himself. "Do you remember what Madame said about the boiling frog?"

"Yes, Uncle."

"I wonder, who was supposed to be the frog? Her? Or the Germans?"

Volkheimer

The engineer is a taciturn, pungent man named Walter Bernd whose pupils are misaligned. The driver is a gap-toothed thirty-year-old they call Neumann One. Werner knows that Volkheimer, their sergeant, cannot be older than twenty, but in the hard pewter-colored light of dawn, he looks twice that. "Partisans are hitting the trains," he explains. "They're organized, and the captain believes they're coordinating their attacks with radios."

"The last technician," says Neumann One, "didn't find anything."

"It's good equipment," says Werner. "I should have them both functioning in an hour."

A gentleness flows into Volkheimer's eyes and hangs there a moment. "Pfennig," he says, looking at Werner, "is nothing like our last technician."

They begin. The Opel bounces down roads that are hardly more than cattle trails. Every few miles they stop and set up a transceiver on some hump or ridge. They leave Bernd and skinny, leering Neumann Two — one with a rifle and the other wearing headphones. Then they drive a few hundred yards, enough to build the base of a triangle, calculating distance all the way, and Werner switches on the primary receiver. He raises the truck's aerial, puts on the headset, and scans the spectra, trying to find anything that is not sanctioned. Any voice that is not allowed.

Along the flat, immense horizon, multiple fires seem always to be burning. Most of the time Werner rides facing backward, looking at land they are leaving, back toward Poland, back into the Reich.

No one shoots at them. Few voices come shearing out of the static, and the ones he does hear are German. At night Neumann One pulls tins of little sausages out of ammunition boxes, and Neumann Two makes tired jokes about whores he remembers or invents, and in nightmares Werner watches the shapes of boys close over Frederick, though when he draws closer, Frederick transforms into Jutta, and she stares at Werner with accusation while the boys carry off her limbs one by one.

Every hour Volkheimer pokes his head into the back of the Opel and meets Werner's eyes. "Nothing?"

Werner shakes his head. He fiddles with the batteries, reconsiders the antennas, triple-checks fuses. At Schulpforta, with Dr. Hauptmann, it was a game. He could guess Volkheimer's frequency; he always knew whether Volkheimer's transmitter was transmitting. Out here he doesn't know how or when or where or even if transmissions are being broadcast; out here he chases ghosts. All they do is expend fuel driving past smoldering cottages and chewed-up artillery pieces and unmarked graves, while Volkheimer passes his giant hand over his close-cropped head, growing more uneasy by the day. From miles away comes the thunder of big guns, and still the German transport trains are being hit, bending tracks and flipping cattle cars and maiming the führer's soldiers and filling his officers with fury.

Is that a partisan there, that old man with the saw cutting trees? That one leaning over the engine of that car? What about those three women collecting water at the creek?

Frosts show up at night, throwing a silver sheet across the landscape, and Werner wakes in the back of the truck with his fingers mashed in his armpits and his breath showing and the tubes of the transceiver glowing a faint blue. How deep will the snow be? Six feet, ten? A hundred?

Miles deep, thinks Werner. We will drive over everything that once was.

Fall

Storms rinse the sky, the beaches, the streets, and a red sun dips into the sea, setting all the west-facing granite in Saint-Malo on fire, and three limousines with wrapped mufflers glide down the rue de la Crosse like wraiths, and a dozen or so German officers, accompanied by men carrying stage lights and movie cameras, climb the steps to the Bastion de la Hollande and stroll the ramparts in the cold.

From his fifth-floor window, Etienne watches them through a brass telescope, nearly twenty in all: captains and majors and even a lieutenant colonel holding his coat at the collar and gesturing at forts on the outer islands, one of the enlisted men trying to light a cigarette in the wind, the others laughing as his hat goes flying over the battlements.

Across the street, from the front door of Claude Levitte's house, three women spill out laughing. Lights burn in Claude's windows, though the rest of the block has no electricity. Someone opens a third-story window and throws out a shot glass, and off it goes spinning, over and over, down toward the rue Vauborel, and out of sight.

Etienne lights a candle and climbs to the sixth floor. Marie-Laure has fallen asleep. From his pocket, he takes a coil of paper and unrolls it. He has already given up trying to crack the code: he has written out the numbers, gridded them, added, multiplied; nothing has come of it. And yet it has. Because Etienne has stopped feeling nauseated in the afternoons; his vision has stayed clear, his heart untroubled. Indeed, it has been over a month since he has had to curl up against the wall in his study and pray that he does not see ghosts shambling through the walls. When Marie-Laure comes through the front door with the bread, when he's opening the tiny scroll in his fingers, lowering his mouth to the microphone, he feels unshakable; he feels alive.

56778. 21. 4567. 1094. 467813.

Then the time and frequency for the next broadcast.

They have been at it for several months, new slips of paper arriving inside a loaf of bread every few days, and lately Etienne plays music. Always at night and never more than a shard of song: sixty or ninety seconds at the most. Debussy or Ravel or Massenet or Charpentier. He sets the microphone in the bell of his electrophone, as he did years before, and lets the record spin.

Who listens? Etienne imagines shortwave receivers disguised as oatmeal boxes or tucked under floorboards, receivers buried beneath flagstones or concealed inside bassinets. He imagines two or three dozen listeners up and down the coast — maybe more tuning in out at sea, captain's sets on free ships hauling tomatoes or refugees or guns — Englishmen who expect the numbers but not the music, who must wonder: *Why?*

Tonight he plays Vivaldi. "L'Autunno — Allegro." A record his brother bought at a shop on the rue Sainte-Marguerite four decades ago for fifty-five centimes.

The harpsichord plucks along, the violins make big baroque flourishes — the low, angled space of the attic brims with sound. Beyond the slates, a block away and thirty yards below, twelve German officers smile for cameras.

Listen to this, thinks Etienne. Hear this.

Someone touches his shoulder. He has to brace himself against the sloping wall to avoid falling over. Marie-Laure stands behind him in her nightdress.

The violins spiral down, then back up. Etienne takes Marie-Laure's hand and together, beneath the low, sloping roof — the record spinning, the transmitter sending it over the ramparts, right through the bodies of the Germans and out to sea — they dance.

He spins her; her fingers flicker through the air. In the candlelight, she looks of another world, her face all freckles, and in the center of the freckles those two eyes hang unmoving like the egg cases of spiders. They do not track him, but they do not unnerve him, either; they seem almost to see into a separate, deeper place, a world that consists only of music.

Graceful. Lean. Coordinated as she whirls, though how she knows what dancing is, he could never guess.

The song plays on. He lets it go too long. The antenna is still up, probably dimly visible against the sky; the whole attic might as well shine like a beacon. But in the candlelight, in the sweet rush of the concerto, Marie-Laure bites her lower lip, and her face gives off a secondary glow, reminding him of the marshes beyond the town walls, in those winter dusks when the sun has set but isn't fully swallowed, and big patches of reeds catch red pools of light and burn — places he used to go with his brother, in what seems like lifetimes ago.

This, he thinks, is what the numbers mean.

The concerto ends. A wasp goes *tap tap tap* along the ceiling. The transmitter remains on, the microphone tucked into the bell of the electrophone as the needle traces the outermost groove. Marie-Laure breathes heavily, smiling.

After she has gone back to sleep, after Etienne has blown out his candle, he kneels for a long time beside his bed. The bony figure of Death rides the streets below, stopping his mount now and then to peer into windows. Horns of fire on his head and smoke leaking from his nostrils and, in his skeletal hand, a list newly charged with addresses. Gazing first at the crew of officers unloading from their limousines into the château.

Then at the glowing rooms of the perfumer Claude Levitte.

Then at the dark tall house of Etienne LeBlanc.

Pass us by, Horseman. Pass this house by.

Sunflowers

They drive a dusty track surrounded by square miles of dying sunflowers so tall that they seem like trees. The stems have dried and stiffened, and the faces bob like praying heads, and as the Opel bellows past, Werner feels as if they are being watched by ten thousand Cyclopic eyes. Neumann One brakes the truck, and Bernd unslings his rifle and takes the second transceiver and wades alone into the stalks to set it up. Werner raises the big antenna and sits in his usual spot in the box of the Opel with his headset on.

Up in the cab, Neumann Two says, "You never scrambled her eggs, you old virgin."

"Shut your mouth," says Neumann One.

"You jerk yourself to sleep at night. Bleed your weasel. Pound your flounder."

"So does half the army. Germans and Russians alike."

"Little pubescent Aryan back there is definitely a flounder pounder."

Over the transceiver, Bernd reads off frequencies. Nothing nothing nothing.

Neumann One says, "The true Aryan is as blond as Hitler, as slim as Göring, and as tall as Goebbels —"

Laughter from Neumann Two. "Fuck if —"

Volkheimer says, "Enough."

It's late afternoon. All day they have moved through this strange and desolate region and have seen nothing but sunflowers. Werner runs the needle through the frequencies, switches bands, retunes the transceiver again, scouring the static. The air swarms with it day and night, a great, sad, sinister Ukrainian static that seems to have been here long before humans figured out how to hear it.

Volkheimer clambers out of the truck and lowers his trousers and pees into the flowers and Werner decides to trim the aerial, but before he does, he hears — as sharp and clear and menacing as the blade of a knife flashing in the sun — a volley of Russian. *Adeen, shest, vosyem.* Every fiber of his nervous system leaps awake.

He turns up the volume as far as it will go and presses the headphones against his ears. Again it comes: *Ponye-something-feshky, shere-something-doroshoi . . .* Volkheimer is looking at him through the open back of the truck shell as though he can sense it, as though he is coming awake for the first time in months, as he did that night out in the snow when Hauptmann fired his pistol, when they realized Werner's transceivers worked.

Werner turns the fine-tune dial fractionally, and abruptly the voice booms into his ears, *Dvee-nat-set, shayst-nat-set, davt-set-adeen,* nonsense, terrible nonsense, pipelined directly into his head; it's like reaching into a sack full of cotton and finding a razor blade inside, everything constant and undeviating and then that one dangerous thing, so sharp you can hardly feel it open your skin.

Volkheimer raps his massive fist on the side of the Opel to quiet the Neumanns, and Werner relays the channel to Bernd on the far transceiver and Bernd finds it and measures the angle and relays it back and now Werner settles in to do the math. The slide rule, the trigonometry, the map. The Russian is still talking when Werner pulls his headset down around his neck. "North northwest."

"How far?"

Only numbers. Pure math.

"One and a half kilometers."

"Are they broadcasting now?"

Werner closes one cup of the headphones over an ear. He nods. Neumann One starts the Opel with a roar and Bernd comes crashing back through the flowers carrying the first transceiver and Werner withdraws the aerial and they grind off the road and directly through the sunflowers, punching them down as they go. The tallest are nearly as tall as the truck, and their big dry heads drum the roof of the cab and the sides of the box.

Neumann One watches the odometer and calls out distances. Volkheimer distributes weapons. Two Karabiner 98Ks. The Walther semiautomatic with the scope. Beside him, Bernd loads cartridges into the magazine of his Mauser. *Bong,* go the sunflowers. *Bong bong bong.* The truck yaws like a ship at sea as Neumann One coaxes it over ruts.

"Eleven hundred meters," calls Neumann One, and Neumann Two scrambles onto the hood of the truck and peers above the field with binoculars. To the south, the flowers give way to a patch of raveled gherkins. Beyond those, ringed by bare dirt, stands a pretty cottage with a thatched roof and stucco walls.

"The line of yarrow. End of the field."

Volkheimer raises his scope. "Any smoke?"

"None."

"An antenna?"

"Hard to say."

"Shut off the motor. On foot from here."

Everything goes quiet.

Volkheimer, Neumann Two, and Bernd carry their weapons into the flowers and are swallowed. Neumann One stays behind the wheel, Werner in the truck shell. No land mines explode in front of them. All around the Opel, the flowers creak on their stems and nod their heliotropic faces as if in some sad accord.

"Fuckers are going to be surprised," whispers Neumann One. His right thigh jogs up and down several times a second. Behind him, Werner raises the aerial as high as he dares and clamps on the headphones and switches on the transceiver. The Russian is reading what sounds like letters of the alphabet. *Peh zheh kah cheh yu myakee znak.* Each utterance seems to rise from the aural cotton for Werner's ears alone, then melts away. Neumann One's vibrating leg shakes the truck lightly, and the sun flares through the remnants of insects smeared across the windows, and a cold wind sets the whole field rustling.

Won't there be sentries? Lookouts? Armed partisans sidling up right now behind the truck? The Russian on the radio is a hornet in each ear, *zvou kaz vukalov* — who knows what horrors he's dispensing, troop positions, train schedules; he might be giving artillery gunners the truck's location right now — and Volkheimer is walking out of the sunflowers, as large a target as a human has ever presented, holding his rifle like a baton; it seems impossible that the cottage could ever accommodate him, as though Volkheimer will engulf the house instead of the other way around.

First the shots come through the air around the headphones. A fraction of a second later, they come through the headphones themselves, so loud that Werner almost tears them off. Then even the static cuts out, and the silence in the headphones feels like something massive moving through space, a ghostly airship slowly descending.

Neumann One opens and closes the bolt of his rifle.

Werner remembers crouching next to his cot with Jutta after the Frenchman would sign off, the windows rattling from some passing coal train, the echo of the broadcast seeming to glimmer in the air for a moment, as though he could reach out and let it float down into his hands.

Volkheimer returns with ink spattered on his face. He raises two huge fingers to his forehead, pushes his helmet back, and Werner can see that it is not ink. "Set the house afire," he says. "Quickly. Don't waste diesel." He looks at Werner. His voice tender, almost melancholy. "Salvage the equipment."

Werner sets down the headphones, puts on his helmet. Swifts swoop out over the sunflowers. His vision makes slow loops, as though something has gone wrong with his balance. Neumann One hums in front of him as he carries a can of fuel through the stalks. They break through the sunflowers toward the cottage, stepping through Aaron's rod, wild carrot, all the leaves browned from frost. Beside the front door a dog lies in the dust, chin on its paws, and for a moment Werner thinks it is only sleeping.

The first dead man is on the floor with an arm trapped beneath him and a crimson mess where his head should be. On the table is a second man: slumped as if sleeping on his ear, only the edges of his wound showing, a whorish purple. Blood that has spread across the table thickens like cooling wax. It looks almost black. Strange to think of his voice still flying through the air, already a country away, growing weaker every mile.

Torn pants, grimy jackets, one of the men in suspenders; they do not wear uniforms.

Neumann One tears down a potato-sack curtain and takes it outside and Werner can hear him splash it with diesel. Neumann Two pulls the suspenders off the second dead man and takes some braided shallots from the lintel and bundles them against his chest and leaves.

In the kitchen, a small brick of cheese sits half eaten. A knife beside it with a faded wooden handle. Werner opens a single cupboard. Inside dwells a den of superstition: jars of dark liquids, unlabeled pain remedies, molasses, tablespoons stuck to the wood, something marked, in Latin, *belladonna,* something else marked with an *X.*

The transmitter is poor, high-frequency: probably salvaged from a Russian tank. It seems little more than a handful of components shoveled into a box. The ground-plane antenna installed beside the cottage might have sent the transmissions thirty miles, if that.

Werner goes out, looks back at the house, bone-white in the failing light. He thinks of the kitchen cupboard with its strange potions. The dog that did not do its job. These partisans may have been involved in some dark forest magic, but they should not have been tinkering with the higher magic of radio. He slings his rifle and carries the big battered transmitter — its leads, its inferior microphone — through the flowers to the Opel, its engine running, Neumann Two and Volkheimer already in the cab. He hears Dr. Hauptmann: *A scientist's work is determined by two things: his interests and those of his time.* Everything has led to this: the death of his father; all those restless hours with Jutta listening to the crystal radio in the attic; Hans and Herribert wearing their red armbands under their shirts so Frau Elena would not see; four hundred dark, glittering nights at Schulpforta building transceivers for Dr. Hauptmann. The destruction of Frederick. Everything leading to this moment as Werner piles the haphazard Cossack equipment into the shell of the truck and sits with his back against the bench and watches the light from the burning cottage rise above the field. Bernd climbs in beside him, rifle in his lap, and neither bothers to close the back door when the Opel roars into gear.

Stones

Sergeant Major von Rumpel is summoned to a warehouse outside Lodz. It is the first time he has traveled since completing his treatments in Stuttgart, and he feels as though the density of his bones has decreased. Six guards in steel helmets wait inside razor wire. Much heel-clicking and saluting ensues. He takes off his coat and steps into a zippered jumpsuit with no pockets. Three dead bolts give way. Through a door, four enlisted men in identical jumpsuits stand behind tables with jeweler's lamps bolted to each. Plywood has been nailed over all the windows.

A dark-haired *Gefreiter* explains the protocol. A first man will pry the stones out of their settings. A second will scrub them one by one in a bath of detergent. A third will weigh each, announce its mass, and pass it to von Rumpel, who will examine the stone through a loupe and call out the clarity — *Included, Slightly Included, Almost Loupe-Clean.* A fifth man, the *Gefreiter,* will record the assessments.

"We'll work in ten-hour shifts until we're done."

Von Rumpel nods. Already his spine feels as if it might splinter. The *Gefreiter* drags a padlocked sack from beneath his table, unthreads a chain from its throat, and upends it onto a velvet-lined tray. Thousands of jewels spill out: emeralds, sapphires, rubies. Citrine. Peridot. Chrysoberyl. Among them twinkle hundreds upon hundreds of little diamonds, most still in necklaces, bracelets, cuff links, or earrings.

The first man carries the tray to his station, sets an engagement ring in his vise, and peels back the prongs with tweezers. Down the line comes the diamond. Von Rumpel counts the other bags beneath the table: nine. "Where," he begins to ask, "did they all —"

But he knows where they came from.

Grotto

Months after the death of Madame Manec, Marie-Laure still waits to hear the old woman come up the stairs, her labored breathing, her sailor's drawl. *Jesus's mother, child, it's freezing!* She never comes.

Shoes at the foot of the bed, beneath the model. Cane in the corner. Down to the first floor, where her knapsack hangs on its peg. Out. Twenty-two paces down the rue Vauborel. Then right for sixteen storm drains. Turn left on the rue Robert Surcouf. Nine more drains to the bakery.

One ordinary loaf, please.

And how is your uncle?

My uncle is well, thank you.

Sometimes the loaf has a white scroll inside and sometimes it does not. Sometimes Madame Ruelle has managed to procure a few groceries for Marie-Laure: cabbage, red peppers, soap. Back to the intersection with the rue d'Estrées. Instead of turning left onto the rue Vauborel, Marie-Laure continues straight. Fifty steps to the ramparts, a hundred or so more along the base of the walls to the mouth of the alley that grows ever narrower.

With her fingers, she finds the lock; from her coat she pulls the iron key Harold Bazin gave her a year before. The water is icy and shin-deep; her toes go numb in an instant. But the grotto itself comprises its own slick universe, and inside this universe spin countless galaxies: here, in the upturned half of a single mussel shell, lives a barnacle and a tiny spindle shell occupied by a still smaller hermit crab. And on the shell of the crab? A yet smaller barnacle. And on that barnacle?

In the damp box of the old kennel, the sound of the sea washes away all other sounds; she tends to the snails as though to plants in a garden. Tide to tide, moment to moment: she comes to listen to the creatures suck and shift and squeak, to think of her father in his cell, of Madame Manec in her field of Queen Anne's lace, of her uncle confined for two decades inside his own house.

Then she feels her way back to the gate and locks it behind her.

That winter the electricity is out more than it is on; Etienne links a pair of marine batteries to the transmitter so that he can broadcast when the power is off. They burn crates and papers and even antique furniture to keep warm. Marie-Laure drags the heavy rag rug from the floor of Madame Manec's apartment all the way to the sixth floor and drapes it over her quilt. Some midnights, her room grows so cold that she half believes she can hear frost settling onto the floor.

Any footfall in the street could be a policeman. Any rumble of an engine could be a detachment sent to haul them away.

Upstairs Etienne broadcasts again and she thinks: I should station myself by the front door in case they come. I could buy him a few minutes. But it is too cold. Far better to stay in bed beneath the weight of the rug and dream herself back into the museum, trail her fingers along remembered walls, make her way across the echoing Grand Gallery toward the key pound. All she has to do is cross the tiled floor and turn left and there Papa will be behind the counter, standing at his key cutter.

He'll say, *What took you so long, bluebird?*

He'll say, *I will never leave you, not in a million years.*

Hunting

In January 1943, Werner finds a second illegal transmission coming from an orchard on which a shell has fallen, cracking most of the trees in half. Two weeks later, he finds a third, then a fourth. Each new find seems only a variation of the last: the triangle closes in, each segment shrinking simultaneously, the vertices growing closer, until they are reduced to a single point, a barn or a cottage or a factory basement or some disgusting encampment in the ice.

"He is broadcasting now?"

"Yes."

"In that shed?"

"Do you see the antenna along the eastern wall?"

Whenever he can, Werner records what the partisans say on magnetic tape. Everybody, he is learning, likes to hear themselves talk. Hubris, like the oldest stories. They raise the antenna too high, broadcast for too many minutes, assume the world offers safety and rationality when of course it does not.

The captain sends word that he is thrilled with their progress; he promises holiday leaves, steaks, brandy. All winter the Opel roves occupied territories, cities that Jutta recorded in their radio log coming to life — Prague, Minsk, Ljubljana.

Sometimes the truck passes a group of prisoners and Volkheimer asks Neumann One to slow. He sits up very straight, looking for any man as large as he is. When he sees one, he raps the dash. Neumann One brakes, and Volkheimer postholes out into the snow, speaks to a guard, and wades in among the prisoners, usually wearing only a shirt against the cold.

"His rifle is in the truck," Neumann One will say. "Left his fucking rifle right here."

Sometimes he's too far away. Other times Werner hears him perfectly. *"Ausziehen,"* Volkheimer will say, his breath pluming out in front of him, and almost every time, the big Russian will understand. Take it off. A strapping Russian boy with the face of someone for whom no remaining thing on earth could be surprising. Except perhaps this: another giant wading toward him.

Off come mittens, a wool shirt, a battered coat. Only when he asks for their boots do their faces change: they shake their head, look up or look down, roll their eyes like frightened horses. To lose their boots, Werner understands, means they will die. But Volkheimer stands and waits, big man against big man, and always the prisoner caves. He stands in his wrecked socks in the trampled snow and tries to make eye contact with the other prisoners, but none will look at him. Volkheimer holds up various items, tries them on, hands them back if they do not fit. Then he stamps back to the truck, and Neumann One drops the Opel into gear.

Creaking ice, villages burning in forests, nights where it becomes too cold even to snow — that winter presents a strange and haunted season during which Werner prowls the static like he used to prowl the alleys with Jutta, pulling her in the wagon through the colonies of Zollverein. A voice materializes out of the distortion in his headphones, then fades, and he goes ferreting after it. There, thinks Werner when he finds it again, *there:* a feeling like shutting your eyes and feeling your way down a mile-long thread until your fingernails find the tiny lump of a knot.

Sometimes days pass after hearing a first transmission before Werner snares the next; they present a problem to solve, something to wrap his mind around: better, surely, than fighting in some stinking, frozen trench, full of lice, the way the old instructors at Schulpforta fought in the first war. This is cleaner, more mechanical, a war waged through the air, invisibly, and the front lines are anywhere.

Isn't there a kind of ravishing delight in the chase of it? The truck bouncing along through the darkness, the first signs of an antenna through the trees?

I hear you.

Needles in the haystack. Thorns in the paw of the lion. He finds them, and Volkheimer plucks them out.

All winter the Germans drive their horses and sledges and tanks and trucks over the same roads, packing down the snow, transforming it into a slick bloodstained ice-cement. And when April finally comes, reeking of sawdust and corpses, the canyon walls of snow give way while the ice on the roads remains stubbornly fixed, a luminous, internecine network of invasion: a record of the crucifixion of Russia.

One night they cross a bridge over the Dnieper with the domes and blooming trees of Kiev looming ahead and ash blowing everywhere and prostitutes bundled in the alleys. In a café, they sit two tables down from an infantryman not much older than Werner. He stares into a newspaper with twitching eyeballs and sips coffee and looks deeply surprised. Astonished.

Werner cannot stop studying him. Finally Neumann One leans over. "Know why he looks like that?"

Werner shakes his head.

"Frostbite took his eyelids. Poor bastard."

Mail does not reach them. Months pass and Werner does not write to his sister.

The Messages

Occupation authorities decree that every house must have a list of its occupants fixed to its door: *M. Etienne LeBlanc, age 62. Mlle Marie-Laure LeBlanc, age 15.* Marie-Laure tortures herself with daydreams of feasts laid out on long tables: platters of sliced pork loin, roasted apples, banana flambé, pineapples with whipped cream.

One morning in the summer of 1943, she walks to the bakery in a slow-falling rain. The queue stretches out the door. When Marie-Laure finally reaches the head of the line, Madame Ruelle takes her hands and speaks very softly. "Ask if he can also read this." Beneath the loaf comes a folded piece of paper. Marie-Laure puts the loaf into her knapsack and bunches the paper in her fist. She passes over a ration ticket, finds her way directly home, and dead-bolts the door behind her.

Etienne shuffles downstairs.

"What does it say, Uncle?"

"It says, *Monsieur Droguet wants his daughter in Saint-Coulomb to know that he is recovering well.*"

"She said it's important."

"What does it mean?"

Marie-Laure removes her knapsack and reaches inside and tears off a hunk of bread. She says, "I think it means that Monsieur Droguet wants his daughter to know that he is all right."

Over the next weeks, more notes come. A birth in Saint-Vincent. A dying grandmother in La Mare. Madame Gardinier in La Rabinais wants her son to know that she forgives him. If secret messages lurk inside these missives — if *Monsieur Fayou had a heart attack and passed gently away* means *Blow up the switching yard at Rennes* — Etienne cannot say. What matters is that people must be listening, that ordinary citizens must have radios, that they seem to need to hear from each other. He never leaves his house, sees no one save Marie-Laure, and yet somehow he has found himself at the nexus of a web of information.

He keys the microphone and reads the numbers, then the messages. He broadcasts them on five different bands, gives instructions for the next transmission, and plays a bit of an old record. At most the whole exercise takes six minutes.

Too long. Almost certainly too long.

Yet no one comes. The two bells do not ring. No German patrols come banging up the stairs to put bullets in their heads.

Although she has them memorized, most nights Marie-Laure asks Etienne to read her the letters from her father. Tonight he sits on the edge of her bed.

Today I saw an oak tree disguised as a chestnut tree.

I know you will do the right thing.

If you ever wish to understand, look inside Etienne's house, inside the house.

"What do you think he means by writing *inside the house* twice?"

"We've been over it so many times, Marie."

"What do you think he is doing right now?"

"Sleeping, child. I am sure of it."

She rolls onto her side, and he hauls the hem of her quilts past her shoulders and blows out the candle and stares into the miniature rooftops and chimneys of the model at the foot of her bed. A memory rises: Etienne was in a field east of the city with his brother. It was the summer when fireflies showed up in Saint-Malo, and their father was very excited, building long-handled nets for his boys and giving them jars with wire to fasten over the tops, and Etienne and Henri raced through the tall grass as the fireflies floated away from them, illuming on and off, always seeming to rise just beyond their reach, as if the earth were smoldering and these were sparks that their footfalls had prodded free.

Henri had said he wanted to put so many beetles in his window that ships could see his bedroom from miles away.

If there are fireflies this summer, they do not come down the rue Vauborel. Now it seems there are only shadows and silence. Silence is the fruit of the occupation; it hangs in branches, seeps from gutters. Madame Guiboux, mother of the shoemaker, has left town. As has old Madame Blanchard. So many windows are dark. It's as if the city has become a library of books in an unknown language, the houses great shelves of illegible volumes, the lamps all extinguished.

But there is the machine in the attic at work again. A spark in the night.

A faint clattering rises from the alley, and Etienne peers through the shutters of Marie-Laure's bedroom, down six stories, and sees the ghost of Madame Manec standing there in the moonlight. She holds out a hand, and sparrows land one by one on her arms, and she tucks each one into her coat.

Loudenvielle

The Pyrenees gleam. A pitted moon stands on their crests as if impaled. Sergeant Major von Rumpel takes a cab through platinum moonlight to a *commissariat* and stands across from a police captain who continually drags the index and middle fingers of his left hand through his considerable mustache.

The French police have made an arrest. Someone has burglarized the chalet of a prominent donor with ties to the Natural History Museum in Paris, and the burglar has been apprehended with a travel case stuffed with gems.

He waits a long time. The captain reviews the fingernails of his left hand, then his right, then his left again. Von Rumpel is feeling very weak tonight, queasy really; the doctor says the treatments are over, that they have made their assault on the tumor and now they must wait, but some mornings he cannot straighten after he finishes tying his shoes.

A car arrives. The captain goes out to greet

it. Von Rumpel watches through the window.

From the backseat, two policemen produce a frail-looking man in a beige suit with a perfect purple bruise around his left eye. Hands cuffed. A spattering of blood on his collar. As though he has just left off playing a villain in some movie. The policemen shepherd the prisoner inside while the captain removes a handbag from the car's trunk.

Von Rumpel takes his white gloves from his pocket. The captain closes his office door, sets the bag atop his desk, and pulls his blinds. Tilts the shade of his desk lamp. In a room somewhere beyond, von Rumpel can hear a cell door clang shut. From the handbag the captain removes an address book, a stack of letters, and a woman's compact. Then he plucks out a false bottom followed by six velvet bundles.

He unwraps them one at a time. The first contains three gorgeous pieces of beryl: pink, fat, hexagonal. Inside the second is a single cluster of aqua-colored Amazonite, gently striated with white. Inside the third is a pear-cut diamond.

A thrill leaps into the tips of von Rumpel's fingers. From a pocket, the captain withdraws a loupe, a look of naked greed blooming on his face. He examines the diamond for a long time, turning it this way and that. Through von Rumpel's mind sail visions of the Führermuseum, glittering cases, bowers beneath pillars, jewels behind glass — and something else too: a faint power, like a low voltage, coming off the stone. Whispering to him, promising to erase his illness.

Finally the captain looks up, the impress of his loupe a tight pink circle around his eye. The lamplight sets a gleam on his wet lips. He places the jewel back on the towel.

From the other side of the desk, von Rumpel picks up the diamond. Just the right weight. Cold in his fingers, even through the cotton of the gloves. Deeply saturated with blue at its edges.

Does he believe?

Dupont has almost kindled a fire inside it. But with the lens to his eye, von Rumpel can see that the stone is identical to the one he examined in the museum two years before. He sets the reproduction back on the desk.

"But at the minimum," the captain says in French, his face falling, "we must X-ray it, no?"

"Do whatever you'd like, by all means. I'll take those letters, please."

Before midnight he is at his hotel. Two fakes. This is progress. Two found, two left to find, and one of the two must be real. For dinner, he orders wild boar cooked with fresh mushrooms. And a full bottle of Bordeaux. Especially during wartime, such things remain important. They are what separate the civilized man from the barbarian.

The hotel is drafty and the dining room is empty, but the waiter is excellent. He pours with grace and steps away. Once in the glass, as dark as blood, the Bordeaux seems almost as though it is a living thing. Von Rumpel takes pleasure in knowing that he is the only person in the world who will have the privilege of tasting it before it is gone.

GRAY

December 1943. Ravines of cold sink between the houses. The only wood left to burn is green and the whole city smells of wood smoke. Walking to the bakery, fifteen-year-old Marie-Laure is as chilled as she has ever been. Indoors, it is little better. Stray snowflakes seem to drift through the rooms, blown through gaps in the walls.

She listens to her great-uncle's footfalls across the ceiling, and his voice — *310 1467 507 2222 576881* — and then her grandfather's song, "Clair de Lune," strains over her like a blue mist.

Airplanes make low, lazy passes over the city. Sometimes they sound so close that Marie-Laure fears they might graze the rooftops, knock over chimneys with their bellies. But no planes crash, no houses explode. Nothing seems to change at all except Marie-Laure grows: she can no longer wear any of the clothes her father carried here in his rucksack three years before. And her shoes pinch; she takes to wearing three pairs of socks and a pair of Etienne's old tasseled loafers.

The rumors are that only essential personnel and those with medical reasons will be allowed to stay in Saint-Malo. "We're not leaving," says Etienne. "Not when we might finally be doing some good. If the doctor won't give us notes, we'll pay for them some other way."

For portions of every day, she manages to lose herself in realms of memory: the faint impressions of the visual world before she was six, when Paris was like a vast kitchen, pyramids of cabbages and carrots everywhere; bakers' stalls overflowing with pastries; fish stacked like cordwood in the fishmongers' booths, the runnels awash in silver scales, alabaster gulls swooping down to carry off entrails. Every corner she turned billowed with color: the greens of leeks, the deep purple glaze of eggplants.

Now her world has turned gray. Gray faces and gray quiet and a gray nervous terror hanging over the queue at the bakery and the only color in the world briefly kindled when Etienne climbs the stairs to the attic, knees cracking, to read one more string of numbers into the ether, to send another of Madame Ruelle's messages, to play a song. That little attic bursting with magenta and aquamarine and gold for five minutes, and then the radio switches off, and the gray rushes back in, and her uncle stumps back down the stairs.

Fever

Maybe it comes from the stew in some nameless Ukrainian kitchen; maybe partisans have poisoned the water; maybe Werner simply sits too long in too many damp places with the headset over his ears. Regardless, the fever comes, and with it terrible diarrhea, and as Werner crouches in the mud behind the Opel, he feels as if he is shitting out the last of his civilization. Whole hours pass during which he can do no more than press his cheek against the wall of the truck shell seeking something cold. Then the shivers take over, hard and fast, and he cannot warm his body; he wants to leap into a fire.

Volkheimer offers coffee; Neumann Two offers the tablets that Werner knows by now are not for backaches. He declines both, and 1943 becomes 1944. Werner has not written Jutta in almost a year. The last letter he has from her is six months old and begins: *Why don't you write?*

Still he manages to find illegal transmissions, one every two weeks or so. He salvages the inferior Soviet equipment, milled from marginal steel, clumsily soldered; it's all so unsystematic. How can they fight a war with such lousy equipment? The resistance is pitched to Werner as supremely organized; they are dangerous, disciplined insurgents; they follow the words of ferocious, lethal leaders. But he sees firsthand how they can be so loosely allied as to be basically ineffectual — they are wretched and filthy; they live in holes. They are ragtag desperadoes with nothing to lose.

And it seems he can never make headway into understanding which theory is closer to the truth. Because really, Werner thinks, they are all insurgents, all partisans, every single person they see. Anyone who is not a German wants the Germans dead, even the most sycophantic of them. They shy away from the truck as it rattles into town; they hide their faces, their families; their shops brim with shoes plucked off the dead.

Look at them.

What he feels on the worst days of that relentless winter — while rust colonizes the truck and rifles and radios, while German divisions retreat all around them — is a deep scorn for all the humans they pass. The smoking, ruined villages, the broken pieces of brick in the street, the frozen corpses, the shattered walls, the upturned cars, the barking dogs, the scurrying rats and lice: how can they live like that? Out here in the forests, in the mountains, in the villages, they are supposed to be pulling up disorder by the root. The total entropy of any system, said Dr. Hauptmann, will decrease only if the entropy of another system will increase. Nature demands symmetry. *Ordnung muss sein.*

And yet what order are they making out here? The suitcases, the queues, the wailing babies, the soldiers pouring back into the cities with eternity in their eyes — in what system is order increasing? Surely not in Kiev, or Lvov, or Warsaw. It's all Hades. There are just so many humans, as if huge Russian factories cast new men every minute. Kill a thousand and we'll make ten thousand more.

February finds them in mountains. Werner shivers in the back of the truck while Neumann One grinds down switchbacks. Trenches snake below them in an endless net, German positions on one side, Russian positions beyond. Thick ribbons of smoke stripe the valley; occasional flares of ordnance fly like shuttlecocks.

Volkheimer unfolds a blanket and wraps it around Werner's shoulders. His blood sloshes back and forth inside him like mercury, and out the windows, in a gap in the mist, the network of trenches and artillery below shows itself very clearly for a moment, and Werner feels he is gazing down into the circuitry of an enormous radio, each soldier down there an electron flowing single file down his own electrical path, with no more say in the matter than an electron has. Then they're around a bend and he feels only the presence of Volkheimer next to him, a cold dusk out the windows, bridge after bridge, hill after hill, all the time descending. Metallic, tattered moonlight shatters across the road, and a white horse stands chewing in a field, and a searchlight rakes the sky, and in the lit window of a mountain cabin, for a split second as they rumble past, Werner sees Jutta seated at a table, the bright faces of other children around her, Frau Elena's needlepoint over the sink, the corpses of a dozen infants heaped in a bin beside the stove.

The Third Stone

He stands in a château outside Amiens, north of Paris. The big old house moans in the dark. The home belongs to a retired paleontologist and von Rumpel believes it is here that the chief of security at the museum in Paris fled during the chaos following the invasion of France three years ago. A peaceful place, insulated by fields, enwombed in hedges. He climbs a staircase to a library. A bookshelf has been peeled open; the strongbox is behind it. The Gestapo safecracker is good: wears a stethoscope, does not bother with a flashlight. In a few minutes, he has it open.

An old handgun, a box of certificates, a stack of tarnished silver coins. And inside a velvet box, a blue pear-cut diamond.

The red heart inside the stone shows itself one second, becomes completely inaccessible the next. Inside von Rumpel, hope braids with desperation; he is almost there. The odds are in his favor, aren't they? But he knows before he sets it under the lamp. That same elation crashing out of him. The diamond is not real; it too is the work of Dupont.

He has found all three fakes. All his luck is spent. The doctor says the tumor is growing again. The prospects of the war are nose-diving — Germany retreats across Russia, across the Ukraine, up the ankle of Italy. Before long, everyone in the Einsatzstab Reichsleiter Rosenberg — the men out there scouring the continent for hidden libraries, concealed prayer scrolls, closeted impressionist paintings — will be handed rifles and sent into the fire. Including von Rumpel.

So long as he keeps it, the keeper of the stone will live forever.

He cannot give up. And yet his hands grow so heavy. His head is a boulder.

One at the museum, one to the home of a museum supporter, one sent with a chief of security. What sort of man would they choose for a third courier? The Gestapo man watches him, his attention on the stone, his left hand on the door of the strongbox. Not for the first time, von Rumpel thinks of the extraordinary jewel safe at the museum. Like a puzzle box. In all his travels, he has seen nothing else like it. Who could have conceived of it?

The Bridge

In a French village far to the south of Saint-Malo, a German truck crossing a bridge is blown up. Six German soldiers die. Terrorists are blamed. *Night and fog,* whisper the women who come by to check on Marie-Laure. *For every Kraut lost, they'll kill ten of us.* Police go door-to-door demanding any able-bodied man come out for a day's work. Dig trenches, unload railway wagons, push barrows of cement bags, construct invasion obstacles in a field or on a beach. Everyone who can must work to strengthen the Atlantic Wall. Etienne stands squinting in the doorway with his doctor's notes in his hand. Cold air blowing over him and fear billowing backward into the hall.

Madame Ruelle whispers that occupation authorities are blaming the attack on an elaborate network of anti-occupation radio broadcasts. She says that crews are busy locking away the beaches behind a network of concertina wire and huge wooden jacks called *chevaux de frise.* Already they have restricted access to the walkways atop the ramparts.

She hands over a loaf and Marie-Laure carries it home. When Etienne breaks it open, there is yet another piece of paper inside. Nine more numbers. "I thought they might take a break," he says.

Marie-Laure is thinking of her father. "Maybe," she says, "it is even more important now?"

He waits until dark. Marie-Laure sits in the mouth of the wardrobe, the false back open, and listens to her uncle switch on the microphone and transmitter in the attic. His mild voice speaks numbers into the garret. Then music plays, soft and low, full of cellos tonight, and it cuts out midstream.

"Uncle?"

It takes him a long time to come down the ladder. He takes her hand. He says, "The war that killed your grandfather killed sixteen million others. One and a half million French boys alone, most of them younger than I was. Two million on the German side. March the dead in a single-file line, and for eleven days and eleven nights, they'd walk past our door. This is not rearranging street signs, what we're doing, Marie. This is not misplacing a letter at the post office. These numbers, they're more than numbers. Do you understand?"

"But we are the good guys. Aren't we, Uncle?"

"I hope so. I hope we are."

Rue des Patriarches

Von Rumpel enters an apartment house in the 5th arrondissement. The simpering landlady on the first floor takes the sheaf of ration tickets he offers and buries them in her housecoat. Cats swarm her ankles. Behind her, an overdecorated flat reeks of dead apple blossoms, confusion, old age.

"When did they leave, Madame?"

"Summer of 1940." She looks as if she might hiss.

"Who pays the rent?"

"I don't know, Monsieur."

"Do the checks come from the Natural History Museum?"

"I can't say."

"When was the last time someone came?"

"No one comes. The checks are mailed."

"From where?"

"I don't know."

"And no one leaves or enters the flat?"

"Not since that summer," she says, and retreats with her vulture face and vulture fingernails into the redolent dark.

Up he goes. A single dead bolt on the fourth floor marks the locksmith's flat. Inside, the windows are boarded over with wood veneer, and an airless, pearly light seeps through the knotholes. As though he has climbed into a dark box hung inside a column of pure light. Cabinets hang open, sofa cushions sit slightly cockeyed, a kitchen chair is toppled on its side. Everything speaks of a hasty departure or a rigorous search or both. A black rim of algae rings the toilet bowl where the water has slipped away. He inspects the bedroom, bathroom, kitchen, some fiendish and immitigable hope flaring within him: *What if — ?*

Along the top of a workbench stand tiny benches, tiny lampposts, tiny trapezoids of polished wood. Little vise, little box of nails, little bottles of glue long since hardened. Beside the bench, beneath a drop cloth, a surprise: a complicated model of the 5th arrondissement. The buildings are unpainted but otherwise beautifully detailed. Shutters, doors, windows, storm drains. No people. A toy?

In the closet hang a few moth-eaten girl's dresses and a sweater on which embroidered goats chew flowers. Dusty pinecones line the windowsill, arranged large to small. On the floor of the kitchen, friction strips have been nailed into the wood. A place of quiet discipline. Calm. Order. A single line of twine runs between the table and the bathroom. A clock stands dead without glass on its face. It's not until he finds three huge spiral-bound folios of Jules Verne in Braille that he solves it.

A safe maker. Brilliant with locks. Lives within walking distance of the museum. Employed there all his adult life. Humble, no visible aspirations for wealth. A blind daughter. Plenty of reasons to be loyal.

"Where are you hiding?" he says aloud to the room. The dust swirls in the strange light.

Inside a bag or a box. Tucked behind a baseboard or stashed in a compartment beneath the floorboards or plastered up inside a wall. He opens the kitchen drawers and checks behind them. But the previous searchers would have checked all of this.

Slowly his attention returns to the scale model of the neighborhood. Hundreds of tiny houses with mansard roofs and balconies. It is this exact neighborhood, he realizes, colorless and depopulated and miniaturized. A tiny spectral version of it. One building in particular appears smoothed and worn by the insistence of fingers: the building he's in. Home.

He puts his eye to street level, becomes a god looming over the Latin Quarter. With two fingers, he could pinch out anyone he chooses, nudge half a city into shadow. Flip it upside down. He sets his fingers atop the roof of the apartment house in which he kneels. Wiggles it back and forth. It lifts free of the model easily, as though designed to do so. He rotates it in front of his eyes: eighteen little windows, six balconies, a tiny entrance door. Down here — behind this window — lurks the little landlady with her cats. And here, on the fourth floor, himself.

On its bottom he finds a tiny hole, not at all unlike the keyhole in the jewel safe in the museum he saw three years before. The house is, he realizes, a container. A receptacle. He plays with it awhile, trying to solve it. Turns it over, tries the bottom, the side.

His heart rate soars. Something wet and feverish rises onto his tongue.

Do you have something inside of you?

Von Rumpel sets the little house on the floor, raises his foot, and crushes it.

WHITE CITY

In April 1944 the Opel rattles into a white city full of empty windows. "Vienna," says Volkheimer, and Neumann Two fulminates about Hapsburg palaces and Wiener schnitzel and girls whose vulvas taste like apple strudel. They sleep in a once stately Old World suite with the furniture shored up against the walls and chicken feathers clogging the marble sinks and newspapers tacked clumsily across the windows. Down below, a switching yard presents a wilderness of train tracks. Werner thinks of Dr. Hauptmann with his curls and fur-lined gloves, whose Viennese youth Werner imagined spent in vibrant cafés where scientists-to-be discussed Bohr and Schopenhauer, where marble statues stared down from ledges like kindly godparents.

Hauptmann, who, presumably, is still in Berlin. Or at the front, like everyone else.

The city commander has no time for them. A subordinate tells Volkheimer there are reports of resistance broadcasts washing out of the Leopoldstadt. Round and round the district they drive. Cold fog hangs in the budding trees, and Werner sits in the back of the truck and shivers. The place smells to him of carnage.

For five days he hears nothing on his transceiver but anthems and recorded propaganda and broadcasts from beleaguered colonels requesting supplies, gasoline, men. It is all unraveling, Werner can feel it; the fabric of the war tearing apart.

"That's the Staatsoper," says Neumann Two one night. The facade of a grand building rises gracefully, pilastered and crenelated. Stately wings soar on either side, somehow both heavy and light. It strikes Werner just then as wondrously futile to build splendid buildings, to make music, to sing songs, to print huge books full of colorful birds in the face of the seismic, engulfing indifference of the world — what pretensions humans have! Why bother to make music when the silence and wind are so much larger? Why light lamps when the darkness will inevitably snuff them? When Russian prisoners are chained by threes and fours to fences while German privates tuck live grenades in their pockets and run?

Opera houses! Cities on the moon! Ridiculous. They would all do better to put their faces on the curbs and wait for the boys who come through the city dragging sledges stacked with corpses.

At midmorning Volkheimer orders them to park in the Augarten. The sun burns away the fog and reveals the first blooms on the trees. Werner can feel the fever flickering inside him, a stove with its door latched. Neumann One, who, if he were not scheduled to die ten weeks from now in the Allied invasion of Normandy, might have become a barber later in life, who would have smelled of talc and whiskey and put his index finger into men's ears to position their heads, whose pants and shirts always would have been covered with clipped hairs, who, in his shop, would have taped postcards of the Alps around the circumference of a big cheap wavery mirror, who would have been faithful to his stout wife for the rest of his life — Neumann One says, "Time for haircuts."

He sets a stool on the sidewalk and throws a mostly clean towel over Bernd's shoulders and snips away. Werner finds a state-sponsored station playing waltzes and sets the speaker in the open back door of the Opel so all can hear. Neumann One cuts Bernd's hair, then Werner's, then pouchy, wrecked Neumann Two's. Werner watches Volkheimer climb onto the stool and close his eyes when a particularly plangent waltz comes on, Volkheimer who has killed a hundred men by now at least, probably more, walking into pathetic radio-transmitting shacks in his huge expropriated boots, sneaking up behind some emaciated Ukrainian with headphones on his ears and a microphone at his lips and shooting him in the back of the head, then going to the truck to tell Werner to collect the transmitter, making the order calmly, sleepily, even with the pieces of the man on the transmitter like that.

Volkheimer who always makes sure there is food for Werner. Who brings him eggs, who shares his broth, whose fondness for Werner remains, it seems, unshakable.

The Augarten proves a thorny place to search, full of narrow streets and tall apartment houses. Transmissions both pass through the buildings and reflect off them. That afternoon, long after the stool has been put away and the waltzes have stopped, while Werner sits with his transceiver listening to nothing, a little redheaded girl in a maroon cape emerges from a doorway, maybe six or seven years old, small for her age, with big clear eyes that remind him of Jutta's. She runs across the street to the park and plays there alone, beneath the budding trees, while her mother stands on the corner and bites the tips of her fingers. The girl climbs into the swing and pendulums back and forth, pumping her legs, and watching her opens some valve in Werner's soul. This is life, he thinks, this is why we live, to play like this on a day when winter is finally releasing its grip.

He waits for Neumann Two to come around the truck and say something crass, to spoil it, but he doesn't, and neither does Bernd, maybe they don't see her at all, maybe this one pure thing will escape their defilement, and the girl sings as she swings, a high song that Werner recognizes, a counting song that girls jumping rope in the alley behind Children's House used to sing, *Eins, zwei, Polizei, drei, vier, Offizier,* and how he would like to join her, push her higher and higher, sing *fünf, sechs, alte Hex, sieben, acht, gute Nacht*! Then her mother calls something Werner cannot hear and takes the girl's hand. They pass around a corner, little velvet cape trailing behind, and are gone.

Not an hour later, he snares something winging in out of the static: a simple broadcast in Swiss German. *Hit nine, transmitting at 1600, this is KX46, do you receive?* He does not understand all of it. Then it goes. Werner crosses the square and tunes the second transceiver himself. When they speak again, he triangulates and plugs the numbers into the equation, then looks up and sees with his naked eyes what looks very much like a wire antenna trailing down the side of an apartment house flanking the square.

So easy.

Already Volkheimer's eyes have come alive, a lion who has caught the scent. As though he and Werner hardly need to speak to communicate.

"See the wire trailing down there?" Werner asks.

Voklheimer glasses the building with binoculars. "That window?"

"Yes."

"It's not too dense in here? All these flats?"

"That's the window," says Werner.

They go in. He does not hear any shots. Five minutes later, they call him up into a fifth-floor flat wallpapered with a dizzying floral print. He expects to be asked to look over the equipment, as usual, but there is none: no corpses, no transmitter, not even a simple listening set. Just ornate lamps and an embroidered sofa and the swarming rococo wallpaper.

"Pry up the floorboards," orders Volkheimer, but after Neumann Two pries up several and peers down, it's clear that the only thing under the boards is decades-old horsehair for insulation.

"Another flat, maybe? Another floor?"

Werner crosses into a bedroom and slides open the window and peers over an iron balcony. What he thought was an antenna is nothing more than a painted rod run up the side of a pilaster, probably meant to anchor a clothesline. Not an antenna at all. But he heard a transmission. Didn't he?

An ache reaches up through the base of his

skull. He laces his hands behind his head and sits on the edge of an unmade bed and looks at the clothes here — a slip folded over the back of a chair, a pewter-backed hairbrush on the bureau, rows of tiny frosted bottles and pots on a vanity, all of it inarticulably feminine to him, mysterious and confusing, in the way Herr Siedler's wife confused him four years before as she hitched up her skirt and knelt in front of her big radio.

A woman's room. Wrinkled sheets, a smell like skin lotion in the air, and a photograph of a young man — nephew? lover? brother? — on a dressing table. Maybe his math was wrong. Maybe the signal scattered off the buildings. Maybe the fever has scrambled his wits. On the wallpaper in front of him, roses appear to drift, rotate, swap places.

"Nothing?" calls Volkheimer from the other room, and Bernd calls back, "Nothing."

In some alternate universe, Werner considers, this woman and Frau Elena could have been friends. A reality more pleasant than this one. Then he sees, hung on the doorknob, a maroon square of velvet, hood attached, a child's cape, and at exactly that moment in the other bedroom, Neumann Two makes a cry like a high, surprised gargle and there is a single shot, then a woman's scream, then more shots, and Volkheimer strides past, hurrying, and the rest follow, and they find Neumann Two standing in front of a closet with both hands on his rifle and the smell of gunpowder all around. On the floor is a woman, one arm swept backward as if she has been refused a dance, and inside the closet is not a radio but a child sitting on her bottom with a bullet through her head. Her moon eyes are open and moist and her mouth is stretched back in an oval of surprise and it is the girl from the swings and she cannot be over seven years old.

Werner waits for the child to blink. Blink, he thinks, blink blink blink. Already Volkheimer is closing the closet door, though it won't close all the way because the girl's foot is sticking out of it, and Bernd is covering the woman on the bed with a blanket, and how could Neumann Two not have known, but of course he didn't, because that is how things are with Neumann Two, with everybody in this unit, in this army, in this world, they do as they're told, they get scared, they move about with only themselves in mind. *Name me someone who does not.*

Neumann One shoulders out, something rancid in his eyes. Neumann Two stands there with his new haircut, his fingers playing senseless trills on the stock of his rifle. "Why did they hide?" he says.

Volkheimer tucks the child's foot gently back inside the closet. "There's no radio here," he says, and shuts the door. Threads of nausea reach up around Werner's windpipe.

Outside, the streetlamps shudder in a late wind. Clouds ride west over the city.

Werner climbs into the Opel, feeling as if the buildings are rearing around him, growing taller and warping. He sits with his forehead against the listening decks and is sick between his shoes.

So really, children, mathematically, all of light is invisible.

Bernd climbs in and pulls the door shut and the Opel comes to life, tilting as it rounds a corner, and Werner can feel the streets rising around them, whorling slowly into an engulfing spiral, into the center of which the truck will arc downward, tracing deeper and deeper all the time.

Twenty Thousand Leagues Under the Sea

On the floor outside Marie-Laure's bedroom door waits something big wrapped in newsprint and twine. From the stairwell, Etienne says, "Happy sixteenth birthday."

She tears away the paper. Two books, one stacked atop the other.

Three years and four months have passed since Papa left Saint-Malo. One thousand two hundred and twenty-four days. Almost four years have passed since she has felt Braille, and yet the letters rise from her memory as if she left off reading yesterday.

Jules. Verne. Twenty. Thousand. Leagues. Part. One. Part. Two.

She throws herself at her great-uncle and hangs her arms around his neck.

"You said you never got to finish. I thought, rather than my reading it to you, maybe you could read it to me?"

"But how — ?"

"Monsieur Hébrard, the bookseller."

"When nothing is available? And they're so

expensive —”

“You have made a lot of friends in this town, Marie-Laure.”

She stretches out on the floor and opens to the first page. “I’m going to start it all over again. From the beginning.”

“Perfect.”

“ ‘Chapter One,’ ” she reads. “ ‘A Shifting Reef.’ ” *The year 1866 was marked by a strange event, an unexplainable occurrence, which is undoubtedly still fresh in everyone’s memory . . .* She gallops through the first ten pages, the story coming back: worldwide curiosity about what must be a mythical sea monster, famed marine biologist Professor Pierre Aronnax setting off to discover the truth. Is it monster or moving reef? Something else? Any page now, Aronnax will plunge over the rail of the frigate; not long afterward, he and the Canadian harpooner Ned Land will find themselves on Captain Nemo’s submarine.

Beyond the carton-covered window, rain sifts down from a platinum-colored sky. A dove scrabbles along the gutter calling *hoo hoo hoo.* Out in the harbor a sturgeon makes a single leap like a silver horse and then is gone.

Telegram

A new garrison commander has arrived on the Emerald Coast, a colonel. Trim, smart, efficient. Won medals at Stalingrad. Wears a monocle. Invariably accompanied by a gorgeous French secretary-interpreter who may or may not have consorted with Russian royalty.

He is average-sized and prematurely gray, but by some contrivance of carriage and posture, he makes the men who stand before him feel smaller. The rumor is that this colonel ran an entire automobile company before the war. That he is a man who understands the power of the German soil, who feels its dark prehistoric vigor thudding in his very cells. That he will never acquiesce.

Every night he sends telegrams from the district office in Saint-Malo. Among the sixteen official communiqués sent on the thirtieth of April, 1944, is a missive to Berlin.

= NOTICE OF TERRORIST BROAD-

CASTS IN CÔTES D'ARMOR WE BELIEVE SAINT-LUNAIRE OR DINARD OR SAINT-MALO OR CANCALE = REQUEST ASSISTANCE TO LOCATE AND ELIMINATE

Dot dot dash dash, off it goes into the wires belted across Europe.

■ ■ ■ ■

Eight: 9 August 1944

■ ■ ■ ■

Fort National

On the third afternoon of the siege of Saint-Malo, the shelling lulls, as though all the artillerymen abruptly fell asleep at their guns. Trees burn, cars burn, houses burn. German soldiers drink wine in blockhouses. A priest in the college cellar scatters holy water on the walls. Two horses, gone mad with fear, kick through the door of the garage in which they've been shut and gallop between the smoldering houses on the Grand Rue.

Around four o'clock, an American field howitzer, two miles away, lets fly a single improperly ranged shell. It sails over the city walls and bursts against the northern parapet of Fort National, where three hundred and eighty Frenchmen are being held against their will with minimal cover. Nine are killed instantly. One of them still clutching the hand of bridge he was playing when the shell struck.

In the Attic

For all of Marie-Laure's four years in Saint-Malo, the bells at St. Vincent's have marked the hours. But now the bells have ceased. She does not know how long she has been trapped in the attic or even if it is day or night. Time is a slippery thing: lose hold of it once, and its string might sail out of your hands forever.

Her thirst becomes so acute, she considers biting into her own arm to drink the liquid that courses there. She takes the cans of food from her great-uncle's coat and sets her lips on their rims. Both taste of tin. Their contents just a millimeter away.

Don't risk it, says the voice of her father. *Don't risk the noise.*

Just one, Papa. I will save the other. The German is gone. Almost certainly he is gone by now.

Why hasn't the trip wire sprung?

Because he cut the wire. Or I slept through the bell. Any of a half dozen other reasons.

Why would he leave when what he seeks is here?

Who knows what he seeks?

You know what he seeks.

I am so hungry, Papa.

Try to think about something else.

Roaring falls of clear, cool water.

You will survive, ma chérie.

How can you know?

Because of the diamond in your coat pocket. Because I left it here to protect you.

All it has done is put me in more danger.

Then why hasn't the house been hit? Why hasn't it caught fire?

It's a rock, Papa. A pebble. There is only luck, bad or good. Chance and physics. Remember?

You are alive.

I am only alive because I have not yet died.

Do not open the can. He will hear you. He will not hesitate to kill you.

How can he kill me if I cannot die?

Round and round the questions run; Marie-Laure's mind threatens to boil over. Just now she has pulled herself up onto the piano bench at the end of the attic and is running her hands over Etienne's transmitter, trying to apprehend its switches and coils — here the phonograph, here the microphone, here one of four leads connected to the pair of batteries — when she hears something below her.

A voice.

Very carefully, she lowers herself off the bench and presses her ear to the floor.

He is directly below her. Urinating into the sixth-floor toilet. Dribbling out a sad intermittent trickle and groaning as though the process causes him torment. Between groans, he calls, *"Das Häuschen fehlt, wo bist du Häuschen?"*

Something is wrong with him.

"Das Häuschen fehlt, wo bist du Häuschen?"

No replies. Whom is he talking to?

From somewhere beyond the house come the thump of distant mortars and the screech of shells hurtling overhead. She listens to the German move from the toilet toward her bedroom. Limping that same limp. Muttering. Unhinged. *Häuschen:* what does it mean?

The springs of her mattress creak; she would know that sound anywhere. Has he been sleeping in her bed all this time? Six deep reports sound one after the other, deeper than antiaircraft guns, farther away. Naval guns. Then come drums, cymbals, the gongs of explosions, drawing a crimson lattice over the roof. The lull is ending.

Abyss in her gut, desert in her throat — Marie-Laure takes one of the cans of food from her coat. The brick and the knife within reach.

Don't.

If I keep listening to you, Papa, I will die of starvation with food in my hands.

Her bedroom below remains quiet. The shells come patiently, each round whizzing over at a predictable interval, scratching a long scarlet parabola over the roof. She uses their noise to open the can. *EEEEEEEEEE* goes the shell, *ding* goes the brick onto the knife, the knife onto the can. Dull terrible detonation somewhere. Shell splinters zinging into the walls of a dozen houses.

EEEEEEEE ding. EEEEEEEE ding. With each blow a prayer. Do not let him hear.

Five bashes and it's leaking liquid. With the sixth, she manages to saw open a quadrant and bend up the lid with the blade of the knife.

She raises it and drinks. Cool, salty: it is beans. Canned cooked green beans. The water they have been boiled in is supremely tasty; her whole body seems to reach up to absorb it. She empties the can. Inside her head, her father has gone quiet.

The Heads

Werner weaves the antenna through the rubbled ceiling and touches it to a twisted pipe. Nothing. On his hands and knees, he drags the aerial around the circumference of the cellar, as though roping Volkheimer into the golden armchair. Nothing. He switches off the dying flashlight and mashes the headset against his good ear and shuts his eyes against the darkness and turns on the repaired transceiver and runs the needle up and down the tuning coil, condensing all his senses into one.

Static static static static static.

Maybe they are buried too deeply. Maybe the rubble of the hotel creates an electromagnetic shadow. Maybe something fundamental is broken in the radio that Werner has not identified. Or maybe the führer's super-scientists have engineered a weapon to end all weapons and this whole corner of Europe is a shattered waste and Werner and Volkheimer are the only ones left.

He takes off the headphones and breaks the connection. The rations are long gone, the canteens are empty, and the sludge in the bottom of the bucket full of paintbrushes is undrinkable. Both he and Volkheimer have gagged down several mouthfuls, and Werner is not sure he can stomach any more.

The battery inside the radio is nearly dead. Once it's gone, they'll have the big American eleven-volt with the black cat printed on the side. And then?

How much oxygen does a person's respiratory system exchange for carbon dioxide every hour? There was a time when Werner would have loved to solve that puzzle. Now he sits with Volkheimer's two stick grenades in his lap, feeling the last bright things inside him fizzle out. Turning the shaft of one and then the other. He'd ignite their fuses just to light this place up, just to see again.

Volkheimer has taken to switching on his field light and focusing its frail beam into the far corner, where eight or nine white plaster heads stand on two shelves, several toppled onto their sides. They look like the heads of mannequins, only more skillfully fashioned, three with mustaches, two bald, one wearing the cap of a soldier. Even with the light off, the heads assume strange power in the dark: pure white, not quite visible but not entirely invisible, embedded into Werner's retinas, almost glowing in the blackness.

Silent and watchful and unblinking.

Tricks of the mind.

Faces, look away.

In the blackness, he crawls toward Volkheimer: a comfort to find his friend's huge knee in the darkness. The rifle beside him. Bernd's corpse somewhere beyond.

Werner says, "Did you ever hear the stories they told about you?"

"Who?"

"The boys at Schulpforta."

"A few I heard."

"Did you like it? Being the Giant? Having everyone afraid of you?"

"It is not so fun being asked how tall you are all the time."

A shell detonates somewhere aboveground. Somewhere out there the city burns, the sea breaks, barnacles beat their feathery arms.

"How tall *are* you?"

Volkheimer snorts once, a bark of a laugh.

"Do you think Bernd was right about the grenades?"

"No," says Volkheimer, his voice coming alert. "They would kill us."

"Even if we built some kind of barrier?"

"We'd be crushed."

Werner tries to make out the heads across the cellar in the blackness. If not the grenades, then what? Does Volkheimer really believe someone is going to come and save them? That they deserve saving?

"So we're just going to wait?"
Volkheimer doesn't answer.
"For how long?"
When the radio batteries die, the American eleven-volt should run the transceiver for one more day. Or he could wire the bulb from Volkheimer's field light to it. The battery will give them one more day of static. Or one more day of light. But they will not need light to use the rifle.

Delirium

A purple fringe flutters around von Rumpel's vision. Something must have gone wrong with the morphine: he may have taken too much. Or else the disease has advanced far enough to alter his sight.

Ash drifts through the window like snow. Is it dawn? The glow in the sky could be the light from fires. Sheets soaked in sweat, his uniform as wet as if he has been swimming in his sleep. Taste of blood in his mouth.

He crawls to the end of the bed and looks at the model. He has studied every square inch of it. Bashed a corner to pieces with the butt of a wine bottle. The structures in it are mostly hollow — the château, the cathedral, the market — but why bother to smash them all when one is missing, the very house he needs?

Out in the forsaken city, every other structure, it seems, is burning or collapsing, but here in front of him is the inverse in miniature: the city remains, but the house he occupies is gone.

Could the girl have carried it out with her when she fled? Possible. The uncle didn't have it when they sent him to Fort National. He was well searched; he carried nothing but his papers — von Rumpel made sure of it.

Somewhere a wall goes to pieces, a thousand kilograms of masonry crashing down.

That the house stands while so many others have been destroyed is evidence enough. The stone must be inside. He simply needs to find it while there is time. Clamp it to his heart and wait for the goddess to thrust her fiery hand through its planes and burn away his afflictions. Burn his way out of this citadel, out of this siege, out of this disease. He will be saved. He simply has to drag himself up from this bed and keep looking. Do it more methodically. As many hours as it takes. Tear the place apart. Begin in the kitchen. One more time.

Water

Marie-Laure hears the springs of her bed groan. Hears the German limp out of her room and go down the stairs. Is he leaving? Giving up?

It starts to rain. Thousands of tiny drops thrum onto the roof. Marie-Laure stands on her tiptoes and presses her ear to the roofing beneath the slates. Listens to the drops trickle down. What was the prayer? The one Madame Manec muttered to herself on Bastille Day as the fireworks went up?

Lord Our God Your Grace is a purifying fire.

She has to marshal her mind. Use perception and logic. As her father would, as Jules Verne's great marine biologist Professor Pierre Aronnax would. The German does not know about the attic. She has the stone in her pocket; she has one can of food. These are advantages.

The rain is good too: it will stifle the fires. Could she capture some of it to drink? Punch a hole in the slates? Use it in some other way?

Maybe to cover her noise?

She knows exactly where the two galvanized buckets are: just inside the door of her room. She can get to them, maybe even carry one back up.

No, carrying it up would be impossible. Too heavy, too noisy, all that water sloshing everywhere. But she could go to one and lower her face into it. She could fill the empty can of beans.

The very thought of her lips against water — the tip of her nose touching its surface — summons up a biological craving beyond anything she has experienced. In her mind she falls into a lake; water fills her ears and mouth; her throat opens. One sip and she could think more clearly. She waits for her father's voice in her head to raise an objection, but none comes.

The distance through the front of the wardrobe, across Henri's room, across the landing, and to her doorway runs twenty-one paces, give or take. She takes the knife and the empty can from the floor and tucks them in her pocket. She creeps down the seven ladder rungs and stays fixed for a long time against the back of the wardrobe. Listening listening listening. The little wooden house is a bump against her ribs as she crouches. Inside its tiny attic, does some tiny likeness of Marie-Laure wait, listening? Does that tiny version of her feel this same thirst?

The only sound is the patter of the rain turning Saint-Malo into mud.

It could be a trick. Maybe he heard her open the can of beans, went noisily downstairs, and climbed quietly back up; maybe he stands outside the big wardrobe with his pistol drawn.

Lord Our God Your Grace is a purifying fire.

She flattens her hands against the back of the wardrobe and slides open the panel. The shirts drag across her face as she crawls through. She sets her hands against the inside of the wardrobe doors and nudges one open.

No gunshot. Nothing. Out the now glassless window, the sound of rain falling on the burning houses is the sound of pebbles being stirred by waves. Marie-Laure steps onto the floor of her grandfather's old bedroom and summons him: a curious boy with lustrous hair who smells of the sea. He's playful, quick-witted, charged with energy; he takes one of her hands, while Etienne finds the other; the house becomes as it was fifty years ago: the boys' well-dressed parents laugh downstairs; a cook shucks oysters in the kitchen; Madame Manec, a young maid, fresh from the countryside, sings on a stepladder as she dusts the chandelier . . .

Papa, you had the keys to everything.

The boys lead her into the hall. She passes the bathroom.

Traces of the German's smell hang in her

bedroom: an odor like vanilla. Beneath it something putrid. She cannot hear anything beyond the rain outside and her own pulse discharging in her temples. She kneels as soundlessly as she can and runs her hands along the grooves of the floor. The sound of her fingertips striking the bucket's side seems louder than the gong of a cathedral bell.

Rain hums against the roof and walls. Drips past the glassless window. All around her wait her pebbles and seashells. Her father's model. Her quilt. Somewhere in here must be her shoes.

She lowers her face and touches her lips to the water's surface. Each swallow seems as loud as a shell burst. One three five; she gulps breathes gulps breathes. Her entire head inside the bucket.

Breathing. Dying. Dreaming.

Does he stir? Is he downstairs? Is he coming back up?

Nine eleven thirteen, she is full. Her whole gut stretches, sloshes; she has had too much. She slips the can into the bucket and lets it fill. Now to retreat without making a sound. Without bumping a wall, the door. Without tripping, without spilling. She turns and begins to crawl, the full can of water in her left hand.

Marie-Laure makes the doorway of her room before she hears him. He is three or four stories below, ransacking one of the rooms; she hears what sounds like a crate of ball bearings get dumped onto the floor. They bounce, clatter, and roll.

She reaches out her right hand, and here, just inside of the doorway, she discovers something big and rectangular and hard, covered with cloth. Her book! The novel! Sitting right here as though her father has placed it for her. The German must have tossed it off her bed. She lifts it as quietly as she can and holds it against the front of her uncle's coat.

Can she make it downstairs?

Can she slip past him and into the street?

But already the water is filling her capillaries, improving the flow of her blood; already she thinks more keenly. She does not want to die; already she has risked too much. Even if she could miraculously slip past the German, there is no promise that the streets will be safer than the house.

She makes it to the landing. Makes it to the threshold of her grandfather's bedroom. Feels her way to the wardrobe, climbs through the open doors, closes them gently behind her.

The Beams

Shells are careening overhead, quaking the cellar like passing freight trains. Werner imagines the American artillerymen: spotters with scopes balanced on rocks or tank treads or hotel railings; firing officers computing wind speed, barrel elevation, air temperature; radiomen with telephone receivers pressed to their ears, calling in targets.

Right three degrees, repeat range. Calm, weary voices directing fire. The same sort of voice God uses, perhaps, when He calls souls to Him. This way, please.

Only numbers. Pure math. You have to accustom yourself to thinking that way. It's the same on their side too.

"My great-grandfather," Volkheimer says all of a sudden, "was a sawyer in the years before steamships, when everything went by sail."

Werner can't be sure in the blackness, but he thinks Volkheimer is standing, running his fingertips along one of the three splintered beams that hold up the ceiling. His knees bent to accommodate his height. Like Atlas about to slip into the traces.

"Back then," Volkheimer says, "all of Europe needed masts for their navies. But most of the countries had cut down their big trees. England, Great-Grandfather said, didn't have a tree worth its wood on the whole island. So the masts for the British and Spanish navies, the Portuguese too, would come from Prussia, from the woods where I grew up. Great-Grandfather knew where all the giants were. Some of those trees would take a crew of five men three days to bring down. First the wedges would go in, like needles, he said, in the hide of an elephant. The biggest trunks could swallow a hundred wedges before they'd creak."

The artillery screams; the cellar shudders.

"Great-Grandfather said he loved to imagine the big trees sledding behind teams of horses across Europe, across rivers, across the sea to Britain, where they'd be stripped and treated and raised up again as masts, where they'd see decades of battle, given a second life, sailing atop the great oceans, until eventually they'd fall and die their second death."

Another shell goes overhead and Werner imagines he hears the wood in the huge beams above him splinter. *That chunk of coal was once a green plant, a fern or reed that lived one million years ago, or maybe two million, or maybe one hundred million. Can you imagine one hundred million years?*

Werner says, "Where I'm from, they dug up trees. Prehistoric ones."

Volkheimer says, "I was desperate to leave."

"I was too."

"And now?"

Bernd molders in the corner. Jutta moves through the world somewhere, watching shadows disentangle themselves from night, watching miners limp past in the dawn. It was enough when Werner was a boy, wasn't it? A world of wildflowers blooming up through the shapes of rusty cast-off parts. A world of berries and carrot peels and Frau Elena's fairy tales. Of the sharp smell of tar, and trains passing, and bees humming in the window boxes. String and spit and wire and a voice on the radio offering a loom on which to spin his dreams.

The Transmitter

It waits on the table tucked against the chimney. The twin marine batteries below it. A strange machine, built years before, to talk to a ghost. As carefully as she can, Marie-Laure crawls to the piano bench and eases herself up. Someone must have a radio — the fire brigade, if one remains, or the resistance, or the Americans hurling missiles at the city. The Germans in their underground forts. Maybe Etienne himself. She tries to imagine him hunched somewhere, his fingers twisting the dials of a phantom radio. Maybe he assumes she is dead. Maybe he needs only to hear a flicker of hope.

She runs her fingers along the stones of the chimney until she finds the lever her uncle installed there. She presses her whole weight on it, and the antenna makes a faint grating noise above the roof as it telescopes upward.

Too loud.

She waits. Counts to one hundred. No sound from downstairs.

Beneath the table, her fingers find switches: one for the microphone, the other for the transmitter, she cannot remember which is which. Switch on one, then the other. Inside the big transmitter, vacuum tubes thrum.

Is it too loud, Papa?

No louder than the breeze. The undertone of the fires.

She traces the lines of the cables until she is sure she has the microphone in her hand.

To shut your eyes is to guess nothing of blindness. Beneath your world of skies and faces and buildings exists a rawer and older world, a place where surface planes disintegrate and sounds ribbon in shoals through the air. Marie-Laure can sit in an attic high above the street and hear lilies rustling in marshes two miles away. She hears Americans scurry across farm fields, directing their huge cannons at the smoke of Saint-Malo; she hears families sniffling around hurricane lamps in cellars, crows hopping from pile to pile, flies landing on corpses in ditches; she hears the tamarinds shiver and the jays shriek and the dune grass burn; she feels the great granite fist, sunk deep into the earth's crust, on which Saint-Malo sits, and the ocean teething at it from all four sides, and the outer islands holding steady against the swirling tides; she hears cows drink from stone troughs and dolphins rise through the green water of the Channel; she hears the bones of dead whales stir five leagues below, their marrow offering a century of food for cities of creatures who will live their whole lives and never once see a photon sent from the sun. She hears her snails in the grotto drag their bodies over the rocks.

Rather than my reading it to you, maybe you could read it to me?

With her free hand, she opens the novel in her lap. Finds the lines with her fingers. Brings the microphone to her lips.

Voice

On the morning of his fourth day trapped beneath whatever is left of the Hotel of Bees, Werner is listening to the repaired transceiver, feathering the tuning knob back and forth, when a girl's voice says directly into his good ear: *At three in the morning I was awakened by a violent blow.* He thinks: It's hunger, the fever, I'm imagining things, my mind is forcing the static to coalesce . . .

She says, *I sat up in bed and tried to hear what was going on, but suddenly I was hurled out into the middle of the room.*

She speaks quiet, perfectly enunciated French; her accent is crisper than Frau Elena's. He grinds the headphones into his ear . . . *Obviously,* she says, *the* Nautilus *had collided with something and then heeled over at a sharp angle . . .*

She rolls her *R*'s, draws out her *S*'s. With each syllable, the voice seems to burrow a bit deeper into his brain. Young, high, hardly more than a whisper. If it is a hallucination, let it be.

One of these icebergs turned and struck the Nautilus *as it was cruising underwater. The iceberg then slipped under its hull and lifted it with an irresistible force into shallower water . . .*

He can hear her wet the top of her mouth with her tongue. *But who was to say that at that moment we wouldn't collide against the underside of the barrier, and thus be horribly squashed between two surfaces of ice?* The static emerges again, threatening to wash her out, and he tries desperately to fight it off; he is a child in his attic dormer, clinging to a dream he does not want to leave, but Jutta has laid a hand on his shoulder and is whispering him awake.

We were suspended in the water, but ten meters on each side of the Nautilus *rose a shining wall of ice. Above and below there was the same wall.*

She stops reading abruptly and the static roars. When she speaks again, her voice has become an urgent hiss: *He is here. He is right below me.*

Then the broadcast cuts out. He feathers the tuner, switches bands: nothing. He takes off the headset and moves in the total blackness toward where Volkheimer sits and grabs what he thinks is his arm. "I heard something. Please . . ."

Volkheimer does not move; he seems made

of wood. Werner yanks with all his strength, but he is too little, too weak; the strength deserts him almost as soon as it came.

"Enough," comes Volkheimer's voice from the blackness. "It won't do any good." Werner sits on the floor. Somewhere in the ruins above them, cats are howling. Starving. As is he. As is Volkheimer.

A boy at Schulpforta once described for Werner a rally at Nuremberg: an ocean of banners and flags, he said, masses of boys teeming in the lights, and the führer himself on an altar a half mile away, spotlights illuminating pillars behind him, the atmosphere oversaturated with meaning and anger and righteousness, Hans Schilzer crazy for it, Herribert Pomsel crazy for it, every boy at Schulpforta crazy for it, and the only person in Werner's life who could see through all that stagecraft was his younger sister. How? How did Jutta understand so much more about how the world worked? While he knew so little?

But who was to say that at that moment we wouldn't collide against the underside of the barrier, and thus be horribly squashed between two surfaces of ice?

He is here. He is right below me.

Do something. Save her.

But God is only a white cold eye, a quarter-moon poised above the smoke, blinking,

blinking, as the city is gradually pounded to dust.

■ ■ ■ ■

Nine:
May 1944

■ ■ ■ ■

Edge of the World

In the back of the Opel, Volkheimer reads aloud to Werner. The paper Jutta has written on seems little more than tissue in his gigantic paws.

> . . . Oh and Herr Siedler the mining official sent a note congratulating you on your successes. He says people are noticing. Does that mean you can come home? Hans Pfeffering says to tell you "a bullet fears the brave" though I maintain that's bad advice. And Frau Elena's toothache is better now but she can't smoke which makes her cranky, did I tell you she started smoking . . .

Over Volkheimer's shoulder, through the cracked rear window of the truck shell, Werner watches a red-haired child in a velvet cape float six feet above the road. She passes through trees and road signs, veers around curves; she is as inescapable as a moon.

Neumann One coaxes the Opel west, and Werner curls beneath the bench in the back and does not move for hours, bundled in a blanket, refusing tea, tinned meat, while the floating child pursues him through the countryside. Dead girl in the sky, dead girl out the window, dead girl three inches away. Two wet eyes and that third eye of the bullet hole never blinking.

They bounce through a string of small green towns where pollarded trees line sleepy canals. A pair of women on bicycles pull off the road and gape at the truck as its passes: some infernal lorry sent to blight their town.

"France," says Bernd.

The canopies of cherry trees drift overhead, pregnant with blossoms. Werner props open the back door and dangles his feet off the rear bumper, his heels just above the flowing road. A horse rolls on its back in grass; five white clouds decorate the sky.

They unload in a town called Épernay, and the hotelkeeper brings wine and chicken legs and broth that Werner manages to keep down. People at the tables around them speak the language that Frau Elena whispered to him as a child. Neumann One is sent to find diesel, and Neumann Two engages Bernd in a debate about whether or not cow intestines were used as inflatable cells inside first-war zeppelins, and three boys in berets peer around a doorpost and ogle Volkheimer with huge eyes. Behind them, six flowering marigolds in the dusk form the shape of the dead girl, then become flowers once more.

The hotelkeeper says, "You would like more?"

Werner cannot shake his head. Just now he's afraid to set down his hands in case they pass right through the table.

They drive all night and stop at dawn at a checkpoint on the northern rim of Brittany. The walled citadel of Saint-Malo blooms out of the distance. The clouds present diffuse bands of tender grays and blues, and below them the ocean does the same.

Volkheimer shows their orders to a sentry. Without asking permission, Werner climbs out of the truck and slips over the low seawall onto the beach. He winds through a series of barricades and makes for the tide line. To his right runs a line of anti-invasion obstacles shaped like a child's jacks, strung with razor wire, extending at least a mile down the shoreline.

No footprints in the sand. Pebbles and bits of weed are strung in scalloped lines. A trio of outer islands bear low stone forts; a green lantern glows on the tip of a jetty. It feels appropriate somehow, to have reached the edge of the continent, to have only the hammered sea left in front of him. As though this is the end point Werner has been moving toward ever since he left Zollverein.

He dips a hand in the water and puts his fingers in his mouth to taste the salt. Someone is shouting his name, but Werner does not turn; he would like nothing more than to stand here all morning and watch the swells move under the light. They're screaming now, Bernd, then Neumann One, and finally Werner turns to see them waving, and he picks his way along the sand and back up through the lines of razor wire toward the Opel.

A dozen people watch. Sentries, a handful of townspeople. Many with hands over their mouths.

"Tread carefully, boy!" Bernd is yelling. "There are mines! Didn't you read the signs?"

Werner climbs into the back of the truck and crosses his arms.

"Have you completely lost it?" asks Neumann Two.

The few souls they see inside the old city press their backs up against walls to allow the battered Opel to pass. Neumann One stops outside a four-story house with pale blue shutters. "The Kreiskommandantur," he announces. Volkheimer goes inside and returns with a colonel in field uniform: the Reichswehr coat and high belt and tall black boots. On his heels come two aides.

"We believe there is a network of them," one aide says. "The encoded numbers are followed by announcements, births and baptisms and engagements and deaths."

"Then there is music, almost always music,"

says the second. "What it means we cannot say."

The colonel drags two fingers along his perfect jawline. Volkheimer gazes at him and then his aides as though assuring worried children that some injustice will be righted. "We'll find them," he says. "It won't take long."

Numbers

Reinhold von Rumpel visits a doctor in Nuremberg. The tumor in the sergeant major's throat, reports the doctor, has grown to four centimeters in diameter. The tumor in the small intestine is harder to measure.

"Three months," says the doctor. "Maybe four."

An hour later, von Rumpel has installed himself at a dinner party. Four months. One hundred and twenty sunrises, one hundred and twenty more times he has to drag his corrupted body out of a bed and button it into a uniform. The officers at the table talk with indignation about other numbers: the Eighth and Fifth German Armies retreat north through Italy, the Tenth Army might be encircled. Rome could be lost.

How many men?

A hundred thousand.

How many vehicles?

Twenty thousand.

Liver is served. Cubes of it with salt and

pepper, showered in a rain of purple gravy. When the plates are taken away, von Rumpel hasn't touched his. Thirty-four hundred marks: all he has left. And three tiny diamonds that he keeps in an envelope inside his billfold. Each perhaps a carat.

A woman at the table enthuses about greyhound racing, the speed, the *charge* she feels watching it. Von Rumpel reaches for the looped handle of his coffee cup, tries to hide the shaking. A waiter touches his arm. "Call for you, sir. From France."

Von Rumpel walks on wobbly legs through a swinging door. The waiter sets a telephone on a table and retreats.

"Sergeant Major? This is Jean Brignon." The name conjures nothing in von Rumpel's memory.

"I have information about the locksmith. Whom you asked about last year?"

"LeBlanc."

"Yes, Daniel LeBlanc. But my cousin, sir. Do you remember? You offered to help? You said that if I found information, you could help him?"

Three couriers, two found, one last puzzle to solve. Von Rumpel dreams of the goddess almost every night: hair made of flames, fingers made of roots. Madness. Even as he stands at the telephone, ivy twines around his neck, climbs into his ears.

"Yes, your cousin. What have you discovered?"

"LeBlanc was accused of conspiracy, something to do with a château in Brittany. Arrested in January 1941 on a tip from a local. They found drawings, skeleton keys. He was also photographed taking measurements in Saint-Malo."

"A camp?"

"I have not been able to find out. The system is rather elaborate."

"What about the informer?"

"A Malouin named Levitte. First name Claude."

Von Rumpel thinks. The blind daughter, the flat on rue des Patriarches. Vacant since June 1940 while the Natural History Museum pays the rent. Where would you run, if you had to run somewhere? If you had something valuable to carry? With a blind daughter in tow? Why Saint-Malo unless someone you trusted lived there?

"My cousin," Jean Brignon is saying. "You'll help?"

"Thank you very much," says von Rumpel, and sets the receiver back in its cradle.

MAY

The last days of May 1944 in Saint-Malo feel to Marie-Laure like the last days of May 1940 in Paris: huge and swollen and redolent. As if every living thing rushes to establish a foothold before some cataclysm arrives. The air on the way to Madame Ruelle's bakery smells of myrtle and magnolia and verbena; wisteria vines erupt in blossom; everywhere hang arcades and curtains and pendants of flowers.

She counts storm drains: at twenty-one she passes the butcher, the sound of a hose splashing onto tile; at twenty-five she is at the bakery. She places a ration coupon on the counter. "One ordinary loaf, please."

"And how is your uncle?" The words are the same, but the voice of Madame Ruelle is different. Galvanized.

"My uncle is well, thank you."

Madame Ruelle does something she has never done: she reaches across the counter and cups Marie-Laure's face in her floury palms. “You amazing child.”

“Are you crying, Madame? Is everything all right?”

“Everything is wonderful, Marie-Laure.” The hands withdraw; the loaf comes to her: heavy, warm, larger than normal. “Tell your uncle that the hour has come. That the mermaids have bleached hair.”

“The mermaids, Madame?”

“They are coming, dear. Within the week. Put out your hands.” From across the counter comes a wet, cool cabbage, as big as a cannonball. Marie-Laure can hardly fit it into the mouth of her knapsack.

“Thank you, Madame.”

“Now get home.”

“Is it clear ahead?”

“As water from the rock. Nothing in your way. Today is a beautiful day. A day to remember.”

The hour has come. *Les sirènes ont les cheveux décolorés.* Her uncle has been hearing rumors on his radio that across the Channel, in England, a tremendous armada is gathering, ship after ship being requisitioned — fishing vessels and ferries retrofitted, equipped with weapons: five thousand boats, eleven thousand airplanes, fifty thousand vehicles.

At the intersection with the rue d’Estrées, she turns not left, toward home, but right. Fifty meters to the ramparts, a hundred or so more along the base of the walls; from her pocket she pulls Harold Bazin's iron key. The beaches have been closed for several months, studded with mines and walled off with razor wire, but here in the old kennel, out of sight of everyone, Marie-Laure can sit among her snails and dream herself into the mind of the great marine biologist Aronnax, both guest of honor and prisoner on Captain Nemo's great machine of curiosity, free of nations and politics, cruising through the kaleidoscopic wonders of the sea. Oh, to be free! To lie once more in the Jardin des Plantes with Papa. To feel his hands on hers, to hear the petals of the tulips tremble in the wind. He made her the glowing hot center of his life; he made her feel as if every step she took was important.

Are you still there, Papa?

They are coming, dear. Within the week.

Hunting (Again)

They search day and night. Saint-Malo, Dinard, Saint-Servan, Saint-Vincent. Neumann One coaxes the battered Opel down streets so narrow that the sides of the truck shell scrape against walls. They pass little gray crêperies with their windows smashed and shuttered boulangeries and empty bistros and hillsides full of conscripted Russians pouring cement and heavy-boned prostitutes carrying water from wells and they find no broadcasts of the sort the colonel's aides described. Werner can receive the BBC from the north and propaganda stations from the south; sometimes he manages to snare random flits of Morse code. But he hears no birth or wedding or death announcements, no numbers, no music.

The room Werner and Bernd are given, on the top floor of a requisitioned hotel in the city within the walls, is like a place that time wants no part of: three-hundred-year-old stucco quatrefoils and palmate capitals and spiraling horns of fruit festoon the ceiling. At night the dead girl from Vienna strides the halls. She does not look at Werner as she passes his open door, but he knows it is he she is hunting.

The hotelkeeper wrings his hands while Volkheimer paces the lobby. Airplanes crawl across the sky, it seems to Werner, incredibly slowly. As if at any moment one will stall and drop into the sea.

"Ours?" asks Neumann One. "Or theirs?"

"Too high to tell."

Werner walks the upstairs corridors. On the top floor, in what is perhaps the hotel's nicest room, he stands in a hexagonal bathtub and wipes grime off a window with the heel of his palm. A few airborne seeds swirl in the wind, then drop into the chasm of shadow between houses. Above him, in the dimness, a nine-foot-long queen bee, with multiple eyes and golden fuzz on her abdomen, curls across the ceiling.

Dear Jutta,

Sorry I have not written these past months. The fever is mostly gone now and you should not worry. I have been feeling very clearheaded lately and what I want to write about today is the sea. It contains so many colors. Silver at dawn, green at noon, dark blue in the evening. Sometimes it looks almost red. Or it will turn the color of old coins. Right now the shadows of clouds are dragging across it, and patches of sunlight are touching down everywhere. White strings of gulls drag over it like beads.

It is my favorite thing, I think, that I have ever seen. Sometimes I catch myself staring at it and forget my duties. It seems big enough to contain everything anyone could ever feel.

Say hello to Frau Elena and the children who are left.

"Clair de Lune"

Tonight they work a section of the old city tucked against the southern ramparts. Rain falls so lightly that it seems indistinguishable from fog. Werner sits in the back of the Opel; Volkheimer drowses on the bench behind him. Bernd is up on the parapet with the first transceiver under a poncho. He has not keyed his handset in hours, which means he is asleep. The only light comes from the amber filament inside Werner's signal meter.

The spectrum is all static and then it is not.

Madame Labas sends word that her daughter is pregnant. Monsieur Ferey sends love to his cousins at Saint-Vincent.

A great gust of static shears past. The voice is like something from a long-ago dream. A half dozen more words flutter through Werner in that Breton accent: *Next broadcast Thursday 2300. Fifty-six seventy-two something . . .* memory coming at Werner like a six-car train out of the darkness, the quality of the transmission and the tenor of the voice matching in every respect the broadcasts of the Frenchman he used to hear, and then a piano plays three single notes, followed by a pair, the chords rising peacefully, each a candle leading deeper into a forest . . . The recognition is immediate. It is as if he has been drowning for as long as he can remember and somebody has fetched him up for air.

Just behind Werner, Volkheimer's eyelids remain closed. Through the separator between the shell and cab, he can see the motionless shoulders of the Neumanns. Werner covers the meter with his hand. The song unspools, grows louder, and he waits for Bernd to key his microphone, to say he has heard.

But nothing comes. Everyone is asleep. And yet hasn't the little shell in which he and Volkheimer sit gone electric?

Now the piano makes a long, familiar run, the pianist playing different scales with each hand — what sounds like three hands, four — the harmonies like steadily thickening pearls on a strand, and Werner sees six-year-old Jutta lean toward him, Frau Elena kneading bread in the background, a crystal radio in his lap, the cords of his soul not yet severed.

The piano rills through its finishing measures, and then the static wallops back.

Did they hear? Can they hear his heart hammering right now against his ribs? There's the rain, falling lightly past the high houses. There's Volkheimer, his chin resting on the acreage of his chest. Frederick said we don't have choices, don't own our lives, but in the end it was Werner who pretended there were no choices, Werner who watched Frederick dump the pail of water at his feet — *I will not* — Werner who stood by as the consequences came raining down. Werner who watched Volkheimer wade into house after house, the same ravening nightmare recurring over and over and over.

He removes the headset and eases past Volkheimer to open the back door. Volkheimer opens one eye, huge, golden, lionlike. He says, *"Nichts?"*

Werner looks up at the stone houses arrayed wall to wall, tall and aloof, their faces damp, their windows dark. No lamplight anywhere. No antennas. The rain falls so softly, almost soundlessly, but to Werner it roars.

He turns. *"Nichts,"* he says. Nothing.

Antenna

An Austrian antiair lieutenant installs a detachment of eight at the Hotel of Bees. Their cook heats oatmeal and bacon in the hotel kitchen while the other seven take apart walls on the fourth floor with sledgehammers. Volkheimer chews slowly, glancing up every now and then to study Werner.

Next broadcast Thursday 2300.

Werner heard the voice everyone was listening for, and what did he do? Lied. Committed treason. How many men might be in danger because of this? And yet when Werner remembers hearing that voice, when he remembers that song flooding his head, he trembles with joy.

Half of northern France is in flames. The beaches are devouring men — Americans, Canadians, Brits, Germans, Russians — and all through Normandy, heavy bombers pulverize country towns. But out here in Saint-Malo, the dune grass grows long and blue; German sailors still run drills in the harbor;

gunners still stockpile ammunition in the tunnels beneath the fort at La Cité.

The Austrians at the Hotel of Bees use a crane to lower an 88-millimeter cannon onto a bastion in the ramparts. They bolt the gun to a cruciform mount and cover it with camouflage tarps. Volkheimer's crew works two nights in a row, and Werner's memory plays tricks on him.

Madame Labas sends word that her daughter is pregnant.

So how, children, does the brain, which lives without a spark of light, build for us a world full of light?

If the Frenchman employs the same transmitter that used to reach all the way to Zollverein, the antenna will be big. Or else there will be hundreds of yards of wire. Either way: something high, something sure to be visible.

On the third night after hearing the broadcast — Thursday — Werner stands in the hexagonal bathtub beneath the queen bee. With the shutters pushed open, he can look to his left over a jumble of slate rooftops. Shearwaters skim the ramparts; sleeves of vapor enshroud the steeple.

Whenever Werner contemplates the old city, it is the chimneys that strike him. They are huge, stacked in rows of twenty and thirty along each block. Not even Berlin had chimneys like that.

Of course. The Frenchman must be using a

chimney.

He hurries down through the lobby and paces the rue des Forgeurs, then the rue de Dinan. Staring up at shutters, gutter lines, looking for cables bracketed to bricks, anything that might give the transmitter away. He walks up and down until his neck aches. He has been gone too long. He will be upbraided. Volkheimer already senses something amiss. But then, right at 2300 hours, Werner sees it, hardly one block from where they parked the Opel: an antenna sliding up alongside a chimney. Not much wider than a broomstick.

It rises perhaps twelve meters and then unfolds as if by magic into a simple *T.*

A high house on the edge of the sea. A spectacularly good location from which to broadcast. From street level, the antenna is all but invisible. He hears Jutta's voice: *I bet he does these broadcasts from a huge mansion, big as this whole colony, a place with a thousand rooms and a thousand servants.* The house is tall and narrow, eleven windows in its facade. Splotched with orange lichen, its foundation furred with moss. Number 4 on the rue Vauborel.

Open your eyes and see what you can with them before they close forever.

He walks fast to the hotel, head down, hands in his pockets.

Big Claude

Levitte the perfumer is flabby and plump, basted in his own self-importance. While he talks, von Rumpel struggles to keep his balance; the intermingling of so many odors in this shop overwhelms. In the course of the past week, he has had to make a show of trips to a dozen different garden estates up and down the Breton coast, forcing his way into summer homes to hunt down paintings and sculptures that either do not exist or do not interest him. All of it to justify his presence here.

Yes, yes, the perfumer is saying, his gaze flitting over von Rumpel's insignia, a few years ago he helped authorities apprehend an out-of-towner who was taking measurements of buildings. He only did what he knew was right.

"Where was he living during those months, this Monsieur LeBlanc?"

The perfumer squints, calculating. His blue-ringed eyes trumpet one message: *I want.*

Give me. All these aching creatures, thinks von Rumpel, toiling under different pressures. But von Rumpel is the predator here. He needs only to be patient. Indefatigable. Remove the obstacles one by one.

When he turns to go, the perfumer's complacency splinters. "Wait, wait, wait."

Von Rumpel keeps one hand on the door. "Where did Monsieur LeBlanc live?"

"With his uncle. Useless man. Off his nut, as they say."

"Where?"

"Right *there.*" He points. "Number four."

Boulangerie

A full day passes before Werner can find an hour to return. A wooden door, iron gate across that. Blue trim on the windows. The morning fog is so dense that he cannot see the roofline. He entertains pipe dreams: the Frenchman will invite him in. They'll drink coffee, discuss his long-ago broadcasts. Maybe they'll investigate some important empirical problem that has been troubling him for years. Maybe he'll show Werner the transmitter.

Laughable. If Werner rings the bell, the old man will assume he's being arrested as a terrorist. That he might be shot where he stands. The antenna on the chimney in itself is cause for execution.

Werner could bang on the door, march the old man away. He would be a hero.

The mist begins to suffuse with light. Somewhere, someone opens a door and closes it again. Werner remembers how Jutta would write her letters in a flurry and scribble

The Professor, France on the envelope and drop them into the mailbox in the square. Imagining her voice might find his ear as his had found hers. One in ten million.

All night he has practiced the French in his head: *Avant la guerre. Je vous ai entendu à la radio.* He will keep his rifle over his shoulder, hands at his sides; he will look small, elfin, no threat at all. The old man will be startled, but his fear will be manageable. He'll listen. But as Werner stands in the slowly dispersing fog at the end of the rue Vauborel, rehearsing what he'll say, the front door of Number 4 opens, and out steps not an eminent old scientist but a girl. A slender, pretty, auburn-haired girl with a very freckled face, in glasses and a gray dress, carrying a knapsack over one shoulder. She heads to her left, making directly for him, and Werner's heart twists in his chest.

The street is too narrow; she will have caught him staring. But her head tracks in a curious way, her face tilted off to one side. Werner sees the roving cane and opaque lenses of her glasses and realizes that she is blind.

Her cane clicks along the cobbles. Already she is twenty paces away. No one seems to be watching; all the curtains are drawn. Fifteen paces away. Her stockings have runs in them and her shoes are too large and the woolen panels of her dress are mottled with stains.

Ten paces, five. She passes within arm's reach, her head slightly higher than his own. Without thinking, hardly understanding what he's doing, Werner follows. The tip of her cane shudders as it knocks against the runnels, finding every storm drain. She walks like a ballerina in dance slippers, her feet as articulate as hands, a little vessel of grace moving out into the fog. She turns right, then left, traverses half a block and steps neatly through the open door of a shop. A rectangular sign above it reads: *Boulangerie.*

Werner stops. Above him, the mist gives way in shreds, and a deep summer blue reveals itself. A woman waters flowers; an old traveler in gabardine walks a poodle. On a bench sits a goitrous and sallow German sergeant major with shadows carved under his eyes. He lowers his paper, stares directly at Werner, then raises his newspaper again.

Why are Werner's hands shaking? Why can't he catch his breath?

The girl emerges from the bakery, steps neatly off the curbstone, and makes straight for him. The poodle squats to relieve itself on the cobbles, and the girl veers neatly to her left to skirt it. She approaches Werner for a second time, her lips working softly, counting to herself — *deux trois quatre* — coming so close he can count the freckles on her nose, smell the loaf of bread in her knapsack. A million droplets of fog bead up on the fuzz of her wool dress and along the warp of her hair, and the light outlines her in silver.

He stands riveted. Her long pale neck seems to him, as it passes, incredibly vulnerable.

She takes no notice of him; she seems to know nothing but the morning. This, he thinks, is the pure they were always lecturing about at Schulpforta.

He presses his back against a wall. The tip of her cane just misses the toe of his boot. Then she's past, dress swaying lightly, cane roving back and forth, and he watches her continue up the street until the fog swallows her.

GROTTO

A German antiair battery shoots an American plane out of the sky. It crashes into the sea off Paramé, and its American pilot wades ashore to be taken prisoner. Etienne sees it as a calamity, but Madame Ruelle radiates glee. "Movie-star handsome," she whispers as she hands Marie-Laure a loaf. "I bet they'll all look like him."

Marie-Laure smiles. Every morning it's the same: the Americans ever closer, the Germans fraying at the seams. Every afternoon Marie-Laure reads to Etienne from part 2 of *Twenty Thousand Leagues,* both of them in new territory now. *Ten thousand leagues in three and a half months,* writes Professor Aronnax. *Where were we going now, and what did the future have in store for us?*

Marie-Laure puts the loaf in her knapsack, leaves the bakery, and winds toward the ramparts to Harold Bazin's grotto. She closes the gate, lifts the hem of her dress, and wades into the shallow pool, praying she does not crush any creatures as she steps.

The tide is rising. She finds barnacles, an anemone as soft as silk; she sets her fingers as lightly as she can on a *Nassarius.* It stops moving immediately, sucking its head and foot inside its shell. Then it resumes, the twin wands of its horns extending, dragging its whorled shell atop the sled of its body.

What do you seek, little snail? Do you live only in this one moment, or do you worry like Professor Aronnax for your future?

When the snail has crossed the pool and started up the far wall, Marie-Laure picks up her cane and climbs out in her dripping oversized loafers. She steps through the gate and is about to lock it behind her when a male voice says, "Good morning, mademoiselle."

She stumbles, almost trips. Her cane goes clattering.

"What's in your sack there?"

He speaks proper French, but she can tell that he is German. His body obstructs the alley. The hem of her dress drips; her shoes squelch out water; to both sides rise sheer walls. She keeps her right fist clenched around a spar of the open gate.

"What is that back there? A hidey-hole?" His voice sounds terribly close, but it's hard to know for certain in a place so congested with echoes. She can feel Madame Ruelle's loaf pulsing on her back like something alive. Lodged inside it — almost certainly — is a coiled-up slip of paper. On which numbers will spell out a death sentence. For her great-uncle, for Madame Ruelle. For them all.

She says, "My cane."

"It has rolled behind you, dear."

Behind the man unspools the alley and then the hanging curtain of ivy and then the city. A place where she could scream and be heard.

"May I pass, monsieur?"

"Of course."

But he does not seem to move. The gate creaks lightly.

"What do you want, monsieur?" Impossible to keep her voice from trembling. If he asks again about the knapsack, her heart will burst.

"What do you do in there?"

"We're not allowed on the beaches."

"So you come here?"

"To collect snails. I must be getting along, monsieur. May I please retrieve my cane?"

"But you have not collected any snails, mademoiselle."

"May I pass?"

"First answer a question about your father."

"Papa?" Something cold inside her grows colder. "Papa will be here any moment."

Now the man laughs, and his laugh echoes up between the walls. "Any moment, you say? Your papa who's in a prison five hundred kilometers away?"

Threads of terror spill through her chest. I

should have listened, Papa. I never should have gone outside.

"Come now, *petite cachotière,*" says the man, "don't look so frightened," and she can hear him reaching for her; she smells rot on his breath, hears oblivion in his voice, and something — a fingertip? — grazes her wrist as she jerks away and clangs the gate shut in his face.

He slips; it takes longer than she expects for him to get to his feet. Marie-Laure turns the key in the lock and pockets it and finds her cane as she retreats into the low space of the kennel. The man's desolate voice pursues her, even as his body remains on the other side of the locked gate.

"Mademoiselle, you made me drop my newspaper. I am just a lowly sergeant major here to ask a question. One simple question and then I will leave."

The tide murmurs; the snails teem. Is the ironwork too narrow for him to squeeze through? Are its hinges strong enough? She prays that they are. The bulk of the rampart holds her in its breadth. Every ten seconds or so, a new sheet of cold seawater comes flowing in. Marie-Laure can hear the man pacing out there, one-pause-two one-pause-two, a lurching hobble. She tries to imagine the watchdogs that Harold Bazin said lived here for centuries: dogs as big as horses. Dogs that ripped the calves off men. She crouches over her knees. She is the Whelk. Armored. Impervious.

AGORAPHOBIA

Thirty minutes. It should take Marie-Laure twenty-one; Etienne has counted many times. Once twenty-three. Often shorter. Never longer.

Thirty-one.

It is a four-minute walk to the bakery. Four there and four back, and somewhere along the way, those other thirteen or fourteen minutes disappear. He knows she usually goes to the sea — she comes back smelling of seaweed, shoes wet, sleeves decorated with algae or sea fennel or the weed Madame Manec called *pioka.* He does not know where she goes exactly, but he has always assured himself that she keeps herself safe. That her curiosity sustains her. That she is more capable in a thousand ways than he is.

Thirty-two minutes. Out his fifth-floor windows, he can see no one. She could be lost, scraping her fingers along walls at the edge of town, drifting farther away every second. She could have stepped in front of a truck, drowned in a puddle, been seized by a mercenary with foulness on his mind. Someone could have found out about the bread, the numbers, the transmitter.

Bakery in flames.

He hurries downstairs and peers out the kitchen door into the alley. Cat sleeping. Trapezoid of sunlight on the east-facing wall. This is all his fault.

Now Etienne hyperventilates. At thirty-four minutes by his wristwatch, he puts on his shoes and a hat that belonged to his father. Stands in the foyer summoning all his resolve. When he last went out, almost twenty-four years ago, he tried to make eye contact, to present what might be considered a normal appearance. But the attacks were sly, unpredictable, devastating; they sneaked up on him like bandits. First a terrible ominousness would fill the air. Then any light, even through closed eyelids, became excruciatingly bright. He could not walk for the thundering of his own feet. Little eyeballs blinked at him from the cobblestones. Corpses stirred in the shadows. When Madame Manec would help him home, he'd crawl into the darkest corner of his bed and belt pillows around his ears. All his energy would go into ignoring the pounding of his own pulse.

His heart beats icily in a faraway cage. Headache coming, he thinks. Terrible terrible terrible headache.

Twenty heartbeats. Thirty-five minutes. He twists the latch, opens the gate. Steps outside.

Nothing

Marie-Laure tries to remember everything she knows about the lock and latch on the gate, everything she has felt with her fingers, everything her father would have told her. Iron rod threaded through three rusted loops, old mortise lock with a rusty cam. Would a gunshot break it? The man calls out now and then as he runs the edge of his newspaper over the bars of the gate. "Arrived in June, not arrested until January. What was he doing all that time? Why was he measuring buildings?"

She crouches against the wall of the grotto, knapsack in her lap. The water surges to her knees: cold, even in July. Can he see her? Carefully Marie-Laure opens her knapsack, breaks open the loaf hidden inside, and fishes with her fingers for the coil of paper. There. She counts to three and slips the piece of paper into her mouth.

"Just tell me," the German calls, "if your father left anything with you or spoke about carrying something for the museum where he used to work. Then I will walk away. I won't tell anyone about this place. God's truth."

The paper disintegrates into mush between her teeth. At her feet, the snails go about their work: chewing, scavenging, sleeping. Their mouths, Etienne has taught her, contain something like thirty teeth per row, eighty rows of teeth, two and a half thousand teeth per snail, grazing, scratching, rasping. High above the ramparts, gulls course through an open sky. God's truth? How long do these intolerable moments last for God? A trillionth of a second? The very life of any creature is a quick-fading spark in fathomless darkness. That's God's truth.

"They have me doing all this busywork," says the German. "A Jean Jouvenet in Saint-Brieuc, six Monets in the area, a Fabergé egg in a manor house near Rennes. I get so tired. Don't you know how long I've searched?"

Why couldn't Papa have stayed? Wasn't she the most important thing? She swallows the pulped shreds of the paper. Then she rocks forward on her heels. "He left me *nothing.*" She is surprised to hear how angry she is. "Nothing! Just a dumb model of this town and a broken promise. Just Madame, who is dead. Just my great-uncle, who is frightened of an ant."

Outside the gate, the German falls quiet. Considering her reply, perhaps. Something in her exasperation convincing him.

"Now," she calls, "you keep your word and go away."

Forty Minutes

Fog gives way to sunshine. It assaults the cobblestones, the houses, the windows. Etienne makes it to the bakery in an icy sweat and cuts to the front of the queue. Madame Ruelle's face looms, moon-white.

"Etienne? But — ?"

Vermilion spots open and close in his vision.

"Marie-Laure —"

"She is not — ?"

Before he can shake his head, Madame Ruelle is lifting the hinged counter and ushering him out; she has him under the arm. The women in the queue are muttering, intrigued or scandalized or both. Madame Ruelle helps him onto the rue Robert Surcouf. The face of Etienne's watch appears to distend. Forty-one minutes? He can hardly do the math. Her hands grip his shoulder.

"Where could she have gone?"

Tongue so dry, thoughts so sluggish. "Sometimes . . . she visits . . . the sea. Before coming home."

"But the beaches are closed. The ramparts too." She looks off over his head. "It must be something else."

They huddle in the middle of the street. Somewhere a hammer rings. War, Etienne thinks distantly, is a bazaar where lives are traded like any other commodity: chocolate or bullets or parachute silk. Has he traded all those numbers for Marie-Laure's life?

"No," he whispers, "she goes to the sea."

"If they find the bread," Madame Ruelle whispers, "we will all die."

He glances again at his watch, but it's a sun burning his retinas. A single side of salted bacon twists in the butcher's otherwise empty window, and three schoolboys stand on a bench watching him, waiting for him to fall, and just as he is certain the morning is about to shatter, Etienne sees in his memory the rusted gate leading to the crumbling kennel beneath the ramparts. A place where he used to play with his brother, Henri, and Harold Bazin. A small dripping cavern where a boy could shout and dream.

Stick-thin, alabaster-pale Etienne LeBlanc runs down the rue de Dinan with Madame Ruelle, the baker's wife, on his heels: the least-robust rescue ever assembled. The cathedral bells chime one two three four, all the way to eight; Etienne turns down the rue du Boyer and reaches the slightly angled base of the ramparts, traveling the paths of his youth, navigating by instinct; he turns right, passes through the curtain of swinging ivy, and ahead, behind the same locked gate, in the grotto, shivering, wet to her thighs, wholly intact, crouches Marie-Laure with the ruins of a loaf of bread in her lap. "You came," she says when she lets them in, when he takes her face in his hands. "You came . . ."

The Girl

Werner thinks of her, whether he wishes to or not. Girl with a cane, girl in a gray dress, girl made of mist. That air of otherworldliness in the snarls of her hair and the fearlessness of her step. She takes up residence inside him, a living doppelgänger to face down the dead Viennese girl who haunts him every night.

Who is she? Daughter of the broadcasting Frenchman? Granddaughter? Why would he endanger her so?

Volkheimer keeps them out in the field, roving villages along the Rance River. It seems certain that the broadcasts will be blamed for something, and Werner will be found out. He thinks of the colonel with his perfect jawline and flared pants; he thinks of the sallow sergeant major eyeing him over the top of the newspaper. Do they already know? Does Volkheimer? What can save him now? There were nights when he'd stare with Jutta out the attic window of Children's House and pray for the ice to grow out from the canals, to reach across the fields and envelop the tiny pit houses, crush the machinery, pave over everything, so they'd wake in the morning to find everything they knew was gone. This is the sort of miracle he needs now.

On the first of August, a lieutenant comes to Volkheimer. The demand for men on the lines, he says, is overwhelming. Anyone not essential to the defense of Saint-Malo must go. He needs at least two. Volkheimer looks them over, each in turn. Bernd too old. Werner the only one who can repair the equipment.

Neumann One. Neumann Two.

An hour later, both are seated in the back of a troop carrier with their rifles between their knees. A great change has occurred in the countenance of Neumann Two, as though he looks not at his former companions but into his last hours on earth. As though he is about to ride in some black chariot at a forty-five-degree angle down into the abyss.

Neumann One raises a single steady hand. His mouth is expressionless, but in the wrinkles at the corners of his eyes, Werner can see despair.

"In the end," murmurs Volkheimer as the truck heaves away, "none of us will avoid it."

That night Volkheimer drives the Opel east along a coastal road toward Cancale, and Bernd takes the first transceiver out to a knoll in a field, and Werner operates the second from the back of the truck, and Volkheimer stays folded into the driver's seat, his huge knees jammed against the wheel. Fires — perhaps on ships — burn far out to sea, and the stars shudder in their constellations. At two twelve A.M., Werner knows, the Frenchman will broadcast again, and Werner will have to switch off the transceiver or else pretend that he hears only static.

He will cover the signal meter with his palm. He will keep his face completely motionless.

Little House

Etienne says he never should have let her take on so much. Never should have put her in such danger. He says she can no longer go outside. In truth, Marie-Laure is relieved. The German haunts her: in nightmares, he's a spider crab three meters high; he clacks his claws and whispers *One simple question* into her ear.

"What about the loaves, Uncle?"

"I will go. I should have been going all along."

On the mornings of the fourth and fifth of August, Etienne stands at the front door mumbling to himself, then pushes open the gate and goes out. Soon afterward, the bell under the third-floor table rings and he comes back in and throws both dead bolts and stands in the foyer breathing as though he has passed through a gauntlet of a thousand dangers.

Aside from the bread, they have almost nothing to eat. Dried peas. Barley. Powdered milk. A last few tins of Madame Manec's vegetables. Marie-Laure's thoughts gallop like bloodhounds over the same questions. First those policemen two years ago: *Mademoiselle, was there no specific thing he mentioned?* Then this limping sergeant major with a dead voice. *Just tell me if your father left anything with you or spoke about carrying something for the museum.*

Papa leaves. Madame Manec leaves. She remembers the voices of their neighbors in Paris when she lost her eyesight: *Like they're cursed.*

She tries to forget the fear, the hunger, the questions. She must live like the snails, moment to moment, centimeter to centimeter. But on the afternoon of the sixth of August, she reads the following lines to Etienne on the davenport in his study: *Was it true that Captain Nemo never left the* Nautilus*? Often I had not seen him for weeks on end. What was he doing during that time? Wasn't it possible that he was carrying out some secret mission completely unknown to me?*

She snaps shut the book. Etienne says, "Don't you want to find out if they're going to escape this time?" But Marie-Laure is reciting in her head the strange third letter from her father, the last one she received.

Remember your birthdays? How there were

always two things on the table when you woke? I'm sorry it turned out like this. If you ever wish to understand, look inside Etienne's house, inside the house. I know you will do the right thing. Though I wish the gift were better.

Mademoiselle, was there no specific thing he mentioned?

May we look at whatever he brought here with him?

He had many keys at the museum.

It's not the transmitter. Etienne is wrong. It was not the radio the German was interested in. It was something else, something he thought only she might know about. And he heard what he wanted to hear. She answered his one question after all.

Just a dumb model of this town.

Which is why he walked away.

Look inside Etienne's house.

"What's wrong?" asks Etienne.

Inside the house.

"I need to rest," she announces, and scrambles up the stairs two at a time, shuts her bedroom door, and thrusts her fingers into the miniature city. Eight hundred and sixty-five buildings. Here, near a corner, waits the tall narrow house at Number 4 rue Vauborel. Her fingers crawl down the facade, find the recess in the front door. She presses inward, and the house slides up and out.

When she shakes it, she hears nothing. But the houses never made any noise when she shook them, did they?

Even with her fingers trembling, it doesn't take Marie-Laure long to solve it. Twist the chimney ninety degrees, slide off the roof panels one two three.

A fourth door, and a fifth, on and on until you reach a thirteenth, a little locked door no bigger than a shoe.

So, asked the children, *how do you know it's really there?*

You have to believe the story.

She turns the little house over. A pear-shaped stone drops into her palm.

Numbers

Allied bombs demolish the rail station. The Germans disable the harbor installations. Airplanes slip in and out of clouds. Etienne hears that wounded Germans are pouring into Saint-Servan, that Americans have captured Mont Saint-Michel, only twenty-five miles away, that liberation is a matter of days. He makes it to the bakery just as Madame Ruelle unlocks the door. She ushers him inside. "They want locations of flak batteries. Coordinates. Can you manage it?"

Etienne groans. "I have Marie-Laure. Why not you, Madame?"

"I don't understand maps, Etienne. Minutes, seconds, declination adjustments? You know these things. All you have to do is find them, plot them, and broadcast the coordinates."

"I'll have to walk around with a compass and a notepad. There's no other way to do it. They'll shoot me."

"It's vital that they receive precise locations

for the guns. Think how many lives it might save. And you'll have to do it tonight. There's talk that tomorrow they will intern all the men in the city between eighteen and sixty. That they're going to check everyone's papers, and every man of fighting age, anyone who could be taking part in the resistance, will be imprisoned at Fort National."

The bakery reels; he is being caught in spiderwebs; they twist around his wrists and thighs, crackle like burning paper when he moves. Every second he becomes more entangled. The bell tied to the bakery door jingles, and someone enters. Madame Ruelle's face seals over like the visor of a knight clanging down.

He nods.

"Good," she says, and tucks the loaf under his arm.

Sea of Flames

It is surfaced by hundreds of facets. Over and over she picks it up only to set it immediately down, as though it burns her fingers. Her father's arrest, the disappearance of Harold Bazin, the death of Madame Manec — could this one rock be the cause of so much sorrow? She hears the wheezy, wine-scented voice of old Dr. Geffard: *Queens might have danced all night wearing it. Wars might have been fought over it.*

The keeper of the stone would live forever, but so long as he kept it, misfortunes would fall on all those he loved one after another in unending rain.

Things are just things. Stories are just stories.

Surely this pebble is what the German seeks. She ought to fling open the shutters and cast it down onto the street. Give it to someone else, anyone else. Slip out of the house and hurl it into the sea.

Etienne climbs the ladder to the attic. She

can hear him cross the floorboards above her and turn on the transmitter. She puts the stone in her pocket and picks up the model house and crosses the hall. But before she makes it to the wardrobe, she stops. Her father must have believed it was real. Why else construct the elaborate puzzle box? Why else leave it behind in Saint-Malo, if not in fear that it could be confiscated during his journey back? Why else leave her behind?

It must at least look like a blue diamond worth twenty million francs. Real enough to convince Papa. And if it looks real, what will her uncle do when she shows it to him? If she tells him that they ought to throw it into the ocean?

She can hear the boy's voice in the museum: *When is the last time you saw someone throw five Eiffel Towers into the sea?*

Who would willingly part with it? And the curse? If the curse is real? And she gives it to him?

But curses are not real. Earth is all magma and continental crust and ocean. Gravity and time. Isn't it? She closes her fist, walks into her room, and replaces the stone inside the model house. Slides the three roof panels back into place. Twists the chimney ninety degrees. Slips the house inside her pocket.

Well after midnight, a magnificent high tide arrives, the largest waves smashing against the bases of the ramparts, the sea green and aerated and networked with seething rafts of moonlit foam. Marie-Laure comes out of dreams to hear Etienne tapping on her bedroom door.

"I'm going out."

"What time is it?"

"Almost dawn. I'll only be an hour."

"Why do you have to go?"

"It's better if you don't know."

"What about curfew?"

"I'll be quick." Her great-uncle. Who has not been quick in the four years she has known him.

"What if the bombing starts?"

"It's almost dawn, Marie. I should go while it's still dark."

"Will they hit any houses, Uncle? When they come?"

"They won't hit any houses."

"Will it be over quickly?"

"Quick as a swallow. You rest, Marie-Laure, and when you wake, I'll be back. You'll see."

"I could read to you a bit? Now that I'm awake? We're so close to the end."

"When I'm back, we'll read. We'll finish it together."

She tries to rest her mind, slow her breathing. Tries not to think about the little house now under her pillow and the terrible burden inside.

"Etienne," Marie-Laure whispers, "are you

ever sorry that we came here? That I got dropped in your lap and you and Madame Manec had to look after me? Did you ever feel like I brought a curse into your life?"

"Marie-Laure," he says without hesitation. He squeezes her hand with both of his. "You are the best thing that has ever come into my life."

Something seems to be banking up in the silence, a tide, a breaker rearing. But Etienne only says a second time, "You rest, and when you wake, I'll be back," and she counts his steps down the stairs.

The Arrest of Etienne LeBlanc

Etienne feels strangely good as he steps outside; he feels strong. He is glad Madame Ruelle has assigned him this final task. He has already transmitted the location of one air-defense battery: a cannon on a shelf of rampart beside the Hotel of Bees. He needs only to take the bearings of two more. Find two known points — he'll choose the cathedral spire and the outer island of Le Petit Bé — then calculate the location of the third and unknown point. Simple triangle. Something other than ghosts on which his mind can fix.

He turns onto the rue d'Estrées, skirts behind the college, makes for the alley behind the Hôtel-Dieu. His legs feel young, his feet light. No one is about. Somewhere the sun eases up behind the fog. The city in the predawn is warm and fragrant and sleepy, and the houses on either side seem almost immaterial. For a moment he has a vision that he's walking the aisle of a vast train carriage, all the other passengers asleep, the train gliding through darkness toward a city teeming with light: glowing archways, gleaming towers, fireworks rising.

As he approaches the dark bulwark of the ramparts, a man in uniform limps toward him out of the blackness.

7 August 1944

Marie-Laure wakes to the concussions of big guns firing. She crosses the landing and opens the wardrobe and, with the tip of her cane, reaches through the hanging shirts and raps three times on the false back wall. Nothing. Then she descends to the fifth floor and knocks on Etienne's door. His bed is empty and cool.

He is not on the second floor, nor in the kitchen. The penny nail beside the door where Madame Manec used to hang the key ring is empty. His shoes are gone.

I'll only be an hour.

She reins in her panic. Important not to assume the worst. In the foyer, she checks the trip wire: intact. Then she tears an end off yesterday's loaf from Madame Ruelle and stands in the kitchen chewing. The water — miraculously — has been turned back on, so she fills the two galvanized buckets and carries them upstairs and sets them in the corner of her bedroom and thinks a moment and walks to the third floor and fills the bathtub to the rim.

Then she opens her novel. Captain Nemo has planted his flag on the South Pole, but if he doesn't move the submarine north soon, they will become trapped in ice. The spring equinox has just passed; they face six months of unrelenting night.

Marie-Laure counts the chapters that remain. Nine. She is tempted to read on, but they are voyaging on the *Nautilus* together, she and Etienne, and as soon as he returns, they will resume. Any moment now.

She rechecks the little house under her pillow and fights the temptation to take out the stone and instead reinstalls the house inside the model city at the foot of her bed. Out the window, a truck roars to life. Gulls pass, braying like donkeys, and in the distance the guns thud again, and the rattling of the truck fades, and Marie-Laure tries to concentrate on rereading a chapter earlier in the novel: make the raised dots form letters, the letters words, the words a world.

In the afternoon, the trip wire quivers, and the bell hidden beneath the third-floor table gives a single ring. In the attic high above her, a muted ring matches it. Marie-Laure lifts her fingers from the page, thinking, At last, but when she winds down the stairs and sets her hand on the dead bolt and calls, "Who is there?" she hears not the quiet voice of Etienne but the oily one of the perfumer Claude Levitte.

"Let me in, please."

Even through the door she can smell him, peppermint, musk, aldehyde. Beneath that: Sweat. Fear.

She undoes both dead bolts and opens the door halfway.

He speaks through the half-open gate. "You need to come with me."

"I am waiting for my great-uncle."

"I have talked to your great-uncle."

"You talked to him? Where?"

Marie-Laure can hear Monsieur Levitte cracking his knuckles one after the next. His lungs toiling inside his chest. "If you could see, mademoiselle, you'd have seen the evacuation orders. They've locked the city gates."

She does not reply.

"They're detaining every man between sixteen and sixty. They've been told to assemble at the tower of the château. Then they will be marched to Fort National at low tide. God be with them."

Out on the rue Vauborel, everything sounds calm. Swallows swoop past the houses, and two doves bicker on a high gutter. A bicyclist goes rattling past. Then quiet. Have they really locked the city gates? Has this man really spoken to Etienne?

"Will you go with them, Monsieur Levitte?"

"I plan not to. You must get to a shelter immediately." Monsieur Levitte sniffs. "Or to the crypts below Notre-Dame at Rocabey. Which is where I sent Madame. It's what your uncle asked me to do. Leave absolutely everything behind, and come with me now."

"Why?"

"Your uncle knows why. Everybody knows why. It's not safe here. Come along."

"But you said the gates to the city are locked."

"Yes, I did, girl, and that's enough questions for now." He sighs. "You are not safe, and I am here to help."

"Uncle says our cellar is safe. He says if it has lasted for five hundred years, it will last a few more nights."

The perfumer clears his throat. She imagines him extending his thick neck to look into the house, the coat on the rack, the crumbs of bread on the kitchen table. Everyone checking to see what everyone else has. Her uncle could not have asked the perfumer to escort her to a shelter — when is the last time Etienne has spoken to Claude Levitte? Again she thinks of the model upstairs, the stone inside. She hears Dr. Geffard's voice: *That something so small could be so beautiful. Worth so much.*

"Houses are burning at Paramé, mademoiselle. They're scuttling ships at the port, they're shelling the cathedral, and there's no water at the hospital. The doctors are washing their hands in wine. Wine!" The edges of Monsieur Levitte's voice flutter. She remembers Madame Manec saying once that every time a theft was reported in town, Monsieur Levitte would go to bed with his billfold stuffed between his buttocks.

Marie-Laure says, "I will stay."

"Christ, girl, must I force you?"

She remembers the German pacing outside Harold Bazin's gate, the edge of his newspaper rattling the bars, and closes the door a fraction. Someone has put the perfumer up to this. "Surely," she says, "my great-uncle and I are not the only people sleeping beneath our own roof tonight."

She tries her best to look impassive. Monsieur Levitte's smell is overpowering.

"Mademoiselle." Pleading now. "Be reasonable. Come with me and leave everything behind."

"You may talk to my great-uncle when he returns." And she bolts the door.

She can hear him standing out there. Working out some cost-benefit analysis. Then he turns and recedes down the street, dragging his fear like a cart behind him. Marie-Laure bends beside the hall table and finds the thread and resets the trip wire. What could he have seen? A coat, half of a loaf of bread? Etienne will be pleased. Out past the kitchen window, swifts swoop for insects, and the filaments of a spiderweb catch the light and shine for an instant and are gone.

And yet: what if the perfumer was telling the truth?

The daylight dulls to gold. A few crickets down in the cellar begin their song: a rhythmic *kree-kree,* evening in August, and Marie-Laure hikes her tattered stockings and goes into the kitchen and tears another hunk from Madame Ruelle's loaf.

Leaflets

Before dark, the Austrians serve pork kidneys with whole tomatoes on hotel china, a single silver bee etched on the rim of every plate. Everyone sits on sandbags or ammunition boxes, and Bernd falls asleep over his bowl, and Volkheimer talks in the corner with the lieutenant about the radio in the cellar, and around the perimeter of the room the Austrians chew steadily beneath their steel helmets. Brisk, experienced men. Men who do not doubt their purpose.

When Werner is done with his food, he lets himself into the top-floor suite and stands in the hexagonal bathtub. He nudges the shutter, and it opens a few centimeters. The evening air is a benediction. Below the window, on one of the bastioned traces on the seaward side of the hotel, waits the big 88. Beyond the gun, beyond the embrasures, ramparts plunge forty feet to the green and white plumes of surf. To his left waits the city, gray and dense. Far in the east, a red glow rises from some battle just out of sight. The Americans have them pinned against the sea.

It seems to Werner that in the space between whatever has happened already and whatever is to come hovers an invisible borderland, the known on one side and the unknown on the other. He thinks of the girl who may or may not be in the city behind him. He envisions her running her cane along the runnels. Facing the world with her barren eyes, her wild hair, her bright face.

At least he protected the secrets of her house. At least he kept her safe.

New orders, signed by the garrison commander himself, have been posted on doors and market stalls and lampposts. *No person must attempt to leave the old city. No one must walk in the streets without special authority.*

Just before Werner closes the shutter, a single airplane comes through the dusk. From its belly issues a flock of white growing slowly larger.

Birds?

The flock is sundering, scattering: it is paper. Thousands of sheets. They gust down the slope of the roof, skitter across the parapets, stick flat in tidal eddies down on the beach.

Werner descends to the lobby, where an Austrian holds one to the light. "It's in French," he says.

Werner takes it. The ink so fresh it smudges beneath his fingers. *Urgent message to the inhabitants of this town,* it says. *Depart immediately to open country.*

Ten:
12 August 1944

Entombed

She is reading again: *Who could possibly calculate the minimum time required for us to get out? Might we not be asphyxiated before the* Nautilus *could surface? Was it destined to perish in this tomb of ice along with all those on board? The situation seemed terrible. But everyone faced it squarely and decided to do their duty to the end . . .*

Werner listens. The crew chops through the icebergs that have trapped their submarine; it cruises north along the coast of South America, past the mouth of the Amazon, only to be chased by giant squid in the Atlantic. The propeller cuts out; Captain Nemo emerges from his cabin for the first time in weeks, looking grim.

Werner hauls himself off the floor, carrying the radio in one hand and dragging the battery in the other. He traverses the cellar until he finds Volkheimer in the gold armchair. He sets down the battery and runs his hand up the big man's arm to his shoulder. Locates his huge head. Clamps the headphones over Volkheimer's ears.

"Can you hear her?" says Werner. "It's a strange and beautiful story, I wish you could understand French. A giant squid has lodged its giant beak into the propeller of the submarine, and now the captain has said they must surface and fight the beasts hand to hand."

Volkheimer draws a slow breath. He does not move.

"She's using the transmitter we were supposed to find. I found it. Weeks ago. They said it was a network of terrorists, but it was just an old man and a girl."

Volkheimer says nothing.

"You knew all along, didn't you? That I knew?"

Volkheimer must not be able to hear Werner through the headphones.

"She keeps saying, 'Help me.' She begs her father, her great-uncle. She says, 'He is here. He will kill me.' "

A moan shudders through the rubble above them, and in the darkness Werner feels as if he is trapped inside the *Nautilus,* twenty meters down, while the tentacles of a dozen angry kraken lash its hull. He knows the transmitter must be high in the house. Close to the shelling. He says, "I saved her only to hear her die."

Volkheimer shows no signs of having understood. Gone or resolved to go: is there much difference? Werner takes back the headphones and sits in the dust beside the battery.

The first mate, she reads, *struggled furiously with other monsters which were climbing up the sides of the* Nautilus. *The crew were flailing away with their axes. Ned, Conseil and I also dug our weapons into their soft bodies. A violent odor of musk filled the air.*

Fort National

Etienne begged his jailers, the guardian of the fort, dozens of his fellow prisoners. "My niece, my great-niece, she's blind, she's alone . . ." He told them he was sixty-three, not sixty, as they claimed, that his papers had been unfairly confiscated, that he was not a terrorist; he wobbled before the *Feldwebel* in charge and stumbled through the few German phrases he could stitch together — *"Sie müssen mich helfen!" "Meine Nichte ist herein dort!"* — but the *Feldwebel* shrugged like everybody else and looked back at the city burning across the water as if to say: what can anyone do in the face of that?

Then the stray American shell struck the fort, and the wounded howled down in the munitions cellar, and the dead were buried under rocks just above the tide line, and Etienne stopped talking.

The tide slips away, then climbs back up. Whatever energy Etienne has left goes into quieting the noise in his head. Sometimes he almost convinces himself that he can see through the smoldering skeletons of the seafront mansions at the northwestern corner of the city to the rooftop of his house. He almost convinces himself it stands. But then it disappears again behind a mantle of smoke.

No pillow, no blanket. The latrine is apocalyptic. Food comes irregularly, carried out from the citadel by the guardian's wife across the quarter mile of rocks at low tide while shells explode in the city behind her. There's never enough. Etienne diverts himself with fantasies of escape. Slip over a wall, swim several hundred meters, drag himself through the shorebreak. Scamper across the mined beach with no cover to one of the locked gates. Absurd.

Out here the prisoners see the shells smash into the city before they hear them. During the last war, Etienne knew artillerymen who could peer through field glasses and discern their shells' damage by the colors thrown skyward. Gray was stone. Brown was soil. Pink was flesh.

He shuts his eyes. He remembers lamplit hours in Monsieur Hébrard's bookshop listening to the first radio he ever heard. He remembers climbing into the choir of the cathedral to listen to Henri's voice as it rose toward the ceiling. He remembers the cramped restaurants with leaded windows and linenfold paneling where his parents took them to dinner; and the corsairs' villas with scalloped friezes and Doric columns and gold coins mortared inside the walls; the storefronts of gunsmiths and shipmasters and money changers and hostelers; the graffiti Henri used to scratch into the stones of ramparts, *I cannot wait to leave, fuck this place.* He remembers the LeBlanc house, his house! Tall and narrow with the staircase spiraling up its center like a spire shell stood on end, where the ghost of his brother occasionally slipped between walls, where Madame Manec lived and died, where not so long ago he could sit on a davenport with Marie-Laure and pretend they flew over the volcanoes of Hawaii, over the cloud forests of Peru, where just a week ago she sat cross-legged on the floor and read to him about a pearl fishery off the coast of Ceylon, Captain Nemo and Aronnax in their diving suits, the impulsive Canadian Ned Land about to hurl his harpoon through the side of a shark . . . All of it is burning. Every memory he ever made.

Above Fort National, the dawn becomes deeply, murderously clear. The Milky Way a fading river. He looks across to the fires. He thinks: The universe is full of fuel.

Captain Nemo's Last Words

By noon on the twelfth of August, Marie-Laure has read seven of the last nine chapters into the microphone. Captain Nemo has freed his ship from the giant squid only to stare into the eye of a hurricane. Pages later, he rammed a warship full of men, passing through its hull, Verne writes, like a sailmaker's needle through cloth. Now the captain plays a mournful, chilling dirge on his organ as the *Nautilus* sleeps in the wastelands of the sea. Three pages are left. If Marie-Laure has brought anyone comfort by broadcasting the story, if her great-uncle, crouched in some dank cellar with a hundred men, tuned her in — if some trio of Americans reclined in the nighttime fields as they cleaned their weapons and traveled the dark gangways of the *Nautilus* with her — she cannot say.

But she is glad to be so near the end.

Downstairs the German has shouted twice in frustration, then fallen silent. Why not, she considers, just slide through the wardrobe and hand the little house to him and find out if he will spare her?

First she will finish. Then she'll decide.

Again she opens the model house and tips the stone into her palm. What would happen if the goddess took away the curse? Would the fires go out, would the earth heal over, would doves return to the windowsills? Would Papa come back?

Fill your lungs. Beat your heart. She keeps the knife beside her. Fingertips pressed to the lines of the novel. The Canadian harpooner Ned Land has found his window for escape. *"The sea's bad,"* he says to Professor Aronnax, *"and the wind's blowing strong . . ."*

"I'm with you, Ned."

"But let me tell you that if we're caught, I'm going to defend myself, even if I die doing it."

"We'll die together, Ned my friend."

Marie-Laure turns on the transmitter. She thinks of the whelks in Harold Bazin's kennel, ten thousand of them; how they cling; how they draw themselves up into the spirals of their shells; how, when they're tucked into that grotto, the gulls cannot come in to carry them up into the sky and drop them on the rocks to break them.

Visitor

Von Rumpel drinks from a bottle of skunked wine he has found in the kitchen. Four days in this house, and how many mistakes he has made! The Sea of Flames could have been in the Paris Museum all along — that simpering mineralogist and the assistant director laughing as he slunk away, duped, fooled, inveigled. Or the perfumer could have betrayed him, taking the diamond from the girl after marching her away. Or Levitte might have walked her right out of the city while she carried it in her ratty knapsack; or the old man could have jammed it up his rectum and is just now shitting it out, twenty million francs in a pile of feces.

Or maybe the stone was never real at all. Maybe it was all hoax, all story.

He had been so certain. Certain he had found the hiding spot, solved the puzzle. Certain the stone would save him. The girl didn't know, the old man was out of the picture — everything was set up perfectly.

What is certain now? Only the murderous bloom inside his body, only the corruption it brings to every cell. In his ears comes the voice of his father: *You are only being tested.*

Someone calls to him in German. *"Ist da wer?"*

Father?

"You in there!"

Von Rumpel listens. Sounds drawing nearer through the smoke. He crawls to the window. Sets his helmet on his head. Thrusts his head over the shattered sill.

A German infantry corporal squints up from the street. "Sir? I didn't expect . . . Is the house clear, sir?"

"Empty, yes. Where are you headed, Corporal?"

"The fortress at La Cité, sir. We are evacuating. Leaving everything. We still hold the château and the Bastion de la Hollande. All other personnel are to fall back."

Von Rumpel braces his chin on the sill, feeling as if his head might separate from his neck and go tumbling down to explode on the street.

"The entire town will be inside the bomb line," the corporal says.

"How long?"

"There will be a cease-fire tomorrow. Noon, they say. To get civilians out. Then they resume the assault."

Von Rumpel says, "We're giving up the city?"

A shell detonates not far away, and the echoes of the blast shunt down between the wrecked houses, and the soldier in the street claps a hand over his helmet. Bits of stone skitter across the cobbles.

He calls, "You are with which unit, Sergeant Major?"

"Continue with your work, Corporal. I'm nearly done here."

Final Sentence

Volkheimer does not stir. The liquid at the bottom of the paint bucket, however toxic it was, is gone. Werner has heard nothing from the girl on any frequency for how long? An hour? More? She read about the *Nautilus* getting sucked down into a whirlpool, waves higher than houses, the submarine standing on end, its steel ribs cracking, and then she read what he assumed was the last line of the book: *Thus, to that question asked six thousand years ago by Ecclesiastes, "That which is far off, and exceeding deep, who can find it out?" only two men now have the right to answer: Captain Nemo and myself.*

Then the transmitter snapped off and the absolute darkness closed around him. For these past days — how many? — it has felt as though the hunger were a hand inside him, thrusting around in the cavity of his chest, reaching up to his shoulder blades, then down into his pelvis. Scraping at his bones. Today, though — or is it tonight? — the hunger peters out like a flame for which no fuel remains. Emptiness and fullness, in the end, somehow the same.

Werner blinks up to see the Viennese girl in her cape descend through the ceiling as if it is no more than a shadow. She carries a paper sack full of withered greens and seats herself amid the rubble. Around her swirls a cloud of bees.

He can see nothing, but he can see her.

She counts on her fingers. *For tripping in line,* she says. *For working too slowly. For arguing over bread. For loitering too long in the camp toilet. For sobbing. For not organizing her things according to protocol.*

It's surely nonsense, yet something hangs inside it, some truth he does not want to allow himself to apprehend, and as she speaks, she ages, silver hair lays down on her head, her collar frays; she becomes an old woman — his understanding of who hovers at the rim of his consciousness.

For complaining of headaches.

For singing.

For speaking at night in her bunk.

For forgetting her birth date during evening muster.

For unloading the shipment too slowly.

For not turning in her keys correctly.

For failing to inform the guard.

For rising from bed too late.

Frau Schwartzenberger — that's who she is. The Jewess in Frederick's elevator.

She runs out of fingers as she counts.

For closing her eyes while being addressed.

For hoarding crusts.

For attempting to enter the park.

For having inflamed hands.

For asking for a cigarette.

For a failure of imagination and in the darkness, it feels as if Werner has reached bottom, as if he has been whirling deeper all this time, like the *Nautilus* sucked under the maelstrom, like his father descending into the pits: a one-way dive from Zollverein past Schulpforta, past the horrors of Russia and Ukraine, past the mother and daughter in Vienna, his ambition and shame becoming one and the same, to the nadir in this basement on the rim of the continent where the apparition chants nonsense — Frau Schwartzenberger walks toward him, transforming herself as she approaches from woman to girl — her hair becomes red again, her skin smooths, a seven-year-old girl presses her face up against his, and in the center of her forehead he can see a hole blacker than the blackness around him, at the bottom of which teems a dark city full of souls, ten thousand, five hundred thousand, all these faces staring up from alleys, from windows, from smoldering parks, and he hears thunder.

Lightning.

Artillery.

The girl evaporates.

The ground quakes. The organs inside his body shake. The beams groan. Then the slow trickle of dust and the shallow, defeated breaths of Volkheimer a meter away.

Music #1

Sometime after midnight on August 13, after surviving in her great-uncle's attic for five days, Marie-Laure holds a record with her left hand while she runs the fingers of her right gently through its grooves, reconstructing the whole song in her head. Each rise and fall. Then she slots the record on the spindle of Etienne's electrophone.

No water for a day and a half. No food for two. The attic smells of heat and dust and confinement and her own urine in the shaving bowl in the corner.

We'll die together, Ned my friend.

The siege, it seems, will never end. Masonry crashes into the streets; the city falls to pieces; still this one house does not fall.

She takes the unopened can out of her great-uncle's coat pocket and sets it in the center of the attic floor. For so long she has saved it. Maybe because it offers some last tie to Madame Manec. Maybe because if she opens it and finds it spoiled, the loss will kill her.

She places the can and brick beneath the piano bench, where she knows she can find them again. Then she double-checks the record on the spindle. Lowers the arm, places the needle at the outside edge. Finds the microphone switch with her left hand, the transmitter switch with her right.

She is going to turn it up as loud as it will go. If the German is in the house, he will hear. He'll hear piano music draining down through the upper stories and cock his head, and then he'll rove the sixth floor like a slavering demon. Eventually he'll set his ear to the doors of the wardrobe, where it will be louder still.

What mazes there are in this world. The branches of trees, the filigree of roots, the matrix of crystals, the streets her father re-created in his models. Mazes in the nodules on murex shells and in the textures of syca-more bark and inside the hollow bones of eagles. None more complicated than the hu-man brain, Etienne would say, what may be the most complex object in existence; one wet kilogram within which spin universes.

She places the microphone into the bell-shaped speaker of the electrophone, switches on the record player, and the plate begins to spin. The attic crackles. In her mind she walks a path in the Jardin des Plantes, the air golden, the wind green, the long fingers of willows drifting across her shoulders. Ahead is her father; he extends a hand, waiting.

The piano starts to play.

Marie-Laure reaches beneath the bench and locates the knife. She crawls along the floor to the top of the seven-rung ladder and sits with her feet dangling and the diamond inside the house in her pocket and the knife in her fist.

She says, "Come and get me."

Music #2

Beneath the stars over the city, everything sleeps. Gunners sleep, nuns in a crypt beneath the cathedral sleep, children in old corsairs' cellars sleep in the laps of sleeping mothers. The doctor in the basement of the Hôtel-Dieu sleeps. Wounded Germans in the tunnels below the fort of La Cité sleep. Behind the walls of Fort National, Etienne sleeps. Everything sleeps save the snails climbing the rocks and the rats scurrying among the piles.

In a hole beneath the ruins of the Hotel of Bees, Werner sleeps too. Only Volkheimer is awake. He sits with the big radio in his lap where Werner has set it and the dying battery between his feet and static whispering in both ears not because he believes he will hear anything but because this is where Werner has left the headphones. Because he does not have the will to push them off. Because he convinced himself hours ago that the plaster heads on the other side of the cellar will kill him if he moves.

Impossibly, the static coalesces into music.

Volkheimer's eyes open as wide as they can. Straining the blackness for every stray photon. A single piano runs up scales. Then back down. He listens to the notes and the silences between them, and then finds himself leading horses through a forest at dawn, trudging through snow behind his great-grandfather, who walks with a saw draped over his huge shoulders, the snow squeaking beneath boots and hooves, all the trees above them whispering and creaking. They reach the edge of a frozen pond, where a pine grows as tall as a cathedral. His great-grandfather goes to his knees like a penitent, fits the saw into a groove in the bark, and begins to cut.

Volkheimer stands. Finds Werner's leg in the darkness, puts the headphones on Werner's ears. "Listen," he says, "listen, listen . . ."

Werner comes awake. Chords float past in transparent riffles. "Clair de Lune." Claire: a girl so clear you can see right through her.

Volkheimer says, "Hook the light to the battery."

"Why?"

"Do it."

Even before the song has stopped playing, Werner disconnects the radio from the battery, unscrews the bezel and bulb from the dead field light, touches it to the leads, and gives them a sphere of light. At the back corner of the cellar, Volkheimer drags blocks of masonry and pieces of timber and shattered sections of wall out of the rubble, stopping now and then only to lean over his knees and catch his breath. He stacks them into a barrier. Then he pulls Werner behind this makeshift bunker, unscrews the base of a grenade and yanks the pull cord to ignite the five-second fuse. Werner sets one hand over his helmet, and Volkheimer throws the grenade at the place where the stairwell used to be.

Music #3

Von Rumpel's daughters were fat, roiling little babies, weren't they? Both of them always dropping their rattles or rubber pacifiers and tangling themselves in blankets, why so tortured, little angels? But they grew! Despite all his absences. And they could sing, especially Veronika. Maybe they weren't going to be famous, but they could sing well enough to please a father. They'd wear their big felt boots and those awful shapeless dresses their mother made for them, primroses and daisies embroidered along the collars, and fold their hands behind their backs, and belt out lyrics they were too young to understand.

> Men cluster to me
> like moths around a flame,
> and if their wings burn,
> I know I'm not to blame.

In what might be a memory or a dream, von Rumpel watches Veronika, the early riser, kneel on the floor of Marie-Laure's room in the predawn darkness and march a doll in a white gown alongside another in a gray suit down the streets of the model city. They turn left, then right, until they reach the steps of the cathedral, where a third doll waits, dressed in black, one arm raised. Wedding or sacrifice, he cannot say. Then Veronika sings so softly that he cannot hear the words, only the melody, less like the sounds made by a human voice and more like the notes made by a piano, and the dolls dance, swaying from foot to foot.

The music stops, and Veronika vanishes. He sits up. The model at the foot of the bed bleeds away and is a long time restoring itself. Somewhere above him, the voice of a young man starts speaking in French about coal.

OUT

For a split second, the space around Werner tears in half, as though the last molecules of oxygen have been ripped out of it. Then shards of stone and wood and metal streak past, ringing against his helmet, sizzling into the wall behind them, and Volkheimer's barricade collapses, and everywhere in the darkness, things scuttle and slide, and he cannot find any air to breathe. But the detonation creates some tectonic shift in the building's rubble, and there is a snap followed by multiple cascades in the darkness. When Werner stops coughing and pushes the debris off his chest, he finds Volkheimer staring up at a single sheared hole of purple light.

Sky. Night sky.

A shaft of starlight slices through the dust and drops along the edge of a mound of rubble to the floor. For a moment Werner inhales it. Then Volkheimer urges him back and climbs halfway up the ruined staircase and begins whaling away at the edges of the hole with a piece of rebar. The iron clangs and his hands lacerate and his six-day beard glows white with dust, but Werner can see that Volkheimer makes quick progress: the sliver of light becomes a violet wedge, wider across than two of Werner's hands.

With one more blow, Volkheimer manages to pulverize a big slab of debris, much of it crashing onto his helmet and shoulders, and then it is simply a matter of scrabbling and climbing. He squeezes his upper body through the hole, his shoulders scraping on the edges, his jacket tearing, hips twisting, and then he's through. He reaches down for Werner, his canvas duffel, and the rifle, and pulls them all up.

They kneel atop what was once an alley. Starlight hangs over everything. No moon Werner can see. Volkheimer turns his bleeding palms up as though to catch the air, to let it seep into his skin like rainwater.

Only two walls of the hotel stand, joined at the corner, bits of plaster attached to the inner wall. Beyond it, houses display their interiors to the night. The rampart behind the hotel remains, though many of its embrasures along the top have been shattered. The sea presents a barely audible wash on the other side. Everything else is rubble and silence. Starlight rains onto every crenellation. How many men decompose in the piles of stone before them? Nine. Maybe more.

They make for the lee of the ramparts, both of them staggering like drunks. When they reach the wall, Volkheimer blinks down at Werner. Then out at the night. His face so dusted white he looks like a colossus made of powder.

Five blocks to the south, is the girl still playing her recording?

Volkheimer says, "Take the rifle. Go."

"And you?"

"Food."

Werner rubs his eyes against the glory of the starlight. He feels no hunger, as if he has rid himself forever of the nuisance of eating. "But will we — ?"

"Go," says Volkheimer again. Werner looks at him a last time: his torn jacket and shovel jaw. The tenderness of his big hands. *What you could be.*

Did he know? All along?

Werner moves from cover to cover. Canvas bag in his left hand, rifle in his right. Five rounds left. In his mind he hears the girl whisper: *He is here. He will kill me.* West down a canyon of rubble, scrambling over bricks and wires and pieces of roof slates, many of them still hot, the streets apparently abandoned, though what eyes might track him from behind shattered windows, German or French or American or British, he cannot say. Possibly the crosshairs of a sniper center on him this very second.

Here a single platform shoe. Here a fretwork wooden chef on his back, holding a board on which remains chalked today's soup. Here great tangled coils of barbed wire. Everywhere the reek of corpses.

Crouching in the lee of what was a tourist gift shop — a few souvenir plates in their racks, each with a different name painted on the rim and arranged alphabetically —Werner locates himself in the city. *Coiffeur Dames* across the street. A bank with no windows. A dead horse, attached to its cart. Here and there an intact building stands without its window glass, the filigreed trails of smoke grown up from its windows like the shadows of ivy that have been ripped away.

What light shines at night! He never knew. Day will blind him.

Werner turns right on what he believes is the rue d'Estrées. Number 4 on the rue Vauborel still stands. Every window on its facade has been broken but the walls are hardly scorched; two of its wooden flower boxes hang on.

He is right below me.

They said what he needed was certainty. Purpose. Clarity. That pigeon-chested commandant Bastian with his grandmother's walk; he said they would strip the hesitation out of him.

We are a volley of bullets, we are can-

nonballs. We are the tip of the sword.

Who is the weakest?

WARDROBE

Von Rumpel wobbles before the mighty cabinet. Peers into the old clothes inside. Waistcoats, striped trousers, moth-chewed chambray shirts with tall collars and comically long sleeves. Boys' clothes, decades old.

What is this room? The big mirrors on the wardrobe doors are spotted black with age, and old leather boots stand beneath a little desk, and a whisk broom hangs from a peg. On the desk stands a photograph of a boy in breeches on a beach at dusk.

Beyond the broken window hangs a windless night. Ashes swirling in starlight. The voice filtering through the ceiling repeats itself . . . *The brain is locked in total darkness, of course, children . . . And yet the world it constructs . . .* lowering in pitch and warping as the batteries die, the lesson slowing as though the young man is exhausted, and then it stops.

Heart galloping, head failing, candle in one hand, pistol in the other, von Rumpel turns again to the wardrobe. Big enough to climb inside. How did such a monstrous thing ever get up to the sixth floor?

He brings the candle closer and sees, in the shadows of the hanging shirts, what he missed on previous inspections: trails through the dust. Made by fingers or knees or both. With the barrel of his pistol, he nudges the clothes. How deep does it go?

He leans all the way inside, and as he does, he hears a chime, twin bells tinkling both above and below. The sound makes him jerk backward, and he knocks his head on the top of the wardrobe, and the candle falls, and von Rumpel lands on his back.

He watches the candle roll, its flame pointing up. Why? What curious principle demands that a candle flame taper always toward the sky?

Five days in this house and no diamond, the last German-controlled port in Brittany nearly lost, the Atlantic Wall with it. Already he has lived beyond the deadline the doctor predicted. And now the tolling of two tiny bells? This is how death comes?

The candle rolls gently. Toward the window. Toward the curtains.

Downstairs the door of the house creaks open. Someone steps inside.

COMRADES

Shattered crockery litters the foyer — impossible to be noiseless as he enters. A kitchen full of debris waits down a corridor. Hallway deep with drifts of ash. Chair overturned. Staircase ahead. Unless she has moved in the past few minutes, she will be high in the house, close to the transmitter.

Rifle in both hands, bag over his shoulder, Werner starts up. At each landing a rushing blackness throws off his vision. Spots open and close at his feet. Books have been thrown down the stairwell, along with papers, cords, bottles, and what might be pieces of antique dollhouses. Second floor third fourth fifth: all in the same state. He has no sense of how much noise he makes or whether it matters.

On the sixth floor, the stairs appear to end. Three half-open doors frame the landing: one to the left, one ahead, one to the right. He goes to his right, rifle up; he expects the flash of gun barrels, the jaws of a demon swinging open. Instead, a broken window illuminates a swaybacked bed. A girl's dress hangs in an armoire. Hundreds of tiny things — pebbles? — line the baseboards. Two buckets stand in a corner, half full of what might be water.

Is he too late? He props Volkheimer's rifle against the bed and raises a bucket and drinks once, twice. Out the window, far beyond the neighboring block, beyond the ramparts, the single light of a boat appears and disappears as it rises and falls on distant swells.

A voice behind him says, "Ah."

Werner turns. In front of him totters a German officer in field dress. The five bars and three diamonds of a sergeant major. Pale and bruised, lean to the point of infirmity, he shambles toward the bed. The right side of his throat spills weirdly above the tightness of his collar. "I do not recommend," he says, "mixing morphine with Beaujolais." A vein on the side of the man's forehead throbs lightly.

"I saw you," says Werner. "In front of the bakery. With a newspaper."

"And you, little Private. I saw you." In his smile Werner recognizes an assumption that they are kindred, comrades. Accomplices. That each has come to this house seeking the same thing.

Behind the sergeant major, across the hall, impossibly: flames. A curtain in the room directly across the landing has caught fire. Already flames are licking the ceiling. The sergeant major loops one finger under his collar and pulls against its tightness. His face gaunt and his teeth maniacal. He sits on the bed. Starlight winks off the barrel of his pistol.

At the foot of the bed, Werner can just make out a low table upon which scaled-down wooden houses crowd together to form a city. Is it Saint-Malo? His eyes flash from the model to the flames across the hall to Volkheimer's rifle leaning against the bed. The officer bends forward and looms over the miniature city like some tormented gargoyle.

Tendrils of black smoke have begun to snake into the hall. "The curtain, sir. It's on fire."

"The cease-fire is scheduled for noon, or so they say," von Rumpel says in an empty voice. "No need to rush. Plenty of time." He jogs the fingers of one hand down a miniature street. "We want the same thing, you and I, Private. But only one of us can have it. And only I know where it is. Which presents a problem for you. Is it here or here or here or here?" He rubs his hands together, then lies back on the bed. He points his pistol at the ceiling. "Is it up there?"

In the room beyond the landing, the burning curtain sloughs off its rod. Maybe it will go out, thinks Werner. Maybe it will go out on its own.

Werner thinks about the men in the sunflowers and a hundred others: each lay dead in his hut or truck or bunker, wearing the look of someone who had caught the tune of a familiar song. A crease between the eyes, a slackness to the mouth. A look that said: So soon? But doesn't it play for everybody too soon?

Firelight plays across the hall. Still on his back, the sergeant major takes the pistol in both hands and opens and closes the breech. "Drink some more," he says, and gestures toward the bucket in Werner's hands. "I can see how thirsty you are. I didn't pee in it, I promise."

Werner sets down the bucket. The sergeant major sits up and tilts his head back and forth as though working out kinks in his neck. Then he aims his gun at Werner's chest. From down the hall, in the direction of the burning curtain, comes a muted clattering, something bouncing down a ladder and striking the floor, and the sergeant major's attention swings toward the noise, and the barrel of his pistol dips.

Werner lunges for Volkheimer's rifle. All your life you wait, and then it finally comes, and are you ready?

The Simultaneity of Instants

The brick claps onto the floor. The voices stop. She can hear a scuffle and then the shot comes like a breach of crimson light: the eruption of Krakatoa. The house briefly riven in two.

Marie-Laure half slides, half falls down the ladder and presses her ear against the false back of the wardrobe. Footsteps hurry across the landing and enter Henri's room. There is a splash and a hiss, and she smells smoke and steam.

Now the footsteps become hesitant; they are different from the sergeant major's. Lighter. Stepping, stopping. Opening the doors of the wardrobe. Thinking. Figuring it out.

She can hear a light brushing sound as he runs his fingers along the back of the wardrobe. She tightens her grip on the handle of the knife.

Three blocks to the east, Frank Volkheimer blinks as he sits in a devastated apartment on the corner of the rue des Lauriers and the rue Thévenard, eating from a tin of sweet yams with his fingers. Across the river mouth, beneath four feet of concrete, an aide holds open the garrison commander's jacket as the colonel swings one arm through one sleeve, then the other. At precisely the same moment, a nineteen-year-old American scout climbing the hillside toward the pillboxes stops and turns and reaches an arm down for the soldier behind him; while, with his cheekbone pressed to a granite paver at Fort National, Etienne LeBlanc decides that if he and Marie-Laure live through this, whatever happens, he will let her pick a place on the equator and they will go, book a ticket, ride a ship, fly an airplane, until they stand together in a rain forest surrounded by flowers they've never smelled, listening to birds they've never heard. Three hundred miles away from Fort National, Reinhold von Rumpel's wife wakes her daughters to go to Mass and contemplates the good looks of her neighbor who has returned from the war without one of his feet. Not all that far from her, Jutta Pfennig sleeps in the ultramarine shadows of the girls' dormitory and dreams of light thickening and settling across a field like snow; and not all that far from Jutta, the führer raises a glass of warm (but never boiled) milk to his lips, a slice of Oldenburg black bread on his plate and a whole apple beside it, his daily breakfast; while in a ravine outside Kiev, two inmates rub their hands in sand because they have become slippery, and then they take up the stretcher again while a sonderkommando stirs the fire below them with a steel pole; a wagtail flits from flagstone to flagstone in a courtyard in Berlin, searching for snails to eat; and at the Napola school at Schulpforta, one hundred and nineteen twelve- and thirteen-year-olds wait in a queue behind a truck to be handed thirty-pound antitank land mines, boys who, in almost exactly one year, marooned amid the Russian advance, the entire school cut off like an island, will be given a box of the Reich's last bitter chocolate and Wehrmacht helmets salvaged from dead soldiers, and then this final harvest of the nation's youth will rush out with the chocolate melting in their guts and overlarge helmets bobbing on their shorn heads and sixty Panzerfaust rocket launchers in their hands in a last spasm of futility to defend a bridge that no longer requires defending, while T-34 tanks from the White Russian army come clicking and rumbling toward them to destroy them all, every last child; dawn in Saint-Malo, and there is a twitch on the other side of the wardrobe — Werner hears Marie-Laure inhale, Marie-Laure hears Werner scrape three fingernails across the wood, a sound not unlike the sound of a record coursing beneath the surface of a

needle, their faces an arm's reach apart.
He says, *"Es-tu là?"*

Are You There?

He is a ghost. He is from some other world. He is Papa, Madame Manec, Etienne; he is everyone who has left her finally coming back. Through the panel he calls, "I am not killing you. I am hearing you. On radio. Is why I come." He pauses, fumbling to translate. "The song, light of the moon?" She almost smiles.

We all come into existence as a single cell, smaller than a speck of dust. Much smaller. Divide. Multiply. Add and subtract. Matter changes hands, atoms flow in and out, molecules pivot, proteins stitch together, mitochondria send out their oxidative dictates; we begin as a microscopic electrical swarm. The lungs the brain the heart. Forty weeks later, six trillion cells get crushed in the vise of our mother's birth canal and we howl. Then the world starts in on us.

Marie-Laure slides open the wardrobe. Werner takes her hand and helps her out.

Her feet find the floor of her grandfather's room.

"Mes souliers," she says. "I have not been able to find my shoes."

SECOND CAN

The girl sits very still in the corner and wraps her coat around her knees. The way she tucks her ankles up against her bottom. The way her fingers flutter through the space around her. Each a thing he hopes never to forget.

Guns boom to the east: the citadel being bombarded again, the citadel bombarding back.

Exhaustion breaks over him. In French he says, "There will be a — a *Waffenruhe.* Stopping in the fighting. At noon. So people can get out of the city. I can get you out."

"And you know this is true?"

"No," he says. "I do not know it is true." Quiet now. He examines his trousers, his dusty coat. The uniform makes him an accomplice in everything this girl hates. "There is water," he says, and crosses to the other sixth-floor room and does not look at von Rumpel's body in her bed and retrieves the second bucket. Her whole head disappears inside its mouth, and her sticklike arms hug its sides as she gulps.

He says, "You are very brave."

She lowers the bucket. "What is your name?"

He tells her. She says, "When I lost my sight, Werner, people said I was brave. When my father left, people said I was brave. But it is not bravery; I have no choice. I wake up and live my life. Don't you do the same?"

He says, "Not in years. But today. Today maybe I did."

Her glasses are gone, and her pupils look like they are full of milk, but strangely they do not unnerve him. He remembers a phrase of Frau Elena's: *belle laide.* Beautiful ugly.

"What day is it?"

He looks around. Scorched curtains and soot fanned across the ceiling and cardboard peeling off the window and the very first pale light of predawn leaking through. "I don't know. It's morning."

A shell screams over the house. He thinks: I only want to sit here with her for a thousand hours. But the shell detonates somewhere and the house creaks and Werner says, "There was a man who used that transmitter you have. Who broadcast lessons about science. When I was a boy. I used to listen to them with my sister."

"That was the voice of my grandfather. You heard him?"

"Many times. We loved them."

The window glows. The slow sandy light of dawn permeates the room. Everything transient and aching; everything tentative. To be here, in this room, high in this house, out of the cellar, with her: it is like medicine.

"I could eat bacon," she says.

"What?"

"I could eat a whole pig."

He smiles. "I could eat a whole cow."

"The woman who used to live here, the housekeeper, she made the most wonderful omelets in the world."

"When I was little," he says, or hopes he says, "we used to pick berries by the Ruhr. My sister and me. We'd find berries as big as our thumbs."

The girl crawls into the wardrobe and climbs a ladder and comes back down clutching a dented tin can. "Can you see what this is?"

"There's no label."

"I didn't think there was."

"Is it food?"

"Let's open it and find out."

With one stroke from the brick, he punctures the can with the tip of the knife. Immediately he can smell it: the perfume is so sweet, so outrageously sweet, that he nearly faints. What is the word? *Pêches. Les pêches.*

The girl leans forward; the freckles seem to bloom across her cheeks as she inhales. "We will share," she says. "For what you did."

He hammers the knife in a second time, saws away at the metal, and bends up the lid. "Careful," he says, and passes it to her. She dips in two fingers, digs up a wet, soft, slippery thing. Then he does the same. That first peach slithers down his throat like rapture. A sunrise in his mouth.

They eat. They drink the syrup. They run their fingers around the inside of the can.

Birds of America

What wonders in this house! She shows him the transmitter in the attic: its double battery, its old-fashioned electrophone, the hand-machined antenna that can be raised and lowered along the chimney by an ingenious system of levers. Even a phonograph record that she says contains her grandfather's voice, lessons in science for children. And the books! The lower floors are blanketed with them — Becquerel, Lavoisier, Fischer — a lifetime of reading. What it would be like to spend ten years in this tall narrow house, shuttered from the world, studying its secrets and reading its volumes and looking at this girl.

"Do you think," he asks, "that Captain Nemo survived the whirlpool?"

Marie-Laure sits on the fifth-floor landing in her oversize coat as though waiting for a train. "No," she says. "Yes. I don't know. I suppose that is the point, no? To make us wonder?" She cocks her head. "He was a madman. And yet I didn't want him to die."

In the corner of her great-uncle's study, amid a tumult of books, he finds a copy of *Birds of America.* A reprint, not nearly as large as the one he saw in Frederick's living room, but dazzling nonetheless: four hundred and thirty-five engravings. He carries it out to the landing. "Has your uncle shown you this?"

"What is it?"

"Birds. Bird after bird after bird."

Outside, shells fly back and forth. "We must get lower in the house," she says. But for a moment they do not move.

California Partridge.

Common Gannet.

Frigate Pelican.

Werner can still see Frederick kneeling at his window, nose to the glass. Little gray bird hopping about in the boughs. *Doesn't look like much, does it?*

"Could I keep a page from this?"

"Why not. We will leave soon, no? When it is safe?"

"At noon."

"How will we know it is time?"

"When they stop shooting."

Airplanes come. Dozens and dozens of them. Werner shivers uncontrollably. Marie-Laure leads him to the first floor, where ash and soot lie a half inch deep over everything, and he pushes capsized furniture out of the way and hauls open the cellar door and they climb down. Somewhere above, thirty bombers let fly their payloads and Werner and Marie-Laure feel the bedrock shake, hear the detonations across the river.

Could he, by some miracle, keep this going? Could they hide here until the war ends? Until the armies finish marching back and forth above their heads, until all they have to do is push open the door and shift some stones aside and the house has become a ruin beside the sea? Until he can hold her fingers in his palms and lead her out into the sunshine? He would walk anywhere to make it happen, bear anything; in a year or three years or ten, France and Germany would not mean what they meant now; they could leave the house and walk to a tourists' restaurant and order a simple meal together and eat it in silence, the comfortable kind of silence lovers are supposed to share.

"Do you know," Marie-Laure asks in a gentle voice, "why he was here? That man upstairs?"

"Because of the radio?" Even as he says it, he wonders.

"Maybe," she says. "Maybe that's why."

In another minute they're asleep.

CEASE-FIRE

Gritty summer light spills through the open trapdoor into the cellar. It might already be afternoon. No guns firing. For a few heartbeats, Werner watches her sleep.

Then they hurry. He cannot find the shoes she asks for, but he finds a pair of men's loafers in a closet and helps her put them on. Over his uniform he pulls on some of Etienne's tweed trousers, along with a shirt whose sleeves are too long. If they run into Germans, he will speak only French, say he is helping her leave the city. If they run into Americans, he will say he is deserting.

"There will be a collection point," he says, "somewhere they're gathering refugees," though he's not sure he says it correctly. He finds a white pillowcase in an upturned cabinet and folds it into her coat pocket. "When it comes time, hold this as high as you can."

"I will try. And my cane?"

"Here."

In the foyer, they hesitate. Neither sure what waits on the other side of the door. He remembers the overheated dance hall from the entrance exams four years before: ladder bolted to the wall, crimson flag with its white circle and black cross below. You step forward; you jump.

Outside, mountains of rubble hunker everywhere. Chimneys stand with their bricks raw to the light. Smoke troweled across the sky. He knows that the shells have been coming from the east, that six days ago the Americans were almost to Paramé, so he moves Marie-Laure in that direction.

Any moment they will be seen, by either Americans or his own army, and made to do something. Work, join, confess, die. From somewhere comes the sound of fire: the sound of dried roses being crumbled in a fist. No other sounds; no motors, no airplanes, no distant pop of gunfire or howling of wounded men or yapping of dogs. He takes her hand to help her over the piles. No shells fall and no rifles crack and the light is soft and shot through with ash.

Jutta, he thinks, I finally listened.

For two blocks they see nobody. Maybe Volkheimer is eating — this is what Werner would like to imagine, gigantic Volkheimer eating by himself at a little table with a view of the sea.

"It's so quiet."

Her voice like a bright, clear window of sky. Her face a field of freckles. He thinks: I don't want to let you go.

"Are they watching us?"

"I don't know. I don't think so."

A block ahead, he sees movement: three women carrying bundles. Marie-Laure pulls at his sleeve. "What is this cross street?"

"The rue des Lauriers."

"Come," she says, and walks with her cane tapping back and forth in her right hand. They turn right and left, past a walnut tree like a giant charred toothpick jammed into the ground, past two crows picking at something unidentifiable, until they reach the base of the ramparts. Airborne creepers of ivy hang from an archway over a narrow alley. Far to his right, Werner can see a woman in blue taffeta drag a great overstuffed suitcase over a curbstone. A boy in pants meant for a younger child follows, beret thrown back on his head, some kind of shiny jacket on.

"There are civilians leaving, mademoiselle. Shall I call to them?"

"I need only a moment." She leads him deeper down the alley. Sweet, unfettered ocean air pours through a gap in the wall he cannot see: the air throbs with it.

At the end of the alley they reach a narrow gate. She reaches inside her coat and produces a key. "Is the tide high?"

He can just see through the gate into a low

space, bounded by a grate on the far side. "There is water down there. We have to hurry."

But she is already passing through the gate and descending into the grotto in her big shoes, moving with confidence, running her fingers along the walls as though they are old friends she thought she might never meet again. The tide pushes a low riffle through the pool, and it washes over her shins and dampens the hem of her dress. From her coat, she takes some small wooden thing and sets it in the water. She speaks lightly, her voice echoing: "You need to tell me, is it in the ocean? It must be in the ocean."

"It is in. We must go, mademoiselle."

"Are you certain it's in the water?"

"Yes."

She climbs out, breathless. Pushes him back through the gate and locks it behind them. He hands her the cane. Then they head back down the alley, her shoes squelching as she goes. Out through the hanging ivy. Turn left. Straight ahead a ragged stream of people crosses an intersection: a woman, a child, two men carrying a third on a stretcher, all three with cigarettes in their mouths.

The darkness returns to Werner's eyes, and he feels faint. Soon his legs will give out. A cat sits in the road licking a paw and smoothing it over its ears and watching him. He thinks of the old broken miners he'd see in

Zollverein, sitting in chairs or on crates, not moving for hours, waiting to die. To men like that, time was a surfeit, a barrel they watched slowly drain. When really, he thinks, it's a glowing puddle you carry in your hands; you should spend all your energy protecting it. Fighting for it. Working so hard not to spill one single drop.

"Now," he says in the clearest French he can muster, "here's the pillowcase. You run your hand along that wall. Can you feel it? You'll reach an intersection, keep going straight. The street looks mostly clear. Keep the pillowcase high. Right out in front like this, do you understand?"

She turns to him and chews her bottom lip. "They will shoot."

"Not with that white flag. Not a girl. There are others ahead. Follow this wall." He sets her hand against it a second time. "Hurry. Remember the pillowcase."

"And you?"

"I will go in the other direction."

She turns her face toward his, and though she cannot see him, he feels he cannot bear her gaze. "Won't you come with me?"

"It will be better for you if no one sees you with me."

"But how will I find you again?"

"I don't know."

She reaches for his hand, sets something in his palm, and squeezes his hand into a fist.

"Goodbye, Werner."

"Goodbye, Marie-Laure."

Then she goes. Every few paces, the tip of her cane strikes a broken stone in the street, and it takes a while to pick her way around it. Step step pause. Step step again. Her cane testing, the wet hem of her dress swinging, the white pillowcase held aloft. He does not look away until she is through the intersection, down the next block, and out of sight.

He waits to hear voices. Guns.

They will help her. They must.

When he opens his hand, there is a little iron key in his palm.

Chocolate

Madame Ruelle finds Marie-Laure that evening in a requisitioned school. She grips her hand and does not let go. The civil affairs people have stacks of confiscated German chocolate in rectangular cartons, and Marie-Laure and Madame Ruelle eat too many to count.

In the morning, the Americans take the château and the last anti-air battery and free the prisoners held at Fort National. Madame Ruelle pulls Etienne out of the processing queue, and he wraps Marie-Laure in his arms. The colonel in his underground fortress across the river holds out for three more days, until an American airplane called a Lightning drops a tank of napalm through an air vent, one shot in a million, and five minutes later, a white sheet comes up on a pole and the siege of Saint-Malo is over. Sweep platoons remove all the incendiary devices they can find, and army photographers go in with their tripods, and a handful of citizens return from farms and fields and cellars to drift through the ruined streets. On August 25, Madame Ruelle is allowed back into the city to check on the condition of the bakery, but Etienne and Marie-Laure travel in the other direction, toward Rennes, where they book a room at a hotel called the Universe with a functioning boiler and each takes a two-hour bath. In the window glass as night falls, he watches her reflection feel its way toward the bed. Her hands press against her face, then fall away.

"We'll go to Paris," he says. "I've never been. You can show it to me."

Light

Werner is captured a mile south of Saint-Malo by three French resistance fighters in streetclothes roving the streets in a lorry. First they believe they have rescued a little white-haired old man. Then they hear his accent, notice the German tunic beneath the antique shirt, and decide they have a spy, a fabulous catch. Then they realize Werner's youth. They hand him off to an American clerk in a requisitioned hotel transformed into a disarmament center. At first Werner worries they're taking him downstairs — please, not another pit — but he is brought to the third floor, where an exhausted interpreter who has been booking German prisoners for a month notes his name and rank, then asks a few rote questions while the clerk rifles through Werner's canvas duffel and hands it back.

"A girl," Werner says in French, "did you see — ?" but the interpreter only smirks and says something to the clerk in English, as though every German soldier he has interviewed has asked about a girl.

He's ushered into a courtyard encircled with razor wire, where eight or nine other Germans sit in their high boots holding battered canteens, one dressed in women's clothes in which he apparently tried to desert. Two NCOs and three privates and no Volkheimer.

At night they serve soup in a cauldron, and he gulps down four helpings from a tin cup. Five minutes later, he is sick in the corner. The soup won't stay down in the morning either. Shoals of clouds swim through the sky. His left ear admits no sound. He lingers over images of Marie-Laure — her hands, her hair — even as he worries that to concentrate on them too long is to risk wearing them out. A day after his arrest, he is marched east in a group of twenty to join a larger group where they are penned in a warehouse. Through the open doors, he cannot see Saint-Malo, but he hears the airplanes, hundreds of them, and a great pall of smoke hangs over the horizon day and night. Twice medics try giving Werner bowls of gruel, but it will not stay down. He's been able to keep nothing in his stomach since the peaches.

Maybe his fever is returning; maybe the sludge they drank in the hotel cellar has poisoned him. Maybe his body is giving up. If he does not eat, he understands, he will die. But when he does eat, he feels as if he will die.

From the warehouse, they are marched to Dinan. Most of the prisoners are boys or middle-aged men, the shattered remains of companies. They carry ponchos, duffels, crates; a few tote brightly colored suitcases claimed from who knows where. Among them walk pairs of men who fought side by side, but most are strangers to one another, and all have seen things they wish to forget. Always there is the sense of a tide behind them, rising, gathering mass, carrying with it a slow and vindictive rage.

He walks in the tweed trousers of Marie-Laure's great-uncle; over his shoulder, he carries his duffel. Eighteen years old. All his life his schoolmasters, his radio, his leaders talked to him about the future. And yet what future remains? The road ahead is blank, and the lines of his thoughts all incline inward: he sees Marie-Laure disappear down the street with her cane like ash blown out of a fire, and a feeling of longing crashes against the underside of his ribs.

On the first of September, Werner cannot get to his feet when he wakes. Two of his fellow prisoners help him to the bathroom and back, then lay him in the grass. A young Canadian in a medic's helmet shines a penlight into Werner's eyes and loads him into a truck, and he is driven some distance and set in a tent full of dying men. A nurse puts fluid into his arm. Spoons a solution into his mouth.

For a week he lives in the strange greenish light beneath the canvas of that huge tent, his duffel clutched in one hand and the hard corners of the little wooden house clamped in the other. When he has the strength, he fiddles with it. Twist the chimney, slide off the three panels of the roof, look inside. Built so cleverly.

Every day, on his right and left, another soul escapes toward the sky, and it sounds to him as if he can hear faraway music, as if a door has been shut on a grand old radio and he can listen only by putting his good ear against the material of his cot, although the music is soft, and there are moments when he is not certain it is there at all.

There is something to be angry at, Werner is sure, but he cannot say what it is.

"Won't eat," says a nurse in English.

Armband of a medic. "Fever?"

"High."

There are more words. Then numbers. In a dream, he sees a bright crystalline night with the canals all frozen and the lanterns of the miners' houses burning and the farmers skating between the fields. He sees a submarine asleep in the lightless depths of the Atlantic; Jutta presses her face to a porthole and breathes on the glass. He half expects to see

Volkheimer's huge hand appear, help him up, and clap him into the Opel.

And Marie-Laure? Can she still feel the pressure of his hand against the webbing between her fingers as he can feel hers?

One night he sits up. In cots around him are a few dozen sick or wounded. A warm September wind pours across the countryside and sets the walls of the tent rippling.

Werner's head swivels lightly on his neck. The wind is strong and gusting stronger, and the corners of the tent strain against their guy ropes, and where the flaps at the two ends come up, he can see trees buck and sway. Everything rustles. Werner zips his old notebook and the little house into his duffel and the man beside him murmurs questions to himself and the rest of the ruined company sleeps. Even Werner's thirst has faded. He feels only the raw, impassive surge of the moonlight as it strikes the tent above him and scatters. Out there, through the open flaps of the tent, clouds hurtle above treetops. Toward Germany, toward home.

Silver and blue, blue and silver.

Sheets of paper tumble down the rows of cots, and in Werner's chest comes a quickening. He sees Frau Elena kneel beside the coal stove and bank up the fire. Children in their beds. Baby Jutta sleeps in her cradle. His father lights a lamp, steps into an elevator, and disappears.

The voice of Volkheimer: *What you could be.*

Werner's body seems to have gone weightless under his blanket, and beyond the flapping tent doors, the trees dance and the clouds keep up their huge billowing march, and he swings first one leg and then the other off the edge of the bed.

"Ernst," says the man beside him. "Ernst." But there is no Ernst; the men in the cots do not reply; the American soldier at the door of the tent sleeps. Werner walks past him into the grass.

The wind moves through his undershirt. He is a kite, a balloon.

Once, he and Jutta built a little sailboat from scraps of wood and carried it to the river. Jutta painted the vessel in ecstatic purples and greens, and she set it on the water with great formality. But the boat sagged as soon as the current got hold of it. It floated downstream, out of reach, and the flat black water swallowed it. Jutta blinked at Werner with wet eyes, pulling at the battered loops of yarn in her sweater.

"It's all right," he told her. "Things hardly ever work on the first try. We'll make another, a better one."

Did they? He hopes they did. He seems to remember a little boat — a more seaworthy one — gliding down a river. It sailed around a bend and left them behind. Didn't it?

The moonlight shines and billows; the broken clouds scud above the trees. Leaves fly everywhere. But the moonlight stays unmoved by the wind, passing through clouds, through air, in what seems to Werner like impossibly slow, imperturbable rays. They hang across the buckling grass.

Why doesn't the wind move the light?

Across the field, an American watches a boy leave the sick tent and move against the background of the trees. He sits up. He raises his hand.

"Stop," he calls.

"Halt," he calls.

But Werner has crossed the edge of the field, where he steps on a trigger land mine set there by his own army three months before, and disappears in a fountain of earth.

Eleven: 1945

Berlin

In January 1945, Frau Elena and the last four girls living at Children's House — the twins, Hannah and Susanne Gerlitz, Claudia Förster, and fifteen-year-old Jutta Pfennig — are transported from Essen to Berlin to work in a machine parts factory.

For ten hours a day, six days a week, they disassemble massive forging presses and stack the usable metal in crates to be loaded onto train cars. Unscrewing, sawing, hauling. Most days Frau Elena works close by, wearing a torn ski jacket she has found, mumbling to herself in French or singing songs from childhood.

They live above a printing company abandoned a month before. Hundreds of crates of misprinted dictionaries are stacked in the halls, and the girls burn them page by page in the potbelly stove.

Yesterday *Dankeswort, Dankesworte, Dankgebet, Dankopfer.*

Today *Frauenverband, Frauenverein, Frauen-*

vorsteher, Frauenwahlrecht.

For meals they have cabbage and barley in the factory canteen at noon, endless ration lines in the evening. Butter is cut into tiny portions: three times a week, they each get a square half the size of a sugar cube. Water comes from a spigot two blocks away. Mothers with infants have no baby clothes, no buggies, and very little cow's milk. Some tear apart bedsheets for diapers; a few find newspapers and fold those into triangles and pin them between their babies' legs.

At least half of the girls working in the factory cannot read or write, so Jutta reads them the letters that come from boyfriends or brothers or fathers at the front. Sometimes she writes responses for them: *And do you remember when we ate pistachios, when we ate those lemon ices shaped like flowers? When you said . . .*

All spring the bombers come, every single night, their only goal seemingly to burn the city to its roots. Most nights the girls hurry to the end of the block and climb into a cramped shelter and are kept awake by the crashing of stonework.

Once in a while, on the walk to the factory, they see bodies, mummies turned to ash, people scorched beyond recognition. Other times, the corpses bear no apparent injuries, and it is these that fill Jutta with dread:

people who look like they are a moment away from rising up and slogging back to work with the rest of them.

But they do not wake.

Once she sees a row of three children facedown, backpacks on their backs. Her first thought is: Wake up. Go to school. Then she thinks: There could be food in those packs.

Claudia Förster stops talking. Whole days pass and she does not say a word. The factory runs out of materials. There are rumors that no one is in charge anymore, that the copper and zinc and stainless steel they've been slaving to collect is being loaded onto train cars and left on sidings for no one.

Mail stops. In late March, the machine parts factory is padlocked, and Frau Elena and the girls are sent to work for a civilian firm cleaning the streets after bombings. They lift broken masonry blocks, shovel dust and shattered glass through strainers. Jutta hears about boys, sixteen- and seventeen-year-olds, terrified, homesick, with trembling eyes, who show up on the doorsteps of their mothers only to be hauled howling out of attics two days later and shot in the street as deserters. Images from her childhood — riding in a wagon behind her brother, picking through trash — return to her. Looking to salvage one shining thing from the mire.

"Werner," she whispers aloud.

In the fall, at Zollverein, she received two

letters announcing his death. Each mentioned a different place of burial. La Fresnais, Cherbourg — she had to look them up. Towns in France. Sometimes, in dreams, she stands with him over a table strewn with gears and belts and motors. *I'm making something,* he says. *I'm working on it.* But he doesn't go on.

By April, the women speak only of the Russians and the things they will do, the vengeance they will seek. Barbarians, they say. Tatars, Russkis, savages, swine. The pigs are in Strasbourg. The ogres are in the suburbs.

Hannah, Susanne, Claudia, and Jutta sleep on the floor in a tangle. Does any goodness linger in this last derelict stronghold? A little. Jutta comes home one afternoon, pasted with dust, to discover that big Claudia Förster has chanced upon a paper bakery box sealed with gold tape. Blots of grease show through the cardboard. Together the girls stare at it. Like something from the unfallen world.

Inside wait fifteen pastries, separated by squares of wax paper and stuffed with strawberry preserves. The four girls and Frau Elena sit in their dripping apartment, a spring rain over the city, all the ash running off the ruins, all the rats peering out of caves made from fallen bricks, and they eat three stale pastries each, none of them saving anything for later, the powdered sugar on their noses, the jelly between their teeth, a giddiness rising and sparkling in their blood.

That cowlike, petrified Claudia could achieve such a miracle, that she would be good enough to share it.

What young women are left dress themselves in rags, cower in basements. Jutta hears that grandmothers are rubbing granddaughters with feces, sawing off their hair with bread knives, anything to make them less appealing to the Russians.

She hears mothers are drowning daughters.

She hears you can smell the blood on them from a mile away.

"Not much longer now," says Frau Elena, her palms out in front of the stove as the water refuses to boil.

The Russians come for them on a cloudless day in May. There are only three of them, and they come only that one time. They break into the printing company below, hunting liquor, but find none and are soon bashing holes in the walls. A crack and a shudder, a bullet zinging off an old dismantled press, and in the upstairs apartment Frau Elena sits in her striped ski parka, an abridged New Testament zipped into the pocket, holding the hands of the girls and moving her lips in soundless prayer.

Jutta allows herself to believe that they won't come up the staircase. For several minutes they don't. Until they do, and their boots thump all the way up.

"Stay calm," Frau Elena tells the girls. Hannah and Susanne and Claudia and Jutta — none of them is older than sixteen. Frau Elena's voice is low and deflated, but it does not seem afraid. Disappointed, maybe. "Stay calm and they won't shoot. I'll make sure to go first. After that they'll be gentler."

Jutta laces her hands behind her head to keep them from shaking. Claudia seems mute, deaf.

"And close your eyes," says Frau Elena.

Hannah sobs.

Jutta says, "I want to see them."

"Keep them open, then."

The footsteps stop at the top of the stairwell. The Russians go into the closet, and they hear the handles of mops being kicked drunkenly and a crate of dictionaries go thudding down the stairs, and then someone rattles the knob. One says something to another and the jamb splinters and the door bangs open.

One is an officer. Two cannot be a day older than seventeen. All are filthy beyond comprehension, but somewhere in the previous hours, they have taken the liberty of splashing themselves with women's perfume. The two boys, in particular, smell toxically of it. They seem partly like sheepish schoolboys and partly like lunatics with an hour left to live. The first has only a rope for a belt and is so thin, he does not have to unknot it to slide off his trousers. The second laughs: a strange, puzzled laugh, as if he does not quite believe the Germans would come to his country and leave a city like this behind. The officer sits by the door with his legs straight out in front of him and peers out into the street. Hannah screams for a half second but quickly muffles it with her own hand.

Frau Elena leads the boys into the other room. She makes a single noise: a cough, as though she has something stuck in her throat.

Claudia goes next. She offers up only moans.

Jutta does not allow herself to make a single sound. Everything is strangely orderly. The officer goes last, trying each of them in turn, and he speaks single words while he is on top of Jutta, his eyes open but not seeing. It is not clear from his compressed, pained face if the words are endearments or insults. Beneath the cologne, he smells like a horse.

Years later, Jutta will hear the words he spoke repeated in her memory — *Kirill, Pavel, Afanasy, Valentin* — and she will decide they were the names of dead soldiers. But she could be wrong.

Before the Russians leave, the youngest fires his weapon into the ceiling twice, and plaster rains gently down onto Jutta, and in the loud reverberating echo, she can hear Susanne on the floor beside her, not sobbing but merely breathing very quietly as she listens to the officer buckle himself back up. Then the three men spill into the street and Frau Elena zips herself into her ski parka, barefoot, rubbing her left arm with her right hand, as if trying to warm that one small segment of herself.

Paris

Etienne rents the same flat on the rue des Patriarches where Marie-Laure grew up. He buys the newspapers every day to scan the lists of released prisoners, and listens incessantly to one of three radios. *De Gaulle* this, *North Africa* that. *Hitler, Roosevelt, Danzig, Bratislava,* all these names, none of them her father's.

Every morning they walk to the Gare d'Austerlitz to wait. A big station clock rattles off a relentless advance of seconds, and Marie-Laure sits beside her great-uncle and listens to the wasted and wretched shamble off the trains.

Etienne sees soldiers with hollows in their cheeks like inverted cups. Thirty-year-olds who look eighty. Men in threadbare suits putting hands to the tops of their heads to take off hats that are no longer there. Marie-Laure deduces what she can from the sounds of their shoes: those are small, those weigh a ton, those hardly exist at all.

In the evenings she reads while Etienne makes phone calls, petitions repatriation authorities, and writes letters. She finds she can sleep only two or three hours at a time. Phantom shells wake her.

"It is merely the autobus," says Etienne, who takes to sleeping on the floor beside her.

Or: "It's just the birds."

Or: "It's nothing, Marie."

Most days, the creaky old malacologist Dr. Geffard waits with them at the Gare d'Austerlitz, sitting upright with his beard and bow tie, smelling of rosemary, of mint, of wine. He calls her Laurette; he talks about how he missed her, how he thought of her every day, how to see her is to believe once more that goodness, more than anything else, is what lasts.

She sits with her shoulder pressed against Etienne's or Dr. Geffard's. Papa might be anywhere. He might be that voice just now drawing nearer. Those footfalls to her right. He might be in a cell, in a ditch, a thousand miles away. He might be long dead.

She goes into the museum on Etienne's arm to talk with various officials, many of whom remember her. The director himself explains that they are searching as hard as they can for her father, that they will continue to help with her housing, her education. There is no mention of the Sea of Flames.

Spring unfurls; communiqués flood the

airwaves. Berlin surrenders; Göring surrenders; the great mysterious vault of Nazism falls open. Parades materialize spontaneously. The others who wait at the Gare d'Austerlitz whisper that one out of every hundred will come back. That you can loop your thumb and forefinger around their necks. That when they take off their shirts, you can see their lungs moving inside their chests.

Every bite of food she takes is a betrayal.

Even those who have returned, she can tell, have returned different, older than they should be, as though they have been on another planet where years pass more quickly.

"There is a chance," Etienne says, "that we will never find out what happened. We have to be prepared for that." Marie-Laure hears Madame Manec: *You must never stop believing.*

All through the summer they wait, Etienne always on one side, Dr. Geffard often on the other. And then, one noon in August, Marie-Laure leads her great-uncle and Dr. Geffard up the long stairs and out into the sunlight and asks if it is safe to cross. They say it is, so she leads them along the quay, through the gates of the Jardin des Plantes.

Along the gravel paths boys shout. Someone not far away plays a saxophone. She stops beside an arbor alive with the sound of bees. The sky seems high and far away. Somewhere, someone is figuring out how to push back the hood of grief, but Marie-Laure cannot. Not yet. The truth is that she is a disabled girl with no home and no parents.

"What now?" asks Etienne. "Lunch?"

"School," she says. "I would like to go to school."

■ ■ ■ ■

Twelve:
1974

■ ■ ■ ■

Volkheimer

Frank Volkheimer's third-floor walk-up in the suburbs of Pforzheim, Germany, possesses three windows. A single billboard, mounted on the cornice of the building across the alley, dominates the view; its surface gleams three yards beyond the glass. Printed on it are processed meats, cold cuts as tall as he is, reds and pinks, gray at the edges, garnished with parsley sprigs the size of shrubs. At night the billboard's four cheerless electric spotlights bathe his apartment in a strange reflected glare.

He is fifty-one years old.

April rain falls slantwise through the billboard's spotlights and Volkheimer's television flickers blue and he ducks habitually as he passes through the doorway between his kitchen and the main room. No children, no pets, no houseplants, few books on the shelves. Just a card table, a mattress, and a single armchair in front of the television where he now sits, a tin of butter cookies in his lap. He eats them one after another, all the floral discs, then the ones shaped like pretzels, and finally the clovers.

On the television, a black horse helps free a man trapped beneath a fallen tree.

Volkheimer installs and repairs rooftop TV antennas. He puts on a blue jumpsuit every morning, faded where it strains over his huge shoulders, too short around the ankles, and walks to work in big black boots. Because he is strong enough to move the big extension ladders by himself, and perhaps also because he rarely speaks, Volkheimer responds to most calls alone. People telephone the branch office to request an installation, or to complain about ghost signals, interference, starlings on the wires, and out goes Volkheimer. He splices a broken line, or pokes a bird's nest off a boom, or elevates an antenna on struts.

Only on the windiest, coldest days does Pforzheim feel like home. Volkheimer likes feeling the air slip under the collar of his jumpsuit, likes seeing the light blown clean by the wind, the far-off hills powdered with snow, the town's trees (all planted in the years after the war, all the same age) glittering with ice. On winter afternoons he moves among the antennas like a sailor through rigging. In the late blue light, he can watch the people in the streets below, hurrying home, and sometimes gulls soar past, white against the dark. The small, secure weight of tools along his belt, the smell of intermittent rain, and the crystalline brilliance of the clouds at dusk: these are the only times when Volkheimer feels marginally whole.

But on most days, especially the warm ones, life exhausts him; the worsening traffic and graffiti and company politics, everyone grousing about bonuses, benefits, overtime. Sometimes, in the slow heat of summer, long before dawn, Volkheimer paces in the harsh dazzle of the billboard lights and feels his loneliness on him like a disease. He sees tall ranks of firs swaying in a storm, hears their heartwood groan. He sees the earthen floor of his childhood home, and the spiderwebbed light of dawn coming through conifers. Other times the eyes of men who are about to die haunt him, and he kills them all over again. Dead man in Lodz. Dead man in Lublin. Dead man in Radom. Dead man in Cracow.

Rain on the windows, rain on the roof. Before he goes to bed, Volkheimer descends three flights of stairs to the atrium to check his mail. He has not checked his mail in over a week, and among two flyers and a paycheck and a single utility bill is a small package from a veterans' service organization located in West Berlin. He carries the mail upstairs and opens the package.

Three different objects have been photographed against the same white background, carefully numbered notecards taped beside each.

14-6962. A canvas soldier's bag, mouse gray, with two padded straps.

14-6963. A little model house, made from wood, partially crushed.

14-6964. A soft-covered rectangular notebook with a single word across the front: *Fragen.*

The house he does not recognize, and the bag could have been any soldier's, but he knows the notebook instantly. *W.P.* inked on the bottom corner. Volkheimer sets two fingers on the photograph as though he could pluck out the notebook and sift through its pages.

He was a just a boy. They all were. Even the largest of them.

The letter explains that the organization is trying to deliver items to next of kin of dead soldiers whose names have been lost. It says they believe that he, Staff Sergeant Frank Volkheimer, served as ranking officer of a unit that included the owner of this bag, a bag that was collected by a United States Army prisoner-of-war processing camp in Bernay, France, in the year 1944.

Does he know to whom these items belonged?

He sets the photographs on the table and stands with his big hands at his sides. He hears jouncing axles, grumbling tailpipes, rain on canvas. Clouds of gnats buzzing. The march of jackboots and the full-throated shouts of boys.

Static, then the guns.

But was it decent to leave him out there like that? Even after he was dead?

What you could be.

He was small. He had white hair and ears that stuck out. He buttoned the collar of his jacket up around his throat when he was cold and drew his hands up inside the sleeves. Volkheimer knows whom those items belonged to.

JUTTA

Jutta Wette teaches sixth-form algebra in Essen: integers, probability, parabolas. Every day she wears the same outfit: black slacks with a nylon blouse — alternately beige, charcoal, or pale blue. Occasionally the canary-yellow one, if she's feeling unrestrained. Her skin is milky and her hair remains white as paper.

Jutta's husband, Albert, is a kind, slow-moving, and balding accountant whose great passion is running model trains in the basement. For a long time Jutta believed she could not get pregnant, and then, one day, when she was thirty-seven years old, she did. Their son, Max, is six, fond of mud, dogs, and questions no one can answer. More than anything lately, Max likes to fold complicated designs of paper airplanes. He comes home from school, kneels on the kitchen floor, and forms airplane after airplane with unswerving, almost frightening devotion, evaluating different wingtips, tails, noses, mostly seeming to love the praxis of it, the transformation of something flat into something that can fly.

It's a Thursday afternoon in early June, the school year nearly over, and they are at the public swimming pool. Slate-colored clouds veil the sky, and children shout in the shallow end, and parents talk or read magazines or doze in their chairs, and everything is normal. Albert stands at the snack counter in his swim trunks, with his little towel draped over his wide back, and contemplates his selection of ice cream.

Max swims awkwardly, windmilling one arm forward and then the other, periodically looking up to make sure his mother is watching. When he's done, he wraps himself in a towel and climbs into the chair beside her. Max is compact and small and his ears stick out. Water droplets shine in his eyelashes. Dusk seeps down through the overcast and a slight chill drops into the air and one by one families leave to walk or bike or ride the bus home. Max plucks crackers out of a cardboard box and crunches them loudly. "I love Leibniz Zoo crackers, Mutti," he says.

"I know, Max."

Albert drives them home in their little NSU Prinz 4, the clutch rattling, and Jutta takes a stack of end-of-term exams from her school bag and grades them at the kitchen table. Albert puts on water for noodles and fries onions. Max takes a clean sheet of paper from the drawing table and starts to fold.

On the front door come knocks, three.

For reasons Jutta does not fully understand, her heartbeat begins to thud in her ears. The point of her pencil hovers over the page. It's only someone at the door — a neighbor or a friend or the little girl, Anna, from down the street, who sits upstairs with Max sometimes and gives him directions for how to best construct elaborate towns out of plastic blocks. But the knock does not sound anything like Anna's.

Max bounds to the door, airplane in hand.

"Who is it, dear?"

Max does not reply, which means it is someone he does not know. She crosses into the hall, and there in her door frame stands a giant.

Max crosses his arms, intrigued and impressed. His airplane on the ground at his feet. The giant takes off his cap. His massive head shines. "Frau Wette?" He wears a tent-sized silver sweatsuit with maroon splashes along the sides, zipper pulled to the base of his throat. Gingerly, he presents a faded canvas duffel bag.

The bullies in the square. Hans and Herribert. His very size invokes them all. This man has come, she thinks, to other doors and not bothered to knock.

"Yes?"

"Your maiden name was Pfennig?"

Even before she nods, before he says, "I have something for you," before she invites him through the screen door, she knows this will be about Werner.

The giant's nylon pants swish as he follows her down the hall. When Albert looks up from the stove, he startles but only says, "Hello," and "Watch your head," and waves his cooking spoon as the giant dodges the light fixture.

When he offers dinner, the giant says yes. Albert pulls the table away from the wall and sets a fourth place. In his wooden chair, Volkheimer reminds Jutta of an image from one of Max's picture books: an elephant squeezed into an airplane seat. The duffel bag he has brought waits on the hall table.

The conversation begins slowly.

He has come several hours on the train.

He walked here from the station.

He does not need sherry, thank you.

Max eats fast, Albert slowly. Jutta tucks her hands beneath her thighs to hide their shaking.

"Once they had the address," Volkheimer says, "I asked if I might deliver it myself. They included a letter, see?" He takes a folded sheet of paper from his pocket.

Outside, cars pass, wrens trill.

A part of Jutta does not want to take the letter. Does not want to hear what this huge man has traveled a long way to say. Weeks go by when Jutta does not allow herself to think of the war, of Frau Elena, of the awful last months in Berlin. Now she can buy pork seven days a week. Now, if the house feels cold she twists a dial in the kitchen, and *voilà*. She does not want to be one of those middle-aged women who thinks of nothing but her own painful history. Sometimes she looks at the eyes of her older colleagues and wonders what they did when the electricity was out, when there were no candles, when the rain came through the ceiling. What they saw. Only rarely does she loosen the seals enough to allow herself to think of Werner. In many ways, her memories of her brother have become things to lock away. A math teacher at Helmoltz-Gymnasium in 1974 does not bring up a brother who attended the National Political Institute of Education at Schulpforta.

Albert says, "In the east, then?"

Volkheimer says, "I was with him at school, then out in the field. We were in Russia. Also Poland, Ukraine, Austria. Then France."

Max crunches a sliced apple. He says, "How tall are you?"

"Max," says Jutta.

Volkheimer smiles.

Albert says, "He was very bright, wasn't he? Jutta's brother?"

Volkheimer says, "Very."

Albert offers a second helping, offers salt, offers sherry again. Albert is younger than

Jutta, and during the war, he ran as a courier in Hamburg between bomb shelters. Nine years old in 1945, still a child.

"The last place I saw him," says Volkheimer, "was in a town on the northern coast of France called Saint-Malo."

From the loam of Jutta's memory rises a sentence: *What I want to write about today is the sea.*

"We spent a month there. I think he might have fallen in love."

Jutta sits straighter in her chair. It's embarrassingly plain how inadequate language is. A town on the northern coast of France? Love? Nothing will be healed in this kitchen. Some griefs can never be put right.

Volkheimer pushes back from the table. "It was not my intention to upset you." He hovers, dwarfing them.

"It's all right," says Albert. "Max, can you please take our guest to the patio? I'll put out some cake."

Max slides open the glass door for Volkheimer, and he ducks through. Jutta sets the plates in the sink. She is suddenly very tired. She only wants the big man to leave and to take the bag with him. She only wants a tide of normality to wash in and cover everything again.

Albert touches her elbow. "Are you all right?"

Jutta does not nod or shake her head, but

slowly drags a hand over both eyebrows.

"I love you, Jutta."

When she looks out the window, Volkheimer is kneeling on the cement beside Max. Max lays down two sheets of paper, and although she cannot hear them, she can see the huge man talking Max through a set of steps. Max watches intently, turning over the sheet when Volkheimer turns it over, matching his folds, wetting one finger, and running it along a crease.

Soon enough, they each have a wide-winged plane with a long forked tail. Volkheimer's sails neatly out across the yard, flying straight and true, and smacks into the fence nose-first. Max claps.

Max kneels on the patio in the dusk, going over his airplane, checking the angle of its wings. Volkheimer kneels beside him, nodding, patient.

Jutta says, "I love you too."

Duffel

Volkheimer is gone. The duffel waits on the hall table. She can hardly look at it.

Jutta helps Max into his pajamas and kisses him good night. She brushes her teeth, avoiding herself in the mirror, and goes back downstairs and stands looking out through the window in their front door. In the basement, Albert is running his trains through his meticulously painted world, beneath the underpass, over his electric drawbridge; it's a small sound up here, but relentless, a sound that penetrates the timbers of the house.

Jutta brings the duffel up to the desk in her bedroom and sets it down on the floor and grades another of her students' exams. Then another. She can hear the trains stop, then resume their monotonous drone.

She tries to grade a third exam but cannot concentrate; the numbers drift across the pages and collect at the bottom in unintelligible piles. She sets the bag in her lap.

When they were first married and Albert

went away on trips for work, Jutta would wake in the predawn hours and remember those first nights after Werner left for Schulpforta and feel all over again the searing pain of his absence.

For something so old, the zipper on the duffel opens smoothly. Inside is a thick envelope and a package covered in newspaper. When she unwraps the newspaper, she finds a model house, tall and narrow, no bigger than her fist.

The envelope contains the notebook she sent him forty years before. His book of questions. That crimped, tiny cursive, each letter sloping slightly farther uphill. Drawings, schematics, pages of lists.

Something that looks like a blender powered by bicycle pedals.

A motor for a model airplane.

Why do some fish have whiskers?

Is it true that all cats are gray when the candles are out?

When lightning strikes the sea, why don't all the fish die?

After three pages, she has to close the notebook. Memories cartwheel out of her head and tumble across the floor. Werner's cot in the attic, the wall above it papered over with her drawings of imaginary cities. The first-aid box and the radio and the wire threaded out the window and through the eave. Downstairs, the trains run through Albert's three-level layout, and in the next room her son wages battles in his sleep, lips murmuring, eyelids flexing, and Jutta wills the numbers to climb back up and find their places on her students' exams.

She reopens the notebook.

Why does a knot hold?

If five cats catch five rats in five minutes, how many cats will it require to catch 100 rats in 100 minutes?

Why does a flag flutter in the wind rather than stand straight out?

Tucked between the last two pages, she finds an old sealed envelope. He has written *For Frederick* across the front. Frederick: the bunkmate Werner used to write about, the boy who loved birds.

He sees what other people don't.

What the war did to dreamers.

When Albert finally comes up, she keeps her head down and pretends to be grading exams. He peels himself out of his clothes and groans lightly as he gets into bed, and switches off his lamp, and says good night, and still she sits.

Saint-Malo

Jutta's grades are in, and Max is off school, and besides, he'd just go to the pool every day, pester his father with riddles, fold three hundred of those airplanes the giant taught him, and wouldn't it be good for him to visit another country, learn some French, see the ocean? She poses these questions to Albert, but both of them know that she is the one who must grant permission. To go herself, to take their son.

On the twenty-sixth of June, an hour before dawn, Albert makes six ham sandwiches and wraps them in foil. Then he drives Jutta and Max to the station in the Prinz 4 and kisses her on the lips, and she boards the train with Werner's notebook and the model house in her purse.

The journey takes all day. By Rennes, the sun has dropped low over the horizon, and the smell of warm manure comes through the open windows, and lines of pollarded trees whisk past. Gulls and crows in equal numbers follow a tractor through its wake of dust. Max eats a second ham sandwich and rereads a comic book, and sheets of yellow flowers glow in the fields, and Jutta wonders if any of them grow over the bones of her brother.

Before dark, a well-dressed man with a prosthetic leg boards the train. He sits beside her and lights a cigarette. Jutta clutches her bag between her knees; she is certain that he was wounded in the war, that he will try to start a conversation, that her deficient French will betray her. Or that Max will say something. Or that the man can already tell. Maybe she smells German.

He'll say, *You did this to me.*

Please. Not in front of my son.

But the train jolts into motion, and the man finishes his cigarette and gives her a preoccupied smile and promptly falls asleep.

She turns the little house over in her fingers. They come into Saint-Malo around midnight, and the cabdriver leaves them at a hotel on the Place Chateaubriand. The clerk accepts the money Albert exchanged for her, and Max leans against her hip, half-asleep, and she is so afraid to try her French that she goes to bed hungry.

In the morning Max pulls her through a gap in the old walls and out onto a beach. He runs across the sand at full tilt, then stops and stares up at the ramparts rearing above him as though imagining pennants and cannons and medieval archers ranged along the parapets.

Jutta cannot tear her eyes away from the ocean. It is emerald green and incomprehensibly large. A single white sail veers out of the harbor. A pair of trawlers on the horizon appear and disappear between waves.

Sometimes I catch myself staring at it and forget my duties. It seems big enough to contain everything anyone could ever feel.

They pay a coin to climb the tower of the château. "Come on," Max says, and charges up the winding narrow stairs, and Jutta huffs along behind, each quarter turn presenting a narrow window of blue sky, Max practically hauling her up the steps.

From the top, they watch the small figures of tourists stroll past shopwindows. She has read about the siege; she has studied photos of the old town before the war. But now, looking across at the huge dignified houses, the hundreds of rooftops, she can see no traces of bombings or craters or crushed buildings. The town appears to have been entirely replaced.

They order galettes for lunch. She expects stares, but no one takes any notice. The waiter seems to neither know nor care that she is German. In the afternoon, she leads Max out through a high arch on the far side of the city called the Porte de Dinan. They cross the quay and climb to a matching headland across the mouth of a river from the old city. Inside the park wait the ruins of a fort overgrown with weeds. Max pauses at all the steep edges along the trail and throws pebbles down into the sea.

Every hundred paces along the path, they come across a big steel cap beneath which a soldier would direct cannon fire at whomever was trying to take the hill. Some of these pillboxes are so scarred by assault that she can hardly imagine the fire and speed and terror of the projectiles showering onto them. A foot of steel looks as if it has been transformed into warm butter and gouged by the fingers of a child.

What it must have sounded like, to stand in there.

Now they are filled with crisps bags, cigarette filters, paper wrappers. American and French flags fly from a hilltop at the center of the park. Here, signs say, Germans holed up in underground tunnels to fight to the last man.

Three teenagers pass laughing and Max watches them with great intensity. On a pocked and lichen-splotched cement wall is bolted a small stone plaque. *Ici a été tué Buy Gaston Marcel agé de 18 ans, mort pour la France le 11 août 1944.* Jutta sits on the ground. The sea is heavy and slate-gray. There are no plaques for the Germans who died here.

Why has she come? What answers did she hope to find? On their second morning, they sit in the Place Chateaubriand across from the historical museum, where sturdy benches face flower beds ringed by shin-high metal half loops. Beneath awnings, tourists browse over blue-and-white-striped sweaters and framed watercolors of corsair ships; a father sings as he puts his arm around a daughter.

Max looks up from his book and says, "Mutti, what goes around the world but stays in a corner?"

"I don't know, Max."

"A postage stamp."

He smiles at her.

She says, "I'll be right back."

The man behind the museum counter is bearded, maybe fifty. Old enough to remember. She opens her purse and unwraps the partially crushed wooden house and says in her best French, "My brother had this. I believe he found it here. During the war."

The man shakes his head, and she returns the house to her purse. Then he asks to see it again. He holds the model under the lamp and turns it so that its recessed front door faces him.

"Oui," he says finally. He gestures for her to wait outside, and a moment later, he locks

the door behind him and leads her and Max down streets narrow and sloping. After a dozen rights and lefts, they stand in front of the house. A real-life counterpart to the little one that Max is right now rotating in his hands.

"Number four rue Vauborel," says the man. "The LeBlanc house. Been subdivided into holiday flats for years."

Lichens splotch the stone; leached minerals have left filigrees of stains. Flower boxes adorn the windows, foaming over with geraniums. Could Werner have made the model? Bought it?

She says, "And was there a girl? Do you know about a girl?"

"Yes, there was a blind girl who lived in this house during the war. My mother told stories about her. As soon as the war ended, she moved away."

Green dots strobe across Jutta's vision; she feels as if she has been staring at the sun.

Max pulls her wrist. "Mutti, Mutti."

"Why," she says, lurching through the French, "would my brother have a miniature reproduction of this house?"

"Maybe the girl who lived here would know? I can find her address for you."

"Mutti, Mutti, look," Max says, and yanks her hard enough to win her attention. She glances down. "I think this little house opens. I think there's a way to open it."

Laboratory

Marie-Laure LeBlanc manages a small laboratory at the Museum of Natural History in Paris and has contributed in significant ways to the study and literature of mollusks: a monograph on the evolutionary rationale for the folds in West African cancellate nutmeg shells; an often-cited paper on the sexual dimorphism of Caribbean volutes. She has named two new subspecies of chitons. As a doctoral student, she traveled to Bora Bora and Bimini; she waded onto reefs in a sun hat with a collecting bucket and harvested snails on three continents.

Marie-Laure is not a collector in the way that Dr. Geffard was, an amasser, always looking to scurry down the scales of order, family, genus, species, and subspecies. She loves to be among the living creatures, whether on the reefs or in her aquaria. To find the snails crawling along the rocks, these tiny wet beings straining calcium from the water and spinning it into polished dreams on their backs — it is enough. More than enough.

She and Etienne traveled while he could. They went to Sardinia and Scotland and rode on the upper deck of a London airport bus as it skimmed below trees. He bought himself two nice transistor radios, died gently in the bathtub at age eighty-two, and left her plenty of money.

Despite hiring an investigator, spending thousands of francs, and poring through reams of German documentation, Marie-Laure and Etienne were never able to determine what exactly happened to her father. They confirmed he had been a prisoner at a labor camp called Breitenau in 1942. And there was a record made by a camp doctor at a subcamp in Kassel, Germany, that a Daniel LeBlanc contracted influenza in the first part of 1943. That's all they have.

Marie-Laure still lives in the flat where she grew up, still walks to the museum. She has had two lovers. The first was a visiting scientist who never returned, and the second was a Canadian named John who scattered things — ties, coins, socks, breath mints — around any room he entered. They met in graduate school; he flitted from lab to lab with a prodigious curiosity but little perseverance. He loved ocean currents and architecture and Charles Dickens, and his variousness made her feel limited, overspecialized. When Marie-

Laure got pregnant, they separated peaceably, with no flamboyance.

Hélène, their daughter, is nineteen now. Short-haired, petite, an aspiring violinist. Self-possessed, the way children of a blind parent tend to be. Hélène lives with her mother, but the three of them — John, Marie-Laure, and Hélène — eat lunch together every Friday.

It was hard to live through the early 1940s in France and not have the war be the center from which the rest of your life spiraled. Marie-Laure still cannot wear shoes that are too large, or smell a boiled turnip, without experiencing revulsion. Neither can she listen to lists of names. Soccer team rosters, citations at the end of journals, introductions at faculty meetings — always they seem to her some vestige of the prison lists that never contained her father's name.

She still counts storm drains: thirty-eight on the walk home from her laboratory. Flowers grow on her tiny wrought-iron balcony, and in summer she can estimate what time of day it is by feeling how wide the petals of the evening primroses have opened. When Hélène is out with her friends and the apartment seems too quiet, Marie-Laure walks to the same brasserie: Le Village Monge, just outside the Jardin des Plantes, and orders roasted duck in honor of Dr. Geffard.

Is she happy? For portions of every day, she

is happy. When she's standing beneath a tree, for instance, listening to the leaves vibrating in the wind, or when she opens a package from a collector and that old ocean odor of shells comes washing out. When she remembers reading Jules Verne to Hélène, and Hélène falling asleep beside her, the hot, hard weight of the girl's head against her ribs.

There are hours, though, when Hélène is late, and anxiety rides up through Marie-Laure's spine, and she leans over a lab table and becomes aware of all the other rooms in the museum around her, the closets full of preserved frogs and eels and worms, the cabinets full of pinned bugs and pressed ferns, the cellars full of bones, and she feels all of a sudden that she works in a mausoleum, that the departments are systematic graveyards, that all these people — the scientists and warders and guards and visitors — occupy galleries of the dead.

But such moments are few and far between. In her laboratory, six saltwater aquariums gurgle reassuringly; on the back wall stand three cabinets with four hundred drawers in each, salvaged years ago from the office of Dr. Geffard. Every fall, she teaches a class to undergraduates, and her students come and go, smelling of salted beef, or cologne, or the gasoline of their motor scooters, and she loves to ask them about their lives, to wonder what adventures they've had, what lusts, what secret follies they carry in their hearts.

One Wednesday evening in July, her assistant knocks quietly on the open door to the laboratory. Tanks bubble and filters hum and aquarium heaters click on or off. He says there is a woman to see her. Marie-Laure keeps both hands on the keys of her Braille typewriter. "A collector?"

"I don't think so, Doctor. She says that she got your address from a museum in Brittany."

First notes of vertigo.

"She has a boy with her. They're waiting at the end of the hall. Shall I tell her to try tomorrow?"

"What does she look like?"

"White hair." He leans closer. "Badly dressed. Skin like poultry. She says she would like to see you about a model house?"

Somewhere behind her Marie-Laure hears the tinkling sound of ten thousand keys quivering on ten thousand hooks.

"Dr. LeBlanc?"

The room has tilted. In a moment she will slide off the edge.

VISITOR

"You learned French as a child," Marie-Laure says, though how she manages to speak, she is not sure.

"Yes. This is my son, Max."

"Guten Tag," murmurs Max. His hand is warm and small.

"He has not learned French as a child," says Marie-Laure, and both women laugh a moment before falling quiet.

The woman says, "I brought something —" Even through its newspaper wrapping, Marie-Laure knows it is the model house; it feels as if this woman has dropped a molten kernel of memory into her hands.

She can barely stand. "Francis," she says to her assistant, "could you show Max something in the museum for a moment? Perhaps the beetles?"

"Of course, Madame."

The woman says something to her son in German.

Francis says, "Shall I close the door?"

"Please."

The latch clicks. Marie-Laure can hear the aquaria bubble and the woman inhale and the rubber stoppers on the stool legs beneath her squeak as she shifts. With her finger, she finds the nicks on the house's sides, the slope of its roof. How often she held it.

"My father made this," she says.

"Do you know how my brother got it?"

Everything whirling through space, taking a lap around the room, then climbing back into Marie-Laure's mind. The boy. The model. Has it never been opened? She sets the house down suddenly, as if it is very hot.

The woman, Jutta, must be watching her very closely. She says, as though apologizing, "Did he take it from you?"

Over time, thinks Marie-Laure, events that seem jumbled either become more confusing or gradually settle into place. The boy saved her life three times over. Once by not exposing Etienne when he should have. Twice by taking that sergeant major out of the way. Three times by helping her out of the city.

"No," she says.

"It was not," says Jutta, reaching the limits of her French, "very easy to be good then."

"I spent a day with him. Less than a day."

Jutta says, "How old were you?"

"Sixteen during the siege. And you?"

"Fifteen. At the end."

"We all grew up before we were grown up.

Did he — ?"
Jutta says, "He died."
Of course. In the stories after the war, all the resistance heroes were dashing, sinewy types who could construct machine guns from paper clips. And the Germans either raised their godlike blond heads through open tank hatches to watch broken cities scroll past, or else were psychopathic, sex-crazed torturers of beautiful Jewesses. Where did the boy fit? He made such a faint presence. It was like being in the room with a feather. But his soul glowed with some fundamental kindness, didn't it?
We used to pick berries by the Ruhr. My sister and me.
She says, "His hands were smaller than mine."
The woman clears her throat. "He was little for his age, always. But he looked out for me. It was hard for him not to do what was expected of him. Have I said this correctly?"
"Perfectly."
The aquaria bubble. The snails eat. What agonies this woman endured, Marie-Laure cannot guess. And the model house? Did Werner let himself back into the grotto to retrieve it? Did he leave the stone inside? She says, "He said that you and he used to listen to my great-uncle's broadcasts. That you could hear them all the way in Germany."
"Your great-uncle — ?"

Now Marie-Laure wonders what memories crawl over the woman across from her. She is about to say more when footfalls in the hall stop outside the laboratory door. Max stumbles through something unintelligible in French. Francis laughs and says, "No, no, *behind* as in the *back* of us, not *behind* as in *derrière*."

Jutta says, "I'm sorry."

Marie-Laure laughs. "It is the obliviousness of our children that saves us."

The door opens and Francis says, "You are all right, madame?"

"Yes, Francis. You may go."

"We'll go too," says Jutta, and she pushes her stool back beneath the lab table. "I wanted you to have the little house. Better with you than with me."

Marie-Laure keeps her hands flat on the lab table. She imagines mother and son as they move toward the door, small hand folded in big hand, and her throat wells. "Wait," she says. "When my great-uncle sold the house, after the war, he traveled back to Saint-Malo, and he salvaged the one remaining recording of my grandfather. It was about the moon."

"I remember. And light? On the other side?"

The creaking floor, the roiling tanks. Snails sliding along glass. Little house on the table between her hands.

"Leave your address with Francis. The

record is very old, but I'll mail it to you. Max might like it."

Paper Airplane

"And Francis said there are forty-two thousand drawers of dried plants, and he showed me the beak of a giant squid and a plesiosaur . . ." The gravel crunches beneath their shoes and Jutta has to lean against a tree.

"Mutti?"

Lights veer toward her, then away. "I'm tired, Max. That's all."

She unfolds the tourist map and tries to understand the way back to their hotel. Few cars are out, and most every window they pass is lit blue from a television. It's the absence of all the bodies, she thinks, that allows us to forget. It's that the sod seals them over.

In the elevator, Max pushes 6 and up they go. The carpeted runner to their room is a river of maroon crossed with gold trapezoids. She hands Max the key, and he fumbles with the lock, then opens the door.

"Did you show the lady how the house opened, Mutti?"

"I think she already knew."

Jutta turns on the television and takes off her shoes. Max opens the balcony doors and folds an airplane with hotel stationery. The half block of Paris that she can see reminds her of the cities she drew as a girl: a hundred houses, a thousand windows, a wheeling flock of birds. On the television, players in blue rush along a field two thousand miles away. The score is three to two. But a goalkeeper has fallen, and a wing has toed the ball just enough that it rolls slowly toward the goal line. No one is there to kick it away. Jutta picks up the phone beside the bed and dials nine numbers and Max launches an airplane over the street. It sails a few dozen feet and hangs for an instant, and then the voice of her husband says hello.

The Key

She sits in her lab touching the *Dosinia* shells one after another in their tray. Memories strobe past: the feel of her father's trouser leg as she'd cling to it. Sand fleas skittering around her knees. Captain Nemo's submarine vibrating with his woeful dirge as it floated through the black.

She shakes the little house, though she knows it will not give itself away.

He went back for it. Carried it out. Died with it. What sort of a boy was he? She remembers how he sat and paged through that book of Etienne's.

Birds, he said. *Bird after bird after bird.*

She sees herself walk out of the smoking city, trailing a white pillowcase. Once she is out of his sight, he turns and lets himself back through Harold Bazin's gate. The rampart a huge crumbling bulwark above him. The sea settling on the far side of the grate. She sees him solve the puzzle of the little house. Maybe he drops the diamond into the pool among the thousands of snails. Then he closes the puzzle box and locks the gate and trots away.

Or he puts the stone back into the house.

Or slips it into his pocket.

From her memory, Dr. Geffard whispers: *That something so small could be so beautiful. Worth so much. Only the strongest people can turn away from feelings like that.*

She twists the chimney ninety degrees. It turns as smoothly as if her father just built it. When she tries to slide off the first of the three wooden roof panels, she finds it stuck. But with the end of a pen, she manages to lever off the panels one two three.

Something drops into her palm.

An iron key.

Sea of Flames

From the molten basements of the world, two hundred miles down, it comes. One crystal in a seam of others. Pure carbon, each atom linked to four equidistant neighbors, perfectly knit, octahedral, unsurpassed in hardness. Already it is old: unfathomably so. Incalculable eons tumble past. The earth shifts, shrugs, stretches. One year, one day, one hour, a great upflow of magma gathers a seam of crystals and drives it toward the surface, mile after burning mile; it cools inside a huge, smoking xenolith of kimberlite, and there it waits. Century after century. Rain, wind, cubic miles of ice. Bedrock becomes boulders, boulders become stones; the ice retreats, a lake forms, and galaxies of freshwater clams flap their million shells at the sun and close and die and the lake seeps away. Stands of prehistoric trees rise and fall and rise again in succession. Until another year, another day, another hour, when a storm claws one particular stone out of a canyon and sends it into a clattering flow of alluvium, where eventually it finds, one evening, the attention of a prince who knows what he is looking for.

It is cut, polished; for a breath, it passes between the hands of men.

Another hour, another day, another year. Lump of carbon no larger than a chestnut. Mantled with algae, bedecked with barnacles. Crawled over by snails. It stirs among the pebbles.

Frederick

He lives with his mother outside west Berlin. Their apartment is a middle unit in a triplex. Its only windows offer a view of sweet-gum trees, a vast and barely used supermarket parking lot, and an expressway beyond.

Frederick sits on the back patio most days and watches the wind drive discarded plastic bags across the lot. Sometimes they spin high into the air and fly unpredictable loops before catching on the branches or disappearing from view. He makes pencil drawings of spirals, messy, heavy-leaded corkscrews. He'll cover a sheet of paper with two or three, then flip it over and fill the other side. The apartment is jammed with them: thousands on the counters, in drawers, on the toilet tank. His mother used to throw the sheets away when Frederick wasn't looking, but lately she has given up.

"Like a factory, that boy," she used to say to friends, and smiled a desperate smile meant to make her appear brave.

Few friends come over now. Few are left.

One Wednesday — but what are Wednesdays to Frederick? — his mother comes in with the mail. "There's a letter," she says, "for you."

Her instinct in the decades since the war has been to hide. Hide herself, hide what happened to her boy. She was not the only widow made to feel as if she had been complicit in an unspeakable crime. Inside the large envelope is a letter and a smaller envelope. The letter comes from a woman in Essen who traces the course of the smaller envelope from her brother to an American prisoner-of-war camp in France, to a military storage facility in New Jersey, to a veterans' service organization in West Berlin. Then to a former sergeant, then to the woman writing the letter.

Werner. She can still picture the boy: white hair, shy hands, a melting smile. Frederick's one friend. Aloud she says, "He was very small."

Frederick's mother shows him the unopened envelope — it is wrinkled, sepia-colored, and old, his name written in small cursive letters — but he shows no interest. She leaves it on the counter as dusk falls, and measures out a cup of rice and sets it to boil, and switches on every lamp and overhead fixture as she always does, not to see, but because she is alone, because the apartments on either side are vacant, and because the lights make her feel as if she is expecting someone.

She purees his vegetables. She puts the spoon in Frederick's mouth and he hums as he swallows: he is happy. She wipes his chin and sets a sheet of paper in front of him and he takes his pencil and begins to draw.

She fills the sink with soapy water. Then she opens the envelope.

Inside is a folded print of two birds in full color. *Aquatic Wood Wagtail. Male 1. Female 2.* Two birds on a stalk of Indian turnip. She peers back into the envelope for a note, an explanation, but finds none.

The day she bought that book for Fredde: the bookseller took so long to wrap it. She did not understand its attraction but knew that her son would love it.

The doctors claim Frederick retains no memories, that his brain maintains only basic functions, but there are moments when she wonders. She flattens out the creases as well as she can and drags the floor lamp closer and places the print before her son. He tilts his head and she tries to convince herself he is studying it. But his eyes are gray and chambered and shallow, and after a moment he returns to his spirals.

When she has finished the dishes, she leads Frederick out onto the elevated patio, as is their routine, where he sits with his bib still around his neck, staring into oblivion. She'll try him again on the bird print tomorrow.

It's fall, and starlings fly in great pulsing swarms above the city. Sometimes she thinks he perks up when he sees them, hears all those wings rushing and rushing and rushing.

As she sits, looking out through the line of trees into the great empty parking lot, a dark shape sweeps through the nimbus of a streetlamp. It disappears and then reemerges, and suddenly and silently it lands on the deck railing not six feet away.

It's an owl. As big as a child. It swivels its neck and blinks its yellow eyes and in her head roars a single thought: *You've come for me.*

Frederick sits up straight.

The owl hears something. It holds there, listening as hard as she has ever seen anything listen. Frederick stares and stares.

Then it goes: three audible wing beats and the darkness swallows it.

"You saw it?" she whispers. "Did you see it, Fredde?"

He keeps his gaze turned toward the shadows. But there are only the plastic bags rustling in the branches above them and the dozens of spheres of artificial light glowing in the parking lot beyond.

"Mutti?" says Frederick. "Mutti?"

"I'm here, Fredde."

She puts her hand on his knee. His fingers lock around the arms of the chair. His whole body becomes rigid. Veins stand out in his neck.

"Frederick? What is it?"

He looks at her. His eyes do not blink. "What are we doing, Mutti?"

"Oh, Fredde. We're just sitting. We're just sitting and looking out at the night."

Thirteen: 2014

She lives to see the century turn. She lives still.

It's a Saturday morning in early March, and her grandson Michel collects her from her flat and walks her through the Jardin des Plantes. Frost glimmers in the air, and Marie-Laure shuffles along with the ball of her cane out in front and her thin hair blown to one side and the leafless canopies of the trees drifting overhead as she imagines schools of Portuguese men-of-war drift, trailing their long tentacles behind them.

Skim ice has formed atop puddles in the gravel paths. Whenever she finds some with her cane, she stops and bends and tries to lift the thin plate without breaking it. As though raising a lens to her eye. Then she sets it carefully back down.

The boy is patient, taking her elbow only when she seems to need it.

They make for the hedge maze in the northwest corner of the gardens. The path they're on begins to ascend, twisting steadily to the left. Climb, pause, catch your breath. Climb again. When they reach the old steel gazebo at the very top, he leads her to its narrow bench and they sit.

No one else here: too cold or too early or both. She listens to the wind sift through the filigree of the crown of the gazebo, and the walls of the maze hold steady around them, Paris murmuring below, the drowsy purr of a Saturday morning.

"You'll be twelve next Saturday, won't you, Michel?"

"Finally."

"You are in a hurry to be twelve?"

"Mother says I can drive the moped when I am twelve."

"Ah." Marie-Laure laughs. "The moped."

Beneath her fingernails, the frost makes billions of tiny diadems and coronas on the slats of the bench, a lattice of dumbfounding complexity.

Michel presses against her side and becomes very quiet. Only his hands are moving. Little clicks rising, buttons being pressed.

"What are you playing?"

"Warlords."

"You play against your computer?"

"Against Jacques."

"Where is Jacques?"

The boy's attention stays on the game. It does not matter where Jacques is: Jacques is inside the game. She sits and her cane flexes against the gravel and the boy clicks his buttons in spasmodic flurries. After a while he exclaims, "Ah!" and the game makes several resolving chirps.

"You're all right?"

"He has killed me." Awareness returns to Michel's voice; he is looking up again. "Jacques, I mean. I am dead."

"In the game?"

"Yes. But I can always begin again."

Below them the wind washes frost from the trees. She concentrates on feeling the sun touch the backs of her hands. On the warmth of her grandson beside her.

"Mamie? Was there something you wanted for your twelfth birthday?"

"There was. A book by Jules Verne."

"The same one Maman read to me? Did you get it?"

"I did. In a way."

"There were lots of complicated fish names in that book."

She laughs. "And corals and mollusks, too."

"Especially mollusks. It's a beautiful morning, Mamie, isn't it?"

"Very beautiful."

People walk the paths of the gardens below, and the wind sings anthems in the hedges, and the big old cedars at the entrance to the maze creak. Marie-Laure imagines the electromagnetic waves traveling into and out of

Michel's machine, bending around them, just as Etienne used to describe, except now a thousand times more crisscross the air than when he lived — maybe a million times more. Torrents of text conversations, tides of cell conversations, of television programs, of e-mail, vast networks of fiber and wire interlaced above and beneath the city, passing through buildings, arcing between transmitters in Metro tunnels, between antennas atop buildings, from lampposts with cellular transmitters in them, commercials for Carrefour and Evian and prebaked toaster pastries flashing into space and back to earth again, *I'm going to be late* and *Maybe we should get reservations?* and *Pick up avocados* and *What did he say?* and ten thousand *I miss you*s, fifty thousand *I love you*s, hate mail and appointment reminders and market updates, jewelry ads, coffee ads, furniture ads flying invisibly over the warrens of Paris, over the battlefields and tombs, over the Ardennes, over the Rhine, over Belgium and Denmark, over the scarred and ever-shifting landscapes we call nations. And is it so hard to believe that souls might also travel those paths? That her father and Etienne and Madame Manec and the German boy named Werner Pfennig might harry the sky in flocks, like egrets, like terns, like starlings? That great shuttles of souls might fly about, faded but audible if you listen closely enough? They flow above the chimneys, ride the sidewalks, slip through your jacket and shirt and breastbone and lungs, and pass out through the other side, the air a library and the record of every life lived, every sentence spoken, every word transmitted still reverberating within it.

Every hour, she thinks, someone for whom the war was memory falls out of the world.

We rise again in the grass. In the flowers. In songs.

Michel takes her arm and they wind back down the path, through the gate onto the rue Cuvier. She passes one storm drain two storm drains three four five, and when they reach her building, she says, "You may leave me here, Michel. You can find your way?"

"Of course."

"Until next week, then."

He kisses her once on each cheek. "Until next week, Mamie."

She listens until his footsteps fade. Until all she can hear are the sighs of cars and the rumble of trains and the sounds of everyone hurrying through the cold.

ACKNOWLEDGMENTS

I am indebted to the American Academy in Rome, to the Idaho Commission on the Arts, and to the John Simon Guggenheim Memorial Foundation. Thank you to Francis Geffard, who brought me to Saint-Malo for the first time. Thank you to Binky Urban and Clare Reihill for their enthusiasm and confidence. And thanks especially to Nan Graham, who waited a decade, then gave this book her heart, her pencil, and so many of her hours.

Additional debts are owed to Jacques Lusseyran's *And There Was Light,* Curzio Malaparte's *Kaputt,* and Michel Tournier's *The Ogre;* to Cort Conley, who kept a steady stream of curated material flowing into my mailbox; to early readers Hal and Jacque Eastman, Matt Crosby, Jessica Sachse, Megan Tweedy, Jon Silverman, Steve Smith, Stefani Nellen, Chris Doerr, Dick Doerr, Michèle Mourembles, Kara Watson, Cheston Knapp, Meg Storey, and Emily Forland; and especially to my mother, Marilyn Doerr, who was my Dr. Geffard, my Jules Verne.

The largest thanks go to Owen and Henry, who have lived with this book all their lives, and to Shauna, without whom this could not exist, and upon whom all this depends.